Once Upon A Star

★

Once Upon A Star

★

NORA ROBERTS
JILL GREGORY
RUTH RYAN LANGAN
MARIANNE WILLMAN

JOVE BOOKS, NEW YORK

A Jove Book / published by arrangement with
the authors

The Penguin Putnam Inc. World Wide Web site address is
http://www.penguinputnam.com

ISBN: 0-7394-0673-6

A JOVE BOOK®
Jove Books are published by The Berkley Publishing Group,
a division of Penguin Putnam Inc.,
375 Hudson Street, New York, New York 10014.
JOVE and the "J" design
are trademarks belonging to Penguin Putnam Inc.

PRINTED IN THE UNITED STATES OF AMERICA

CONTENTS

Once Upon A Star

EVER AFTER

★

Nora Roberts

To my sisters in magic—
Ruth, Marianne, and Jill

1

"THIS," THE OLD woman said, "is for you."

Allena studied the pendant that swung gently from the thickly braided links of a silver chain. Really, she'd only come in to browse. Her budget didn't allow for impulse buys—which were, of course, the most fun and the most satisfying. And her affection for all things impulsive was the very reason she couldn't afford to indulge herself.

She shouldn't have entered the shop at all. But who could resist a tiny little place tucked into the waterfront of a charming Irish village? Especially a place called Charms and Cures.

Certainly not Allena Kennedy.

"It's beautiful, but I—"

"There's only one." The woman's eyes were faded and blue, like the sea that slapped and spewed against the stone wall barely a stone's throw from the door. Her hair was steel gray and bundled into a bun that lay heavy on her thin neck.

She wore a fascinating rattle of chains and pins, but there was nothing, Allena thought, like the pendant she held in her bony fingers. "Only one?"

"The silver was cured in Dagda's Cauldron over the Midsummer's fire and carved by the finger of Merlin. He that was Arthur's."

"Merlin?"

Allena was a sucker for tales of magic and heroics. Her stepsister Margaret would have sniffed and said no, she was simply a sucker.

"The high king's sorcerer wandered through Ireland in his time. It was here he found the Giant's Dance, and coveting it for Arthur, floated it away over the Irish Sea to Britain. But while he took magic from this land, some he also left." Watching Allena, she set the pendant swaying. "Here is some, and it belongs to you."

"Well, I really can't . . ." But Allena trailed off, her gaze locked on the pendant. It was a long oval, dulled and tarnished a bit, and centered in it was a carving in the shape of a bursting star.

It seemed to catch the murky, cloud-filtered light coming through the small shop window, hold it, expand it, so that it glittered hypnotically in Allena's eyes. It seemed the star shimmered.

"I just came in to look around."

"Sure and if you don't look, you can't find, can you? You came looking, all the way from America."

She'd come, Allena tried to remember, to assist Margaret with the tour group. Margaret's business, A Civilized Adventure, was very successful—and very regimented. Everyone said that Allena needed some regimentation. And Margaret had been clear, brutally clear, that this opportunity was her last chance.

"Be organized, be prepared, and be on time," Margaret had told her as she'd sat behind her polished desk in her perfectly terrifying and perfectly ordered office in New York. "If you can manage that, there might be a chance for you. If you can't, I wash my hands of you, Lena."

It wouldn't be the first time someone had washed their

hands of her. In the past three years she'd lost three jobs. Well, four, but it didn't seem necessary to count those hideous two days she'd spent as assistant to her uncle's mother-in-law's sister.

It wasn't as if she'd spilled ink on the white Valentino gown on purpose. And if the Social Dragon hadn't insisted that she use a fountain pen—I mean, really—for all correspondence, there wouldn't have been ink to spill.

But that wasn't the point, she reminded herself as she stared at the pendant. She'd lost that job and all the others, and now Margaret was giving her a chance to prove she wasn't a complete moron.

Which, Allena feared, she probably was.

"You need to find your place."

Blinking, Allena managed to tear her gaze away from the pendant and look back into the old woman's eyes. They seemed so kind and wise. "Maybe I don't have one."

"Oh, there now, each of us has one, but there are those who don't fit so easily into the world the way others see it. And us. You've only been looking in the wrong places. Till now. This," she said again, "belongs to you."

"I really can't afford it." There was apology in her voice, even as she reached out. Just to touch. And touching, she felt heat from the silver, and terrible longing inside her. A thrill raced up her spine even as something heavy seemed to settle over her heart.

It couldn't hurt to try it on. Surely there was no harm in just seeing how it looked on her, how it felt.

As if in a dream, she took the chain from the old woman, slipped it around her neck. The heaviness in her heart shifted. For a moment, the light through the window strengthened, beamed brilliantly over the trinkets and pots of herbs and odd little stones crammed on the shelves and counters.

An image swam into her mind, an image of knights and dragons, of wild wind and water, of a circle of stones standing alone under a black and raging sky.

Then a shadow that was a man, standing still as the stones, as if waiting.

In her heart she knew he waited for her, as no one had before and no one would after. And would wait, eternally.

Allena closed her hand over the pendant, ran her thumb over the star. Joy burst through her, clear as the sunlight. Ah, she thought. Of course. It's mine. Just as I'm his, and he's mine.

"How much is it?" she heard herself say, and knew no price would be too dear.

"Ten pounds, as a token."

"Ten?" She was already reaching for her purse. "It has to be worth more." A king's ransom, a sorcerer's spell, a lover's dream.

"It is, of course." But the woman merely held out her hand for the single note. "And so are you. Go on your journey, *a chuid,* and see."

"Thank you."

"You're a good lass," the woman said as Allena walked to the door. And when it shut, her smile turned bright and crafty. "He won't be pleased, but you'll bring him 'round by Midsummer's Eve. And if you need a bit of help, well, that will be my pleasure."

Outside, Allena stared at the sea wall, the dock, the line of cottages as if coming out of a dream. Odd, she thought, hadn't that all been wonderfully odd? She traced a finger over the pendant again. Only one, cast in Dagda's Cauldron, carved by Merlin.

Of course, Margaret would sneer and tell her that the old woman had a dozen more in the stockroom ready to pass them off to birdbrained tourists. And Margaret, as always, was probably right. But it didn't matter.

She had the pendant and a wonderful story to go with it. And all for ten pounds. Quite a bargain.

She glanced up now, wincing. The sky was heavy with clouds, and all of them were thick and gray. Margaret would not be pleased that the weather wasn't falling in line with today's plans. The ferry ride to the island had been meticulously arranged.

Tea and scones would be served on the trip over, while Margaret lectured her twenty-person group on the history of the place they were about to visit. It had been Allena's job to type up Margaret's notes and print the handouts.

First stop would be the visitors' center for orientation. There would be a tour of a ruined abbey and graveyard, which Allena looked forward to, then lunch, picnic style, which the hotel had provided in hampers. Lunch was to last precisely sixty minutes.

They would then visit the beehive cottages, and Margaret would deliver a lecture on their history and purpose. The group would be allotted an hour to wander on their own, into the village, the shops, down to the beach, before gathering at four-thirty on the dot for high tea at the restored castle, with, naturally, another lecture on that particular spot.

It was Allena's job to keep all of Margaret's lecture notes in order, to help herd the group, to watch valuables, to haul parcels should there be any, and to generally make herself available for any and all menial chores.

For this she would be paid a reasonable salary by Margaret's definition. But, more important, it was explained, she would receive training and experience that, her family hoped, would teach her responsibility and maturity. Which, by the age of twenty-five, she should have learned already.

There was no point in explaining that she didn't want to be responsible and mature if it turned her into another Margaret. Here she was, four days into her first tour and already something inside her was screaming to run away.

Dutifully, she quashed the rebellion, glanced at her watch. Stared at it, dumbfounded.

That couldn't be. It was impossible. She'd only meant to slip into the shop for a few minutes. She couldn't possibly have spent an hour in there. She couldn't—oh, God, she *couldn't* have missed the ferry.

Margaret would murder her.

Gripping the strap of her bag, she began to run.

She had long, dancer's legs and a slim build. The sturdy walking shoes Margaret had ordered her to buy slapped pavement on her race to the ferry dock. Her bag bounced heavily against her hip. Inside was everything ordered from the Civilized Adventure directive and a great deal more.

The wind kicked in from the sea and sent her short blond hair into alarmed spikes around her sharp-boned face. The alarm was in her eyes, gray as the clouds, as well. It turned quickly to despair and self-disgust when she reached the dock and saw the ferry chugging away.

"Damn it!" Allena grabbed her own hair and pulled viciously. "That's it and that's all. I might as well jump in and drown myself." Which would be more pleasant, she had no doubt, than the icy lecture Margaret would deliver.

She'd be fired, of course, there was no doubt of it. But she was used to that little by-product of her professional endeavors. The method of termination would be torture.

Unless . . . There had to be another way to get to the island. If she could get there, throw herself on Margaret's stingy supply of mercy, work like a dog, forfeit her salary. Make an excuse. Surely she'd be able to come up with some reason for missing the damn ferry.

She looked around frantically. There were boats, and if there were boats, there were people who drove boats. She'd hire a boat, pay whatever it cost.

"Are you lost, then?"

Startled, she lifted a hand, closed it tight over her pendant. There was a young man—hardly more than a boy, really, she noted—standing beside a small white boat. He wore a cap over his straw-colored hair and watched her out of laughing green eyes.

"No, not lost, late. I was supposed to be on the ferry." She gestured, then let her arms fall. "I lost track of time."

"Well, time's not such a matter in the scheme of things."

"It is to my sister. I work for her." Quickly now, she headed down toward him where the sea lapped the shore. "Is this your boat, or your father's?"

"Aye, it happens it's mine."

It was small, but to her inexperienced eye looked cheerful. She had to hope that made it seaworthy. "Could you take me over? I need to catch up. I'll pay whatever you need."

It was just that sort of statement, Allena thought the minute the words left her mouth, that would make Margaret cringe. But then bargaining wasn't a priority at the moment. Survival was.

"I'll take you where you need to be." His eyes sparkled as he held out a hand. "For ten pounds."

"Today everything's ten pounds." She reached for her purse, but he shook his head.

"It was your hand I was reaching for, lady, not payment. Payment comes when you get where you're going."

"Oh, thanks." She put her hand in his and let him help her into the boat.

She sat starboard on a little bench while he cast off. Closing her eyes with relief, she listened to the boy whistle as he went about settling to stern and starting the motor. "I'm very grateful," she began. "My sister's going to be furious with me. I don't know what I was thinking of."

He turned the boat, a slow and smooth motion. "And couldn't she have waited just a bit?"

"Margaret?" The thought made Allena smile. "It wouldn't have occurred to her."

The bow lifted, and the little boat picked up speed. "It would have occurred to you," he said, and then they were skimming over the water.

Thrilled, she turned her face to the wind. Oh, this was better, much better, than any tame ferry ride, lecture included. It was almost worth the price she would pay at the end, and she didn't mean the pounds.

"Do you fish?" she called out to him.

"When they're biting."

"It must be wonderful to do what you want, when you want. And to live so near the water. Do you love it?"

"I've a fondness for it, yes. Men put restrictions on men. That's an odd thing to my way of thinking."

"I have a terrible time with restrictions. I can never remember them." The boat leaped, bounced hard and made her laugh. "At this rate, we'll beat the ferry."

The idea of that, the image of her standing on shore and giving Margaret a smug look when the ferry docked, entertained Allena so much she didn't give a thought to the shiver of lightning overhead or the sudden, ominous roar of the sea.

When the rain began to pelt her, she looked around again, shocked that she could see nothing but water, the rise and fall of it, the curtain that closed off light.

"Oh, she won't like this a bit. Are we nearly there?"

"Nearly, aye, nearly." His voice was a kind of crooning that smoothed nerves before they could fray. "Do you see there, through the storm? There, just ahead, is where you need to be."

She turned. Through the rain and wind, she saw the darker shadow of land, a rise of hills, the dip of valley in shapes only. But she knew, she already knew.

"It's beautiful," she murmured.

Like smoke, it drifted closer. She could see the crash of surf now and the cliffs that hulked high above. Then in the flash of lightning, she thought, just for an instant, she saw a man.

Before she could speak, the boat was rocking in the surf, and the boy leaping out into the thrashing water to pull them to shore.

"I can't thank you enough, really." Drenched, euphoric, she climbed out onto the wet sand. "You'll wait for the storm to pass, won't you?" she asked as she dug for her wallet.

"I'll wait until it's time to go. You'll find your way, lady. Through the rain. The path's there."

"Thanks." She passed the note into his hand. She'd go to the visitors' center, take shelter, find Margaret and do penance. "If you come up with me, I'll buy you some tea. You can dry off."

"Oh, I'm used to the wet. Someone's waiting for you," he said, then climbed back into his boat.

"Yes, of course." She started to run, then stopped. She hadn't even asked his name. "I'm sorry, but—" When she rushed back, there was nothing there but the crash of water against the shore.

Alarmed that he'd sailed back into that rising storm, she

called out, began to hurry along what she could see of the shore to try to find him. Lightning flashed overhead, more vicious than exciting now, and the wind slapped at her like a furious hand.

Hunching against it, she jogged up the rise, onto a path. She'd get to shelter, tell someone about the boy. What had she been thinking of, not insisting that he come with her and wait until the weather cleared?

She stumbled, fell, jarring her bones with the impact, panting to catch her breath as the world went suddenly mad around her. Everything was howling wind, blasting lights, booming thunder. She struggled to her feet and pushed on.

It wasn't fear she felt, and that baffled her. She should be terrified. Why instead was she exhilarated? Where did this wicked thrill of anticipation, of *knowledge*, come from?

She had to keep going. There was something, someone, waiting. If she could just keep going.

The way was steep, the rain blinding. Somewhere along the way she lost her bag, but didn't notice.

In the next flash of light, she saw it. The circle of stones, rising out of the rough ground like dancers trapped in time. In her head, or perhaps her heart, she heard the song buried inside them.

With something like joy, she rushed forward, her hand around the pendant.

The song rose, like a crescendo, filling her, washing over her like a wave.

And as she reached the circle, took her first step inside, lightning struck the center, the bolt as clear and well defined as a flaming arrow. She watched the blue fire rise in a tower, higher, higher still, until it seemed to pierce the low-hanging clouds. She felt the iced heat of it on her skin, in her bones. The power of it hammered her heart.

And she fainted.

2

THE STORM MADE him restless. Part of the tempest seemed to be inside him, churning, crashing, waiting to strike out. He couldn't work. His concentration was fractured. He had no desire to read, to putter, to simply be. And all of those things were why he had come back to the island.

Or so he told himself.

His family had held the land, worked it, guarded it, for generations. The O'Neils of Dolman had planted their seed here, spilled their blood and the blood of their enemies for as far back as time was marked. And further still, back into the murky time that was told only in songs.

Leaving here, going to Dublin to study, and to work, had been Conal's rebellion, his escape from what others so blithely accepted as his fate. He would not, as he'd told his father, be the passive pawn in the chess game of his own destiny.

He would make his destiny.

And yet, here he was, in the cottage where the O'Neils had lived and died, where his own father had passed the last day of his life only months before. Telling himself it had been his choice didn't seem quite so certain on a day where the wind lashed and screamed and the same violence of nature seemed to thrash inside him.

The dog, Hugh, which had been his father's companion for the last year of his life, paced from window to window, ears pricked up and a low sound rumbling in his throat, more whimper than growl.

Whatever was brewing, the dog sensed it as well, so that his big gray bulk streamed through the cottage like blown smoke. Conal gave a soft command in Gaelic, and Hugh came over, bumping his big head under Conal's big hand.

There they stood, watching the storm together, the large gray dog and the tall, broad-shouldered man, each with a wary expression. Conal felt the dog shudder. Nerves or anticipation? Something, all Conal could think, was out there in the storm.

Waiting.

"The hell with it. Let's see what it is."

Even as he spoke, the dog leaped toward the door, prancing with impatience as Conal tugged a long black slicker off the peg. He swirled it on over rough boots and rougher jeans and a black sweater that had seen too many washings.

When he opened the door, the dog shot out, straight into the jaws of the gale. "Hugh! *Cuir uait!*"

And though the dog did stop, skidding in the wet, he didn't bound back to Conal's side. Instead he stood, ears still pricked, despite the pounding rain, as if to say *hurry!*

Cursing under his breath, Conal picked up his own pace, and let the dog take the lead.

His black hair, nearly shoulder-length and heavy now with rain, streamed back in the wind from a sharply-honed face. He had the high, long cheekbones of the Celts, a narrow, almost aristocratic nose, and a well-defined mouth that could look, as it did now, hard as granite. His eyes were a deep and passionate blue.

His mother had said they were eyes that saw too much, and still looked for more.

Now they peered through the rain, and down, as Hugh climbed, at the turbulent toss of the sea. With the storm, the day was almost black as night, and he cursed again at his own foolishness in being out in it.

He lost sight of Hugh around a turn on the cliff path. More irritated than alarmed, he called the dog again, but all that answered was the low-throated, urgent bark. Perfect, was all Conal could think. Now the both of us will likely slip off the edge and bash our brains on the rocks.

He almost turned away, at that point very nearly retreated, for the dog was surefooted and knew his way home. But he wanted to go on—too much wanted to go on. As if something was tugging him forward, luring him on, higher and higher still, to where the shadow of the stone dance stood, singing through the wind.

Because part of him believed it, part of him he had never been able to fully quiet, he deliberately turned away. He would go home, build up the fire, and have a glass of whiskey in front of it until the storm blew itself out.

Then the howl came, a wild and primitive call that spoke of wolves and eerie moonlight. The shudder that ran down Conal's spine was as primal as the call. Grimly now, he continued up the path to see what caused young Hugh to bay.

The stones rose, gleaming with wet, haloed by the lightning strikes so that they almost seemed to glow. A scent came to him, ozone and perfume. Hot, sweet, and seductive.

The dog sat, his handsome head thrown back, his great throat rippling with his feral call. There was something in it, Conal thought, that was somehow triumphant.

"The stones don't need guarding," Conal muttered. He strode forward, intending to grab the dog by the collar and drag them both back to the warmth of the cottage.

And saw that it wasn't the stones Hugh guarded, but the woman who lay between them.

Half in and half out of the circle, with one arm stretched

toward the center, she lay on her side almost as if sleeping. For a moment he thought he imagined her, and wanted to believe he did. But when he reached her side, his fingers instinctively going to her throat to check her pulse, he felt the warm beat of life.

At his touch her lashes fluttered. Her eyes opened. They were gray as the stones and met his with a sudden and impossible awareness. A smile curved her lips, parted them as she lifted a hand to his cheek.

"There you are," she said, and with a sigh closed her eyes again. Her hand slid away from his cheek to fall onto the rain-trampled grass.

Delirious, he told himself, and most likely a lunatic. Who else would climb the cliffs in a storm? Ignoring the fact that he'd done so himself, he turned her over, seeing no choice but to cart her back to the cottage.

And when he started to gather her into his arms, he saw the pendant, saw the carving on it in another spit of lightning.

His belly pitched. His heart gave one violent knock against his chest, like an angry fist.

"Damn it."

He stayed crouched as he was, closing his eyes while the rain battered both of them.

She woke slowly, as if floating lazily through layers of thin, white clouds. A feeling of well-being cushioned her, like satin pillows edged with the softest of lace. Savoring it, she lay still while sunlight played on her eyelids, cruised warm over her face. She could smell smoke, a pleasant, earthy scent, and another fragrance, a bit darker, that was man.

She enjoyed that mix, and when she opened her eyes, her first thought was she'd never been happier in her life.

It lasted seconds only, that sensation of joy and safety, of contentment and place. Then she shot up in bed, confused, alarmed, lost.

Margaret! She'd missed the ferry. The boat. The boy in the boat. And the storm. She'd gotten caught in it and had lost her way. She couldn't quite remember, couldn't quite separate the blurry images.

Stones, higher than a man and ringed in a circle. The blue fire that burned in the center without scorching the grass. The wild scream of the wind. The low hum of the stones.

A wolf howling. Then a man. Tall, dark, fierce, with eyes as blue as that impossible fire. Such anger in his face. But it hadn't frightened her. It had amused her. How strange.

Dreams, of course. Just dreams. She'd been in some sort of accident.

Now she was in someone's house, someone's bed. A simple room, she thought, looking around to orient herself. No, not simple, she corrected, spartan. Plain white walls, bare wood floor, no curtains at the window. There was a dresser, a table and lamp and the bed. As far as she could tell, there was nothing else in the room but herself.

Gingerly now, she touched her head to see if there were bumps or cuts, but found nothing to worry her. Using the same caution, she turned back the sheet, let out a little sigh of relief. Whatever sort of accident there'd been, it didn't appear to have hurt her.

Then she gaped, realizing she wore nothing but a shirt, and it wasn't her own. A man's shirt, faded blue cotton, frayed at the cuffs. And huge.

Okay, that was okay. She'd been caught in the storm. Obviously she had gotten soaked. She had to be grateful that someone had taken care of her.

When she climbed out of bed, the shirt hung halfway to her knees. Modest enough. At her first step, the dog came to the door. Her heart gave a little hitch, then settled.

"So at least you're real. Aren't you handsome?" She held out a hand and had the pleasure of him coming to her to rub his body against her legs. "And friendly. Good to know. Where's everyone else?"

With one hand on the dog's head, she walked to the bedroom door and discovered a living area that was every bit as spartan. A couch and chair, a low burning fire, a couple of tables. With some relief she saw her clothes laid over a screen in front of the fire.

A check found them still damp. So, she hadn't been asleep—unconscious—for long. The practical thing to do, now that she'd apparently done everything impractical, was to find her rescuer, thank him, wait for her clothes to dry, then track down Margaret and beg for mercy.

The last part would be unpleasant, and probably fruitless, but it had to be done.

Bolstering herself for the task, Allena went to the door, opened it. And let out a soft cry of sheer delight.

The watery sunlight shimmered over the hills, and the hills rolled up green in one direction, tumbled down in the other toward the rock-strewn shore. The sea reared and crashed, the walls of waves high and wonderful. She had an urge to rush out, to the edge of the slope, and watch the water rage.

Just outside the cottage was a garden gone wild so that flowers tangled with weeds and tumbled over themselves. The smell of them, of the air, of the sea had her gulping in air, holding her breath as if to keep that single sharp taste inside her forever.

Unable to resist, she stepped out, the dog beside her, and lifted her face to the sky.

Oh, this place! Was there ever a more perfect spot? If it were hers, she would stand here every morning and thank God for it.

Beside her, the dog let out one quiet woof, at which she rested her hand on his head again and glanced over at the little building, with its rough stone, thatched roof, wide-open windows.

She started to smile, then the door of it opened. The man who came out stopped as she did, stared as she did. Then with his mouth hard set, he started forward.

His face swam in front of her. The crash of the sea filled her head with roaring. Dizzy, she held out a hand to him, much as she had to the dog.

She saw his mouth move, thought she heard him swear, but she was already pitching forward into the dark.

3

SHE LOOKED LIKE a faerie, standing there in a wavery sunbeam. Tall and slender, her bright hair cropped short, her eyes long-lidded, tilted at the tips, and enormous.

Not a beauty. Her face was too sharp for true beauty, and her mouth a bit top-heavy. But it was an intriguing face, even in rest.

He'd thought about it even after he'd dumped her in bed after carrying her in from the storm. Undressing her had been an annoying necessity, which he'd handled with the aloof detachment of a doctor. Then, once she was dry and settled, he'd left her, without a backward glance, to burn off some of the anger in work.

He worked very well in a temper.

He didn't want her here. He didn't want her. And, he told himself, he wouldn't have her, no matter what the fates decreed.

He was his own man.

But now when he came out, saw her standing in the

doorway, in the sunlight, he felt the shock of it sweep through him—longing, possession, recognition, delight, and despair. All of those in one hard wave rose inside him, swamped him.

Before he could gain his feet, she was swaying.

He didn't manage to catch her. Oh, in the storybooks, he imagined, his feet would have grown wings and he'd have flown across the yard to pluck her nimbly into his arms before she swooned. But as it was, she slid to the ground, melted wax pooling into the cup and taking all the candle as well, before he'd closed half the distance.

By the time he reached her, those long gray eyes were already opening again, cloudy and dazed. She stared at him, the corners of her mouth trembling up.

"I guess I'm not steady yet," she said in that pretty American voice. "I know it's a cliché and predictable, but I have to say it—where am I?"

She looked ridiculously appealing, lying there between the flowers, and made him all too aware she wore nothing but one of his shirts. "You're on O'Neil land."

"I got lost—a bad habit of mine. The storm came up so fast."

"Why are you here?"

"Oh, I got separated from the group. Well, I was late—another bad habit—and missed the ferry. But the boy brought me in his boat." She sat up then. "I hope he's all right. He must be, as he seemed to know what he was doing and it was such a quick trip anyway. Is the visitors' center far?"

"The visitors' center?"

"I should be able to catch up with them, though it won't do me a lot of good. Margaret'll fire me, and I deserve it."

"And who is Margaret?"

"My stepsister. She owns A Civilized Adventure. I'm working for her—or I did work for her for the last twenty-three days." She let out a breath, tried the smile again. "I'm sorry. I'm Allena Kennedy, the moron. Thank you for helping me."

He glanced down at the hand she held out, then with

some reluctance took it. Instead of shaking it, he pulled her to her feet. "I've a feeling you're more lost than you know, Miss Kennedy, as there's no visitors' center here on Dolman Island."

"Dolman? But that's not right." The hand in his flexed, balled into a little fist of nerves. "I'm not supposed to be on Dolman Island. Oh, damn it. Damn it! It's my fault. I wasn't specific with the boy. He seemed to know where I was going, was supposed to be going. Or maybe he got turned around in the storm, too. I hope he's all right."

She paused, looked around, sighed. "Not just fired," she murmured. "Disinherited, banished, and mortified all in one morning. I guess all I can do is go back to the hotel and wait to face the music."

"Well, it won't be today."

"Excuse me?"

Conal looked out to sea, studying the crashing wall of waves. "You won't find your way back today, and likely not tomorrow, as there's more coming our way."

"But—" She was talking to his back as he walked inside as though he hadn't just sealed her doom. "I have to get back. She'll be worried."

"There'll be no ferry service in these seas, and no boatman with a brain in his head would chance the trip back to the mainland."

She sat on the arm of a chair, closed her eyes. "Well, that caps it. Is there a phone? Could I use your phone to call the hotel and leave a message?"

"The phones are out."

"Of course they are." She watched him go to the fire to add some bricks of turf. Her clothes hung on the screen like a recrimination. "Mr. O'Neil?"

"Conal." He straightened, turned to her. "All the women I undress and put into bed call me Conal."

It was a test, deliberately provocative. But she didn't flush or fire. Instead her eyes lit with humor. "All the men who undress me and put me into bed call me Lena."

"I prefer Allena."

"Really? So do I, but it seems to be too many syllables

for most people. Anyway, Conal, is there a hotel or a bed-and-breakfast where I can stay until the ferry's running again?''

"There's no hotel on Dolman. It's a rare tourist who comes this far. And the nearest village, of which there are but three, is more than eight kilometers away.''

She gave him a level look. "Am I staying here?''

"Apparently.''

She nodded, rubbing her hand absently over Hugh's broad back as she took stock of her surroundings. "I appreciate it, and I'll try not to be a nuisance.''

"It's a bit late for that, but we'll deal with it.'' When her only response was to lift her eyebrows and stare steadily, he felt a tug of shame. "Can you make a proper pot of tea?''

"Yes.''

He gestured toward the kitchen that was separated from the living area by a short counter. "The makings are in there. I've a few things to see to, then we'll talk this out over a cup.''

"Fine.'' The word was rigidly and properly polite. Only the single gunshot bang of a cupboard door as he started out again told him she was miffed.

She'd make the damn tea, she thought, jerking the faucet on to fill the kettle, which was no easy matter since the cast-iron sink was loaded with dishes. And she'd be grateful for Conal O'Neil's hospitality, however reluctantly, however *rudely* given.

Was it her fault she'd ended up on the wrong island? Was it her fault she'd gotten turned around in a storm and passed out and had to be carted back to his house? Was it her fault she had nowhere else to go?

Well, yes. She rolled her eyes and began to empty the dishes out of the sink so that she could fill it with soapy water and wash them. Yes, technically it *was* her fault. Which just made it all the more annoying.

When she got back to New York she would be jobless. Again. And once more she'd be the object of pity, puzzlement, and pursed lips. And that was her fault, too. Her

family expected her to fail now—flighty, scatterbrained
Lena.

Worse, she realized, was that she expected it, too.

The problem was she wasn't particularly good at anything. She had no real skill, no craft, and no driving ambitions.

She wasn't lazy, though she knew Margaret would dis-
agree. Work didn't frighten her. Business did.

But that was tomorrow's problem, she reminded herself
as she dealt with the dishes and waited for the kettle to
boil. Today's problem was Conal O'Neil and how to handle
the situation she'd put them both into.

A situation, she thought, as she went about stacking
dishes, wiping counters, heating the teapot, that should have
been thrilling. A storm-swept island; a handsome, brooding
man; a cozy, if rustic, cottage isolated from the world.

This, she decided, perking up, was an adventure. She was
going to find a way to enjoy it before the axe fell.

When Conal came back in, the old teapot was sitting
snugly in a frayed and faded cozy. Cups and saucers were
set on the table, and the table scrubbed clean. The sink was
empty, the counters sparkling, and the chocolate biscuits
he'd had in a tin were arranged prettily on a plate.

"I was hungry." She was already nibbling on one. "I
hope you don't mind."

"No." He'd nearly forgotten what it was like to sit down
and have tea in tidiness. Her little temper snap appeared to
be over as well, he noted. She looked quietly at home in
his kitchen, in his shirt.

"So." She sat down to pour. The one thing she was good
at was conversation. She'd often been told she was too
good at it. "You live here alone?"

"I do."

"With your dog."

"Hugh. He was my father's. My father died some
months back."

She didn't say she was sorry, as so many—too many—
would have. But her eyes said it, and that made it matter
more. "It's a beautiful spot. A perfect spot. That's what I

was thinking before I fell into your garden. You grew up here?''

"I did.''

"I grew up in New York, in the city. It never fit, some-how.'' She studied him over her teacup. "This fits you. It's wonderful to find the right fit. Everyone in my family fits except me. My parents and Margaret and James—my brother and sister. Their mother died when Margaret was twelve and James ten. Their father met my mother a couple of years later, then they married and had me.''

"And you're Cinderella?''

"No, nothing as romantic as that.'' But she sighed and thought how lovely it would be. "Just the misfit. They're all brilliant, you see. Every one of them. My father's a doctor, a surgeon. My mother's a lawyer. James is a wildly successful cosmetic surgeon, and Margaret has her own business with A Civilized Adventure.''

"Who would want an adventure civilized?''

"Yes.'' Delighted, Allena slapped a palm on the table. "That's exactly what I thought. I mean, wouldn't regi-menting it mean it wasn't an adventure at all? But saying that to Margaret earned me a twenty-minute lecture, and since her business is thriving, there you go.''

The light was already shifting, he noted, as a new sea of clouds washed in. But there was enough of the sun yet to sprinkle over her hair, into her eyes. And make his fingers itch for a pencil.

He knew just what he would do with her, exactly how it would be. Planning it, he let his gaze wander over her. And nearly jolted when he saw the pendant. He'd all but forgotten it.

"Where did you get that?''

She'd seen those vivid blue eyes travel down, had felt a shiver of response, and now another of relief that—she hoped—it was the pendant that interested him.

"This? It's the heart of my problem.''

She'd meant it as a joke, but his gaze returned to her face, all but seared the flesh with the heat of it. "Where did you get it?''

Though the edge to his voice puzzled her, she shrugged. "There was a little shop near the waterfront. The display window was just crammed with things. Wonderful things. Magic."

"Magic."

"Elves and dragons, books and jewelry in lovely, fascinating shapes. A hodgepodge, but a crafty one. Irresistible. I only meant to go in for a minute. I had time before we were to meet at the ferry. But the old woman showed me this, and somehow while we were talking, time just went away. I didn't mean to buy it, either. But I do a lot of things I don't mean to do."

"You don't know what it is?"

"No." She closed her hand over it, felt that low vibration that couldn't be there, blinked as something tried to slide in on the edge of her vision. "It feels old, but it can't be old, not valuably old, because it only cost ten pounds."

"Value's different for one than for another." He reached out. It was irresistible. With his eyes steady and level he closed his hand over hers that held the pendant.

The jolt snapped into her, sharp as an electric current. The air seemed to turn the blue of lightning. She was on her feet, her head tipping back to keep her eyes locked with his as he shoved back from the table with enough violence to send his chair crashing.

That same violence was in him when his mouth crushed hers. The need, so bright, so strong, so right, whipped through her even as the wind rushed sudden and sharp through the window at her back. Her hand fisted in his hair, her body lifted itself to his.

And fit.

The pounding of her heart was like a song, each note a thrill. Here, with him, it was enough, even if the world crumbled to dust around them.

He couldn't stop. The taste of her was like water, cool and clean, after a lifetime of thirst. Empty pockets he hadn't known he carried inside him filled, bulged, overflowed. His blood was a rage of heat, his body weak with wanting. He gathered the back of the shirt in his bunched fingers, prepared to rip.

Then they dropped the pendant they held between them to reach for each other. And he snapped back as if from a blow.

"This is not what I want." He took her shoulders, intending to shake her, but only held her. She looked dazed. Faerie-struck. "This is not what I'll accept."

"Would you let me go?" Her voice was low, but it didn't quaver. When he did, and stepped back, she let out a short, quiet breath. There was no point in being a coward, she told herself.

"I have a couple of choices here," she began. "One is I hit my head when I fell and I have a concussion. The other is that I just fell in love with you. I think I prefer the concussion theory, and I imagine you do, too."

"You didn't hit your head." He jammed his hands in his pockets and strode away from her. The room was suddenly too small. "And people don't fall in love in an instant, over one kiss."

"Sensible ones don't. I'm not sensible. Ask anyone." But if there was ever a time to try to be, it was now.

"I think I should get dressed, take a walk, clear my head or whatever."

"Another's storm's brewing."

Allena tugged her clothes off the screen. "You're telling me," she muttered and marched into the bedroom.

4

CONAL WASN'T IN the cottage when she came out again, but Hugh sat by the fire as if waiting for her. He got up as she came through and pranced to the door, turning his big head so that his eyes met hers.

"Want a walk? Me, too."

It was a pity about the gardens, Allena thought as she paused between them. She'd have enjoyed getting down into them, yanking out those choking weeds, pinching off deadheads. An hour's pleasant work, she thought, maybe two, and instead of looking wild and neglected, those tumbling blossoms would just look wild. Which is what was needed here.

Not her job, she told herself, not her home, not her place. She cast an eye at the little outbuilding. He was probably in there doing . . . whatever the hell he did. And doing it, she imagined, angrily.

Why was there so much anger in him?

Not her problem, she thought, not her business, not her man.

26

Though for a moment, when their hands and mouths were joined, he had seemed to be.

I don't want this. I don't want you.

He'd made himself very clear. And she was tired of finding herself plopped down where she wasn't wanted.

The wind raced in off the sea, driving thick black-edged clouds toward the island. As she began to walk, she could see the pale and hopeful blue being gradually, inevitably consumed.

Conal was right. A storm was coming.

Walking along the shoreline couldn't do any harm. She wouldn't climb the hills, though she longed to. She would just stick to the long curve of surf and sand and enjoy the jittery thrill of watching the fierce waves crash.

Hugh seemed content to walk at her side. Almost, she thought, like a guard.

Eight kilometers to the nearest village, she remembered. That wasn't so very far. She could wait for the weather to clear, then walk it if Conal wouldn't drive her. There'd been a truck parked between the cottage and the outbuilding, a sleek and modern thing, anachronistic but surely serviceable.

Why had he kissed her like that?

No, that wasn't right. It hadn't been his doing. It had simply happened, to both of them. For both of them. There'd been a roar in her head, in her blood, that she'd never experienced before. More than passion, she thought now, more than lust. It was a kind of desperate recognition.

There you are. Finally. At last.

That, of course, was ridiculous, but she had no other way to explain what had spurted to life inside her. And what had spread from that first hot gush felt like love.

You couldn't love what you didn't know. You couldn't love where there was no understanding, no foundation, no history. Her head told her all these sensible, rational things. And her heart laughed at them.

It didn't matter. She could be conflicted, puzzled, annoyed, even willing to accept. But it didn't matter when he didn't want her or what had flamed to life between them.

She stopped, let the wind beat its frantic wings over her, let the spray from the waves fly on her. Overhead a gull, white as the moon, let out its triumphant scream and streamed off in the current of electric air.

Oh, she envied that freedom, for the heart of flight was inside her. To simply fly away, wherever the wind took her. And to know that when she landed, it would be her place, her time, her triumph.

But you have to live in the present, don't you, Lena? Her mother's patient and puzzled voice murmured in her ear. *You have to apply yourself, to pay attention. You can't keep drifting this way and make something of yourself. It's time you focused on a career, put your considerable energy into making your mark.*

And under that voice, unsaid, was *You disappoint me.*

"I know it. I'm sorry. It's awful. I wish I could tell you how awful it is to know I'm your only failure."

She would do better, Allena promised herself. She'd talk Margaret into giving her a second chance. Somehow. Then she'd work harder, pay more attention, be responsible, be practical.

Be miserable.

The dog bumped his head against her leg, rubbed his warm fur against her. The small gesture comforted her and turning away from the water, she continued to walk along its verge.

She'd come out to clear her head, she reminded herself, not to fill it with more problems. Surely there couldn't be a more perfect spot for easing heart and mind. Under those threatening skies, the rough hills shone, the wicked cliffs gleamed. Wildflowers, dots and splashes of color, tangled in the green and gray, and she saw a shadowy spread of purple that was heather.

She wanted to gather it, fill her arms with it, bury her face in the scent. Delighted with the idea, she turned to scramble over rocks where sprigs of it thrived in the thin soil, then higher to mounds bumpy and thick until the fragrance of it overpowered éven the primitive perfume of the sea.

When her arms were full, she wanted more. Laughing, she hurried along a narrow path. Then stopped dead. Startled, she shook her head. She heard the oddest hum. She started to step forward again, and couldn't. Simply couldn't. It was as if a wall of glass stood between her and the next slope of rock and flowers.

"My God, what is this?"

She lifted a trembling hand, sending sprigs of heather falling, then flying free in the wind. She felt no barrier, but only a kind of heat when her hand pressed the air. And try as she might, she couldn't push through it.

Lightning burst. Thunder rolled. Through it, she heard the sound of her name. She looked down to the beach, half expecting to see dragons or sorcerers. But it was only Conal, standing with his legs spread, his hair flying, and his eyes annoyed.

"Come down from there. You've no business clambering up the rocks when a storm's breaking."

What a picture she made. He'd come after her out of responsibility, he liked to think. But he'd been dumbstruck when he'd seen her walking the cliff path in the eerie light, her hair fluttering, her arms overflowing with flowers. It made him want to climb after her, to whirl her and her flowers into his arms, to press his mouth to hers again while the wind whipped savagely over them.

Because he wanted it, could all but taste her, his tone was blade-sharp when she met him on the beach. "Have you no more sense than to pick flowers in such weather?"

"Apparently not. Would you walk down there?"

"What?"

"Just humor me, and walk down the beach five more feet."

"Maybe you did rattle your brains." He started to grab her hand, pull her away, but she took a nimble step aside.

"Please. It'll only take you a minute."

He hissed out an oath, then strode off, one foot, two, three. His abrupt halt had Allena closing her eyes, shivering once. "You can't do it, can you? You can't go any farther than that. Neither could I." She opened her eyes again, met his furious ones when he turned. "What does it mean?"

"It means we deal with it. We'll go back. I've no desire to find myself drenched to the skin a second time in one day."

He said nothing on the way back, and she let him have his silence. The first fat drops of rain splattered as they reached the cottage door.

"Do you have anything to put these in?" she asked him. "They'll need water, and I'd like to keep my hands busy while you explain things to me."

He shrugged, made a vague gesture toward the kitchen, then went to add more turf to the fire.

It was a downpour. The wind rose to a howl, and she began to gather vases and bottles and bowls. When he remained silent, scowling into the fire, she heated up the tea.

He glanced over when she poured the cups, then went into the kitchen himself to take out a bottle of whiskey. A healthy dollop went into his own tea, then he lifted a brow, holding the bottle over hers.

"Well, why not?"

But when it was laced, she picked up the flowers instead of the cup and began to tuck them into vases. "What is this place? Who are you?"

"I've told you that already."

"You gave me names." The homey task calmed her, as she'd known it would. When her gaze lifted to his again, it was direct and patient. "That's not what I meant."

He studied her, then nodded. Whether she could handle it or not, she deserved to know. "Do you know how far out in the sea you are?"

"A mile, two?"

"More than ten."

"Ten? But it couldn't have taken more than twenty minutes to get here—and in rough weather."

"More than ten miles out is Dolman Island from the southwest coast of Ireland. Here we straddle the Atlantic and Celtic Seas. Some say the silkies come here, to shed their hides and sun on the rocks in human form. And the faeries come out of their rafts under the hills to dance in the moonlight.''

Allena slipped the stems of shorter blossoms into a squat bottle. ''Do you say it?''

''Some say,'' he continued without answering, ''that my great-grandmother left her raft, her palace under the hill, and pledged herself to my great-grandfather on the night of the summer solstice while they stood by the king stone of the dance on the cliffs. One hundred years ago. As a hundred years before, another with my blood stood with his woman in that same place to pledge. And a century before that as well, and always on that same night in that same place when the star shows itself.''

She touched her pendant. ''This star?''

''They say.''

''And in two days it's the solstice, and your turn?''

''If I believed my great-grandmother was other than a simple woman, that I have elfin blood in my veins and could be directed to pledge to a woman because of the way a star shines through the stones, I wouldn't be in this place.''

''I see.'' She nodded and carried one of the vases into the living room to set it on a table. ''So you're here to prove that everything you've just told me is nonsense.''

''Can you believe otherwise?''

She had no idea what she believed, but had a feeling there was a great deal, a very great deal, that she *could* believe. ''Why couldn't I walk away from here, Conal? Why couldn't you?''

She left the question hanging, walked back into the kitchen. She took a sip of her tea, felt the hot flow of whiskey slide into her, then began to select her other arrangements and put them where she liked. ''It would be hard for you, being told this story since you were a child, being expected to accept it.''

''Can you accept it?'' he demanded. ''Can you just shrug off education and reason and accept that you're to belong to me because a legend says so?''

''I would've said no.'' Pleasing herself, she set bottles

of heather on the narrow stone mantel over the simmering fire. "I would have been intrigued, amused, maybe a little thrilled at the idea of it all. Then I would have laughed it off. I would have," she said as she turned to face him. "Until I kissed you and felt what I felt inside me, and inside you."

"Desire's an easy thing."

"That's right, and if that had been it, if that had been all, we'd both have acted on it. If that had been all, you wouldn't be angry now, with yourself and with me."

"You're awfully bloody calm about it."

"I know." She smiled then, couldn't help herself. "Isn't that odd? But then, I'm odd. Everyone says so. Lena, the duck out of water, the square peg, the fumbler always just off center. But I don't feel odd or out of place here. So it's easier for me to be calm."

Nor did she look out of place, he thought, wandering through the cottage placing her flowers. "I don't believe in magic."

"And I've looked for it all my life." She took a sprig of heather, held it out to him. "So, I'll make you a promise."

"You don't owe me promises. You don't owe me anything."

"It's free. I won't hold you with legends or magic. When I can leave, if that's what you want, I'll go."

"Why?"

"I'm in love with you, and love doesn't cling."

Humbled, he took the heather, slipped it into her hair. "Allena, it takes clear eyes to recognize what's in the heart so easily. I don't have them. I'll hurt you." He skimmed his fingers down her cheek. "And I find I'd rather not."

"I'm fairly sturdy. I've never been in love before, Conal, and I might be terrible at it. But right now it suits me, and that's enough."

He refused to believe anything could be so simple. "I'm drawn to you. I want my hands on you. I want you under me. If that's all, it might not be enough for you, or for me in the end. So it's best to stand back."

He walked to the peg, tugged down his slicker. "I need to work," he said, and went out into the rain.

It would be more than she'd had, she realized, and knew that if necessary, she could make it enough.

The storm was only a grumble when he came back. Evening was falling, soft and misty. The first thing he noticed when he stepped inside, was the scent. Something hot and rich that reminded his stomach it was empty.

Then he noticed the little changes in the living room. Just a few subtle touches: a table shifted, cushions smoothed. He wouldn't have noticed the dust, but he noticed the absence of it, and the faint tang of polish.

She'd kept the fire going, and the light, mixed with that of the candles she'd found and set about, was welcoming. She'd put music on as well and was humming along to it as she worked in the kitchen.

Even as he hung up his slicker, the tension he'd carried through his work simply slid off his shoulders.

"I made some soup," she called out. "I hunted up some herbs from the kitchen bed, foraged around in here. You didn't have a lot to work with, so it's pretty basic."

"It smells fine. I'm grateful."

"Well, we have to eat, don't we?"

"You wouldn't say that so easy if I'd been the one doing the cooking." She'd already set the table, making the mismatched plates and bowls look cheerful and clever instead of careless. There were candles there, too, and one of the bottles of wine he'd brought from Dublin stood breathing on the counter.

She was making biscuits.

"Allena, you needn't have gone to such trouble."

"Oh, I like puttering around. Cooking's kind of a hobby." She poured him wine. "Actually, I took lessons. I took a lot of lessons. This time I thought maybe I'd be a chef or open my own restaurant."

"And?"

"There's a lot more to running a restaurant than cooking. I'm horrible at business. As for the chef idea, I realized you had to cook pretty much the same things night after night, and on demand, to suit the menu, you know? So, it turned into one of my many hobbies.'' She slipped the biscuits into the oven. ''But at least this one has a practical purpose. So.'' She dusted her hands on the dishcloth she'd tucked into her waistband. ''I hope you're hungry.''

He flashed a grin that made her heart leap. ''I'm next to starving.''

''Good.'' She set out the dish of cheese and olives she'd put together. ''Then you won't be critical.''

Where he would have ladled the soup straight from the kettle, she poured it into a thick white bowl. Already she'd hunted out the glass dish his mother had used for butter and that he hadn't seen for years. The biscuits went in a basket lined with a cloth of blue and white checks. When she started to serve the soup, he laid a hand over hers.

''I'll do it. Sit.''

The scents alone were enough to make him weep in gratitude. The first taste of herbed broth thick with hunks of vegetables made him close his eyes in pleasure.

When he opened them again, she was watching him with amused delight. ''I like your hobby,'' he told her. ''I hope you'll feel free to indulge yourself with it as long as you're here.''

She selected a biscuit, studied it. It was so gratifying to see him smile. ''That's very generous of you.''

''I've been living on my own poor skills for some months now.'' His eyes met hers, held. ''You make me realize what I've missed. I'm a moody man, Allena.''

''Really?'' Her voice was so mild the insult nearly slipped by him. But he was quick.

He laughed, shook his head, and spooned up more soup. ''It won't be a quiet couple of days, I'm thinking.''

5

He slept in his studio. It seemed the wisest course.

He wanted her, and that was a problem. He had no doubt she would have shared the bed with him, shared herself with him. As much as he would have preferred that to the chilly and narrow cot crammed into his work space, it didn't seem fair to take advantage of her romantic notions.

She fancied herself in love with him.

It was baffling, really, to think that a woman could make such a decision, state it right out, in a fingersnap of time. But then, Allena Kennedy wasn't like any of the other women who'd passed in and out of his life. A complicated package, she was, he thought. It would have been easy to dismiss her as a simple, almost foolish sort. At a first and casual glance.

But Conal wasn't one for casual glances. There were layers to her—thoughtful, bubbling, passionate, and compassionate layers. Odd, wasn't it? he mused, that she didn't seem to recognize them in herself.

That lack of awareness added one more layer, and that was sweetness.

Absently, with his eyes still gritty from a restless night, he began to sketch. Allena Kennedy from New York City, the square peg in what appeared to be a family of conformists. The woman who had yet to find herself, yet seemed perfectly content to deal with where she'd landed. A modern woman, certainly, but one who still accepted tales of magic.

No, more than accepted, he thought now. She embraced them. As if she'd just been waiting to be told where it was she'd been going all along.

That he wouldn't do, refused to do. All his life he'd been told this day would come. He wouldn't passively fall in, give up his own will. He had come back to this place at this time to prove it.

And he could almost hear the fates giggling.

Scowling, he studied what he'd drawn. It was Allena with her long eyes and sharp bones, the short and shaggy hair that suited that angular face and slender neck. And at her back, he'd sketched in the hint of faerie wings.

They suited her as well.

It annoyed the hell out of him.

Conal tossed the pad aside. He had work to do, and he'd get to it as soon as he'd had some tea.

The wind was still up. The morning sun was slipping through the stacked clouds to dance over the water. The only thunder now was the crash and boom of waves on the shore. He loved the look of it, that changing and capricious sea. His years in Dublin hadn't been able to feed this single need in him, for the water and the sky and the rough and simple land that was his.

However often he left, wherever he went, he would always be drawn back. For here was heart and soul.

Turning away from the sea, he saw her.

She knelt in the garden, flowers rioting around her and the quiet morning sun shimmering over her hair. Her face was turned away from him, but he could see it in his mind. She would have that half-dreaming, contented look in her eyes as she tugged away the weeds he'd ignored.

Already the flowers looked cheerful, as if pleased with the attention after weeks of neglect.

There was smoke pluming from the chimney, a broom propped against the front wall. She'd dug a basket out of God knew where, and in this she tossed the weeds. Her feet were bare.

Warmth slid into him before he could stop it and murmured *welcome* in his ear.

"You don't have to do that."

She looked up at his voice, and she was indeed happy. "They needed it. Besides, I love flowers. I have pots of them all over my apartment, but this is so much better. I've never seen snapdragons so big." She traced a finger on a spike of butter-yellow blooms. "They always make me think of Alice."

"Alice?"

"In Wonderland. I've already made tea." She got to her feet, then winced at the dirt on the knees of her trousers. "I guess I should've been more careful. It's not like I have a vast wardrobe to choose from at the moment. So. How do you like your eggs?"

He started to tell her she wasn't obliged to cook his breakfast. But he remembered just how fine the soup had been the night before. "Scrambled would be nice, if it's no trouble."

"None, and it's the least I can do for kicking you out of your own bed." She stepped up to the door, then turned. Her eyes were eloquent, and patient. "You could have stayed."

"I know it."

She held his gaze another moment, then nodded. "You had some bacon in your freezer. I took it out last night to thaw. Oh, and your shower dripped. It just needed a new washer."

He paused at the doorway, remembered, as he hadn't in years, to wipe his feet. "You fixed the shower?"

"Well, it dripped." She was already walking into the

kitchen. "You probably want to clean up. I'll get breakfast started."

He scratched the back of his neck. "I'm grateful."

She slanted him a look. "So am I."

When he went into the bedroom, she did a quick dance, hugged herself. Oh, she loved this place. It was a storybook, and she was right in the middle of it. She'd awakened that morning half believing it had all been a dream. But then she'd opened her eyes to that misty early light, had smelled the faint drift of smoke from the dying fire, the tang of heather she'd put beside the bed.

It was a dream. The most wonderful, the most real dream she'd ever had. And she was going to keep it.

He didn't want it, didn't want her. But that could change. There were two days yet to open his heart. How could his stay closed when hers was so full? Love was nothing like she'd expected it to be.

It was so much more brilliant.

She needed the hope, the faith, that on one of the days left to her he would wake up and feel what she did.

Love, she discovered, was so huge it filled every space inside with brightness. There was no room for shadows, for doubts.

She was in love, with the man, with the place, with the promise. It wasn't just in the rush of an instant, though there was that thrill as well. But twined with it was a lovely, settled comfort, an ease of being, of knowing. And that was something she wanted for him.

For once in her life, she vowed, she wouldn't fail. She would not lose.

Closing her eyes, she touched the star that hung between her breasts. "I'll make it happen," she whispered, then with a happy sigh, she started breakfast.

He didn't know what to make of it. He couldn't have said just what state the bathroom had been in before, but he was dead certain it hadn't sparkled. There may or may not have been fresh towels out the last time he'd seen it. But he thought not. There hadn't been a bottle of flowers on the windowsill.

The shower had dripped, that he remembered. He'd meant to get to that.

He could be certain that it was a great deal more pleasant to shower and shave in a room where the porcelain gleamed and the air smelled faintly of lemon and flowers.

Because of it, he guiltily wiped up after himself and hung the towel to dry instead of tossing it on the floor.

The bedroom showed her touch as well. The bed was tidily made, the pillows fluffed up. She'd opened the windows wide to bring in the sun and the breeze. It made him realize he'd lived entirely too long with dust and dark.

Then he stepped out. She was singing in the kitchen. A pretty voice. And the scents that wafted to him were those of childhood. Bread toasting, bacon frying.

There was a rumble he recognized as the washer spinning a load. He could only shake his head.

"How long have you been up and about?" he asked her.

"I woke up at dawn." She turned to pass him a mug of tea over the counter. "It was so gorgeous I couldn't get back to sleep. I've been piddling."

"You've a rare knack for piddling."

"My father calls it nervous energy. Oh, I let Hugh out. He bolted to the door the minute my feet hit the floor, so I figured that was the routine."

"He likes to run around in the mornings. Dog piddling, I suppose."

It made her laugh as she scooped his eggs from skillet to plate. "He's terrific company. I felt very safe and snug with him curled up at the foot of the bed last night."

"He's deserted me for a pretty face." He sat, then caught her hand. "Where's yours?"

"I had something earlier. I'll let you eat in peace. My father hates to be chattered at over breakfast. I'll just hang out the wash."

"I'm not your father. Would you sit? Please." He waited until she took a seat and for the first time noticed nerves in the way she linked her fingers together. Now what was that about? "Allena, do you think I expect you to cater to me this way? Cook and serve and tidy?"

"No, of course not." The lift had gone out of her voice, out of her eyes. "I've overstepped. I'm always doing that. I didn't think."

"That's not what I meant. Not at all." His eyes were keen, part of his gift, and they saw how her shoulders had braced, her body tensed. "What are you doing? Waiting for the lecture?" With a shake of his head, he began to eat. "They've done what they could, haven't they, to stifle you? Why is it people are always so desperate to mold another into their vision, their way? I'm saying only that you're not obliged to cook my meals and scrub my bath. While you're here you should do what pleases you."

"I guess I have been."

"Fine. You won't hear any complaints from me. I don't know what you've done with these humble eggs unless it's magic."

She relaxed again. "Thyme and dill, from your very neglected herb bed. If I had a house, I'd plant herbs, and gardens." Imagining it, she propped her chin on her fist. "I'd have stepping-stones wandering through it, with a little bench so you could just stop and sit and look. It would be best if it was near the water so I could hear the beat of it the way I did last night. Pounding, like a quickened heart."

She blinked out of the image, found him staring at her. "What? Oh, I was running on again." She started to get up, but he took her hand a second time.

"Come with me."

He got to his feet, pulled her to hers. "The dishes—"

"Can wait. This can't."

He'd already started it that morning with the sketch. In his head, it was all but finished, and the energy of it was driving him, so he strode quickly out of the house, toward his studio. She had to run to keep up.

"Conal, slow down. I'm not going anywhere."

Ignoring her, he shoved open the door, pulled her in after him. "Stand by the window."

But she was already moving in, eyes wide and delighted. "You're an artist. This is wonderful. You sculpt."

The single room was nearly as big as the main area of the cottage. And much more cramped. A worktable stood in the center, crowded with tools and hunks of stone, pots of clay. A half dozen sketch pads were tossed around. Shelves and smaller tables were jammed with examples of his work. Mystical, magical creatures that danced and flew.

A blue mermaid combed her hair on a rock. A white dragon breathed fire. Faeries no bigger than her thumb ringed in a circle with faces sly. A sorcerer nearly as tall as she, held his arms high and wept.

"They're all so alive, so vivid." She couldn't help herself, she had to touch, and so she ran her finger down the rippling hair of the mermaid. "I've seen this before," she murmured. "Not quite this, but the same feeling of it, but in bronze. At a gallery in New York."

She looked over then where he was impatiently flipping through a sketch pad. "I've seen your work in New York. You must be famous."

His answer was a grunt.

"I wanted to buy it—the mermaid. I was with my mother, and I couldn't because she'd have reminded me I couldn't afford the price. I went back the next day, because I couldn't stop thinking about it, but it was already sold."

"In front of the window, turn to me."

"That was two years ago, and I've thought about her a dozen times since. Isn't it amazing that she was yours?"

Muttering an oath, he strode to her, pulled her to the window. "Lift your head, like that. Hold it there. And be quiet."

"Are you going to draw me?"

"No, I'm after building a boat here. Of course I'm drawing you. Now be quiet for one bloody minute."

She shut her mouth, but couldn't do anything about the grin that trembled on her lips. And that, he thought, was precisely what he wanted. Just that trace of humor, of energy, of personal delight.

He would do a clay model, he thought, and cast her in

bronze. Something that gleamed gold and warmed to the touch. She wasn't for stone or wood. He did three quick studies of her face, moving around her for a change of angle. Then he lowered his pad.

"I need the line of your body. Your shape. Take off your clothes."

"Excuse me?"

"I have to see how you're made. The clothes are in the way of you."

"You want me to pose nude?"

With an effort, he brought himself back from his plans, met her eyes. "If this was a matter of sex, I wouldn't have slept on that rock in the corner last night. You've my word I won't touch you. But I have to see you."

"If this was a matter of sex, I wouldn't be so nervous. Okay." She shut her eyes a minute, bolstered her courage. "I'm like a bowl of fruit," she told herself and unbuttoned her shirt.

When she slipped it off, folded it, set it aside, Conal lifted a brow. "No, you're like a woman. If I wanted a bowl of fruit, I'd get one."

6

SHE WAS SLIM, leaning toward angular, and exactly right. Eyes narrowed, mind focused, he flipped up a fresh page and began.

"No, keep your head up," he ordered, faintly irritated that she should be so exactly right. "Hold your arms back. Just a bit more. Palms down and flat. No, you're not a flaming penguin, spread your fingers a little. Ah."

It was then he noticed the faint flush spreading over her skin, the stiffness in her movements. Moron, he told himself and bit back a sigh. Of course she was nervous and embarrassed. And he'd done nothing to put her at ease.

He'd grown too used, he supposed, to professional models who undraped without a thought. She liked to talk, so he would let her talk.

"Tell me about these lessons of yours."

"What?"

"The lessons. You said you'd taken a number of lessons on this and that. What was it you studied?"

She pressed her lips together, fought back the foolish urge to cross her arms over her breasts. "I thought you said I wasn't supposed to talk."

"Now I'm saying you can."

She heard the exasperation, rolled her eyes. What was she, a mind reader? "I, ah, took art lessons."

"Did you now? Turn to the right just a bit. And what did you learn from them?"

"That I'm not an artist." She smiled a little. "I'm told I have a good eye for color and shapes and aesthetics, but no great skill with the execution."

Yes, it was better when she talked. Her face became mobile again. Alive again. "That discouraged you?"

"Not really. I draw now and then when I'm in the mood."

"Another hobby?"

"Oh, I'm loaded with them. Like music. I took music lessons."

Ah, she was relaxing. The doe-in-the-crosshairs look was fading from her eyes. "What's your instrument?"

"The flute. I'm reasonably adept, but I'm never going to have a chair with the Philharmonic."

She shrugged, and he bit back a sharp order for her not to change the line.

"I took a course in computer programming, and that was a complete wash. As most of my business courses were, which scuttled the idea I had of opening a little craft shop. I could handle the craft part, but not the shop part."

Her gaze was drawn back to the mermaid. She coveted that, not just the piece itself, but the talent and vision that had created it.

"Stand on your toes. That's it, that's lovely. Hold a minute. Why don't you take on a partner?"

"For what?"

"The shop, if it's what you want. Someone business-minded."

"Mostly because I have enough business sense to know I could never afford the rent in New York, the start-up costs." She moved a shoulder. "Overhead, equipment, stock. I guess running a business is a study in stress. Margaret always says so."

Ah, he thought, the inestimable Margaret, whom he'd already decided to detest. "What do you care what she says? No, that's not right. It's not quite right. Turn around. You have a beautiful back."

"I do?" Surprise had her turning her head to look at him.

"There! Hold that. Lower your chin a little more to your shoulder, keep your eyes on me."

That was what he wanted. No shyness here. Coyness was something different altogether. There was a hint of that in the upward angle of her gaze, the tilt of her head. And just a bit of smugness as well, in the slight curve of her lips.

Allena of the Faeries, he thought, already eager to begin in clay. He ripped the sheets off the pad, began tacking them to the wall.

"I'll do better with you as well as the sketches. Relax a minute while I prep the clay." As he passed, he touched a hand absently to her shoulder. He stopped. "Christ, you're cold. Why didn't you say something?"

She was turning toward him, a slow shift of her body. "I didn't notice."

"I didn't think to keep the fire going." His hand skimmed over her shoulder, fingers tracing the blade where he imagined wings. "I'll build one now." Even as he spoke he was leaning toward her, his eyes locked on hers. Her lips parted, and he could feel the flutter of her breath.

He jerked back, like a man snapping out of a dream. Lifted his hand, then held them both up, away from her. "I said I wouldn't touch you. I'm sorry."

The rising wave of anticipation in her broke, then vanished as he walked away to yank a blanket from the cot. "I wish you weren't. Sorry, I mean."

He stood with the table between them, the blanket in his hands, and felt like a man drowning. There was no shyness in her now, nor coyness. But the patience was there, and the promise.

"I don't want this need for you. Do you understand?"

"You want me to say yes." She was laid bare now, she realized. Much more than her body laid bare. "It would make it easier if I said that I understand. But I can't, I don't. I want that need, Conal. And you."

"Another place, another time," he murmured. "There'd be no need to understand. Another place, another time, I'd want it as well."

"This is here," she said quietly. "And this is now. It's still your choice."

He wanted to be sure of it, wanted to know there was nothing but her. "Will you take that off?"

She lifted a hand to the pendant, her last shield. Saying nothing, she slipped the chain over her head, then walked to the table, set it down. "Do you think I'll feel differently without it?"

"There's no magic between us now. We're only who and what we are." He stepped to her, swept the blanket around her shoulders. "It's as much your choice as mine, Allena. You've a right to say no."

"Then . . ." She laid her hands on his shoulders, brought her lips to within a breath of his. "I've also a right to say yes."

It was she who closed that tenuous distance so mouths and bodies met. And she who let the blanket drop when her arms went around him.

She gave, completely, utterly. All the love, so newly discovered in her heart, poured out for him. Her lips seduced, her hands soothed, her body yielded.

There was a choice. She had made hers, but he still had his own. To draw back, step away and refuse. Or to gather close and take. Before his blood could take over, before it was all need and heat, he took her face in his hands until their eyes met again.

"With no promises, Allena."

He suffered. She could see the clouds and worry in his eyes, and said what she hoped would comfort. And be the truth as well. "And no regrets."

His thumbs skimmed over her cheeks, tracing the shape

of her face as skillfully as he'd drawn it on paper. "Be with me, then."

The cot was hard and narrow, but might have been a bed of rose petals as they lay on it. The air was chill, still damp from the storm, but she felt only warmth when his body covered hers.

Here. At last.

He knew his hands were big, the palms rough and calloused from his work, and very often careless. He would not be careless with her, would not rush through the moment they offered each other. So he touched her, gently, giving himself the pleasure of the body he'd sketched. Long limbs, long bones, and soft white skin. Her sigh was like music, the song his name.

She tugged off his sweater, sighing again when flesh met flesh, and again murmuring his name against the pulse of his own throat. With only that, she gave him the sweetness he'd denied himself. Whatever he had of that simple gift inside him, he offered back.

Under him she lifted and moved as if they'd danced this dance together for a lifetime. Flowed with and against him, now fluid, now strong. And the quickening pulse that rose in her was like his own.

Her scent was soap, her taste fresh as rain.

He watched her glide up, the faerie again, soaring on one long spread of wings. As she crested, her eyes opened, met his. And she smiled.

No one had brought her so much, or shown her how much she had to offer. Her body quivered from the thrill of it, and in her heart was the boundless joy of finding home.

She arched up, opened so he would fill her. As he slid inside her, the beauty dazzled, and the power hummed.

While they took each other, neither noticed the star carved in silver, glowing blue as flame.

She lay over him now, snug under his arm with her cheek upon his chest. It was lovely to hear how his heart still

48 ★ Nora Roberts

pounded. A kind of rage, she thought, though he'd been the most tender of lovers.

No one could have shown her that kind of caring if there wasn't caring inside. And that, she thought, closing her eyes, was enough.

"You're cold," he murmured.

"Am not." She snuggled against him and would have frozen to the bone before she let him move. But she lifted her head so she could grin at him.

"Allena Kennedy." His fingers trailed lightly down the back of her neck. "You look smug."

"I feel smug. Do you mind?"

"I would be a foolish man to mind."

She bent down to kiss his chin, a sweet and casual gesture that moved him. "And Conal O'Neil is not a foolish man. Or is he?" She angled her head. "If we can't go beyond a certain point and walk to the village, wouldn't it follow that no one from the village can come here?"

"I suppose it would."

"Then let's do something foolish. Let's go swim naked in the sea."

"You want to swim naked in the sea?"

"I've always wanted to. I just realized it this minute." She rolled off the cot and tugged at his hand. "Come be foolish with me, Conal."

"*Leannan,* the first wave'll flatten you."

"Will not." *Leannan.* She had no idea what it meant, but it sounded tender, and made her want to dance. She raked both hands through her hair, then the light of challenge lighted her eyes. "Race you."

She darted off like a rabbit and had him scrambling up. "Wait. Damn it, the seas are too rough for you."

Bird bones, he thought, snatching up the blanket on his way. She would crack half a dozen of them in minutes.

No, she didn't run like a rabbit, he realized. She ran like a bloody gazelle, with long, loping strides that had her nearly at the foaming surf. He called out her name, rushing after her. His heart simply stopped when she raced into the water and dived under its towering wall.

"Sweet Jesus."

He'd gotten no farther than the beach when she surfaced, laughing. "Oh, it's cold!" She struggled to the shallows, slicking her hair back, lifted her face, her arms. For the second time his heart stopped, but now it had nothing to do with alarm.

"You're a vision, Allena."

"No one's ever said that to me before." She held out a hand. "No one's ever looked at me the way you do. Ride the sea with me."

It had been, he decided, much too long since he'd been foolish. "Hold on, then."

It tossed them up, a rush of power. It sucked them down into a blind, thundering world. The tumult of it was freedom, a cocky dare to fate. Wrapped around each other, they spun as the waves rolled over them.

Breathless, they surfaced, only to plunge in again. Her scream wasn't one of fear, but a cry of victory as, latched around him, she was swept into the air again.

"You'll drown us both!" he shouted, but his eyes were lit with wicked humor.

"I won't. I can't. Nothing but wonders today. Once more." She locked her arms around his neck. "Let's go under just once more."

To her shrieking delight, he snatched her off her feet and dived into the cresting wave with her.

When they stumbled out, panting, their hands were linked.

"Your teeth are chattering."

"I know. I loved it." But she snuggled into the blanket he wrapped around them both. "I've never done anything like that. I guess you've done it dozens of times."

"Not with the likes of you."

It was, she thought, the perfect thing to say. She held the words to her for a moment even as she held him. Hard against her heart.

"What does *leannan* mean?"

"Hmm?" Her head was on his shoulder, her arms linked

around his waist. Everything inside him was completely at peace.

"*Leannan*. You said that to me, I wondered what it means."

His hand paused in midstroke on her hair. "It's a casual term," he said carefully. "A bit of an endearment, is all. 'Sweetheart' would be the closest."

"I like it."

He closed his eyes. "Allena, you ask for too little."

And hope for everything, she thought. "You shouldn't worry, Conal. I'm not. Now, before we both turn blue out here, I'll make fresh tea, and you'll build up the fire." She kissed him. "Right after I pick up some of these shells."

She wiggled away, leaving him holding the blanket and shaking his head. Most of the shells that littered the beach had been broken by the waves, but that didn't appear to bother her. He left her to it and went into the studio to tug on his jeans.

She had a pile of shells when he came back, offering her his sweater and her pendant.

"I won't wear it if it bothers you."

"It's yours." Deliberately, as if challenging the fates, he slipped it around her neck. "Here, put this on before you freeze."

She bundled into it, then crouched to put the shells into the blanket. "I love you, Conal, whether I'm wearing it or not. And since loving you makes me happy, it shouldn't worry you."

She rose. "Don't spoil it," she murmured. "Let's just take today, then see about tomorrow."

"All right." He took her hand, brought it to his lips. "I'll give you a promise after all."

"I'll take it."

"Today will always be precious to me, and so will you."

7

SHE DUG OUT an ancient pair of Conal's jeans, found a hunk of frayed rope, and went to work with scissors. As a fashion statement the chopped jeans, rough belt, and baggy sweater said Island Shipwreck, but they did the job.

As he insisted on making the tea this time around, she busied herself hanging the wash. And dreaming.

It could be just this way, she thought. Long, wonderful days together. Conal would work in his studio, and she'd tend the house, the gardens . . . and, oh, the children when they came along.

She would paint the shutters and the little back porch. She'd put an arbor in front, plant roses—the only roses she would have—so that they'd climb up and twine and ramble and it would be like walking through a fairy tale every time she went into the house.

And it would be her fairy tale, ever after.

They would need to add rooms, of course, for those children. A second floor, she imagined, with dormer windows.

Another bath, a bigger kitchen, but nothing that would take away from the lovely cottage-by-the-sea feeling.

She'd make wonderful meals, keep the windows spar-kling, sew curtains that would flutter in the breeze.

She stopped, pegging a sheet that flapped wetly. Her mother would be appalled. Household chores were some-thing you hired other people to do because you had a ca-reer. You were a professional . . . something.

Of course, it was all just fantasy, she told herself as she moved down the clothesline. She had to make a living somehow. But she'd worry about that later. For now, she was going to enjoy the moment, the thrilling rush of being in love, the jittery ache of waiting to be loved in return.

They would have today, and their tomorrow. Whatever happened after, she'd have no regrets.

With the last of the laundry hung, she stepped back, lifted the basket to rest it on her hip. She saw Hugh pranc-ing down the hill.

"Well, so you decided to come home. What have you got there?" Her eyes widened as she recognized the brown bulk he carried in his mouth. "My bag!"

She dropped the basket and rushed to him. And Hugh, sensing a game, began to race in circles around her.

Conal watched from the doorway. The tea was steeping in the pot, and he'd been about to call to her. Now he simply stood.

Sheets billowed like sails in the wind. He caught the clean, wet scent of them, and the drift of rosemary and lemon balm from the herb bed she'd weeded that morning. Her laughter lifted up, bright and delighted, as she raced with the dog.

His tattered old jeans hung on her, though she'd hacked them off to above her ankles. She'd rolled up the cuffs, pushed up the sleeves on his sweater, but now as she ran around with Hugh, they'd come down again and fell over her hands. She hadn't put on her shoes.

She was a joy to watch. And when, he wondered, had he stopped letting joy into his life? The shadow of his fate had grown longer with each passing year. He'd huddled under it, he thought now, telling himself he was standing clear.

He had let no one touch him, let nothing be important to him but his work. He had estranged himself from his father and his home. Those had been his choices, and his right. Now, watching Allena play tug-of-war with the big dog in a yard filled with sun and sailing white sheets, he wondered for the first time what he'd missed along the way.

And still, whatever he'd missed, she was here.

The pendant was here.

The solstice was closing in.

He could refuse it. He could deny it. However much this woman called to his blood, he would, at the end of that longest day, determine his own fate.

It would not be magic that forced his destiny, but his own will.

He saw Allena yank, Hugh release. She stumbled back, clutching something to her chest, then landed hard on her back. Conal was out the door and across the yard in a single skipping heartbeat.

"Are you hurt?" He issued one sharp order to the dog in Gaelic that had Hugh hanging his head.

"Of course not." She started to sit up, but Conal was already gathering her, stroking, murmuring something in Gaelic that sounded lovely. Loving. Her heart did one long, slow cartwheel. "Conal."

"The damn dog probably outweighs you, and you've bones like a bird."

"We were just playing. There, now, you've hurt Hugh's feelings. Come here, baby, it's okay."

While Conal sat back on his heels and scowled, she hugged and cuddled the dog. "It's all right. He didn't mean it, whatever it was. Did you, Conal?"

Conal caught the sidelong glance the dog sent him, and had to call it smug. "I did."

She only laughed and kissed Hugh's nose. "Such a smart dog, such a good dog," she crooned. "He found my bag and brought it home. I, on the other hand, am a moron. I forgot all about it."

Conal studied the oversized purse. It was wet, filthy, and now riddled with teeth marks. That didn't seem to bother her a bit. "It's taken a beating."

"I must've dropped it in the storm. Everything's in here. My passport, my credit cards, my ticket. My makeup." She hugged the bag, thrilled to have her lipstick back. "Oh, and dozens of things. Including my copy of Margaret's itinerary. Do you think the phone's working now?"

Without waiting for him to answer, she leaped up. "I can call her hotel, let her know I'm all right. She must be frantic."

She dashed into the house, clutching the bag, and Conal stayed as he was.

He didn't want the phones to be working. He didn't want that to break their bubble. Realizing it left him shaken. Here, he thought, at the first chance to reach out of their world, she'd run to do it.

Of course she had. He pressed his fingers to his eyes. Wouldn't he have done the same? She had a life beyond this, beyond him. The romance of it had swept her away for a while, just as it had nearly swept him. She would get her feet back under her and move on. That was as it should be. And what he wanted.

But when he rose to go after her, there was an ache inside him that hadn't been there before.

"I got through." Allena sent him a brilliant smile. She stood by the counter, the phone in her hand and what appeared to be half her worldly goods dumped on the table. "She's checked in, and they're going to ring her room. I only hope she didn't call my parents. I'd hate to think they'd—Margaret! Oh, I'm so glad you're—"

She broke off again, and Conal watched the light in her eyes go dim. "Yes, I know. I'm so sorry. I missed the ferry and . . ."

Saying nothing, he moved past her and got down mugs for tea. He had no intention of leaving her to her privacy.

"Yes, you're right, it was irresponsible. Inexcusable, yes, that, too, to leave you shorthanded this way. I tried to . . ."

He saw the moment she gave up, when her shoulders

slumped and her face went carefully blank. "I understand. No, of course, you can't be expected to keep me on after this. Oh, yes, I know it was against your better judgment in the first place. You were very clear about that. I'm sorry I let you down. Yes, again."

Shame, fatigue, resignation closed in on her, a dingy fog of failure. She shut her eyes. "No, Margaret, excuses don't matter when people are depending on you. Did you call Mom and Dad? No, you're right. What would have been the point?"

"Bloody bitch," Conal muttered. They'd just see how Margaret liked being on the other end of a tongue-lashing, he decided, and grabbed the phone out of Allena's hand. The buzz of the dial tone left him no victim for his outrage.

"She had to go," Allena managed. "Schedule. I should—Excuse me."

"No, damned if I will." He took her shoulders in a firm grip before she could escape. There were tears on her lashes. He wanted Margaret's neck in his hands. "You'll not go off to lick your wounds. Why did you take that from her?"

"She was right. I was irresponsible. She has every reason to fire me. She'd never have taken me on in the first place without family pressure."

"Family pressure? Bugger it. Where was her family concern? Did she ask if you were all right? What had happened? Where you were? Did she once ask you why?"

"No."

A tear spilled over, slid down her cheek and inflamed him. "Where is your anger?" he demanded.

"What good does it do to be angry?" Wearily, she brushed the tear away. "I brought it on myself. I don't care about the job. That's the problem, really. I don't care about it. I wouldn't have taken it if I'd had a choice. Margaret's probably right. I bungle this way on purpose."

"Margaret is a jackass."

"No, really, she's not." She managed a wobbly grin. "She's just very disciplined and goal-oriented. Well, there's no use whining about it." She patted his hand, then moved away to pour the tea. "I'll call my parents after I've settled down a little, explain . . . oh, God."

Pressing her palms to the counter, she squeezed her eyes shut. "I *hate* disappointing them this way. Over and over, like a cycle I can't break. If I could just do something, if I could just be good at something."

Shaking her head, she went to the refrigerator to take out last night's soup to heat for lunch. "You don't know how much I envy you your talent and your confidence in it. My mother always said if I'd just focus my energies instead of scattering them a dozen different ways, I'd move beyond mediocre."

"It should have shamed her to say such a thing to you."

Surprised by the violence in his tone, she turned back. "She didn't mean it the way I made it sound. You have to understand, they're all so smart and clever and, well, dedicated to what they do. My father's chief of surgery, my mother's a partner in one of the most prestigious law firms on the East Coast. And I can't do *anything.*"

There was the anger. It whipped through her as she slammed the pot on the stove. Pleased to see it, Conal folded his arms, leaned back, and watched it build.

"There's James with his glossy practice and his gorgeous trophy wife and certified genius child, who's a complete brat, by the way, but everyone says she's simply precocious. As if precocious and rude are synonymous. And Margaret with her perfect office and her perfect wardrobe and her perfect home and her perfectly detestable husband, who won't see anything but art films and collects coins."

She dumped soup into the pot. "And every Thanksgiving they all sit around patting each other on the back over how successful and brilliant they are. Then they look at me as if I'm some sort of alien who got dumped on the doorstep and had to be taken in for humanitarian purposes. And I can't be a doctor or a lawyer or a goddamn Indian chief no matter how hard I try because I just can't *do* anything."

"Now *you* should be ashamed."

"What?" She pressed her fingers to her temples. Temper

made her dizzy, and fuzzy-headed, which is why she usually tried to avoid it. "What?"

"Come here." He grabbed her hand, pulled her into the living room. "What did you do here?"

"About what?"

"What are the things you did in here?"

"I . . . dusted?"

"To hell and back again with the dust, Allena. Look here at your flowers and candles and your bowl of broken shells. And out here."

He dragged her to the door, shoved it open. "Here's a garden that was suffering from neglect until the morning. Where's the sand that was all over the walk that I didn't even notice until it was gone? There are sheets drying in the wind out back and soup heating in the kitchen. The bloody shower doesn't drip now. Who did those things?"

"Anyone can sweep a walk, Conal."

"Not everyone thinks to. Not everyone cares to. And not everyone finds pleasure in the doing of it. In one day you made a home out of this place, and it hasn't been one in too long, so that I'd all but forgotten the feel of a home around me. Do you think that's nothing? Do you think there's no value in that?"

"It's just . . . ordinary," she said for lack of a better word. "I can't make a career out of picking wildflowers."

"A living can be made where you find it, if a living must be made. You've a need to pick wildflowers and seashells, Allena. And there are those who are grateful for it, and notice the difference you make."

If she hadn't loved him already, she would have fallen at that moment with his words still echoing and his eyes dark with impatience. "That's the kindest thing anyone's ever said to me." She laid her hands on his cheeks. "The very kindest." Softly, she touched her lips to his. "Thank you."

Before he could speak, she shook her head, then rested it on his shoulder.

8

THEY SHUT OUT the world. Turned off time. Conal would have bristled at the idea that they were making a kind of magic, but for Allena there was no other word for it.

She posed for him again, in the studio where the afternoon sun slanted through the windows. And she watched herself be born in clay.

Because she asked, he told her of his years in Dublin. His studies and his work. The lean student years when he'd lived on tinned food and art. Then the recognition that had come, like a miracle, in a dingy gallery.

The first sale had given him the luxury of time, room to work without the constant worry of paying the rent. And the sales that followed had given him the luxury of choice, so that he'd been able to afford a studio of his own.

Still, though he spoke of it easily, she noticed that when he talked of Dublin, he didn't refer to it as home. But she said nothing.

Later, when he'd covered the clay with a damp cloth and

washed in the little sink, they went for a walk along the shore. They spoke of a hundred things, but never once of the star she wore against her heart, or the stone circle that threw its shadows from the cliff.

They made love while the sun was still bright, and the warmth of it glowed on her skin when she rose over him.

As the day moved to evening, the light remained, shimmering as though it would never give way to night. She entertained herself mending the old lace curtains she'd found on a shelf in the closet while Conal sketched and the dog curled into a nap on the floor between them.

She had the most expressive face, he thought. Dreamy now as she sat and sewed. Everything she felt moved into her eyes of soft, clear gray. The witch behind those eyes had yet to wake. And when she did, he imagined that any man she cast them on would be spellbound.

How easily she had settled in—to him, his home, his life. Without a break of rhythm, he thought, and with such contentment. And how easy it would be to settle in to her. Even with these edgy flashes of need and desire, there was a comfort beneath.

What was he to do about her? Where was he to put these feelings she'd brought to life inside him? And how was he to know if they were real?

"Conal?" She spoke quietly. His troubled thoughts were like a humming in the air, a warning. "Can't you put it aside for now? Can't you be content to wait and see?"

"No." It irritated him that she'd read his mood in his silence. "Letting others shape your life is your way, not mine."

Her hand jerked, as if it had been slapped, then continued to move smoothly. "Yes, you're right. I've spent my life trying to please people I love, and it hasn't gotten me anywhere. They don't love me enough to accept me."

He felt a hitch in his gut, as if he'd shoved her away when he should have taken hold. "Allena."

"No, it's all right. They do love me, under it all, just not as much, or in the same way, or . . . however I love them. They want things for me that I'm not capable of—

or that I just don't want for myself enough to make a real effort. I can't put restrictions on my feelings. I'm not made that way.''

"And I can.'' He rose, paced. "It's not a matter of feelings, but of being. I can't and won't be led. I care for you more than should be possible in this short a time.''

"And because of that you don't trust what's happened, what's happening between us.'' She nodded and, clipping the thread, set her needle aside. "That's reasonable.''

"What do you know of reason?'' he demanded. "You're the damnedest, most irrational woman I've ever met.''

She smiled at that, quick and bright. "It's so much easier to recognize reason when you have so little yourself.''

His lips twitched, but he sat down. "How can you be so calm in the middle of all this?''

"I've had the most amazing two days of my life, the most exciting, the most beautiful.'' She spread her hands. "Nothing can ever take that away from me now that I've had it. And I'll have one more. One more long and wonderful day. So . . .'' She got to her feet, stretched. "I think I'll get a glass of wine and go outside and watch the stars come out.''

"No.'' He took her hand, rose. "I'll get the wine.''

It was a perfect night, the sky as clear as glass. The sea swept in, drew back, then burst again in a shower of water that caught those last shimmers of day and sparkled like jewels.

"You should have benches,'' Allena began. "Here and here, with curved seats and high backs, in cedar that would go silver in the weather.''

He wondered why he hadn't thought of it himself, for he loved to sit and watch the sea. "What else would you have, were you me?''

"Well, I'd put big pots near the benches and fill them with flowers that spilled out and spiked up. Dark blue crocks,'' she decided, then slanted him a look. "You could make them.''

"I suppose I could. Flowerpots.'' The idea was amusing.

No one had ever expected flowerpots from him before. He skimmed a hand over her hair as he sipped his wine and realized he would enjoy making them for her, would like to see her pleasure in them.

"Dark blue," she repeated, "to match the shutters when they're fixed up with the paint I found in the laundry room."

"Now I'm painting shutters?"

"No, no, no, your talents are much too lofty for such mundane chores. You make the pots, sturdy ones, and I'll paint the shutters."

"I know when someone's laughing at me."

She merely sent him a sly wink and walked down toward the water. "Do you know what I'm supposed to be doing tonight?"

"What would that be?"

"I should be manning the slide projector for Margaret's after-dinner lecture on megalithic sites."

"Well, then, you've had a narrow escape, haven't you?"

"You're telling me. Do you know what I'm going to do instead?"

"Ah, come back inside and make wild love with me?"

She laughed and spun in a circle. "I'm definitely putting that on the schedule. But first, I'm going to build a sand castle."

"A sand castle, is it?"

"A grand one," she claimed and plopped down on the beach to begin. "The construction of sand castles is one of my many talents. Of course, I'd do better work if I had a spade and a bucket. Both of which," she added, looking up at him from under her lashes, "can be found in the laundry room."

"And I suppose, as my talent for this particular art is in doubt, I'm delegated to fetch."

"Your legs are longer, so you'll get there and back faster."

"Can't argue with that."

He brought back the garden spade and the mop bucket, along with the bottle of wine.

As the first bold stars came to life, he sat and watched her build her castle of sand.

"You need a tower on that end," he told her. "You've left it undefended."

"It's a castle, not a fortress, and my little world here is at peace. However, I'd think a famous artist could manage to build a tower if he saw the need for one."

He finished off his glass of wine, screwed the stem in the sand, and picked up the challenge.

She added more turrets, carefully shaping, then smoothing them with the edge of her spade. And driven by his obviously superior talent with his hands, began to add to the structure, elaborately.

"And what, I'd like to know, is that lump you've got there?"

"It's the stables, or will be when I'm finished."

"It's out of proportion." He started to reach over to show her, but she slapped his hand away. "As you like, but your horses would have to be the size of Hugh to fit in there."

She sniffed, rocked back on her heels. Damn it, he was right. "I'm not finished," she said coolly. She scooped up more sand and worked it in. "And what is that supposed to be?"

"It will be the drawbridge."

"A drawbridge?" Delighted, she leaned over to study the platform he fashioned with his quick, clever hands. "Oh, that's wonderful. You're definitely sand castle–skilled. I know just what it needs."

She scrambled up and raced to the house. She came back with some wooden kitchen matches and a bit of red ribbon that she'd cut in a triangle.

"Chain would be better, but we'll be innovative." She poked the tip of the long match into the side of the drawbridge, slid the other end into the castle wall. "Fortunately, the royal family here is having a ball, so the drawbridge stays down." She set a second match in the other side.

She broke a third match, looped her ribbon around it,

then hoisted her makeshift flag on the topmost tower. "Now that's a sand castle."

She plucked up the bottle of wine and poured for both of them. "To Dolman Castle." A dream, she thought, they'd made together.

After clinking her glass to his, she drew up her knees and looked out to sea. "It's a beautiful night. So many stars. You can't see sky like this in New York, just slices of it, pieces between buildings, so you forget how big it is."

"When I was a boy, I used to come out at night and sit here."

She turned her head, rested her cheek on her knee. "What else did you do when you were a boy?"

"Climbed the cliffs, played with my friends in the village, worked very hard to get out of chores that would have taken less time and less effort than the eluding of them took. Fished with my father."

He fell into silence, and the depth of it had Allena reaching out to take his hand. "You miss him."

"I left him, alone. I didn't know he was ill that last year. He never told me, never once asked me to come back and tend to him. He died by himself rather than ask me for that."

"He knew you'd come back."

"He should have told me. I could've brought him to Dublin, gotten him to hospital, for treatments, specialists."

"It's always so much harder on the ones who're left behind," she murmured. "He wanted to be here, Conal. To die here."

"Oh, aye, to die here, that was his choice. And knowing he was ill, and frail, he climbed the cliffs. And there at the stone dance is where his heart gave out. That was his choice."

"It makes you angry."

"It makes me helpless, which is the same thing to me. So I miss him, and I regret the time and distance that was between us—the time and distance I put between us. I sent him money instead of myself. And he left me all he had. The cottage, and Hugh.''

He turned to her then and pulled the chain at her neck until the pendant slid clear. ''And this. He left this for me in that small wood box you see on the dresser in the bedroom.''

The shiver raced over her skin, chill and damp. ''I don't understand.''

''His mother had given it to him on his eighteenth birthday, as it had been given to her. And he gave it to my mother on the day he asked her to marry him, at the stone circle, as is the O'Neil tradition. She wore it always. And gave it back to him, to hold for me, on the night she died.''

Cured in Dagda's Cauldron. Carved by the finger of Merlin. ''It's yours,'' she murmured.

''No. No longer mine, never mine as I refused it. The day I buried my father, I came here and I threw this into the sea. That, I told myself, was the end of things.''

There's only one, the old woman had told her. It belonged to her. She had found it, or it had found her. And led her, Allena thought, to him. How could she feel anything but joy at knowing it? And how, being who he was, could Conal feel anything but anger?

For her it was a key. For him a lock.

Allena touched his cheek. ''I don't know how to comfort you.''

''Neither do I.'' He rose, pulled her to her feet. ''No more of this tonight. No more castles and stars. I want what's real. My need is real enough.'' He swept her up. ''And so are you.''

9

SHE COULDN'T SLEEP. No matter how short the night, she couldn't bear to waste it in dreams. So she lay quiet, and wakeful, reliving every moment of the day that had passed.

They'd ended it, she thought now, with love. Not the slow and tender sort they'd brought each other the first time. There'd been a desperation in Conal when he carried her into bed from the beach. A kind of fierce urgency that had streaked from him and into her so that her hands had been as impatient as his, her mouth as hungry.

And her body, she thought, oh, her body had been so very alive.

That kind of craving was another sort of beauty, wasn't it? A need that deep, that strong, that *willful* could dig deep and lasting roots.

Why wouldn't he let himself love her?

She turned to him, and in sleep he drew her against him. *I'm here*, she wanted to say. *I belong here. I know it.*

But she kept the words inside her, and simply took his

mouth with hers. Soft, seductive, drawing what she needed and giving back. Slow and silky, a mating of lips and tongues. The heat from bodies wrapped close weighing heavy on the limbs.

He drifted into desire as a man drifts through mists. The air was thick, and sweet, and she was there for him. Warm and willing. And real.

He heard her breath catch and sigh out, felt her heart beat to match the rhythm of his own. And she moved against him, under him, bewitching in the dark.

When he slid into her, she took him in with a welcome that was home. Together they lifted and fell, steady and smooth. Mouths met again as he felt her rise up to peak, as he lost himself, gave himself. And emptied.

"Allena." He said her name, only her name as he once more gathered her against him. Comforted, settled, he slipped back into sleep never knowing that she wept.

Before dawn she rose, afraid that if she stayed beside him any longer in the dark she would ask—more afraid that if he offered some pale substitute for love and life-times, she would snatch at it, pitifully.

She dressed in silence and went out to wait for the dawn of the longest day.

There was no moon now, and no stars, nothing to break that endless, spreading dark. She could see the fall of land, the rise of sea, and to the west the powerful shadows of the jagged cliffs where the stone circle stood, and waited.

The pendant weighed heavy on her neck.

Only hours left, she thought. She wouldn't lose hope, though it was hard in this dark and lonely hour to cling to it. She'd been sent here, brought here, it didn't matter. What mattered was that she was here, and here she had found all the answers she needed.

She had to believe that Conal would find his in the day that was left to them.

She watched dawn break, a slow, almost sly shifting of light that gave the sky a polish. Mists slipped and slid over the ground, rose into the air like a damp curtain. And there, in the east, it flamed, gold, then spread to red over sky and water, brighter, and brighter still, until the world woke.

The air went from gray to the shimmer of a pearl.

On the beach, the castle had been swamped by the tide. And seeing what could be so easily washed away broke her heart a little.

She turned away from it and went back inside.

She needed to keep her hands busy, her mind busy. She could do nothing about the state of her heart, but she wouldn't mope, today of all days.

When Hugh came padding out, she opened the door so he could race through. She put on the kettle for tea. She already knew how Conal liked his, almost viciously strong with no sugar or cream to dilute the punch.

While it steeped, she got a small pot from a cupboard. Conal had mentioned there were berries ripening this time of year. If she could find them, and there were enough, they'd have fresh fruit for breakfast.

She went out the back, past the herb garden and a huge shrub covered with dozens of conical purple blossoms that smelled like potpourri. She wondered how they would look dried and spearing out of a big copper urn.

Ground fog played around her ankles as she walked and made her think it was something like wading in a shallow river. The wind didn't reach it, but fluttered at her hair as she climbed the gentle rise behind the cottage. Far off was the sound of Hugh's deep-throated bark, and somewhere nearer, the liquid trill of a bird. Over it all was the forever sound of the sea.

On impulse, she slipped off her shoes to walk barefoot over the cool, wet grass.

The hill dipped, then rose again. Steeper now, with the mist thickening like layers of filmy curtain. She glanced back once, saw the cottage was merely a silhouette behind the fog. A prickle over her skin had her pausing, nearly turning back. Then she heard the dog bark again, just up ahead.

She called out to him, turned in the direction of his bark, and kept climbing. On the top of the next rise was a scattering of trees sculpted by wind, and with them the bushes, brambles, and berries she hunted.

Pleased with her find, she set down her shoes and began to pick. And taste. And climb still higher to where the ripest grew. She would make pancakes, she thought, and mix the berries in the batter.

Her pot was half full when she scrambled up on a rock to reach a solitary bush pregnant with fat fruit of rich and deep purple.

"The most tempting are always the ones just out of reach."

Allena's breath caught, and she nearly overturned her pot when she saw the woman standing on the rough track on the other side of the bush.

Her hair was dark and hung past her waist. Her eyes were the moody green of the ocean at dawn. She smiled and rested her hand on Hugh's head as he sat patiently beside her.

"I didn't know anyone was here." Could be here, she thought. "I—" She looked back now, with some alarm, and couldn't see the cottage. "I walked farther than I realized."

"It's a good morning for a walk, and for berry picking. Those you have there'd make a fine mixed jam."

"I've picked too many. I wasn't paying attention."

The woman's face softened. "Sure, you can never pick too many as long as someone eats them. Don't fret," she said quietly. "He's sleeping still. His mind's quiet when he sleeps."

Allena let out a long breath. "Who are you?"

"Whoever you need me to be. An old woman in a shop, a young boy in a boat."

"Oh." Surrendering to shaky legs, she sat on the rock. "God."

"It shouldn't worry you. There's no harm meant. Not to you, or to him. He's part of me."

"His great-grandmother. He said—they say—"

The woman's smile widened. "They do indeed."

Struggling for composure, Allena reached under her

sweater, drew out the pendant. "This is yours."

"It belongs to whom it belongs to . . . until it belongs to another."

"Conal said he threw it into the sea."

"Such a temper that boy has." Her laugh was light and rich as cream over whiskey. "It does me proud. He could throw it to the moon, and still it would come to whom it belongs to when it was time. This time is yours."

"He doesn't want to love me."

"Oh, child." She touched Allena's cheek, and it was like the brush of wings. "Love can't be wanted away. It simply is, and you already know that. You have a patient heart."

"Sometimes patience is just cowardice."

"That's wise." The woman nodded, obviously pleased, and helped herself to one of the berries in the pot. "And true as well. But already you understand him, and are coming to understand yourself, which is always a more difficult matter. That's considerable for such a short time. And you love him."

"Yes, I love him. But he won't accept love through magic."

"Tonight, when the longest day meets the shortest night, when the star cuts through with power and light, the choice you make, both you and he, will be what was always meant to be."

Then she took Allena's face in her hands, kissed both her cheeks. "Your heart will know," she said and slipped into the mist like a ghost.

"How?" Allena closed her eyes. "You didn't give us enough time."

When Hugh bumped his head against her legs, she bent down to bury her face in his neck. "Not enough time," she murmured. "Not enough to mope about it, either. I don't know what to do, except the next thing. I guess that's breakfast."

She wandered back the way she had come, with Hugh for company on this trip. The fog was already burning off at the edges and drawing into itself. It seemed that fate had decreed one more clear day for her.

When the cottage came into view, she saw Conal on the little back porch, waiting for her.

"You worried me." He walked out to meet her, knowing his sense of relief was out of proportion. "What are you doing, roaming away in the mist?"

"Berries." She held up the pot. "You'll never guess what I . . ." She trailed off as his gaze tracked down to the pendant.

"I'll never guess what?"

No, she thought, she couldn't tell him what had happened, whom she had seen. Not when the shadows were in his eyes, and her heart was sinking because of them. "What I'm going to make for breakfast."

He dipped a hand into the pot. "Berries?"

"Watch," she told him and took her gatherings into the house. "And learn."

He did watch, and it soothed him. He'd wakened reaching for her, and that had disturbed him. How could a man spend one night with a woman, then find his bed so cold, so empty when she wasn't in it? Then that panic, that drawing down in the gut, when he hadn't been able to find her. Now she was here, mixing her batter in a bowl, and the world was right again.

Was there a name for this other than love?

"You really need a griddle." She set the bowl aside to heat a skillet. "But we'll make do."

"Allena."

"Hmm?" She glanced back. Something in his eyes made her dizzy. "Yes?" When she turned, the pendant swung, and caught at the sunlight.

The star seemed to flash straight into his eyes, taunting him. Without moving, Conal took a deliberate step back. No, he would not speak of love.

"Where are your shoes?"

"My shoes?" He'd spoken with such gentle affection that her eyes stung as she looked down at her own bare feet. "I must have left them behind. Silly of me."

"So you wander barefoot through the dew, pretty Allena?"

Words strangled in her throat. She threw her arms around him, burying her face at his shoulder as emotions whirled inside her.

"Allena." He pressed his lips to her hair and wished, for both of them, he could break this last chain that held his heart. "What am I to do about you?"

Love me. Just love me. I can handle all of the rest. "I can make you happy. If only you'd let me, I can make you happy."

"And what of you? There are two of us here. How can you believe, and accept, all I've told you and be willing to change your life for it?" He drew her back, touched a fingertip to the pendant. "How can you, Allena, so easily accept this?"

"Because it belongs to me." She let out a shaky breath, then took one in, and her voice was stronger. "Until it belongs to another."

Steadier, she took a ladle from a drawer and spooned batter into the skillet. "You think I'm naive, and gullible, and so needy for love that I'll believe anything that offers the possibility of it?"

"I think you have a soft heart."

"And a malleable one?" The cool gaze she sent him was a surprise, as was her nod. "You may be right. Trying to fit yourself into forms so that the people you love will love you back the way you want keeps the heart malleable. And while I hope to be done with that, while I'm going to try to be done with that, I prefer having a heart that accepts imprints from others."

A patient heart, she thought, but by God if it was a cowardly one.

Deftly, she flipped the pancakes. "What hardened yours, Conal?"

"You've good aim when you decide to notch the arrow."

"Maybe I haven't reached into the quiver often enough." But she would now. Movements smooth and unhurried, she turned the pancakes onto a platter, spooned more batter into the pan. "Why don't you ever speak of your mother?"

Bull's-eye, he thought, and said nothing as she set him a place at the table.

"I have a right to know."

"You do, yes."

She got out honey, cinnamon, poured the tea. "Sit down. Your breakfast will get cold."

With a half laugh, he did as she asked. She was a puzzle, and why had he believed he'd already solved her? He waited until she'd emptied the skillet, turned it off, and come to the table to join him.

"My mother was from the near village," he began. "Her father was a fisherman, and her mother died in childbirth when my own mother was a girl. The baby died as well, so my mother was the youngest and the only daughter and pampered, she told me, by her father and brothers."

"You have uncles in the village?"

"I do. Three, and their families. Though some of the younger have gone to the mainland or beyond. My father was an only child."

She drizzled honey on her pancakes, passed the bottle to Conal. He had family, she thought, and still kept so much alone. "So you have cousins here, too?"

"Some number of them. We played together when I was a boy. It was from them that I first heard of what runs in me. I thought it a story, like others you hear, like silkies and mermaids and faerie forts."

He ate because it was there and she'd gone to the trouble to make it. "My mother liked to draw, to sketch, and she taught me how to see things. How to make what you see come out in pencil and chalk. My father, he loved the sea, and thought I would follow him there. But she gave me clay for my eighth birthday. And I . . ."

He paused, lifted his hands, stared at them through narrowed eyes. They were very like his father's. Big, blunt, and with strength in them. But they had never been made for casting nets.

"The shaping of it, the finding what was inside it . . . I

was compelled to see. And wood, carving away at it until you could show others what you'd seen in it. She understood that. She knew that.''

"Your father was disappointed?''

"Puzzled more, I think.'' Conal moved his shoulders, picked up his fork again. "How could a man make a living, after all, whittling at wood or chipping at hunks of rock? But it pleased my mother, so he let it be. For her, and I learned later, because in his mind my fate was already set. So whether I sculpted or fished wouldn't matter in the end.''

When he fell silent, looked back at the pendant, Allena slipped it under her sweater. And feeling the quiet heat of it against her heart, waited for him to continue.

10

"AFTER ME, MY parents tried for more children. Twice my mother miscarried, and the second, late in her term . . . damaged her. I was young, but I remember her having to stay in bed a long time and how pale she was even when she could get up. My father set a chair out for her, so she could be outside and watch the sea. She was never well after that, but I didn't know."

"You were just a boy." When she touched a hand to his, he looked down, smiled a little.

"Soft heart, Allena." He turned his hand over, squeezed hers once, then released. "She was ill the summer I was twelve. Three times that spring, my father took her on the ferry, and I stayed with my cousins. She was dying, and no one could find a way to save her. Part of me knew that, but I pushed it out of my mind. Every time she came home again, I was certain it was all right."

"Poor little boy," Allena murmured.

"He doesn't deserve as much sympathy as you think. That summer, when I was twelve, she walked down to the

74

sea with me. She should've been in bed, but she wouldn't go. She told me of the stone dance and the star and my place in it. She showed me the pendant you're wearing now, though I'd seen it countless times before. She closed my hand around it with her own, and I felt it breathe.

"I was so angry. I wasn't different from the other lads I knew, no different from my cousins and playmates. Why would she say so? She told me I was young to have it passed on to me, but she and my father had discussed it. He'd agreed to let her do it, in her time and her own way. She wanted to give me the pendant before she left us."

"You didn't want it."

"No, by God, I didn't. I wanted her. I wanted things to be as they were. When she was well and I was nothing more than a lad running over the hills. I wanted her singing in the kitchen again, the way she did before she was ill."

Everything inside her ached for him, but when she reached out, Conal waved her off. "I shouted at her, and I ran from her. She called after me, and tried to come after me, but I was strong and healthy and she wasn't. Even when I heard her weeping, I didn't look back. I went and hid in my uncle's boat shed. It wasn't till the next morning that my father found me.

"He didn't take a strap to me as I might have expected, or drag me home by the ear as I deserved. He just sat down beside me, pulled me against him, and told me my mother had died in the night."

His eyes were vivid as they met Allena's. She wondered that the force of them didn't burn away the tears that swam in her own. "I loved her. And my last words to her were the bitter jabs of an angry child."

"Do you think—oh, Conal, can you possibly believe those words are what she took with her?"

"I left her alone."

"And you still blame a frightened and confused twelve-year-old boy for that? Shame on you for your lack of compassion."

Her words jolted him. He rose as she did. "Years later, when I was a man, I did the same with my father."

"That's self-indulgent and untrue." Briskly, she stacked plates, carried them to the sink. It wasn't sympathy he needed, she realized. But plain, hard truth. "You told me yourself you didn't know he was ill. He didn't tell you."

She ran the water hot, poured detergent into it, stared hard at the rising foam. "You curse the idea you have—what did you call it—elfin blood—but you sure as hell appear to enjoy the notion of playing God."

If she'd thrown the skillet at his head he'd have been less shocked. "That's easy for you to say, when you can walk away from all of this tomorrow."

"That's right, I can." She turned the faucet off and turned to him. "I can, finally, do whatever I want to do. I can thank you for that, for helping me see what I was letting happen, for showing me that I have something of value to give. And I want to give it, Conal. I want to make a home and a family and a life for someone who values me, who understands me and who loves me. I won't take less ever again. But you will. You're still hiding in the boat shed, only now you call it a studio."

Vile and hateful words rose up in his throat. But he was no longer a young boy, and he rejected them for the sharper blade of ice. "I've told you what you asked to know. I understand what you want, but you have no understanding of what I need."

He walked out, letting the door slap shut behind him.

"You're wrong," she said quietly. "I do understand."

She kept herself busy through the morning. If she did indeed go away the next day, she would leave something of herself behind. He wouldn't be allowed to forget her.

She hung the curtains she'd mended, pleased when the sunlight filtered through the lace into patterns on the floor. In the laundry room she found tools and brushes and everything she needed. With a kind of defiance she hauled it all outside. She was going to scrape and paint the damn shutters.

The work calmed her, and that malleable heart she'd spoken of began to ache. Now and then she glanced over at the studio. He was in there, she knew. Where else would he be? Though part of her wanted to give up, to go to him, she did understand his needs.

He needed time.

"But it's running out," she murmured. Stepping back, she studied the results of her labors. The paint gleamed wet and blue, and behind the windows the lace fluttered in the breeze.

Now that it was done and there was nothing else, her body seemed to cave in on itself with fatigue. Nearly stumbling with it, she went into the house. She would lie down for a little while, catch up on the sleep she'd lost the night before.

Just an hour, she told herself and, stretching out on the bed, went under fast and deep.

Conal stepped back from his own work. His hands were smeared with clay to the wrists, and his eyes half blind with concentration.

Allena of the Faeries. She stood tall, slim, her head cocked slyly over one shoulder, her eyes long and her mouth bowed with secrets. She wasn't beautiful, nor was she meant to be. But how could anyone look away?

How could he?

Her wings were spread as if she would fly off at any moment. Or fold them again and stay, if you asked her.

He wouldn't ask her. Not when she was bound by something that was beyond both of them.

God, she'd infuriated him. He went to the sink, began to scrub his hands and arms. Snipping and sniping at him that way, telling him what he thought and felt. He had a mind of his own and he'd made it up. He'd done nothing but tell her the truth of that, of everything, from the beginning.

He wanted peace and quiet and his work. And his pride, he thought, as his hands dripped water. The pride that refused to accept that his path was already cut. In the end, would he be left with only that?

The emptiness stretched out before him, staggeringly

deep. Were these, then, after all, his choices? All or nothing? Acceptance or loneliness?

Hands unsteady, he picked up a towel, drying off as he turned and studied the clay figure. "You already know, don't you? You knew from the first."

He tossed the towel aside, strode to the door. The light shifted, dimmed even as he yanked it open. Storm clouds crept in, already shadowing the sea.

He turned for the cottage, and what he saw stopped him in his tracks. She'd painted the shutters, was all he could think. The curtains she'd hung danced gaily in the rising wind. She'd hung a basket beside the door and filled it with flowers.

How was a man to resist such a woman?

How could it be a trap when she'd left everything, even herself, unlocked and unguarded?

All or nothing? Why should he live with nothing?

He strode toward the cottage and three steps from the door found the way barred to him. "No." Denial, and a lick of fear, roughened his voice as he shoved uselessly at the air. "Damn you! You'd keep me from her now?"

He called out to her, but her name was whisked away by the rising wind, and the first drops of rain pelted down.

"All right, then. So be it." Panting, he stepped back. "We'll see what comes at the end of the day."

So he went through the storm to the place that called to his blood.

She woke with a start, the sound of her own name in her ears. And woke in the dark.

"Conal?" Disoriented, she climbed out of bed, reached for the lamp. But no light beamed when she turned the switch. A storm, she thought blearily. It was storming. She needed to close the windows.

She fumbled for the candle, then her hand jerked and knocked it off the little table.

Dark? How could it be dark?

Time. What time was it? Frantically she searched for the candle, found a match. Before she could light it, lightning flashed and she saw the dial of the little wind-up clock.

Eleven o'clock.

No! It was impossible. She'd slept away all but the last hour of the longest day.

"Conal?" She rushed out of the room, out of the house, into the wind. Rain drenched her as she ran to his studio, fought to open the door.

Gone. He was gone. Struggling against despair, she felt along the wall for the shelves, and on the shelves for the flashlight she'd seen there.

The thin beam made her sigh with relief, then her breath caught again at what stood in the line of that light.

Her own face, her own body, made fanciful with wings. Did he see her that way? Clever and confident and lovely?

"I feel that way. For the first time in my life, I feel that way."

Slowly, she shut the light off, set it aside. She knew where he'd gone, and understood, somehow, that she was meant to find her own way there, as he had, in the dark.

The world went wild as she walked, as wild as the day she had come to this place. The ground shook, and the sky split, and the sea roared like a dragon.

Instead of fear, all she felt was the thrill of being part of it. This day wouldn't pass into night without her. Closing her hand over the star between her breasts, she followed the route that was clear as a map in her head.

Steep and rough was the path that cut through rock, and slippery with wet. But she never hesitated, never faltered. The stones loomed above, giants dancing in the tempest. In its heart, the midsummer fire burned, bright and gold, despite the driving rain.

And facing it, the shadow that was a man.

Her heart, as she'd been told, knew.

"Conal."

He turned to her. His eyes were fierce as if whatever wild was in the night pranced in him as well. "Allena."

"No, I've something to say." She walked forward, unhurried though the air trembled. "There's always a choice, Conal, always another direction. Do you think I'd want you without your heart? Do you think I'd hold you with this?''

In a violent move she pulled the pendant from around her neck and threw it.

''No!'' He grabbed for it, but the star only brushed his fingertips before it landed inside the circle. ''Can you cast it off so easily? And me with it?''

''If I have to. I can go, make a life without you, and part of me will always grieve. Or I can stay, make a home with you, bear your children, and love you for everything you are. Those are my choices. You have yours.''

She held out her arms. ''There's nothing but me here to hold you. There never was.''

Emotions tumbled through him, end over end. ''Twice I've let the people I loved go without telling them. Even when I came here tonight I thought I might do so again.''

He pushed dripping hair away from his face. ''I'm a moody man, Allena.''

''So you told me once before. I never would have known it otherwise.''

His breath came out in a half laugh. ''You'd slap at me at such a time?'' He took a step toward her. ''You painted the shutters.''

''So what?''

''I'll make you pots in dark blue, to fill with your flowers.''

''Why?''

''Because I love you.''

She opened her mouth, closed it again, took a careful breath. ''Because I painted the shutters?''

''Yes. Because you would think to. Because you mended my mother's curtains. Because you pick berries. Because you swim naked in the sea. Because you look at me and see who I am. Whatever brought you here, brought us here, doesn't matter. What I feel for you is all there is. Please, God, don't leave me.''

''Conal.'' The storm, inside her and around her, quieted. ''You only have to ask.''

''They say there's magic here, but it's you who brought it. Would you take me, Allena?'' He reached for her hand, clasped it. "And give yourself to me. Make that home and that life and those children with me. I pledge to you I'll love you, and I'll treasure you, ever hour of every day." He lifted her hand, pressed his lips to it. "I'd lost something, and you brought it back to me. You've brought me my heart."

So, she thought, he'd found the key after all. "I'll take you, Conal, and give myself to you." Her eyes were dry and clear and steady. "And everything we make, we'll make together. I promise to love you now and ever after."

As she wrapped her arms around him, the mists cleared. In the dark sea of the sky a star began to pulse. The fire shimmered down to a pool of gold flame, tipped red as ruby. The air went sharp and cool so the stones stood out like a carving in glass.

And they sang in whispers.

"Do you hear it?" Allena murmured.

"Yes. There." He turned her, held her close to his side as the shimmering beam from the midsummer star shot through the stones and like an arrow pinned its light to its mate on the ground.

The pendant burst blue, a clean fire, star-shaped and brilliant. While star joined star, the circle was the world, full of light and sound and power.

Then the longest day passed, slipping into the shortest night. The light rippled, softened, faded. The stones sighed to silence.

Conal drew her farther into the circle. The fire rose up again, and shot sparks into her eyes, stroked warmth over his skin. He bent to pick up the pendant, and slipping the chain around her neck, sealed the promise.

"This belongs to you, and so do I."

"It belongs to me." She pressed their joined hands against it. "Until it belongs to another. I'll always be yours."

She kissed him there, inside the echo of magic, then stepped back. "Come home," she said.

●　　　●　　　●

Some say that the faeries came out of their raft to celebrate and danced round the midsummer fire while the star showered the last of its light. But those who had magic in their hearts and had pledged it left the circle, walked from the cliffs and along the quiet beach to the cottage with dark blue shutters that waited by the sea.

CATCH A FALLING STAR

STAR

★

Jill Gregory

To Marianne, Nora, and Ruth—
and friendship that shines brighter than any star

And to Larry and Rachel—
with all my love

1

"COME TO THE window, my lady, I beg you. Perhaps you will see a falling star and can make a wish, and all of this will vanish like a bad dream."

Else, the youngest of Princess Lianna's ladies-in-waiting, spoke through tears. She turned from the castle window and gazed imploringly at the slender, sable-haired princess, who sat with legs curled beneath her on the gilded bed before the fire. The princess's chamber was filled with women, all weeping, with reddened cheeks and eyes and faces damp with tears. Only Lianna herself, lovely and regal in her sapphire silk gown trimmed in gold thread, remained dry-eyed and composed, her heart-shaped face as calm as a new day.

"A falling star? A wish?" Despite the churning of her stomach, Lianna gave her head a shake, sending her dark locks flying about her pale face. She even smiled grimly at Else as she sprang catlike off the bed, her gown billowing about her. "If I only had the chance, I would wish Ambrose the Barbarian a bloody death and an eternity in hellfire!''

She paced to the window, peering out at the silent black sky aglitter with a thousand stars. Not one fell from its destined place. There would be no help there. ''Wishes and stars and magic will not avail me now,'' she said softly, half to herself. ''Nothing will.''

A half-remembered spell of her grandmother's floated through her mind, tinkling like a fairy song. *Comes the night of a falling star . . .*

The rest danced away into the recesses of her memory, a chant from long-ago days of childhood. But she was no longer a child, Lianna reminded herself, her fingers tightening upon her skirt. She was a woman, full-grown, pledged to wed.

Old spells and rhymes could not save her from that.

She turned from the window, her shoulders straight and determined. ''Falling star or no, I am going to marry the Barbarian come morn, and that is that.''

Her old nurse, Meeg, sunk in a chair in the corner, let out a wail, the sound echoing through the firelit chamber where velvet bed hangings and rich tapestries and fragrant rushes softened the chill coming off the old stone walls of the castle. Lianna's mouth trembled as she turned to gaze at the old woman. Meeg had been lady-in-waiting to her grandmother, a great lady renowned for her goodness and her magic, whom Lianna only dimly remembered, with fondness and awe. But Meeg had told her stories about her grandmother and helped her to see that she, Lianna, had inherited the knack for magic that blessed the women of her family, skipping every other generation, then returning afresh. It was Meeg who had raised her like a mother since she was twelve years old when her own mother had died giving birth to a stillborn son. Meeg, who had crooned to her when she had nightmares, encouraged her interest in the healing arts and simple spells, taught her to listen to the whispers of her own heart and follow the sigh of the wind. Now, weak as a baby bird and nearly blind, the old woman refused all of the fine gifts Lianna sought to give her, would not even wear the ermine robe Lianna had ordered made for her—save on state occasions—and still made up her own bed, swept her floor, spent hours at embroidery all done by touch and instinct—refusing to rest and lie about as Lianna kept insisting she had earned the right to do.

"Oh, Meeg," the girl said softly, kneeling beside the woman and wrapping her arms around her. "Do not weep for me—I am not afraid of Ambrose." She repressed a shudder, thinking of the bridegroom she had not yet met, the fearsome warlord known as the Barbarian. "He cannot be as bad as they say." She bit her lip, praying her words would prove true. "And even if he is, I still must do what I can for Penmarren, and for my father. Another battle, waged either against Ambrose or Loth, will kill him. This way, there will be peace with Ambrose, and he will protect Penmarren from Prince Loth. It is the only way to save my father—and our kingdom."

"We must delay, child. There is always the chance that Prince Constantine might return."

Lianna shook her head. Her cousin Constantine, Prince of Wyborn, had been trying to raise an army in the east, an army that could match the strength of Loth or Ambrose, and to bring that army to Penmarren's aid. But all the spring and summer and autumn had passed, and he had not returned, nor sent word. "We do not know what has become of him. Now we cannot wait any longer. If I do not wed Ambrose on the morrow, he will tear Penmarren apart like a wild dog. Or leave us to Loth, which will be just as bad." Her lips tightened. "This is the only way."

"But you . . . *you,* my beautiful little one, will be shackled to a barbarian." Her voice cracking, Meeg tore her fingers from her wet dumpling of a face and stared into the princess's wide-set violet eyes, her own eyes filled with pain. "A man whose castle is cursed, who they say eats the hearts of his enemies for breakfast—who takes no prisoners on the battlefield, a man who they say . . . who they say . . ."

She straggled off, choking on the rest.

"A man who they say killed his first wife," Lianna com-

88 * Jill Gregory

pleted for her quietly. She saw Else press her white lips
together and Kira and Gwenlyn wring their hands. Her own
blood pounded in her ears as she spoke the words, yet she
struggled to keep her face composed and her voice steady.
"Rumors."

She was pleased that she managed to sound brisk and
unconcerned. "He cannot be as brutal as they say. If everything that is said about him were true, he would be the
devil himself. No, I am not afraid. Let Ambrose be afraid
of *me*," she added with a toss of her head. "Didn't I tame
and ride the wildest steed in our kingdom? Didn't I once
spear a boar that had felled three men? Haven't I broken
hearts of knights and princes from lands as far away as
Galeron? Let Ambrose the Barbarian fear *me!*"

The women exchanged hopeful glances despite their mis-
givings, taking heart from her bravery. Though they knew
what she said was true, they couldn't help but fear for her.
She was slender, delicate, yet as fiery as a candle's flame.
Lianna had grown up wild and free, racing through the trees
and meadows of the gentle land like a fairy child, eluding
those set to guard her, making friends with every creature
she encountered, playing at sword fighting with sticks and
branches, stealing destriers from the stables to test their
speed, returning home to the castle at nightfall with muddy
gown and dirt-streaked face, leaves in her hair and scrapes
upon knees, toes, and bare feet.

Her mother, Queen Felice, had disapproved of her antics
and made no attempt to hide her displeasure, but the king
delighted in her bravery and curiosity and warm, impulsive
nature, and she was allowed to roam at will—until she began to grow into womanhood.

When her mother died shortly after Lianna's twelfth
summer, the king had become more protective, and Lianna,
sensing his heavy heart and heightened concern, had allowed herself to wander less and less. She had applied herself to mastering her royal duties and threw herself into
becoming her father's friend and confidante as well as his
daughter, hoping to lessen his loneliness.

She had grown into a beautiful, independent young

woman, beloved by her people, respected by even her father's most somber advisers.

But a man like Ambrose the Barbarian—he would see nothing but a trophy to be displayed in his castle, a vessel to bear his heir, a princess of indisputably royal blood who would buy a bastard duke respectability and greater power. The woman who had served Lianna all her life shuddered to think what would become of her when she was locked away in Crow's Keep, in the cold and distant kingdom of Blackenstar, as Ambrose's wife—and his prisoner.

A knock at the door made every woman turn in dread.

"Your Highness, your father the king requests your presence in his chambers." Her father's servant, Ulf, bowed low, his seamed old face as grim as those of all the others in the castle.

Lianna was only too glad to escape. It was a strain to keep up her spirits in front of those who cared for her. How she wished she could be alone—alone to try to master her fear and her own crawling dread. She had been raised every inch a princess and knew her duty. She was not the first royal daughter to be given over to an enemy as a trophy of war—or in this case, as a prize that would bring peace. If it would save her father and her people, she would gladly suffer the fate of being Ambrose's bride. What choice did she have?

Yet she was only human and she couldn't help but be afraid. The stories told about Ambrose were fearsome. He was a warrior, first and foremost, a man born a bastard youngest son of a fierce nobleman, a man who had wrested his kingdom from a series of half brothers and brutish warlords who had quarreled over pieces of it, all of them slabbering to have it all. His reputation on the battlefield was legendary, his ruthlessness the stuff of stories told to frighten children into obedient behavior, his cruelty, lust for women, and crude disregard of civilized behavior were all part and parcel of his dark legend.

And, a small scared voice inside reminded her, *he killed his first wife when she'd been unable to give him a child.*

A shudder rippled through her as she made her way

through the long, torchlit hall, across the solar, to the king's chambers. Ambrose might be a crude barbarian, but she was a princess. She would not cower before him, nor weep, nor seek to escape her fate. She would do her duty with her head held high, and she would not let anyone—least of all the beast she was to marry—see her quail or quiver.

"Lianna, child. My dear child.'' Her father stroked her head as she bent over his bed and kissed his cheek. The sight of him so weak and frail flooded her with pain. As a little girl she had known her father to be tall and strong, with his shock of white hair and ruddy face, his merry smile. But a battle wound had left him lame in one leg, with a creeping sickness that kept him confined to his bed. In the last skirmish, when Penmarren had been forced to drive Loth's men from their southern border, he had been carried onto the field in a litter.

Only his captain-of-arms, the brave soldier Rufus, had saved him from a death blow.

"Don't fear for me, Father.'' Lianna spoke soothingly. "As I told my ladies, I am not afraid. Well, not very afraid,'' she added with a trembling smile. "It will be all right.''

"I hope and pray that is so, child.'' The king waved his hand, dismissing the servants hovering nearby in the gilded chamber. "Leave us,'' he commanded.

When they were alone and Lianna had seated herself comfortably upon the edge of his bed, he struggled to a sitting position and huffed as she propped tasseled pillows behind him.

"Listen to me, Lianna. Don't fuss with me, child. I have news—hopeful news.''

For the first time she noted that his cheeks were flushed and his eyes bright. Her heart jolted in her chest. "Constantine?'' she whispered, scarcely daring to hope.

He nodded and grasped her hand. "He is coming. By all that is holy, he is coming. Not in time to stop the wedding, I fear, but if all goes well, my dear, you will be Ambrose's bride for no more than a fortnight—at most!'' He spoke in a whisper, as if fearful that even the walls might have ears.

Lianna's heart began to thud. Constantine and his army were coming to save her from a lifetime wed to Ambrose. She had only to wait, to endure—to stay alive for the brief time she was married to the Barbarian, and then she could return home in honor to Penmarren.

"Such wonderful news, Father!" Her eyes glowed. "Tell me all of what he said," she urged eagerly.

"Your cousin has gathered an army—a mighty army, Lianna—one that is nearly twice the strength of Loth's and very near in size and ferocity to that of Ambrose! He has been beyond the Crystal Sea and has found fighting men as fearsome as any Ambrose might boast, and they have sworn allegiance to him. They have to cross the sea and make their way through Dunhelm, amass horses and weapons and supplies, but they are coming. No one is to know," the king added quickly. "If Ambrose were to suspect what is afoot, it would be disastrous for us all—and very dangerous for you, my child."

Lianna's eyes sparked violet fire, and she nodded. "We won't speak of it again, Father. But what am I to do? How can I help? Surely while I am in the Barbarian's keep there is some way that I can be of use to Constantine."

"No. That's too dangerous. It is bad enough that you must go off with that monster." His voice trembled, and fury and helplessness shone from his sunken blue eyes, still sharp despite his sickness. "If I were a younger man, and stronger, I would never allow him within a mile of these castle walls, much less to dare demand your hand in marriage. He's nothing but a bastard, a blackguard, a murd—" He broke off, his face purple, his breath coming heavily in his chest.

He'd been about to say "murderer," Lianna knew. Her hand shook a little as she touched his arm. "Hush, Father. Don't upset yourself. It does no good to think what could have been or should be. My marriage to this man will buy time to keep our kingdom safe."

"But Constantine will come for you, I swear it." His white brows drew together. "So be ready, girl. We'll get word to you somehow and you must be ready to flee, or to hide—whatever is called for when the hour draws near.''

''I will be ready.'' Lianna's mind was already leaping ahead to the day when the gates of the Barbarian's keep would be flung down, when Constantine and his army would crash through and storm the castle, when perhaps even the bastard Ambrose himself would be slain.

''If only we could delay the wedding.'' Her father's tone was heavy. ''But at the least, we can try to keep the Barbarian here for several more days, drunk and entertained with wedding feasts and festivities.''

He fell silent. Lianna knew they were both thinking the same thing. Such things would delay her being taken from Penmarren, carried off to the dark, distant, and forbidding Blackenstar, but it would not delay the wedding night itself. The moment when she would be alone with Ambrose in their marriage bed, when he would claim her in the most elemental way as his bride.

''I am not afraid,'' she whispered as steadily as she could. ''I know what must be done. And he won't dare harm me—not until I bear him a child, the heir he is rumored to want so badly. And long before then, Constantine will have rescued me and perhaps will even have run the Barbarian through like the wild pig that he is—''

She broke off as urgent knocking sounded at the door. Not the brisk polite rapping with which Ulf had summoned her to her father's side, but forceful and repeated *thwacks* that sounded as if they would smash the door to bits.

''Come in!'' the king bellowed, and Lianna looked up in astonishment as the door burst open and a broad, gold-haired soldier with a scar that slashed across the entire left side of his fleshy face strode into the king's lamplit chamber like a lion invading another's den. He was not one of her father's knights. He was clearly Ambrose's man. His river-green eyes, colder than the frost that clung to the winter trees outside the window, swept the room and fell upon Lianna, then shifted to the glaring king.

Two more soldiers followed him into the room, men equally as large, with expressions equally as grim.

''King Penmarren,'' the scar-faced soldier rasped in a

thick voice, "Duke Ambrose has received news. He must ride this very night to Blackenstar to protect his eastern border—we leave within the hour. Your daughter . . ." He riveted his sharp gaze upon Lianna, who had jumped up, her hands to her throat.

"Ah, this must be the dark beauty we've heard about." Lusty approval glistened in his eyes. "My lady, you will wed the duke at once and depart with us now. Come." He stepped toward her, stretching out an arm. "I will take you to Ambrose—"

Lianna jerked back out of reach and stared at him in wide-eyed astonishment. "I am not going anywhere with you."

"By all that's holy, how dare you try to lay your hands upon my daughter!" the king roared. He struggled upward in the bed, his voice rising in a harsh command. "Guards! Guards, restrain this man!"

Three soldiers of Penmarren rushed in. Two grabbed the gold-haired man, each by one arm, and the third planted himself between the intruder and the king and princess.

"Fools, do you think you can stop me? Stop any of us? Think hard, Penmarren. You don't want to fight Ambrose, do you? You've struck a bargain—now keep it!"

The soldier's voice was a barely disguised sneer. "Your pitiful troops are scattered, protecting your borders from Loth. What do you have here? Fifty men? One hundred at most? We have three hundred fighting men encamped in your fields and forests, all at alert, awaiting only the call to battle. We could take the castle and burn the village before the sun is near to rising. Ambrose's men are trained to fight in darkness, snow, and storm."

"What do you want?" the king croaked.

"We want what we came for, Your Highness. Your daughter as bride to Ambrose. Then we'll send one hundred of those men to fortify your borders against Loth. And we'll be gone."

"I agreed to the marriage, but it is to take place tomorrow. Not tonight. You can't expect me to turn my daughter over to Ambrose and let him ride off with her in the dead of night to a battle.''

"I've no time to waste with you!'' The gold-haired man shook off the king's guards and lunged forward, shoving aside the soldier who stood between him and the king. In a flash, he had a dagger in his hand, its glinting blade only inches from the king's chest.

"Ambrose gave me orders to fetch his betrothed. If you want them married before they ride for Blackenstar, you'd best rouse your cardinal from his bed and get him down to the courtyard quick-like, because as soon as Ambrose hits his saddle, we are off—*with* your daughter. With or without your permission—Your Highness!''

Trembling all over, Lianna stared at the dagger pointed at her father's chest. Leave Penmarren tonight? Be dragged off like a prisoner? Like a prize of war—without a proper wedding, or her ladies-in-waiting to accompany her, or even a chance to bid her father a solemn farewell, much less time to pack her belongings?

"This is outrageous!'' the king sputtered, but as another half dozen of Ambrose's soldiers charged in, unsheathing their swords to hold off the guards, Lianna realized that there was nothing any of them could do to stop the events that Ambrose the Barbarian had set in motion.

"Father, don't disturb yourself,'' she cried, knowing that resistance would only lead to full-scale bloodshed and battle. "I . . . I will go. It is only a few hours sooner,'' she finished on a ragged breath and suddenly thrust herself forward, between her father and the man who held the dagger.

"Put your weapon away. Do you think I would let you hurt my father?'' she demanded. Her hand came up, and the soldier's eyes flickered down to the dagger she gripped, a gold-and-ruby-handled dagger with a blade that shone in the lantern light.

Ambrose's soldier grinned. "They said you were feisty. Ambrose will have his hands full with you, my lady.'' His grin widening, he sheathed his own weapon.

"Come, then, Princess, I will take you to your husband.''

"He is not my husband yet,'' Lianna retorted. But at the

same moment she realized the uselessness of the situation. Ambrose had made up his mind, and he was obviously accustomed to having things his way. In this situation, neither she, nor her father, nor anyone else in Penmarren could stop him.

Until Constantine arrived.

Up to that point, all she could do was her duty—and avoid endangering her father and those in the castle any further.

"Tell the men to put down their swords, and I will go with you." Her tone was quiet but full of command.

The man gave a signal, and Ambrose's soldiers lowered their weapons. Penmarren's guards swarmed around the king's bedside.

"Father, I will see you in the courtyard," Lianna said softly. For a moment their eyes met and held. Lianna did her best to silently reassure him, though her own heart was pounding and her chest was so tight she could scarcely draw breath.

"I will . . . bring the cardinal," he whispered hoarsely and held out his thin, blue-veined hand.

She clutched it, her slender fingers clinging to his gnarled ones, and then as the gold-haired soldier growled impatiently, she turned with a rustle of her skirts and sailed out the door.

"This way, my lady." The man jerked a thick arm toward the great hall. He put a hand at her back and swept her along before him, his pace forcing her almost to run. "Hurry, now. There's a good girl. There's no time to waste."

"Then by all means," Lianna said breathlessly, her face every bit as grim and set as his as he propelled her along the narrow corridor, "let us find your cursed Barbarian. When I lay eyes on him, there is much I wish to say!"

2

"JUST AS YOU asked, Ambrose—I've brought her. I give you Princess Lianna."

With a laugh, the gold-haired soldier thrust her forward toward the man seated at a long trestle table in an anteroom off the great hall. The man had been scribbling swiftly upon a map, but at the soldier's words he halted his task, and lifted his head sharply.

Lianna was frozen to the spot. As she met his cold, hard gaze, both panic and surprise rose in her like drowning tides.

A great strapping giant gazed back at her, a giant with the broadest shoulders she'd ever seen and raven-black hair as startlingly dark as her own.

May the angels save me, she thought wildly. The man was pure warrior, more rugged than an oak. He couldn't be more than thirty, but he looked to be the toughest, strongest man she had ever seen—and the most handsome. His chest beneath its dark plum tunic was massive and thick with muscles, and beneath his cropped black hair, ice-gray eyes glinted like shards in the torchlight that threw dancing amber shafts across the table where he sat.

She caught her breath. She had not expected him to be handsome. But he was—brutally, swarthily handsome. There was something dangerous and alive and vibrant about him, something magnetic that came not so much from the harsh lines of his face, the keen, deep-set eyes, that aggressive nose and chin, but from the sheer power and raw forcefulness that seemed to emanate from him. It radiated from those gray eyes and that immense body like dark slashes of lightning.

She could find no trace of emotion, neither pity nor amiability—and certainly not even a flicker of gentleness—in the impassive way he studied her. Unlike other men she had met, who openly revealed their admiration of her charms, Ambrose the Barbarian showed nothing upon that handsome countenance but swift, ruthless appraisal.

Lianna's pulse raced. She wanted to stride forward and slap him as his gaze boldly swept up and down the curves of her body, as if he were seeing everything that was hidden beneath the elegant sapphire gown. He took in her slender waist, the swell of her breasts, and his expression remained unchanged—but his eyes darkened to the color of smoke.

His gaze missed nothing and at last came to rest upon her pale, defiant face and the sable hair that fell loose and tumbling past her shoulders.

"Satisfied?" Lianna asked between clenched teeth.

To her surprise, amusement flickered across his swarthy features as he stood, towering before her like an implacable mountain.

But he made no answer.

His silence unnerved her even more than the imposing sight of him.

She'd planned to be elaborately gowned and coiffed when she first met this man, protected by dazzling jewels and royal raiment and all her carefully cultivated dignity— wrapped in her power and position, using them as a shield against this bastard warrior who was so far beneath her. Never had she thought to meet him face-to-face like this—

breathless, her hair flying, her heart pounding as uncertainty and panic collided within her.

She struggled for composure, but it was difficult to feel composed when he was regarding her as if she were a chunk of ham brought forth on a platter for his inspection before he picked up his knife to dine.

"I demand to know the meaning of this, Duke Ambrose." She took a deep breath. "Why have I been literally dragged from my father's side, forced to meet you here, and informed that we are leaving Penmarren within the—"

"Bring the horses now, Beorn. I'll meet you in the courtyard shortly with my bride." Ambrose cut her off without preamble, shifting his intense glance to the soldier. "What of the cardinal?"

"They're fetching him."

Ambrose nodded. "Make haste, then," he said curtly, and the gold-haired soldier hurried out, leaving them alone in the antechamber.

Swiftly the barbarian duke strode around the table.

Lianna had to fight the urge to back away. In his rich purple tunic of heavy wool, fastened at the shoulder by a distinctive star-shaped brooch of gold, onyx, and rubies, with that powerful body and harsh, thoughtful face, he was formidable—he might have been a young dark prince, born to command. Not the ragged, coarse bastard she had envisioned but a leader of men, a warrior/ruler who looked every inch as royal as she—and a hundredfold more dangerous.

"Silence," Ambrose said softly. "Good. I don't like chatter in a woman."

"Do you really think I care what you like?" she asked haughtily as he paused less than a foot from her.

Surprise flickered momentarily in those intent gray eyes, and perhaps another shadow of amusement, but just as quickly vanished. Ambrose had no time or patience for spoiled princesses, however beautiful they might be. And this one was the most beautiful he'd ever beheld, with her gorgeous spill of velvety hair and those eyes like amethyst stars. But she was not a prize to be cherished and indulged, he thought harshly. She was a necessity—a weapon of sorts—and all that mattered was that they be wed and she be ensconced under guard in the keep as soon as possible. His holdings, all that he'd fought for his entire life, were being threatened by an old enemy, his clever cousin Sandar of Kenelm, who had planned a surprise attack meant to wrest Blackenstar away. He needed to reach his land's eastern border without delay to make sure that Sandar failed.

And that he paid.

Ambrose also needed to learn how Sandar had discovered he was to be away at this time fetching his royal bride, with a large portion of his army dispersed—and thus temporarily vulnerable.

It reeked of treachery. If there was indeed a traitor in his camp, he, too, must be found. And made to pay.

So he looked at the lovely black-haired girl glaring at him and spoke brusquely. "You are as beautiful as they say, I suppose, if one cares for such an elegant, icy type of female." He ignored her gasp and continued calmly. "And you are clearly royal. It shows in every inch of you. That is good, for it's the reason I chose you." A slight pause, and his eyes narrowed upon her. "But they tell me you also possess powers. Is this true?"

Lianna drew in her breath. How dare he! Her magic was a difficult subject. Her mother had hated her powers, perhaps because she herself didn't possess them, and from the time she was a child Lianna had learned to keep them quiet, nearly hidden, as a matter of course. Even after her mother's death, she rarely openly displayed the few small gifts she possessed. But everyone seemed to know of them all the same.

"There is some magic in me, my lord duke," she said stiffly. "Not enough to turn you into a toad, I'm afraid."

For one brief moment a grin tugged at those hard lips, then his expression turned cool once more. "Be advised, when you reach Blackenstar, you may do what you will with small, harmless charms and tricks, but I will not have you practicing spells or employing potions. That is forbidden. Do you understand?''

"And if I disobey? Punishment by death?'' she retorted, but then recoiled as the blood drained from his face and every muscle in his body went rigid.

She suddenly remembered the first wife, the one he was rumored to have killed, and her mocking remark rang through her head like an ominously tolling bell.

Ambrose spoke with dangerous quiet. "You have an undaunted spirit, Princess—as well as beauty, royal blood, and power. Use them wisely and do not anger me, and you will live a long and contented life.''

"They say you anger readily, my lord. That may not be an easy thing to avoid.''

"They say many things about me, Lianna. Some are even true.'' His voice was rough. "You'll have to make your own judgments.''

"I already have,'' she murmured sweetly, but there was contempt dripping from the words.

He gripped her arm and yanked her closer, so close she gasped. His touch sent a sizzling warmth through her. She would have jerked away, but she knew her strength was no match for his and so she went still, gazing up into his eyes, her lips parting.

He smelled of sweat and leather and horses. There was the dark shadow of beard on his lean jaw. She had never been quite this intimately close to a man before, even those who had dared to kiss her—chaste, temperate kisses, hesitant, almost meek. There was nothing meek about Ambrose the Barbarian. His eyes glinted like coals in the torchlight. They ignited something inside her: fear, perhaps—or was it fascination?

Lianna knew better than to struggle. She would not break free, not if he didn't want her to. She nearly whimpered because her skin burned hot where his strong fingers touched.

He was entirely too powerful. Too close. Too handsome.

She swallowed and kept silent, though it took all of her will to meet those hard, stern eyes.

"I learned long ago never to judge early, or in igno-rance," he said softly. "Such blunders prove fatal. You'd be wise to remember that."

Waves of fear enveloped her, but Lianna lifted her chin and spoke with all the calm she could muster. "Are you threatening me, my lord?"

"Who would threaten such a fine royal lady?" he asked silkily, the clamp of his fingers tightening. His gray eyes raked her as her own eyes widened. "As brides go, you have all the attributes I seek. And yet I tend to prefer a woman who thinks before she speaks, who does not delib-erately try to offend, but rather tries to please." He swept an arm around her waist, pressing her up against him, let-ting her feel his superior strength. Indeed, he could break her in two if he chose, and they both knew it. "Still, my spoiled, sharp-tongued princess, if you learn to mind your tongue and please me in our marriage bed, you'll do. Aye, my lady Lianna, you'll do."

She drew in her breath, her face flushed a vivid pink. "How dare you," she whispered, in a voice as cold and furious as midwinter snow.

He met those wide, flashing eyes, his own hard as gran-ite. "If it's wooing and pretty words you want, you won't get them from me. I've neither the time nor the nature to indulge such things. This is a business arrangement, Prin-cess, one you've been raised to understand. If you don't know what this marriage is about, don't blame me for it— and don't expect me to coddle you. I am first and foremost a warrior and I've got a battle to fight. A savage one, at that."

He pushed her away. But as he began to wheel toward the table, Lianna grabbed his arm.

"Coddle?" she flashed. Her fingers gripped hard, terri-fying muscle, but she rushed on anyway, driven by an anger that was deep and scorching. "I'd never expect that, my lord duke—especially not from a man like you! Only a barbarian would treat his intended bride with such callous-ness as you have shown this night—"

"Exactly." His nod was weary. "I am what I am. You do understand. Now go."

"Go?"

"Go to your chambers and ready yourself for the journey. Take what belongings you can gather in the next few moments. There isn't much time, so seize that which is most precious to you, and the rest will be sent for later."

"But my ladies-in-waiting! They must pack for themselves as well as for me . . ."

"No ladies-in-waiting, Princess. They'll be sent for later, when Crow's Keep is once more secure. For now, you'll have to manage like a soldier."

Desperation surged through her. "Why don't you go and fight your battle and then come back to Penmarren, and we'll have a proper civilized wedding ceremony—oh!"

He seized her so suddenly that she gulped back the rest of her words, nearly choking on them. His strength seemed to pulse through her, dazzling her senses, weakening her knees. She who had been taught to use a sword by her father's own man-at-arms, who had killed a boar, who had met with equanimity kings and counts and rulers from lands near and far, found herself trembling as she stared into the lean, dark face of this barbarian from Blackenstar.

"There is *nothing* proper or civilized about me, Princess. The sooner you understand that, the better off you'll be. Now, I have no more time to waste chattering with you—either go and pack what you can and meet me in the courtyard in the blink of an eye, or you and your precious kingdom of Penmarren will know exactly what kind of barbarian I really am."

Her chest constricted with fear, Lianna read the furious determination in his face. "You're hurting me," she whispered.

He glanced down, as if unaware, at the spot where he gripped her wrists, his strong fingers digging into her flesh. With an oath muttered under his breath, he released her.

"Go!"

She went. She turned and swept toward the corridor, refusing to run, refusing to look desperate and afraid, though heaven knew that was how she felt. As she reached the outer hall, she heard his voice call sharply behind her.

"Don't make me come looking for you, Princess! I have urgent business, and if you cause me a moment's delay, it will not go well for you or for those you hold dear."

Lianna did run then. She fled through the great hall and the solar, up a short flight of stairs, and down the corridor that led to her own quarters. All the castle was aflurry about her—guards and servants running, shouting, colliding, as the news spread from the tower to the cellar that the Barbarian of Blackenstar was leaving at any moment and taking the Princess Lianna with him.

"Princess . . . is it true?" Else gasped, her face whiter than the snows that still clung to the winter trees beyond the window.

"Please, by the stars, no!" Meeg whispered, but one look at Lianna's taut, pale face, and she dropped her head into her hands.

"I must get to the courtyard. I am to be married at once and leave immediately after for Blackenstar." She managed to say it without bursting into tears, though they clogged her throat and burned behind her eyelids. It would not do to collapse in a quivering heap now—it would not serve her father, her kingdom, or herself. What was it her mother had always told her?

You do not have what it takes to be a true princess, Lianna. Running through the woods like a squirrel. You lack dignity. Grace. A princess never speaks without considering her words or acts without considering the effects of her deeds. You are impulsive, emotional, and unreliable. You disappoint me.

"I must take only some clothing and necessities. Else, Bronwen, help me, if you please. Fill my trunk—quickly. I am to meet Ambrose immediately, or he will . . . he will . . ." Her voice faded, but she summoned it back. "I must go down without delay," she finished desperately.

Else and Bronwen began frantically tossing clothing, boxes of jewels, colored hose, snoods, and other belongings into a silver-edged trunk.

"A marriage gown," Meeg gasped out. "Surely you must have time to don your marriage gown."

"No time," Lianna muttered, dragging her crimson velvet cloak from its peg and throwing it around her shoulders. "We will be riding for Blackenstar as soon as the wedding is done. I dare not make him come in search of me, or who knows what those I leave behind will suffer. The man is a beast. 'Barbarian' is too kind a word for him . . . He is . . ."

She stopped short. The horror and pain on her nurse's beloved face made her curse her own tongue. "He is not that bad, dearest," she whispered. "He is quite handsome, at least. I am sure we shall deal well together."

But it was a lie, and every woman in the room knew it, especially Meeg. She caught Princess Lianna's lovely face in her doughy hands and spoke to her so softly no one else could hear.

"Take care, Lianna. Watch your tongue, child, I beg you. Do not anger him. He is a dangerous man."

A dangerous man? Lianna bit back a hysterical laugh. That was true a hundredfold. She wanted to claim that she wouldn't be intimidated by any man—least of all a graceless bastard who didn't deserve the noble title of duke that he had snatched for himself, but she knew such rash words would only alarm Meeg further.

"I will take care, Meeg," she promised softly, a catch in her throat. "Do not fear for me. I promise you—all will be well."

All will be well—when Constantine comes for me, she finished silently, grimly. Then she was running down the hall again, the manservant Ludd following with her trunk and all her ladies trailing after, weeping.

The night whipped around her in a flurry of icy, bitter winds. Wrapped in her crimson cloak, a few wild strands of hair escaping from her hood to fly about her face, she shivered and prayed that she would survive the hours ahead.

They'd been riding nearly all the night, it seemed to her, and she wondered that dawn had not yet begun to glimmer on the horizon. But, no, darkness still shrouded the great dark forest through which they rode—she could not even see the stars—and the cold was unrelenting.

Behind her in the saddle, the Barbarian's large, well-muscled frame was warm and hard, but his arms around her were every bit as unrelenting as the cold.

Lianna knew that if she were riding alone or in a litter she might well have frozen to death by now. It grated on her to be grateful to him for anything—after all, she would be in her own soft, warm, and very safe featherbed right now if not for him—but she had to acknowledge that she was thankful for the very solid bulk of his body behind her, for his warmth and strength, which partly shielded her from the fierce night wind, and for his arms, which held her upright in the saddle—for she was so weary, her body aching and exhausted, that without his grip, she was certain she would slide right off the horse and simply die of cold and misery upon the forest floor.

As they rode, the wedding itself whirled through her mind, a blur that seemed more like a dream than a real event. She saw her father's face, ashen and furious as he gave her away to the Barbarian of Blackenstar, and the cardinal, his collar askew, his voice trembling at the unexpected late-night turn of events, concern for her glistening in his sad, ancient eyes as he guided Ambrose and her through the sacred vows.

With torchlight smoking in the courtyard, and incense burning, and women muttering prayers, Ambrose's men had chafed impatiently, horses had snorted and pranced, and the groom himself, cloaked, wearing hauberk and sword, had barked out his vows in a quick, rough tone that had made Lianna repeat hers with deliberate slowness. Then just as they'd finished and Ambrose had scooped her up in his arms and hoisted her into the saddle, Meeg had pushed forward, breaking free of the knot of women and going straight to the Barbarian himself.

"Duke Ambrose!"

He'd turned back, staring at the short, heavy woman with the seamed face and faded eyes.

"Lady, I have no time—-"

"Be good to her." It was an order—gruff, quick—yet oddly pleading. "My Lianna. If you dare to hurt her, I will hunt you down myself. She's a good child. Her heart is pure. If you hurt her—"

"Ease your mind, old woman. I will not harm her." Ambrose spoke so softly that Lianna was certain only she and Meeg had heard. "Go to your bed and rest easy. She will not suffer at my hands."

Meeg stared at him as the seconds beat on, precious seconds, while horses whinnied, men seethed to be off, the wind whipped at the nobles and servants gathered in the courtyard to see their princess wed.

Then Meeg nodded and stepped back. The king cried, "Have courage, my daughter!" and with one last glimpse of her father's anguished face, Lianna was swept away upon the Barbarian's black destrier, and she could only gaze back in longing at her beloved castle as the dark night closed around her.

Since then they'd been riding for hours. Or perhaps days . . .

Lianna didn't realize she'd fallen asleep until she felt herself being lifted down from the steed. Her eyes fluttered open and for a moment she stared in confusion at the swarthily handsome face so close to hers.

"She needs rest." The man's words came to her as if from a great distance. His voice was deep, not at all unpleasant. "Or else I'll have another dead bride on my hands."

A chill pierced her, and she came fully awake, her heart lurching.

"Ambrose."

"Yes, Princess." He was carrying her in his arms, she realized, and then she saw that the great forest had given way to a hamlet, and a churning black river flowed to her right. To her left was a cluster of ramshackle buildings that huddled like stooped monsters in the night.

"Where are we?"

"An inn in Kyrdwyk where it will be safe to spend what

remains of the night. No more than three or four hours—
then we'll have to ride again.''

She moaned and tried to struggle free of his arms. ''Put
me down. I can walk.''

''I doubt it.''

She realized he was right. Her body ached and weariness
dragged at her so that she could scarcely see or think. But
she detested her own weakness and vowed he should not
know of it.

''You underestimate me. I am well able to—''

''If you're going to argue with me every time you speak,
there is going to be real trouble between us.'' He strode
into the inn, where a man in a greasy dark tunic and cap
raced down the stairs, staring in stupefaction.

''A dozen of my men and I need quarters for the night.
Others will be camped outside. They'll need food in the
morning. See that you have enough for all.''

''Aye, sir, my lord. As you wish. Let me show you to a
room.''

Goggle-eyed at the sight of the large, armed, and obviously dangerous soldiers who stomped into the tiny inn, the
landlord stumbled over his own feet as he led the dark-
haired duke to the best room of his house.

Entering the musty, low-ceilinged chamber, Ambrose
gave it a swift glance. It had a hearth. That was something.
But not much. The mattress was of straw, the planked floor
sticky with spilled ale, the blankets moth-eaten and nearly
threadbare.

But the fire would warm the woman in his arms and the
bed would afford her some much-needed sleep, and those
were his chief concerns at the moment.

He had to reach Blackenstar before the invaders from the
east did, but he couldn't afford to kill his bride getting
there.

''Sleep while you may.'' He tossed her down upon the
bed, noting how swiftly she bounced up to glare at him.

''Build a fire and bring the lady some refreshment,'' he
ordered the landlord over his shoulder and then left the dim

chamber to find William and Beorn and set out orders for the men.

Lianna wanted no refreshment, only sleep. As the fire sprang to life in the hearth, and the landlord bowed and scraped his way out the door, she huddled in her gown and cloak upon the lumpy mattress, which smelled like a pig had been the last to lie upon it. She thought briefly, longingly, of her own bed made of softest feathers, her room delicately scented with rushes and sweet spices, of the hot spiced drink Else brought her each night in the winter before she retired. Then she pushed the thoughts away.

Those days were gone—for now. If she ever wanted to return to Castle Penmarren, to her life there as her father's daughter and a princess held in esteem by her people, she had first to get through the next fortnight wed to the Barbarian.

And that meant getting through her wedding night.

She had expected it would take place in Penmarren Castle, at least. Not here in some filthy inn on the road, in the middle of the night, with the smell of pig nearly choking her.

She must have drifted off into sleep again, because suddenly she was jerked awake by a heavy form dropping down beside her and the bed dipping low with a resounding creak.

Ambrose sprawled alongside her, fully clothed, the long, heavy length of him taking up nearly the entire bed.

In shock she recoiled and tried to shift herself away from any contact with him, but she mistook the width of the bed. With a strangled cry, she tumbled over the edge to land with a most unprincesslike thud upon the floor.

3

A DEEP RUMBLE of laughter shook the rafters of the chamber.

"Come back to bed, Princess. I've already swallowed three virgins whole for my supper—I won't eat you alive, at least not tonight."

Her cheeks burned. And her rump ached. Not to mention her elbow. She wanted to march out of the room and demand that the landlord give her another chamber—but she couldn't. Ambrose was her husband and there was no escaping him.

Not until Constantine came and, with any luck, lopped off his head.

So she rose with all the dignity she could muster, yanked her cloak tight about her shoulders, and tried to avoid her husband's eyes as she began to carefully settle herself upon the bed once more, but he reached out a giant arm and before she could move he tugged her unceremoniously down beside him, clamped an arm across her chest, and drew her close by his side.

"Next time you fall out of bed you might injure your-self," he growled. "Then the world would say I raised my hand to you on our bridal night." ·

Staring into his eyes, Lianna saw that they were tinged with amusement, but also a shadow of bitterness. "I'd best keep you close or my reputation will suffer," he said softly.

A strange dizziness assailed her at his nearness. Some-thing about him made her senses reel. *Fear*, she told her-self. *Dread.*

"I wouldn't worry, my lord," she said with honeyed sweetness, "your reputation could not sink much lower than it already has."

She felt him move beside her, the bunch of powerful muscles, the catlike spring as he came up in one smooth, powerful motion. He had removed his hauberk but wore tunic and cloak as he loomed over her, his face dark and harsh in the dancing glow of the fire.

"You're wrong, Princess." He spoke in a low tone. "It could."

Lianna didn't dare try to move. She couldn't escape him if she tried. He hadn't yet touched her, or tried to hold her there, but if she moved, he would, sure as a lion would pin down a lamb.

"D-do what you want with me, then." She took a deep breath. "I know what is expected of me as your w-wife. G-go ahead."

She squeezed her eyes tight shut and braced herself for the worst.

Nothing happened.

She waited, sensing him above her, hearing his soft breathing, aware of the sizzling air that seemed to tingle around her.

She braced herself to be roughly touched, grabbed, her cloak and gown ripped, flung to the floor, but . . . nothing happened.

She opened her eyes.

Ambrose was just as he had been before. Except for one thing. Now his gray eyes no longer glittered threateningly. In the waving firelight that sent golden-orange shadows through the dingy room, they shone with faint amusement.

Was he *laughing*—at *her*?

"What are you waiting for?" she bit out between clenched teeth. "Midsummer's Eve?"

A low rumble of laughter sounded deep in his chest. "I've a fierce battle to plan and win, Lianna. My castle is endangered. And our road is not without peril. I think—for now—for this one night, at least—I am able to withstand your many and considerable charms," he chuckled.

So he did not mean to . . . he would not . . . she didn't have to . . .

She carefully hid the relief that surged through her. Thank the heavens she would be spared having to couple with this monstrous creature—at least for tonight. If a tiny bit of disappointment nibbled at the corners of her heart she pushed it away. Why should she feel disappointment? Because Ambrose the Barbarian wasn't so tempted by her beauty and femininity that he would forget the very real troubles besetting him and wish only to kiss her, touch her, and bed her?

That was preposterous. She didn't want him even to look at her, much less place those large, rough hands upon her . . . much less . . .

She pushed that thought away, too, deciding that fatigue was turning her mind to mush and confusing her thoughts with nonsense.

She struggled up to a sitting position then, half fearing that he would try to push her down, but he leaned back and allowed her to rise. Her hood dangled down her back and her black hair tumbled in her face as she stared into those deep, disconcertingly intelligent eyes. "Very wise to set your priorities, my lord. My father taught me when I was young that if a man wants to hold on to his kingdom he should consider well his choices and his actions. If your land is being threatened, and your castle is at risk I agree that nothing else can possibly be as important as . . ."

He reached out and pushed her back down onto the straw mattress, and a hand clamped over her mouth.

"Ye gods, woman, do you always talk so much? I may have to kiss you just to keep you quiet!"

"That won't . . . be necessary."

Ambrose lifted one dark brow. "Frightened?"

"Of you, my lord?" Lianna forced a laugh, though she felt none too confident sprawled on the bed with him nearly atop her. "H-hardly!"

It was his turn to laugh. Suddenly his hands pinioned hers above her head and he leaned closer, his weight pressing down over her. "Prove it, my brave lady." Gray eyes gleamed down into hers. "Let me kiss you."

Lianna's blood pounded in her ears. "But you said . . ."

"One kiss—only one."

Her gaze dropped from those gleaming eyes to the hard, implacable mouth. Heat twisted through her. She squirmed in a futile effort to break free, then went still. "I cannot stop you," she whispered bitterly.

"Yes. You can, Princess." He released her hands, and his knuckle moved downward to gently brush her cheek. "If you are afraid, simply tell me no."

"I'm *not* afraid. I've never met the man to make me afraid . . ."

"Then your answer is yes."

Slowly, he leaned down. Close, closer. His eyes glinted silver, his breath whispered on her cheek. One big hand slid through her hair, stirring a strange feeling in the pit of her stomach. "Yes?" he persisted, his mouth an inch from hers.

Suddenly the room was no longer cold—it was hot, dizzyingly hot. Gazing into that darkly handsome face, she trembled, and felt the fire of his lips though they were still a breath away from hers. She tried to form her lips to speak the word "no."

"Yes," she heard herself whisper and knew that she was in terrible trouble now, drawn forward toward something she couldn't name—or resist.

Ambrose's head dipped lower and his lips swooped down upon hers. Firm, masculine lips—yet warm, yielding. Commanding. He laid claim to her mouth with a kiss that was hungry and intense, a warrior's kiss, giving no quarter. Without warning, his tongue darted inside her parted lips—searching, branding.

Conquering.

Lianna moaned at the shocking pleasure that invaded her senses. The dingy room vanished, the strange inn, even the straw bed. There was only Ambrose, only the kiss, only the flame of it eating her up, sparking a spiraling pleasure inside her. His hand moved through her hair, slid down to cup her nape. A delicious melting sensation rolled through her.

The kiss never ended, he merely deepened it and continued, plundering with sure, smooth strokes that demolished her defenses.

But when his hand slipped inside her cloak to close about her breast, shock struck her, and sense rushed back. "N-no!" She struggled free of the fierce pleasure. "Stop . . . Ambrose . . . stop."

She pressed hard against his chest and he drew back at last, his hand dropping, his mouth ceasing its relentless assault.

Why, his breath was coming as fast as hers, Lianna noted as she stared wild-eyed at him. And there was a flush to his swarthy skin.

"You . . . promised. Just one . . . kiss!"

"You *are* afraid," he taunted softly, a smile curling his lips. He reached for her again.

"No!"

"Then one more . . ."

"*No!*"

Ambrose sighed and released her. Reluctantly, he shifted in the bed, leaving a slight space between them. "As you wish." There was a tinge of mockery in his voice, and something else—regret. "We'll finish this game at Crow's Keep, then—when I have sent Sandar to a bloody grave." He grinned at her.

"You are very sure of yourself," Lianna said breathlessly, her heart still pounding from the soul-stirring heat of his kiss.

114 ★ Jill Gregory

"I know my strong points." Again the swift grin that transformed his dark face and stunned her almost as much as the kiss had. One hand reached out and gently tugged on a gleaming black curl that framed her face.

"Sleep then, Princess. Gather your strength. The ride we've just completed from Penmarren is child's play compared with what lies ahead."

And before she could speak, the grin faded and he settled down on his side, facing her, and closed his eyes.

It took a few moments for Lianna's breath to calm, for her heartbeat to slow and steady. Soundlessly, she raised up on one elbow and studied the man beside her. Impossibly handsome, she thought helplessly, as the firelight gilded his strong features, glinted off the dark sheen of his cropped hair. Impossibly powerful, she thought in dismay, recalling the heady, dizzying effects of his kiss.

She studied his closed eyes, with their unexpectedly thick lashes. For some reason, every time those eyes flickered over her, she felt a jolt. Like lightning striking her. Strange. She'd never felt any such thing before, not when any of the noble or royal suitors who had come to court had looked at her. Not a one.

It is naught but fear, she told herself, and settled her head gingerly upon the pillow once more. *And loathing. Nothing more.*

But when he'd kissed her—such strange feelings had churned through her. Why, oh, why, had she accepted his dare? He'd stirred up emotions and sensations inside her she hadn't known were there. And what if . . . the next time he kissed her, touched her, claimed her fully as his wife, those sensations returned?

She tossed fitfully, but as the fire hissed and danced, and night crept toward morning, eventually fatigue stole over her. Now that she wasn't cold any longer, now that the warmth of the fire and of the kiss and of the man lying beside her had banished the ice in her blood, she felt sleep coming to claim her, dragging her down.

She must sleep while she could. Or she wouldn't be strong enough to endure a fortnight wed to this man, who shifted suddenly in his sleep and dropped his powerful arm across her. A man with no scruples, she reminded herself, a bastard with not a drop of royal blood in his veins, a man who made her flesh crawl every time he looked at her. Well, perhaps not crawl . . . more like *tingle.*

Morning came in a blink.

They rode for two more days and nights—with only brief intervals of rest, meals, and sleep. By the time they reached Blackenstar, Lianna could only stare blearily at the forbidding, mountainous country through which they traveled, at the dark forests whose trees loomed taller, denser, and more threateningly than any she had seen in Penmarren.

They left the mountains behind late in the day, and as dusk approached and thick, glistening snowflakes began to fall, they reached a frozen river and then rolling farmland frosted with ice. Not long after that, they came to a village and heard the sounds of the sea. Beyond the cottages and workshops and the local inn, with smoke curling from the chimneys to dissipate in the dark slate sky, Lianna had her first glimpse of Crow's Keep.

Her heart constricted at the sight of the great stone castle rising from the rocky cliffs at the very edge of the sea.

With its weathered gray stone, looming towers, and fortified battlements all flying the star-shaped black-and-crimson flags of Blackenstar, the huge keep looked chillingly impregnable. A fine silver mist clung to the tower and dwindled down over the bailey, and the iron gates appeared as forbidding as those leading to a dungeon. High above, black crows circled and squawked, swooping from treetop to battlements, their dark wings beating against wind and sky.

Ambrose spoke from behind her in the saddle, his arms snug around her waist, his deep voice carrying over the wind.

"I'll leave you at the gate. My seneschal, Randolph, will show you to your quarters and acquaint you with all you need to know."

"Do you mean that you are going into battle now—this

very night?'' Half turning in the saddle, she stared at him
incredulously. Weariness tugged at every bone in her body.
She marveled at his strength to proceed straight into battle
after their grueling ride.

''I must catch Sandar unawares before he can cross the
Crystal Sea. There is no way in hell I will let him reach
within arrow's distance of Crow's Keep or the village.''
Then he spoke again, in her ear.

''Do I take it that you regret the postponement of our
first real night together as husband and wife?''

''I am thankful for it!''

He laughed, which made Lianna immediately try to
squirm forward, as far away from his muscled body as she
could, but Ambrose's arms tightened around her waist and
drew her back.

''When I return we'll make up for the time we've lost.''

''Not if your battle leaves you dead—or grievously
wounded!''

''Ah, your concern touches me, Princess.''

She twisted around to look at him and saw that beneath
his dark brows, Ambrose the Barbarian's gray eyes glinted
silver as the mist.

''Does it indeed? I am surprised that anything could
touch you, my lord,'' she retorted in her haughtiest tones.

''Those daggers from your eyes could kill me if they
reached my heart. If I but *had* a heart,'' he mused.

''Daggers? Really, my lord.'' She spoke coldly, in the
manner her mother would have employed when addressing
a stableboy. ''Indeed, I wish you safe journey.''

''You lie, Princess. You know you hope that Sandar runs
me through.'' He caught her chin in his hand and raised it,
forcing her to meet his eyes. ''Why don't you just say it?''

''That would be unfitting speech for a princess of royal
blood.''

To her chagrin, he threw back his head and laughed.
''I am pleased to see that I have got my money's worth
with this bargain. Go ahead. Be just as royal and haughty
as you want. Especially when you're in my bed.'' His
voice grew deeper, huskier. ''I've conquered every petty

king and noble who has sneered at me, and I'll conquer you, too."

"How dare you . . ."

"This is as far as I'll go."

He pulled the destrier to a sudden halt and swung off the steed with surprising litheness for such a large man. Without a word he swept Lianna down beside him.

All around her the company drew up. They were near the portcullis, where soldiers in armor guarded the gates, awaiting orders from their duke.

The wind blasted around Lianna, slicing right through the heavy velvet cloak, whipping her hood back like a banner.

"William—you stay behind." Ambrose addressed a stout, bearded man with hair and whiskers the color of summer wheat who spurred his horse forward at the duke's words. "Guard my lady and the keep well! Take her to Randolph and see that she is made comfortable and shown the respect due her."

Sir William saluted sharply and rode toward the gate to await the lady of the castle.

Lianna began to stride toward him, but Ambrose gripped her wrist and tugged her back.

She was conscious of the men on horseback all around them, watching, smiling, as their duke prepared to bid farewell to his bride.

"Not so fast, my lady. I have something for you before we part." To her surprise, he removed the gold-and-ruby star-brooch from the shoulder of his cloak and pinned it to hers.

"It is a bridal gift. I command you to wear it always. It is a symbol that you are under my protection."

"But who is to protect me from you?" She gazed defiantly up at him as the wind tore at her hair.

"No one can protect you from me." Ambrose pulled her closer. She shivered and his hands tightened at her waist. His voice dropped. "No doubt a chaste public kiss is appropriate even for royalty," he said slowly. "Am I correct?"

She was unnerved by his touch, by the way his eyes gleamed at her through the cold mist, but she nodded with outward calm. "You are correct. Most proper of all would be for you to kiss my hand—oh!"

Her startled cry was cut off as he swept her into his arms and his lips clamped down to claim hers. Heat and dazzling confusion suffused her as Ambrose the Barbarian roughly and thoroughly kissed her, holding her taut against him, his warm mouth waging a lusty battle against hers, his arms locking her entire body against his.

Struggling would be undignified and unbecoming a princess, Lianna thought dimly before she couldn't think at all. She felt as if she was drowning, drowning in a hot sea of sparkling pleasure as his hand fisted in her hair and his mouth set hers afire.

The dark keep, the men on horseback, the mist, and the sea—all blurred to nothingness as the man she had wed against her will held her in arms of iron and kissed her to the depths of her soul.

When he drew back, Lianna could only stare blankly up at him, her eyes wide and glazed, her lips swollen and parted.

She couldn't speak. Couldn't break the spell.

Heaven help her, what evil magic was this? She wanted him to kiss her again!

But he only smiled, his eyes dancing as snowflakes melted upon her upturned face. He spoke so that only she could hear his words.

"I'll be back before you can miss me, Lianna. And I'll teach you about all the things a proper, true-blood princess doesn't know."

As he vaulted back upon the destrier, the laughter and shouts of his men rang out. Then he was off, straight through the village again, toward the dark wood that bordered the sea, his soldiers thundering after him.

Still shaken, her face hot despite the numbing cold, Lianna walked with as much dignity as she could muster toward those massive gates. William and the soldiers manning them bowed their heads in deference as the portcullis lifted and the new lady of the castle passed through into the great courtyard of Crow's Keep.

4

AMBROSE'S KISS HAD chased all thoughts out of her mind—including her fears about this castle—but as the thunder of hoofbeats faded and the keep loomed before her, and servants and scullery maids peeped out at her in silent awe, and knights and pages and stableboys hurried forth to get a glimpse of her, she once more had to fight off a sense of dread.

The castle was much more stark than Penmarren. Everything was well ordered, large and spacious, with tapestries upon the walls, and tables and chests inlaid with gold and precious jewels, but there was a chill that seemed to mist from the stone walls, a sense of foreboding that clung to the recessed shadows of the great hall.

Surely the rumors that the place was cursed were as baseless as the one that claimed Ambrose had murdered his wife, Lianna told herself as she proceeded with the seneschal, Randolph, through the great hall.

At any rate, it would do her no good to appear afraid.

It was easy for Lianna to meet those who lived and worked in the castle, to greet the cook, Berta, and the scullery maids, the pages and the squires, and the men-at-arms who guarded the keep. She knew the role of lady of the castle well, and it took no effort for her to smile, nod, and murmur questions or instructions to those who bowed or curtsied as she passed.

But during all that time, and especially that evening as she prepared herself for bed, she could not forget the parting kiss that Ambrose had bestowed upon her.

She sat by the window in the lofty bedchamber she had been given, drawing her silver hairbrush through her hair and thinking about that moment when his lips had seared hers.

She'd had many suitors—tall, short, fair, dark- or russet-haired, young, old, kindly or stern—and one or two had even been bold enough to kiss her when no one was about and when, eager to discover what it was like, she had made it known that she was willing.

But none of them had kissed her like that. None of them had affected her like that. None of them had ever clouded her brain, assaulted her heart, made her blood pound like a tempestuous sea in her ears.

Only Ambrose.

A barbarian.

She was ashamed. He was not worthy of whatever feelings had begun to alight in her heart toward him. He was all that she had been raised to despise. He had in effect forced her at swordpoint to marry him!

And she would have her revenge when Constantine came to free her.

But for some reason she found little comfort in that notion tonight. She wondered where Ambrose was, how he fared against Sandar. If he was hurt.

The thought tore through her and she caught her breath, taken aback by the pain that sliced her heart.

Surely she would not care if Ambrose had been hurt, even if he were dead. She would celebrate. Wouldn't she?

She closed her eyes and remembered again the feel of

his steely arms around her, the deep roughness of his voice—and his mouth, bruising and hungry upon hers as he bade her farewell.

Her sleep that night was uneasy. She was in a strange bed, in a keep rumored to be cursed, with crows flapping at her window—and a husband far afield, fighting an enemy.

He had many enemies, this barbarian.

She wondered, just before sleep claimed her at last, if he had ever had a friend.

The next two days dragged by. Each hour Lianna found herself listening for the thunder of hoofbeats that would signal Ambrose's return. It did not come.

She took her meals alone in her room. They were served by a stoop-shouldered stern-faced woman named Marthe, who uttered not a word but only nodded or shook her head when Lianna spoke to her. She wondered if the servants were all so fearful of Ambrose that they dared not speak lest they offend him or someone who would report to him.

She thought of her own beloved nurse, of Else and Gwenlyn and Kira—and her heart ached with missing them.

On the second afternoon, she felt as if the walls of the castle were closing in upon her. She threw her cloak over her simple gown of cream-colored wool, tucked her braid inside the hood, and headed toward the bailey. The star-brooch winked at her shoulder as she hurried through the halls and all she passed bent their heads or bowed as she went by.

Their deference, born of fear, Lianna guessed, increased her desperation to be alone, to have time to think about what she could do in this time when Ambrose was gone that might help Constantine.

Perhaps there were maps, documents showing the placement of Ambrose's troops, how many men he commanded, where he might be vulnerable.

Surely there must be something she could do to help Penmarren defeat him. She needed to get away alone for a while to think and plan. And perhaps she could gather some herbs, even now, in the dead of winter. Even dead roots would serve for some of her healing draughts. She'd not had time to pack her herbs and healing medicines when she'd left Penmarren, and she didn't like being without them.

An idea came to her in a flash. Perhaps she would come across a plant that could be useful during Constantine's attack. Kittle plants or umsbar weed, which could be used to make a sleeping draught—something tasteless but powerful to slip into the ale drunk by Blackenstar's knights—and by the Barbarian Duke himself on the day Constantine stormed the castle.

Her stomach clenched at the thought, but she pushed the unease away. Whatever she could do to help Constantine and Penmarren—and to free herself from Ambrose—she must do. It was not wrong, she told herself, heading out toward the bailey with a brisk step. It was her duty.

But when she stepped out into the courtyard, making for the stable, she was dismayed to see William bearing down on her.

"Yes?" She stared at him questioningly, though she knew full well why he was there.

"Does my lady wish to leave the protection of the castle grounds? It is not advisable."

"Oh? Am I a prisoner?" It wasn't as if she could escape—she was much too far from Penmarren to try reaching it alone on horseback.

"Of course not, my lady." William smiled. "But you are our honored duchess, and if you wish to ride out, I must accompany you. The duke ordered me to guard you well, and I must obey those orders. Besides," he added with a slight bow, "it is a pleasure to protect so lovely a lady."

"I wonder what he would do to you should you fail in your duty." Lianna kept walking toward the stables, and the knight easily kept pace with her. "You are frightened of him, are you not?"

"Frightened, my lady?" William sounded amused. "No. But I respect him. I owe him. Why, he has made me his captain-of-arms when I have served him for fewer years than others—like Beorn. He has granted me an estate—farmland and a manor house—when the wars are finished and Blackenstar is secure. I will carry out whatever service he asks of me without hesitation.''

Lianna doubted that Ambrose could inspire loyalty. Fear, yes. That she could imagine. William was merely too wise to say so, however—and besides, no man liked to admit fear of another. She surveyed him closely, but could read only calm in his expression. ''The servant woman, Marthe. Do you know her? *She* is fearful even to speak! I can only imagine what she has suffered in the duke's employ.''

''Marthe.'' Sir William halted before the stable doors, and Lianna did, too, turning to face him. The knight shook his head, his face somber. ''No, my lady. You mistake the matter.''

''It is true. She does not speak.''

''Aye, that is true, but not because she is fearful of Duke Ambrose. She is devoted to him. Marthe was attacked—ravaged—when she was a young maid in his father's court. She worked in the old duke's household, and one day she was returning from the village with her parcels and was set upon by men traveling along the road. She was grievously hurt, but she recovered—except after that day, and the horrors she experienced, she never spoke again.''

''Oh.'' Lianna bit her lip, her heart going out to the silent stick of a woman who had served her meals since she'd arrived. ''I see.''

''If it were not for Duke Ambrose, no one knows what might have become of her. He was only a lad of sixteen summers at the time, but he set out to find the men and bring them to justice. Which he did, I might add. He killed them all.''

Lianna sucked in her breath. ''I see,'' she repeated shakily. Perhaps Ambrose was not such a complete brute as he had been painted. He had cared enough for a servant girl to punish the men who had harmed her. That didn't fit with the legends told of him from forest to sea.

''And if it weren't for Ambrose, who knows what would

have become of Marthe?'' William continued in his quiet way. "She was too ill and skittish to work for some time, and afterward, when she didn't speak, many might have sent her packing as useless. But Ambrose found a place for her in a manor house where she could serve a gentle and quiet lady. And when he himself became duke, he brought her back to his own household. He has always made certain she had a livelihood, food to eat, shelter, and no one is allowed to mistreat her. I know few men who would take such pains for a servant, but Ambrose is loyal to all those who are loyal to him.''

"Well, yes. It would seem so.'' Lianna was too stunned by all she'd heard to think of anything else to say. She needed time, time to mull over what William had told her.

They went into the stables together and he helped her to mount a splendid white mare, then he himself took a dun horse with the thickest mane she had ever seen. Lianna waited until they had ridden out past the gates before she gave a low cry.

"What is wrong, my lady?''

"I have forgotten my gloves, and the air is cold.'' She shivered. The air *was* cold, but her gloves were shoved deep inside the pockets of her velvet cloak. There was no need for William to know that, however.

"Would you kindly go back to the hall and ask Marthe to fetch them for me? If you please?''

The knight hesitated, eyeing her uneasily, but he could hardly tell the duke's bride to fetch her own gloves. "Perhaps you'd care to ride back within the gates while I do so?'' he said at last.

Lianna gave a laugh and flashed him her most brilliant smile. "The guards are right there watching,'' she pointed out. "Where do you think I might flee, Sir William, in the twinkling you will be gone? And with the guards to see my every move?''

He warmed under the power of that sunny smile.

"Very well, my lady. I will return, as you say, in a twinkling.''

And I will be gone in a twinkling, Lianna thought, but she kept the bright smile upon her face.

She waited only until he had dismounted in the yard and disappeared inside the castle before kicking the mare and galloping straight for the belt of trees that lined the road.

"My lady! Halt! Halt!" The guards ran after her, calling for her to stop, shouting for Sir William, but she was off like the wind, her hood blowing back, her braid bouncing free, her sights set on the glorious shadowy depths of the forest.

Moments later, she found a curving track that led along a rocky outcropping, and this she followed, knowing that the rocks would leave no telltale hoofprints for Sir William to follow. Many was the time she had escaped her nurse, her ladies-in-waiting, or one of the soldiers sent to guard her on her expeditions in search of berries or healing herbs. She had long ago mastered all the tricks involved in eluding those who would follow her.

And on this bright, cold day her tricks worked like a charm, just as they always had. In a short time she found herself deep within the shadows of the forest, surrounded by the bare winter trees, her mare picking its way along a rutted path glossy with patches of melting snow.

When she spotted the dull purple roots of umsbar weed straggling beside a rock, she dismounted and began to gather some, careful not to crush them. Looking around, she found kittle as well, peeking out from some dead leaves clustered at the base of a pine, and filled the deep pockets of her cloak. She had just spotted some dead lavender at the rim of a gully when she heard a woman's scream.

Her head flew up and she listened, her heart thudding. A man's shout followed, quickly joined by more, and above all, the continuous, bloodcurdling shrieks of the woman.

The fracas came from straight ahead, just beyond a thicket of pines. Leaving her mare, Lianna dashed through the trees at a run, her kid boots making little noise on the forest floor, but when she reached the clearing beyond the trees, she skidded to a halt and her hand groped for the dagger hidden in the folds of her gown.

Three men—outlaws by the look of their filthy, tattered clothes, scarred and cruel faces, and the knives and sticks they brandished—had attacked a peddler's wagon. The peddler and his gray-haired wife were frantically trying to beat them off as their terrified horse reared and whinnied. Even as she watched, one of the outlaws dashed in and swung a stick at the man, knocking him to the ground.

The woman screamed again as the outlaw arced his blade at her husband. At the last moment he rolled aside, nearly under the horse's hooves, but the knife slashed his arm and blood spilled into the earth as he howled in agony.

"Halt!" Lianna darted forward, her dagger clenched, her eyes blazing at the outlaws closing in upon the fallen man.

They paused, staring at her, as startled as if she had sprung down from the very sky.

Then the one who had slashed the peddler grinned tooth-lessly, and the others joined him.

"What's this, lads? A pretty maid joins the fun. Our luck is truly in, I say!"

The woman and her husband stared in shock as the outlaws turned their attention upon the lovely young woman whose elegant face was flushed with fury.

"Welcome, beauty," the tallest of the three muttered. They left the man lying on his side and fanned out as they approached her—two of them gripping knives, the shortest man clenching a long stick whose tip had been sharpened to an evil point. "Put down that shiny blade and come join us," the tall one barked. "There's no turning away now."

"Stand back." Fear clawed at Lianna, nearly overriding the outrage that had filled her when she saw the plight of the peddler and his wife. But she refused to step back even a pace as the men advanced.

"Come no closer," she warned. "I order you to leave this place at once—in the name of Ambrose, Duke of Blackenstar."

These words made the outlaws laugh. They did pause, though, and surveyed Lianna with uproarious amusement. The burly man brandished his knife overhead.

"I don't see no Duke of Blackenstar. Do you, Werric?"

"All I sees is a wisp of a woman who looks like she'll be as tasty a morsel as any I've known."

The tall one, obviously the leader, stepped forward, his black eyes glistening like chunks of coal. "You two see to the peddler," he ordered, his gaze riveted on Lianna. "Kill him and take whatever gold or silver you find. Do what you want with that screeching woman. This tasty morsel is mine."

Lianna's blood froze. She could hear the woman in the wagon weeping as if from a long way off. She saw the peddler struggling to gain his feet, but he swayed and fell into a pool of his own blood. "I am under the protection of the Duke of Blackenstar," she said desperately. "If you harm me, or these people traveling his roads, you'll have his wrath to deal with. See here?" She touched the star-brooch glittering at her shoulder. "I wear the brooch of Blackenstar. You'd best beware!"

A flicker of doubt crossed their faces.

"Go now—while you still may!" she commanded, and prayed through the frantic drumming of her heart that they would be cowed enough in that moment to obey.

But the leader began to curse, and his hands tightened on his knife. "I might be feared of a man, but not of a brooch. Or of any woman who thinks to trick me. I'll take you, my fine lady, *and* your star-brooch. It'll fetch a handsome price in the marketplace."

And with that, he leapt toward her. Lianna slashed out with the dagger and caught him in the stomach. With a strangled gurgle of surprise and pain, he stared at her, then down at the blood pouring from the wound. Then he fell to his knees, the knife slipping from his slack fingers.

"Kill . . . her!" he rasped as the other two rushed forward.

The old woman staggered down from the wagon and picked up a rock, shrieking as she headed into the battle. Lianna scarcely had time to notice. The outlaw with the stick struck her full across the shoulders, a whacking blow that sent her reeling sideways into a tree.

Before she could recover, the third outlaw seized her arm

and wrenched her jeweled dagger from her. Holding his knife in one hand and her dagger in the other, he grinned grotesquely and came at her.

Through the terror sweeping over her, she heard a great roar, felt a whooshing rush behind her, and before she knew what was happening, the clearing was filled with a great charging horse and Ambrose leaned low in the saddle, bearing down upon the outlaw like a dark bolt of fire.

The man shrieked and tried to parry the blow, but Ambrose drove the glittering sword through his heart with one swift thrust.

Screams. Blood. Death.

Through a fog of horror, Lianna watched as the outlaw tumbled into the dirt and Ambrose spun his horse toward the other two, for the leader, bloodied and hurt, had grabbed his knife and hurled himself to his feet, his face savage with fury as he returned to the fray.

Two against one.

There was nothing to do but watch, her heart in her throat, as the duke fought both of them—his face calm, determined, and utterly ruthless. Neither man stood a chance, Lianna realized after that first awful moment. Ambrose fought with single-minded purpose and sublime skill, and before the peddler's woman even had time to run to her husband and kneel at his side, it was over.

The outlaws lay dead beneath the clouded sky, and Ambrose himself turned his destrier and surveyed Lianna as though he would like to run her through as well.

For a long moment she met his harsh gaze, unable to look away, shaken by the way he had fought for her, killed for her, and fully aware of what would have happened if he had not come when he had. And then the sobs of the woman penetrated her shock.

With a choked cry, she ran to the wagon and knelt beside the fallen man.

"There, now, let me see." She spoke quietly to the weeping woman, who raised a grimy, pockmarked face to her.

The knife wound was deep. The man had lost much blood and lay in a faint.

She heard Ambrose approach behind her, but focused her attention on the peddler. The ancient spells came easily to her lips as she pulled a sprig of umsbar from her pocket, crushed it between her fingers, and sprinkled the coarse brown powder on the wound. She asked the woman for bandages and salve, if they carried any in the wagon, then returned her attention to the fallen man as his wife went in search of them.

The moments blurred as Lianna ministered to the man, and by the time the wound was bound up they had been joined in the clearing by Sir William and Beorn and half a dozen other knights, who stood silently behind Ambrose and watched.

Gently Lianna lay her hands upon the man's brow and closed her eyes. Her lips moved, the old spells of healing sprang forth sweet as song.

At last she felt the faint, hot pulsing beneath her fingertips, and at the same moment she heard him moan. She opened her eyes.

Another groan came from the man.

"Will he live, then, my lady?" The woman clasped her hands to her throat.

Lianna nodded wearily, her vision dazed. She was utterly drained.

"He can recover in the hall. My men will take him to the keep." Ambrose turned and quietly gave orders to Sir William, then lifted Lianna to her feet. She sagged against him, her knees buckling at the weakness that assailed her.

Without a word, Ambrose lifted her and set her upon his destrier.

"My mare," she murmured softly. "Back there."

"William will fetch her." Ambrose spoke curtly, tightly controlled anger in his voice.

He swung up behind her, and once again they rode together toward the castle.

They did not speak until they were nearly at the gates. Then Ambrose addressed her, his voice so cold it was like a bucket of icy spring water poured over her.

"Why did you run away? Did you really think you could travel back to Penmarren in safety on your own? You would never have reached the border. And if you had—and your father took you in, I would have made war on your people. Is that what you wanted?"

"No . . . I wasn't going to run away. I would never bring your anger down upon my people!" Lianna cried. Her head was swimming—the result of conjuring up the spells, of the deep concentration needed to ensure the man's healing. She fought to think and speak coherently.

"I only wanted some time alone. In the open air. I am used to going about freely out-of-doors . . . gathering herbs and medicines . . ."

"I told you the first night we met that I would have you brew no potions."

"Not potions—herbal draughts, healing medicines. You said I might do as I pleased . . ."

"Not that." They reached the portcullis and the guards opened the gate, saluting.

Lianna turned in the saddle and risked a glance at his face. It was thunderous.

"Go to your quarters and await me there. You will not be allowed out of your rooms without my leave. A guard will be posted."

"You can't keep me a prisoner!"

"Can't I?" His mocking smile made Lianna wish to strike him. "You will see what it means to cross me."

Lianna couldn't reach the castle soon enough. She refused even to look at him when he helped her down from the horse, his hands tight at her waist as he set her upon the ground. Though she was dizzy from the weariness besetting her, the same weariness that always drained her after the exertion of the healing spells, she held her head high and walked swiftly and with dignity straight into the hall, never once looking back.

She knew exactly what she was going to do.

5

DARKNESS CLOAKED HER chamber when she awoke.

Candles flickered, streaming pale ribbons of light upon the walls, the rush-strewn floor, the crimson bed hangings. Pushing herself up slowly in the bed, Lianna gazed about her, relieved to see that she was alone.

Her head was clearer than it had been, thank heavens. Sleep had cured her of the aftermath of the magic. But she felt fear and panic churning within her. She was a prisoner, not only of the keep but of her own chambers. She who loved to roam the woods and hills, to feel the breeze flying through her hair, was locked here within these dank old stone walls.

Until Ambrose granted permission for her to leave.

Cold sweat broke out upon her skin, and she had to force herself to remain calm.

Someone—Marthe, no doubt—had left a tray for her on the table near the window. She had no appetite, but to distract herself from her predicament she tiptoed barefoot across the room and found on the tray thick slabs of bread, a wedge of cheese, a dish of eggs in jelly, and a plate of sliced venison and turnips. She tasted a bite of bread, then a sip from the goblet of wine that stood beside the plate.

She turned to the window and stared out at the magnificent star-bright night.

Else's plea the night she was taken from her home flashed into her mind. *Come to the window, my lady, I beg you. Perhaps you will see a falling star and can make a wish, and all of this will vanish like a bad dream.*

Again the faint shiver of memory ran through her, and a distant song tinkled somewhere in her brain. Her grandmother's spells—something about a falling star and . . . a curse? Had there been something about a curse in that same spell? And dreams . . . coming true . . .

She closed her eyes and felt the gentle stroke of her grandmother's beautiful hands upon her hair, heard that low, witch-husky voice as if it whispered in her ear once again. *Comes the night of a falling star . . .*

No. This time it was different.

Catch yourself a falling star. . . . And love will . . .

The sound of the door opening banished the fragile wisp of memory and everything else except the hot tension that flooded the room as she whirled and saw Ambrose's large frame filling the doorway.

"You slept a long while, Princess."

"I fear not long enough."

Lianna moved from the window, holding her head high, eyeing him with the haughtiness her mother had reserved for the lowest of stableboys. She remembered now what she must do, what she had vowed silently to do when he had carried her back to this keep as his prisoner.

She would aid Constantine in every way possible. She would find a means of ensuring that Ambrose the Barbarian lost everything he craved in the world—and threatened no one ever again.

"You didn't touch your supper." Ambrose stalked into the room and kicked the door closed behind him.

"Supper? Too common a word, my lord," she chided

tightly. "Why, this repast is a veritable feast. I thought prisoners were served up stale bread and water."

"That can be arranged."

She nodded coolly. "Of that I have no doubt."

As his gaze raked her, she became suddenly aware that she wore only a sheer ivory sleeping gown, with pale lemon flowers embroidered upon it. Marthe must have helped her out of her day garments, just as she had helped her into bed. Vaguely Lianna remembered the woman's somber gray face swimming before her, but that was all.

But now it was Ambrose who stood there, studying her, a hard dark gleam in his eyes that Lianna didn't care for. A gleam that made her throat tighten and her own heartbeat race.

With fear, she told herself. *Nothing more.* But a heady excitement like that of too much wine seemed to burst inside her chest.

"I am not well, my lord. If you must lecture me, let it be on the morrow. I am in need of sleep."

"It is not a lecture I had in mind for you, bride." Ambrose came closer. One big hand reached out and captured her hair, twining through the loose, lustrous black curls.

"And you do not look sickly to me. You look quite lovely."

"The aftereffects of my magic—"

"Are gone," he finished for her, his tone taking on a firm note. "It is clear that sleep has refreshed you. Your eyes are as bright and clear as ever, your cheeks delectably flushed. You look as lovely as I have ever seen you."

Lianna caught her breath. "Well, I . . . I . . . have no wish to speak to you at the moment."

"We needn't speak." He took another step forward.

Lianna backed up. "Then good night."

"It will be a good night," Ambrose agreed and advanced again.

Lianna retreated two more steps to counter his forward ones, only to come sharply up against the window embrasure. She gasped as he closed in upon her and seized her by the arms.

"Wait, my lord—"

"Wait?" Ambrose pulled her closer, one muscular arm snaking around her waist. There was a tautness about his mouth, a tension in his powerful limbs, that filled Lianna with a kind of strange and wonderful panic. "For what should I wait, Princess? My battle is over. Sandar is defeated, his ships burned. The keep is safe—for now."

"Then . . . you should celebrate. There is wine . . ."

"I intend to celebrate. With my beautiful—and disobedient—bride." Suddenly he swung her toward the velvet-covered bed and sent her sprawling backward upon it.

Before she could spring up, he was upon her, pinning her beneath him. His eyes gleamed silver in the candlelight and anger stamped his face.

"You may be royal, Lianna, but you are also foolhardy. You might have been killed today if I hadn't returned in time, found you in time. You were told to stay in the keep, to let Sir William guard you, yet you ran off—straight into danger. You were told—no, *forbidden*—to mix potions, yet you were gathering plants and herbs for just that purpose. If it is taming you want and need, Princess, I'll damn well give it to you!"

"Let me go!" Lianna struggled futilely beneath him. He was far too powerful, and though she twisted and writhed and kicked, it was all to no avail. Her hair straggled across her face, her breath came in deep, gasping rasps, but Ambrose held her down easily, his weight pressing her relentlessly into the softness of the bed, his hard face showing no sign of pity for her helplessness.

"If you don't release me right this very moment, I will . . . I will . . ."

"Yes?" Ambrose asked, his lip curling.

She stared up at him, a red film of rage across her eyes. "I will turn you into a worm and mash you up and feed you to a falcon!" she gasped.

He laughed, the sound rumbling clear up to the rafters.

"You dare to laugh? You think I won't?" she fumed, frustrated by a strand of hair that fell and lingered across her eyes.

"You, Lianna, are a healer," he said at last, gazing into her eyes with a piercing intensity that nearly took her breath away. "Not a sorceress. I may be a bastard and not royal-born, but I am not stupid. I saw what you did with that man back there. I heard the spells."

He brushed the wayward lock of hair out of her eyes, smoothing it away from her creamy cheeks.

Lianna stared at him. "Then you know I never planned to use those plants and herbs to concoct any dark potions!"

Her words made sense. He admitted it. No doubt she only wanted to find healing plants, but Ambrose couldn't afford to take chances. Not after what had happened with Madeline.

He resolved to take the herbs and plants she'd gathered to the wise woman of the village, who knew such things, and make certain they could not be used for poisons or potions that addled the senses.

As he stared down at her, still frantically struggling beneath him, he couldn't help but feel a rush of admiration for her courage. She was hopelessly outmatched in this battle, yet she still fought with both her body and her mind.

He hadn't expected to get such a fiery beauty when he'd set his sights on the princess of Penmarren. He needed a royal bride, someone to bring respectability to his title so that his heir might rule in peace one day, without this incessant fighting. He needed someone who could help him to end this vicious curse of war and strife that seemed to shadow all who tried to lay claim to power in this land.

He'd had no personal hopes of a woman who would interest him beyond the usual reasons men were interested in women.

But this one not only interested him—she enticed him. Something his pale, secretive first bride in their very brief marriage never had done.

With her eyes bright as the flowers that grew in the mountains of Blackenstar, her creamy skin and ripe lips that were pinker than sunrise, she was the most sensuous female he'd ever seen. And her velvety hair—how did it happen that it always smelled like roses? Was that some magic, too?

"If you don't stop struggling you'll wear yourself out and be no use to me at all this evening," he told her gruffly and was intrigued to see her lovely eyes shoot sparks of even hotter blue fire.

"Barbarian! I will never stop struggling. If you're going to treat me like a hostage, a prisoner, like a serf here to serve your pleasure, then I will behave like one and fight you with my every breath!"

"I think you would," he growled, meeting her fierce glare with a thoughtful look. "Woman, if you show this much passion when we consummate our marriage vows, you just might tire me out."

But he laughed as he said it and suddenly released her arms. He shifted off her and Lianna shot upright, sweeping her hair back from her face. She sprang off the bed and across the room, her breasts rising and falling in such a way that Ambrose could not take his eyes off her.

He came slowly to his feet. She was magnificent. Slender and elegant in her chemise, which clung to her pretty white breasts and rounded hips. Beautiful, proud, elegant—and frightened. Though she fought to keep from showing it, he saw that behind the sparkle in her eyes there was a tinge of fear. Her lips trembled, though she stood straight and tall—a delicate yet formidable warrior woman.

She would never admit her fear. He could see that. She would rather die than beg him to be gentle.

He had bedded many women in his time, all of them willing—eager, even—for his touch. Yet this one, his bride, feared him, despised him. He knew she considered him beneath her. He wanted suddenly to command her senses, her mind, her body, to melt her ice with fire and have her come eagerly into his arms and his bed.

He went to her, moving slowly so as not to frighten her any more than she already was. He saw her back up apace, then stop herself, no doubt knowing that she couldn't escape him a step at a time.

"Lianna." He reached out and cupped that dainty chin in his fingers, forcing her head up. The candlelight spilled over her, setting her pale skin aglow.

"Be calm. I've no intention of hurting you."

"You already have!"

He raised his brows. "I have not."

She hated to admit it, but it was true. He had curbed his strength carefully and had done her no harm. Yet.

"Perhaps it is your pride that is hurt," he said and ran a finger along the sumptuous curve of her lip.

She trembled all over. And a new fear consumed her as she stared into Ambrose's eyes. He would see that she herself was torn—torn between a strange, heated attraction to him and a desire to flee. Something piercing and brilliant in those silver-gray eyes seemed able to read her soul, her heart.

She struggled for the frosty dignity that would be her only protection.

"I told you once—at the inn—that I know my duty, and I do," she said quickly. "But there is no need to rush into anything, my lord. Is there? You must be fatigued from your battle . . ."

"I am not."

"And perhaps injured . . ."

"Nary a scratch."

"And we scarcely know each other!" she rushed on.

"That can be easily remedied."

He was grinning at her! Lianna's heart flipped over, and she cursed it for a traitor.

She ought to be furious with him at the way he'd treated her tonight, and yet . . .

There was a weakness in her knees that made her actually long to lean into him, to feel his arms snug around her again. Surely, surely, he couldn't read that in her eyes.

"Wait . . . my lord." In desperation, she wrenched away and retreated to the window. Beyond, the darkness gleamed, a half-moon glistened in a pale curve of light, and the stars glittered pure as crystals. "Look at the night. It is so lovely. Perhaps if we gaze out for a while at the moon . . . and the . . . sky . . . we will see a falling star," Lianna chattered, scarcely knowing what she said.

Ambrose pulled her away from the window and into his

arms. "Now why would I care to see a falling star, Lianna, when I can gaze into your eyes?" he said softly.

Her skin burned where he touched her. This odd tingling sensation, the leaping in her heart, had never happened before—not when any of her suitors had touched her, looked at her, complimented her. Confusion warred with panic in her head, and Lianna found herself gazing up at him in desperate appeal.

"Kind w-words, my lord, but . . . they say if you make a wish upon a falling star, it will come true . . ."

"What would you wish for, Lianna? I would know."

"Wish for?"

He nodded, and his hand slid down through her curls, slowly, gently, and cupped her nape. His fingers were strong and warm against her skin, sending delicious shivers down her arms.

"I would wish. . . ." Suddenly the words burst from her. "That you would not stand so close to me . . . or hold me so . . ."

"But you are my lawful wife," he reminded her, his voice low, firm, and not the least bit reassuring. "And you are ready to do your duty. You married me of your own free will and in good faith, and I can do with you as I please. Whatever I please."

She sucked in her breath, every inch of her tensing. "Then I would wish that you were human and not a barbarous monster!"

She tried to pull away from him, but found herself inexorably caught, held, imprisoned by arms far stronger than any that had ever touched her. "I would wish that you would show patience, mercy, understanding, that I could somehow touch your heart . . . if you had a heart!"

"Touch my heart?" He stared down into her eyes, his own glinting with amusement. He leaned closer, his strong, handsome face only inches from hers. "You have a better chance to *catch* a falling star, Lianna, than you do to touch a warrior's heart."

"That, my lord, is obvious," she cried, and kicked at

him, but instead of releasing her, he only grunted, then laughed and tightened his hold.

"Come," he said, and swept her off her feet, cradling her against his chest. "There have been enough words between us this evening. I am a warrior, Lianna, a brute and a barbarian, as you say—and for a man like me, words are of little use. To stay alive, I must act."

He set her down upon the bed, not ungently, but neither did he give her a chance to roll away. Even as she tried to bolt, he pinioned her once again, clasping her wrists above her head, gazing into her eyes with unmistakable determination.

"You have every right," Lianna said between gritted teeth. "So do what you will. For Penmarren's sake, I gladly sacrifice myself to your base needs, your low animal . . ."

She made a moaning sound deep in her throat as his mouth came down upon hers and incinerated her words. And not only her words. Her bones, her blood, her soul. The kiss was deep, roaringly hot, vanquishing.

His mouth worked clever magic. His body pressed her down, down into the velvet covers. And her heart soared as never before when his hands roved over her with strokes of unexpected gentleness.

As if drawn onto a battlefield, Lianna found herself waging a war of heat and desire. Determined to feel nothing, to want nothing from him but to be finished with him and left alone, she found herself swiftly caught up in a maelstrom of emotions so stormy and riotous she could scarcely think. Her arms flung around his neck, she pulled him close, closer, and as his tongue thrust boldly into her mouth, she quivered as if he'd shot an arrow through her. She was kissing him back before she knew what had happened, writhing beneath him, not to escape but to satisfy an exquisite urge that grew more insistent with every touch.

"So beautiful." His lips scorched lightly along her throat. She trembled. "Let me look at you, Lianna." His voice was excitingly deep. "Let me love you."

He leaned back slowly and she sat up, her breath coming in shallow gasps. They gazed into each other's eyes, neither of them able to look away. "I want to see all of you," he said huskily and instead of wishing to flee from those gleaming eyes, Lianna angled forward as he touched a hand to the neckline of her delicate gown.

She shivered as he removed the ivory gown. The warm light of his eyes pleased her, and experimentally, she tossed her head, letting her long sable curls swirl around her shoulders and over her breasts. To her delight, a muscle clenched in Ambrose's jaw, and his eyes darkened to the color of smoke.

"Your turn," she heard herself whisper, amazed by her own boldness. She reached for his tunic and removed it, then gazed at him in wonder.

He was splendid. So splendid. All steel and bronzed muscle, his stomach flat, his chest broad and powerful, furred with soft, dark hair that invited her fingers to touch it.

But even as she did so, she realized that his warrior's patience was wearing thin. He made a growling sound deep in his throat and snatched her to him, tangling his hands in her hair, pressing his mouth against her breast.

Her startled gasp quickly turned to a moan of dizzy pleasure. Sweet sensations such as she had never known swept through her as he laid her down among the silk and velvet pillows and with his roughened hands and seeking mouth set about exploring every tingling inch of her.

Her breasts ached as his palms rubbed against them, building to a slow torment. How could such strength be curbed into such tantalizing gentleness? she wondered as thought buckled beneath waves of pure, sleek pleasure. Pulling him down upon her, closer, ever closer, Lianna pressed wild kisses against his flesh. Reason, time, dignity vanished. There were only Ambrose and her—the two of them alone in the whole wide world, only passion and fire and bliss so sweet her blood sang with it.

Her throat quivered as he stroked it. Gently, surely. Seductively. Flames licked through her. Lianna clutched at him, her own hunger building, building to a consuming arc of fire. The length of her body grew aroused and torturously sensitive as he rained moist, hot kisses upon all its secret

places, and she cried out, begging him wordlessly, trem-
blingly, to fulfill the promise of those kisses, to relieve the
almost painful ache that had begun to rock her with primitive need and longing.

He laughed low in his throat and continued to torment
her with knowing hands and ruthless mouth. He held her,
opened her, took her, inch by inch conquering her body,
melting her defenses, storming her soul.

There upon the velvet-covered bed, by firelight and
moonlight and starlight, they discovered each other, princess and warrior. They were locked in a sweet, rough battle
that was as ancient as the earth and from which there was
no retreat.

They waged the battle long and hard into the night—
until victory claimed them—a fierce, wild victory sweet-
ened with joy. Lianna felt herself exploding again and
again, brilliant colors and sensations tearing through her,
Ambrose's strong arms and hard thighs clenched her, holding her earthbound while her senses soared and her heart
throbbed at his every touch, kiss, and thrust.

He drove her to the brink of madness and sent her top-
pling over. She set him afire as he'd never been afire before.
He buried his face in her hair, plunged inside her and
stormed every battlement. Bodies linked, hearts racing,
blood pounding, they wrested shattering fulfillment from
each other's arms.

Outside the castle walls, the moon sailed across the sky,
the stars winked and glowed. Within Lianna's bedchamber,
the fire in the hearth gilded their sweat-slicked skin with
palest gold. Spent and shaken, they lay together across the
bed, all in a heap, and at last—at long, long last—at peace.

6

Calm and lianna's senses slowly returned. She became aware that she was entangled with Ambrose, arms and legs entwined, linked, touching so intimately that it was no wonder she still felt the flush of heat.

She felt no urge to move or escape. This alarmed her, and she lifted a hand to her heart. What in heaven's name had come over her?

She had lost her mind, become crazed. Over a *barbarian.*

This wasn't the way it was supposed to happen. She was supposed to have given herself to him with reluctance and silent revulsion. She was not supposed to have enjoyed even one moment of it.

But she had thrown herself into their union with such passionate desire—no, *need*—that a pink blush stole over her naked form as she remembered it.

You hate this man. You loathe him. He forced you to this marriage, he is a bloodthirsty bastard who takes what he wants and lives by the sword and . . .

143

He made you feel more alive than you ever have before. He made you forget you're a princess and feel like a woman. He made you want him with all of your soul, want him so deeply and powerfully that you gave yourself to him, to this enemy, with abandon—and, may the angels save you—with joy.

She swallowed a cry in her throat and slid off the bed, extricating herself carefully from Ambrose's heavy limbs. Shivering, for the fire had died down, she pulled on her sleeping gown and then lifted her cloak from its peg and wrapped it around her. The star-brooch glinted at her shoulder as she crept to the window and stared out at the purple sky.

She wanted to hate him, this man who had swept her from her home and brought her to this accursed castle. But he was not what she had expected. She remembered how he had laughed at her when she'd fallen off the bed in the inn. The way he'd fought the men who would have harmed her in the forest, killing them with single-minded fury. The way he'd plundered her mouth with sweet kisses and awakened her body to glorious pleasure as they tossed upon the bed like cresting waves across a burning sea.

Her wish—if she had but seen a falling star—would have been to touch his heart. But, heaven help her, he had touched hers.

If she wasn't careful—most careful—she would find herself in love with him.

"*No,*" Lianna whispered, scarcely realizing that she spoke aloud until the next moment, when she heard his voice beside her.

"*No, what,* Princess?"

How long had she been gazing at nothingness, lost in dreamy thought? She'd never even heard him rouse himself from the bed or don his tunic. As she glanced up at him, so darkly handsome in the dim room, her heart ached, and she searched his somber face for some of the same emotions that she felt.

But she found none. Ambrose looked like the fierce warrior he was—strong, cold, aloof. And in a hurry to be gone.

"I was thinking aloud." Her reply was soft, and she knew that a ridiculous blush was staining her cheeks.

"Oh?" For an instant she thought he was trying to search her mind, as she sought to search his. His gaze settled on her, warming, but then, just as quickly, it grew cool.

"You should return to the bed. The air is chill."

Instead of obeying him, she merely pulled the cloak closer around her.

"Stubborn as always, I see."

He spoke evenly, yet he found himself exerting every measure of self-discipline he possessed to steel himself against the beauty that radiated from her. It smote his heart to gaze at her and remember the feel of her in his arms, the sweet, enticing warmth of her beneath him, the scent of roses and woman that had filled his nostrils as he loved her. If he was not careful, he thought in alarm, he would find himself thinking of her when he had no business to be thinking of anything but the matters at hand. Whether fighting or leading war councils, he could not afford to be distracted by thoughts of a woman—any woman, even one as spectacular as this one.

"I must leave you," he said curtly. If he didn't leave soon, he would carry her to that bed and make love to her again. And again. By all that was holy, he wanted to do just that. "William is to ride out on a scouting mission at first light, and I have need to speak with him before he goes."

Then his gaze fell upon the roots and plants protruding from the pocket of her cloak. Frowning, he snatched them before Lianna could protest.

"There is a crone in the village who knows of the healing arts. She will tell me if these are to be used solely in innocent medicines—or if they could be used for ill purposes as well."

"So you doubt my word?"

"I doubt everyone's word, lady. It is why I still live today."

They had made love to each other in that bed, kissed, touched, held each other in the most intimate of ways, and he doubted her word over a simple matter of herbs?

"What did she do with her plants and herbs, Ambrose?" she asked quietly, her dark hair swaying back from her face as she lifted her eyes to his. "Your first wife—did she try to poison you?"

Anger pulsed through his veins. He set the plants down upon a low table. "How do you know about my wife's dabblings?"

"So it's true, then? Mine was only a guess, since you are so wary of that which I've gathered. But . . ." Lianna took a deep breath. "Is that why you killed her?" she continued, as steadily as she could. Her eyes were glued to his face. "Because she tried to poison you?"

His hands tightened into fists. "So you think it still," he said, his voice low, harsh. "Even after—"

He broke off, his mouth white with anger. Had he been about to say "even after last night"? Lianna would never know, for instead of completing the sentence, he seized her arm.

"You must fear me, then." Granite eyes pierced her. "For if it were true, I could kill you as well. As easily as a hawk swallows a mouse."

"You're trying to frighten me." Lianna spoke calmly, but the slight quaver in her voice gave her away.

"Do you know how she died?" Ambrose asked brutally. "She fell—from the parapet in my bedchamber."

"Fell?" It was a whisper. "Or was pushed?"

"What do you think?"

She stared into that stern, hard face, with its harsh lines and the dark stubble across his jaw. Studying the gray shards of his eyes, she remembered how tender had been his kisses in the night, the care he had taken not to hurt her.

"She fell." The words came from her in a cool, soft breath, edged with certainty.

Ambrose slowly nodded. The tension went out of his shoulders, and a flicker of relief lightened those penetrating eyes.

"Actually," he said, "she jumped."

"Jumped?"

"Madeline became so caught up in her potions and strange medicines—trying to ensure that she would bear my child—that she grew desperate." He sighed, released her arm, and raked a hand through his hair. "Never mind. It doesn't matter."

"Yes, it does matter. Please tell me."

He hesitated, but the urgency in her gaze, and something in her voice, made him sigh again and lead her to the gold-cushioned bench beneath the window. They sat side by side, and as the candles sputtered low, casting pale, glimmering shadows across their faces, he spoke to her in a low, grim tone.

"We were not often together in the three brief months of our marriage. I was called away to battle more than I was home. The nights we spent together were rare and did not result immediately in prospects for a future heir. Madeline was impatient, then she became distressed." Ambrose shook his head. "Her women told me later, when I questioned them, that it was all she could think about, talk about. Our marriage had been arranged, of course, like yours and mine. But unlike you, Lianna, she had been eager for it. She was a quiet, fragile-looking thing, but she was ambitious. She sought the power and glory of being duchess of such a great kingdom as Blackenstar, and she wanted to ensure her position by giving me an heir."

"I understand," Lianna said softly. "Go on." Without thinking, she reached out and touched his hand.

Ambrose jumped as if she'd bitten him, then glanced at her sympathetic face. Slowly he twined his fingers through hers and continued. "The sooner the better, that is how Madeline felt. But when this didn't happen . . ." His mouth twisted. "She sought out the crone in the village who had knowledge of potions that could help a woman in this matter. And she tried them—but to no avail. Then"—his voice hardened—"according to her women, she heard of a gypsy band passing through the village, and she had them brought to her. Madeline questioned one of the gypsy women—all this while I was away fighting my eldest half brother,

Eoric," he added darkly, "and though she was supposedly warned of possible ill effects, she mixed a potion meant to ensure that she would be able to beget a child. But the effects of this potion were powerful—and immediate."

A silence fell in which the only sounds were the low hiss and sputter of the dying candles. Lianna held her breath, waiting for him to continue. He did, gazing not at her but at the few glinting embers that remained of the fire.

"Madeline became crazed. She ran about, blathering, shrieking, seeing things that were not there. She needed to fly, she said, to get away, and she ran to the parapet. To fly, she screamed. Beorn was here, and even he could not stop her in time . . ."

He broke off.

Lianna squeezed his hand. "I'm sorry," she whispered.

"I didn't love her." Ambrose shrugged his massive shoulders. "As I said, I arranged the marriage much as I did ours. Her father was a count—she was of good stock, wealthy, a fine match—and the count's lands bordered the farthest tip of my southern border. That increased the security of Blackenstar, at least in one tiny corner of this great meandering land. I wanted the marriage for that reason, and though I barely knew her, I would have given my life to protect her." He spoke fiercely. "She was *mine* to protect, like Blackenstar, like this keep."

Suddenly he surged to his feet and stalked across the chamber.

"Never have I known peace in my own land, Lianna. *Never.*" He spun about and returned to loom over her. "Ever since I was a boy, I've had to fight, fight with my half brothers and my cousins over every scrap of food. I fought with them over which horse I'd be riding, which pallet I'd sleep upon, which regiment I'd have the right to lead. We were raised like a pack of dogs—my father encouraged us to hate each other, distrust each other, fight each other, plot against each other—always with the doctrine drummed into our heads that only the strongest can lead, and even from the first, deep down, we all knew we were really fighting over who would one day rule Black-enstar.''

Silent, horrified, Lianna watched his face. She who had grown up under the shadow of her mother's disapproval, yet with every luxury granted her, and those around her who cared for her every wish, tried to imagine the household he described. Her pity grew as his story continued.

"My mother died when I was five. I was the youngest and the smallest. If I hadn't become the toughest I would surely have starved. I very nearly did. But I learned to fight—oh, yes, I learned it well. Eventually, when my father was killed in battle and Blackenstar went up for grabs, slices of land being tussled over like meaty bones, I went to war with each of my brothers. And they with me.''

"And you won.''

He nodded grimly. "So far. But Kenneth and Duncan still have formidable armies and greedy hearts. They are not satisfied with the lands I granted them when we made peace. They will attack again—unless I am so strong, so firmly entrenched as the duke of Blackenstar that they see no hope whatever in challenging me.''

"And that,'' Lianna spoke softly, "is why you married me.''

She pulled the cloak more tightly around her again, for it was not yet dawn and the room was still chilly.

"If your wife is royal, as royal as can be,'' she went on quietly, "and you are a strong ruler and fighter, as strong as can be, then few men will question your ability or authority. Or your heir's,'' she added, and saw him nod.

"You are wise as well as beautiful, Lianna. Yes, it is of my heir that I think. I'd never want my child to go through what I have—forced to fight continuously for what is his, never knowing a time of peace in which to build and let the land and the people prosper. My people have already endured year after year of turmoil and war.''

He reached out an arm and pulled her to her feet, his eyes riveted on hers. "With you by my side, no one will dare question me. I'll wear the mantle of the warrior duke, the Barbarian, and fight all I must, but I hope that by the time my son is grown, he can turn his attention to making the land and the people—and the House of Blackenstar—great and prosperous. And peaceful. I might be a bastard, but my son will be a true-born ruler of men, descended from a line of kings. Then I can end this damned curse—''

"Curse? So there is a curse?''

"Surely you know the tale.''

A shiver danced down her spine. "Well, I knew the rumors. And then I felt it—I felt it in the walls the first moment I set foot inside the keep.''

His eyes glittered. "They say that Morgan le Fey cursed the keep in a fit of rage after Merlin himself paid her a visit here—and warned her to keep her evil magic far from King Arthur. I don't say that I believe it, but there does seem to be something, something that prevents Blackenstar from ever knowing peace, something that keeps us in turmoil, always fighting, with those of us who share the same blood remaining enemies instead of becoming allies.''

Faintly her grandmother's voice whispered in her head, pure and musical as the notes of a harp: *Comes the night of a falling star . . .*

"I must go.'' Abruptly the intimate mood was gone. Dawn was breaking over the mountains of Blackenstar, delicate streaks of lilac and peach hazed with gold lightening the horizon. Banishing the stars. And Ambrose was no more the bold lover, nor the surprising confidant. He was all warrior. He released her arm, scowling, and swung toward the door.

"Beorn will guard you henceforth.''

"I don't care for Beorn and I don't need a guard.''

"Would that that were true.'' Ambrose eyed her from the door. "If in the following days you cause no further trouble, I'll allow you to send for your ladies-in-waiting and will provide an escort for them.''

He opened the door, then suddenly remembered the plants. He stalked to the low table where he'd set them and stared down at them as Lianna watched, her stomach clenching.

Then, without a word, he spun about and left.

Was this a sign of trust? Lianna wondered, as she gazed after him in confusion. Had something changed between them?

Everything had changed between them.

Everything she thought and felt about Ambrose the Barbarian, and about Blackenstar, was not as it had been before.

Except for one thing.

Constantine was still coming—to destroy this keep and the duke who had spent his whole life fighting for it.

And she must stand by and watch.

7

Lɪᴀɴɴᴀ sᴘᴇɴᴛ ᴛʜᴇ next few days in a state of wonder, doubt, and bewilderment. Each time she saw Ambrose, her pulse quickened, her heart leapt. How could this be?

Tormented, she tried to avoid him. She visited the village—accompanied by and closely watched by Beorn, per Ambrose's orders—where all the people she encountered watched her in awe, and she found that contrary to hating and fearing Ambrose, the people there respected him and wished him well on his marriage.

"Now, if Master Eoric had become duke of Blackenstar, we'd be in a sad pickle," one old woman huffed as she leaned on a rough bark stick. "He was always a vicious boy. But Duke Ambrose, though he be as fierce in battle as they come, is fair and has a care for the rest of us. I hope you give him many fine sons, my lady," she told Lianna before bowing past and going on her way.

In the keep, preparations began for a great feast. Ambrose wished to celebrate their marriage with a grand ball

152

and had invited all the nobles, gentry, and villagers to join in the festivities. The serving maids scurried this way and that, polishing, scrubbing, airing, dusting, and in the kitchens the cook and Marthe and countless others toiled night and day.

Lianna supervised and approved all of the food for the feast—there would be mutton and venison and sauced duckling, sweetmeats, and honey cakes and fruit, and dark, soft bread and silver goblets brimming with spiced wine.

She managed to see little of Ambrose during the days and found her heart heavy for it. But each midnight, when the stars glimmered and the silver moon sailed across the tranquil sky, he came to her chambers. Always there was that strange distance between them, the moments of unease and jousting with their words, and then they would come together, and he would kiss her, touch her hair with gentle fingers, and it would all begin again—the strange magic he worked on her, the undoing of all her resolve to despise him. Her heart opened like a flower and her body burned at his touch, and she couldn't hate him. And she was certain from the way he held her, stroked her, gazed at her with those keen eyes, that he did not in the least hate her.

So she found that though she did not hate him, *could* not hate him, she couldn't love him either, Lianna told herself on the fourth morning as she swallowed a crust of bread, nibbled at a bit of cake, and turned her attention to dressing for the day.

He was known far and wide as a ruthless enemy, she reminded herself, a fierce warrior who showed no mercy, a bloodthirsty fiend feared by the weak and the powerful alike.

Yet now she knew that the rumors were not all to be believed, that Ambrose fought only to hold the vast kingdom that was his, that he was as much a victim of his enemies as her father had been of Ambrose himself.

And then, the day before the ball, the moment she had begun to dread arrived.

The message came.

It came as Marthe was dressing her hair for dinner, coiling it into a tight coronet atop her head. Lianna glanced up at the knock upon the door, and when a towheaded page entered, he bowed low.

"My lady, two knights have arrived from the court of King Penmarren. One of them wishes to present himself before you. The duke received him before riding out to the hunt, and he has given leave. The knight bade me tell you he brings news of your father and of your homeland and begs for an audience."

Her heart stopped. Lianna stared at the youth, unable to utter a word.

"My lady?"

"Yes, yes. I will see him. Tell him I shall meet with him in the garden." Lianna jumped up from the velvet bench before Marthe could wind the gold ribbons through her hair. With her amber silk gown rustling, she snatched her cloak from its peg and rushed to the door, then reminded herself that she was a princess and a duchess and she should walk with dignity and grace. It had been many years since she had forgotten that lesson.

Ambrose, what have you wrought? she thought in frustration. She deliberately slowed her steps and straightened her shoulders, aware that Beorn, who had been stationed near her door, followed at a discreet distance.

But she was bursting with impatience by the time she reached the great hall. She headed toward the corridor that led to the kitchens and the garden, but was stopped by the peddler and his wife, who called to her when she would have hurried past.

Despite her impatience, she paused to greet them, noting that the man was nearly well and would be able to travel soon.

"Bless you, my lady." The woman curtsied low before her, but Lianna raised her, smiled, and wished them good health.

She reached the garden at last, hoping that here at least she would have an opportunity to talk with the knight in private. Beorn would be near, but she would request him to stand back a little distance. So long as he saw that she could not flee into the woods or toward some possible danger, he would not impose himself closer. Or so she hoped. It seemed to her that Beorn disliked her as much as she disliked him. So he would guard her, but from afar.

The winter garden was gloomy and gray—the stone benches, urns empty of blooms, the shrubs and trees naked and shivering in the light wind that blew down from the north. Beyond and to her right, the sea churned and crested and roared, and the salt tang of it filled her nostrils as she wandered the pathways, searching for her father's man.

He appeared from down a tree-lined path. Sir Gryford had guarded her father's litter when last he had been carried into battle. Middle-aged, paunchy now, and dark-bearded, he came toward her, limping slightly from a wound he had suffered in that same battle.

"My lady, it gives me joy to see you are well." He knelt and kissed her hand, but Lianna quickly raised him. She searched his face. Even here, where they seemed to be alone, she knew they could not speak freely.

To be overheard would spell disaster—and certain death.

"My father—is he well? And Meeg?"

He assured her of their good health and good wishes. "And Constantine, my cousin?" Lianna asked with as much casualness as she could muster.

She held her breath waiting for his reply.

"He is well and strong. He has returned from his journey and is eager to serve your father in every way."

"How good of him." Lianna clutched her cloak more tightly around her as her blood turned to ice. Constantine was back, and Gryford had come to tell her that the attack was imminent.

"Let us . . . walk a little through the garden," she managed to say through trembling lips, and then glanced over at Beorn, who stood watching from beneath the bare branches of an ancient, gnarled tree.

"I am well guarded by my father's man—and cannot possibly escape the gates," she said to Beorn. "You needn't follow me like a nursemaid if there is other business you might attend to."

She expected him to assert his orders to stay close by her at all times, but to her surprise, he saluted. "Aye, my lady, there is a matter I need to see about, and you're in no danger here. The duke won't mind if I loosen the leash just for a little while. But take care—if you play any tricks, it will come down on both of our heads." A grin spread across his scarred, fleshy face, and then he turned and stalked back toward the bailey with swift strides.

"My lady, come, let us walk. This way." Gryford gripped her arm and began leading her purposefully toward the rocky path that wound out of the garden, toward the craggy cliffs and paths that bordered the sea.

She followed silently, her heart tight in her chest. All she could think was that Constantine was coming and battle was near, and a vision of Ambrose fighting that massive army within the borders of his precious Blackenstar weighed upon her like a boulder.

But her thoughts were interrupted when Gryford suddenly veered from the path and led her higher, toward the towering cliff that overlooked that dangerous winter sea.

"Quick, my lady. This way. Ahead, past those trees, behind the rocks, there is Emmett with our horses. Two horses, his and mine. I'll stay behind—he is to take you at once to Constantine."

Lianna heard a sound behind her and looked back in alarm, but saw nothing, no one, except a crow lift from the branch of a furze bush and soar toward the tower of the keep.

"But what of you, Sir Gryford?" she asked as she breathlessly picked her way up a rocky path tangled with dead brush and stones.

"I'll hide myself until the battle commences and I can serve your father and Constantine from here within the keep. Don't you fret about me, Princess—it's you we must get safe away, lest the Barbarian use you as a hostage once he learns what is afoot."

He's not a barbarian, she wanted to cry, but she held her tongue. "Tell me, Sir Gryford, where am I to meet

Constantine? And when—and where—is he planning to stage the attack?''

"He is marching on Blackenstar even as we speak. He will await you on the Hill of Rivalen to take you into safety. If all goes as planned, the battle will commence tomorrow at dawn.''

Dawn. Only this very dawn, she had been lying in Ambrose's arms while his lips trailed kisses across her shoulder. Tomorrow, he would be at war with her cousin and her father. The keep would be under siege.

"No. *No!*''

"What, my lady? What is amiss?'' The aging knight was as out of breath as she. They paused at the crest of a cliff that overlooked the wild sea, and he turned to her, studying her drawn, pale face, the wide, panicked eyes. "Do not fear, Princess. You will be far and away—safe from the battle,'' he assured her.

"I don't want a battle, Sir Gryford. There must not be any attack. I must go to Constantine and stop him!''

"Stop him?'' Sir Gryford gaped at her, thunderstruck. "But the Barbarian took you from Penmarren, forced you to—''

"I won't leave him. I won't have him fighting Constantine or my father or anyone!'' *I love him,* she thought, but she bit back the words. How could she tell Sir Gryford this when she had not yet told Ambrose? She had only just discovered it herself.

"Come, we must hurry and reach Constantine before Ambrose discovers something.'' Frantic, she grasped his arm. "He has spies everywhere, and if he were to learn of this, he would be certain I had betrayed him—''

Suddenly a tall figure sprang out from the rocks behind her, knocking her aside. With a cry, Lianna found herself sprawled across the rough path, and then she saw Beorn hurling himself straight at Sir Gryford. The knight never had a chance. Beorn drove a knife through his heart as Lianna screamed. The sound echoed round and round, and before it had faded, Beorn yanked his knife out and dragged the knight to the precipice of the cliff. As Lianna watched in frozen horror, he threw Sir Gryford into the icy green waters far below.

Stunned and sick, Lianna struggled to her knees. Beorn spun back from the edge of the cliff and came toward her, his face wearing a triumphant sneer.

"*That* takes care of *that*, my lady," he said pleasantly. He was deadly calm, scarcely out of breath. The sun glinted off his bright gold hair. "Now it's time to take care of you."

Marthe's scream was a hoarse, rusty sound that grated through every corner of the kitchen. The peddler and his wife, eating bread and cheese at the table, stared in terror at the serving woman who stood at the door, her mouth open, and terrible low keening sounds emerging as though she were gazing at the devil. Half a dozen other servants stood rooted to the spot, petrified that the woman who had never uttered so much as a whisper had let out that blood-curdling scream.

The peddler's wife was the only one to move. She rushed to the door. "What? What is it?" she demanded.

Marthe lifted an arm and pointed.

When the woman looked up, she could just make out the rocky outcropping where someone—a dark-haired woman in blue—lay sprawled upon the ground. And at the same time, she saw a huge broad-shouldered man toss another man into the sea.

"It's my lady! That's her—up there!" she shrieked.

A commotion began in the kitchen, an uproar of shouts, prayers, questions—with everyone shoving toward the door. Suddenly Duke Ambrose strode into their midst.

"What goes on here?"

"My lord!" The peddler's wife stumbled toward him and fell to her knees. "I beg you—my lady is in danger!"

"What are you talking about, woman? Do you mean my wife?" Ambrose grabbed her arm and dragged her to her feet. "Where? Where is Lianna?"

"Upon the . . . ground . . . my lord." It was Marthe who answered him, slowly, in a rasping whisper, each word a

struggle. He turned in shock to stare at her. "The . . . cliff—
up there . . . a man . . . *hurt* her. He . . . killed the man . . .
threw him over . . ."

Ambrose's skin turned ashen. Fear churned through him,
stronger than any emotion he'd ever known. "Where, Marthe? Show me where, damn it!"

The peddler's wife rushed back to the doorway.
"There—she was there! You see? The gray rocks, above
the gardens—I saw it, too—the man who threw the other
into the sea—"

She broke off, trembling, lifting terrified eyes to the
duke.

Ambrose's keen stare raked the cliffside. His blood froze
in his veins. No one was there.

8

"YOU'RE MAD."

"Mad, is it? Think what you want, Princess. I know exactly what I'm doing."

Beorn suddenly dragged her off the path he'd taken and pushed her across a small ledge toward what she saw was the entrance to a cave.

"This is where you'll be staying until all the fighting's done. Then the new duke of Blackenstar will be back to claim you." His mouth curled into a smile. "As a royal bride, you'll serve me every bit as well as you did Ambrose."

"You think that *you* are going to become the new duke of Blackenstar?" Lianna's throat closed with horror. "You mean to kill Ambrose, don't you?" she whispered, a sick panic washing through her.

"I wouldn't put that fine a point on it," Beorn growled. "I only mean to see to it that he dies in this battle with Constantine—one way or another. Ah, yes, my lady." Beorn's lips curled into an ugly smile. "I followed you and that old knight, heard most every word. This attack planned

160

by Prince Constantine—it'll serve me. Aye, it'll serve me damned well.''

"Traitor,'' she whispered, her fists clenching at her sides.

Beorn shrugged. "It's his own fault—naming William captain-of-arms instead of me. He granted William land and a title. Not me. I've served him nearly thrice as long, and this is the way I'm rewarded? Assigned to protect both of his wives, a lady's guard.'' He snorted contemptuously, but beneath the scorn there was raw fury blazing in his eyes.

Her arms were bruised where he had grabbed her, held her helpless as he'd forced her away from the cliff and along another twisted path that wound back into the mountain along the coast and near the cave. If only she could get past him, back to the path. She could scream, try to rouse the attention of the guards, or someone at the castle, though the roar of the sea and the squawking of the crows might well drown out her cry. But as Beorn pulled a length of rope from the pocket of his heavy green cloak, she shrank back.

"You can't tie me up and leave me here, cave or no. I'll freeze!''

"That's a chance we'll have to take, won't we, my lady?''

He advanced on her.

"Why?'' Lianna forced herself to hold her ground, to stand firm as he approached, swaggering a little in his eagerness.

"Why must you betray Ambrose in this way? If you want recognition for all of your service, I can help you. I'll speak to Ambrose on your behalf. He'll listen to me.''

"Aye, he'll listen to you. He has a soft spot for you, that he does.'' The gold-haired soldier nodded, his voice thick with contempt. "Not like that other one, the poor stupid wench.''

"Madeline?''

"It's her fault, all this.'' Beorn grimaced. "If she hadn't taken those potions and gone mad like she did—trying to fly off the parapet—I'd have been captain-of-arms instead of William. Ambrose held me accountable for her dying.

He didn't say it." His eyes glittered. Black rage thrummed through his voice. "But I know he did."

"That's not true—he would have told you if it were. He thinks highly of you. He set you to guard me. He wouldn't have entrusted you with the care of another wife if he didn't trust you. After all, I escaped Sir William only days ago. He has not been faulted—"

"You didn't die after escaping the guard of Sir William," Beorn snarled. "If you had, it would have gone badly for him."

"But now . . . if I disappear," Lianna rushed on desperately, "Ambrose will hold you responsible once again. You were set to guard me today. He'll question you. You can't possibly get away with—"

"I'll tell him that your father's men overpowered me and ran off with you. By then, word of the coming attack might well have reached him, and he'll realize you betrayed him."

"I haven't!"

Beorn continued as though she hadn't spoken. "He won't want you back, my lady," he said softly. "He'll want you dead. Along with Constantine—and your father. Ambrose doesn't like betrayal." His green eyes shone. "You ought to be glad. It will make Constantine's job easier for it. Ambrose never was one to let himself get tied in knots over a woman, not him—not even when Madeline died, much as he regretted that. But he will, I would wager, get tied in knots over you. He'll be distracted in battle, as he's never been before. And I'll see to it that he finds himself in harm's way, with men loyal to me surrounding him, men who will let him be outnumbered and fall."

"How can you hate him so?"

"I didn't always hate him," Beorn told her, lifting the rope, stepping closer. "I admired him. Until he promoted William over me. Until he went soft—over you."

Suddenly he ripped the star-brooch off her cloak and clenched it in his fist. "He wore this always. *Always.* A symbol of Blackenstar. Until he brought you here. When he gave you this brooch, as a symbol that you were under his protection, I knew something had changed with him. He never gave it to Duchess Madeline. He cared for you even then, when you first reached Blackenstar. More so now. I've seen it when he looks at you. You are his weakness. Now you are my hostage.'' His lip curled. ''And soon you'll be my bride. You, my lady, will help me forge a treaty with Constantine and with Penmarren, and then you will remain by my side, adding legitimacy to my reign.''

Lianna snatched the brooch back from him, holding it tight within her hand. ''I'd rather jump into the sea and sink beside Sir Gryford than help you in any way!''

''No, my lady, you would not. For if you don't cooperate with me, your precious father will die. And that nurse you're so fond of. I have men in place inside Penmarren even now,'' he sneered. ''On my orders they'll kill those you hold dear. Only if you do my bidding will they be safe.''

A red fog swirled before her eyes. She struggled to remain calm, to think clearly. ''Monster!'' she gasped. Her hand plunged into her cloak pocket for her dagger, but Beorn only laughed aloud. ''Drop it to the ground,'' he ordered. ''If you don't obey me, I'll send word for those you love to be killed.''

She gripped it still.

''Drop it now.'' His scarred face flushed. ''The duke might have patience for you, Princess, but I do not. If you don't value their lives . . .'' He shrugged.

Biting back a sob, Lianna dropped the dagger. It clattered down among the rocks.

Suddenly there was a great noise below. Horses, shouts.

Then Ambrose's voice rang out—he sounded as if he were on a path nearby, just below the cave.

''Lianna!'' The urgency of his tone sent a sharp wave of love through her. ''Lianna—answer me!''

In a flash, Beorn had her imprisoned, his huge hand pressed against her mouth, preventing her from crying out, while his other arm clamped her body to his. Uselessly she struggled to free herself, but was unable to budge him.

"Duchess Lianna!" Another voice called out, more distant.

And another. "Are you hurt? Duchess Lianna!"

The shouts of Ambrose's knights drifted to her above the frenzied roar of the sea, and tears stung her eyes at her helplessness to answer.

Then Ambrose's voice came again—he sounded as if he were now directly below the ledge, on the path that wound around the cliff.

"Lianna!"

She heard the fear, the desperation underlying his commanding tone, and her heart broke in two.

Suddenly she remembered the star-brooch clenched in her fist. With all her strength she hurled it toward the tip of the ledge that overhung the path. It struck a rock, rolled, then tumbled over the edge, glittering in open space for one heart-stopping moment before it disappeared from sight.

Ambrose heard a slight clatter and glanced up. A small glimmering rock hurtled down toward him. On instinct, his arm shot out and caught the shining stone.

Only it wasn't a stone. It was a star. The star-brooch he had given to Lianna.

His mouth grim, he wheeled his destrier toward the path leading to the upper ledge, dropping the brooch into his pocket.

Sounds of a scuffle reached him as he drew near, and he spurred the destrier on. Reaching the path, he saw Lianna struggling mightily as Beorn attempted to drag her into a cave.

"Release her!" He was already swinging out of the saddle, striding toward them. "What the devil are you doing, Beorn? You were set to guard her, not to—"

Only then did he see the stark terror upon Lianna's face.

"What have you done to her?" Ambrose's stride quickened. His eyes were dark as thunder. "If you've hurt her, I'll kill you."

But before he could reach them and tear Lianna from the soldier's grasp, Beorn hurled the woman away, straight at

Ambrose. Ambrose caught her and held her steady.

"You dare treat my bride this way? Beorn, have you gone mad?"

He glanced down at Lianna, trembling like a spring leaf in his arms. "Whatever has happened," he said in a quiet, soothing tone, "I will make him pay. Stand aside now while I deal with him—"

He broke off as he saw that Beorn had drawn his sword. With his face taut and determined, the gold-haired soldier advanced.

"Deal with me, Ambrose? You think *you* shall deal with me? I, my lord duke, am going to deal with *you*. I've been wanting to do this ever since you passed me over for captain-of-arms. This isn't exactly the way I had planned things, but it will give me great pleasure to run you through here and now."

Ambrose thrust Lianna behind him and regarded the other man with steely eyes. "So you were the traitor. I thought of others, Beorn. Never you." His sigh was heavy. "You alerted Sandar when I went to Penmarren. You told him how my troops were dispersed, where and when we might be vulnerable to attack. Tell me, what did he promise you?"

"He promised me captain-of-arms of his whole army, for one thing—but that's not all. The kingdom of Pye for my own!" Beorn bragged.

"Too bad he failed. But even if he hadn't, you're not going to be alive long enough to have enjoyed any of it."

"Don't count on that." Beorn gripped his sword tighter. "I am a match for you, whether you know it or not. I know your skill, your great skill," he mocked, "and I'm not afraid to fight you. You'll be afraid before we're done. But first there is something you should know," he added slyly. "Your lovely bride has been conspiring with your enemies. Even now an army is marching on Blackenstar."

"No!" Stepping up beside Ambrose, Lianna clutched at his cloak. "I did not conspire! Not . . . exactly. I can explain . . ."

She broke off, her heart sinking at the expression on his

face. Shock. Pain. And then a coldness unlike anything she had ever seen. His gaze flicked back and forth between her and Beorn, sharp as a hawk.

"Ambrose, let me but explain," she begged. "There is not much time."

"That's true. Even as we speak, her cousin, Prince Constantine of Wyborn, is coming to rescue her from the barbarian duke of Blackenstar!" Beorn's mouth twisted. "She would see you dead. And now, yes, indeed she will—but not at Constantine's hand. At mine!"

He lunged forward so swiftly that Lianna screamed.

In a blink Ambrose thrust her aside and drew his sword. Even as Beorn closed in, Ambrose swung the glittering blade. The swords clashed. Beorn laughed.

Lianna gasped as she watched Ambrose cut his sword again, even more fiercely, at the soldier.

They fought ruthlessly. Single-mindedly. Grunting, dodging, charging, parrying with blinding speed. The blades glittered in the sunlight, and Lianna watched in horror as Beorn's thrust nearly went home, and then Ambrose drove forward with impossible strength and dizzying speed, and only narrowly missed running the gold-haired soldier through.

The sun dipped and faded in the graying winter sky, the crows flapped their great black wings and squawked, and the two men struggled and grunted and circled one another on the rocky ledge high above the sea. Ambrose fought with savage, dazzling skill and a strength that would have terrified any other man, while Beorn thrust and parried with a rough-edged skill every bit as ruthless and unrelenting.

It ended as suddenly as it had begun. A mighty thrust, a groan, blood spurting like a fountain. Beorn toppled over, sprawling across the ledge, his green eyes staring sightlessly toward the heavens as Ambrose slid his bloodied sword out of his enemy's chest.

Slowly Ambrose turned to Lianna.

"You're hurt." She started toward him, distraught by the blood staining his cloak, but he pushed her away.

"Is it true, Lianna? What he said? Did you conspire against me?"

"Yes." There was a dull roaring in her ears. A crushing anguish in her heart. Never had she seen such pain as she saw now upon his lean, handsome face. "But it isn't what you think," she rushed on, her voice trembling. "I knew that Constantine was raising an army . . ."

"*Duke Ambrose!*" A flame-haired knight on a gray horse charged into the clearing. "A scout has just ridden in from the west country. A great army is on the march—making its way, he believes, toward the Hill of Rivalen. A thousand men, armed to the hilt, with giant horses and—"

The knight broke off, staring in stupefaction at Beorn's bloodied form and then at the tall, hard-eyed duke.

"Call every man to arms. We will assemble at Lansdowne Point and stop them there. Send word to Masson in the south and to the troops quartered in the Low Country." Ambrose fired off his orders in a tone of deadly calm. "We ride within the hour."

He wiped his bloodied sword on his cloak. When the man continued to stare at him as if dazed, Ambrose shouted, "Ride, man! Ride!"

The knight disappeared in a spray of small stones, and Ambrose returned the sword to its scabbard and silently mounted his horse. Her heart breaking into a thousand pieces at the sight of his grim, weary face, the heaviness of his shoulders, Lianna stumbled forward.

"Wait. Ambrose, please. Wait! I can explain."

"Explain? There is no need. You have what you want, Princess. This might well mean the destruction of the House of Blackenstar. You can go home to Penmarren and leave us to be picked apart by the crows and whatever other scavengers happen by. But I vow it will not happen while I still breathe," he growled, a terrible icy fury claiming his features.

A sob broke from Lianna, but Ambrose wheeled his horse away, and even as the horn sounded from far below, trumpeting the alarm, and the clamor to arms began in the bailey and all through the keep, he charged down the path

toward the soldiers gathering in the yard. It was her last
glimpse of him—a tall, strapping giant sitting straight in
the saddle, galloping away from her and toward the coming
battle.

9

"HELP ME, SIR Emmett! Quick, help me to mount that horse!"

Lianna flew toward the young knight from her father's court as he stared at her in astonishment, scarcely recognizing the dignified princess he had known in Penmarren. Her hair had tumbled down from its stiff coronet, her face was streaked with tears and dirt, and the hem of her gown was torn.

"Princess Lianna—what are you doing—"

"Help me!" Lianna commanded as she skidded to a halt before Sir Gryford's dun. Frantic, she sprang into the saddle with the knight's assistance and spurred the horse forward, leaving the stunned knight to vault onto his mount and follow as best he could.

"But where is Sir Gryford?" he called after her.

"Dead," Lianna called back. "Dead!"

It was a blur to her, the mad dash down the perilous slopes, across the bailey, through the gates. The gates had already been raised while Ambrose's men hoisted their banners, gathered their armor, and prepared to ride out, and the guards manning the portcullis merely stared in shock at the princess and the knight who flew after her.

Back in the courtyard, Ambrose stared after the dark-haired girl on the huge destrier as she galloped like the wind away from the keep.

His eyes followed her, wasting precious seconds as he memorized that slim, lovely figure riding hard as a soldier on an urgent mission.

A terrible pain assailed him, a pain unlike any he had ever known. Only his tremendous self-discipline overcame the grief that rent him, and he tore his gaze from his fleeing bride at last and turned his attention to the men under his command.

''To Lansdowne Point!'' he shouted. The world was a bleak, ugly, faithless place, but he could not escape his duty. Or his fate.

He spurred his destrier toward the gate as horses sidled, banners lifted, swords smote the air, and with one shout, one voice that roared through woods and cliffs alike, his men surged in a faceless sea behind him.

It was nightfall when Lianna and Sir Emmett neared the Hill of Rivalen. She was by now too weary and weak even to glance at her surroundings, and she heard as if from a great distance her companion whistle, then whistle again. As if conjured up from the very air, a troop of ten men materialized through the trees, closing around them.

''The princess of Penmarren seeks the refuge of her cousin, Prince Constantine,'' the young knight barked to the fierce, heavy-bearded men.

Warriors, Lianna noted with a shiver. They had the tough and seasoned look of formidable men, a true match for even Ambrose's experienced troops. Her throat was thick with silent sobs, her heart heavy as the darkening sky.

She was escorted to a tent at the crest of the hill and ushered inside.

Constantine, golden-haired, strong, fit, and handsome, hurried to embrace her.

"Cousin! I am sorry to see you looking so weary. Are you ill? You're shaking," he said sharply. "You must be starved. There's bread and soup . . .''

"No, Constantine, nothing. I want nothing—only your ear. You must listen to me!''

"Yes, Lianna, I shall. But first you must sit. And eat. You're trembling.''

He drew her in, tried to pour her wine and offered her bread, but Lianna clutched at his tunic and demanded that he be silent.

"There is no time. You must call off this battle. And come with me now to find Ambrose—to help me explain.''

Constantine's thin face puckered in concern. "Have you gone mad, Lianna? Yes, I shall find Ambrose. At dawn. We will converge, his army and mine, and I will teach him not to threaten my uncle and steal my cousin . . .''

"No." Through a swimming weariness and despair, Lianna's determination rose. She pushed her wild hair out of her eyes and seized Constantine's arm. "No, no battle! I don't want this war. I don't want to return to Penmarren. I love Ambrose.'' The words rushed out, frantic and fevered. "I love him, do you hear me? You must come with me—not to fight him—but to make peace!''

Constantine stared down at her pale, desperate face, stunned into silence.

"Peace? With the Barbarian?'' he asked at last, incredulously, and then caught her as she swooned, falling straight into his arms.

In the thickest, blackest hours of the night, the small party reached the pass that led to Lansdowne Point. Once they had traveled the narrow pathway cutting through the hillside, they would come to an open plain in sight of where Ambrose's men were encamped.

There were few sounds, save the hooting of an owl and the scurrying of unseen creatures in the dense brush. A light snow began to fall as Lianna and Constantine, Sir Emmett, and five of Constantine's soldiers rode silently along the narrow track beneath moon and stars.

It was just as they emerged upon the plain that the night exploded with the sounds of charging horses, and danger suddenly vibrated through the frosty air.

A dozen men surrounded them, swords drawn, glistening in the silvered moonlight. Drawing in her breath, Lianna found herself gazing into her husband's cold, furious face.

"Ambrose," she managed to whisper, a catch in her throat.

Constantine had forced her to eat a few morsels before they'd departed, but the strain and exertion of the day and the long, arduous hours in the saddle had left her weak and aching.

But there was hope and determination in her face when she gazed across her horse's graceful head at the tall warrior before her, sitting his destrier with such unconscious grace.

"I must speak to you."

"There is nothing for either of us to say." He spoke over his shoulder then to William, one of the dozen knights. "Take this woman to the camp and guard her well. She is my hostage now."

But before William could spur his mount forward, Lianna slipped down from the saddle and ran toward Ambrose's destrier.

"My lord, I won't go with him. I must speak with you—alone. We come in peace—"

"Peace!" He gave a fierce bark of laughter.

"William, take her away from here before I can no longer be responsible for what I do. I can't bear the sight of her!"

The words cut her to the quick, and Lianna choked back a cry. Her eyes pleading, she reached up to try to touch him, implore him, but he wheeled his horse away from her so abruptly that she stumbled.

Instantly Constantine vaulted from his saddle and was at her side. "You *are* nothing but a damned barbarian," he said to Ambrose as he steadied Lianna, slipping an arm around her waist. "I told her it was no use trying to—"

Before he could finish, Ambrose had leapt to the ground,

grabbed him by the throat, and shoved him up against a tree.

"My only question is should I kill you here and now, or wait until full battle begins." His voice was a murderous snarl. Suddenly the tip of his sword pressed ever so lightly against the prince's throat.

"Ambrose—no!" In vain Lianna tried to pull him off Constantine, but she may as well have tried to uproot an oak. "Listen to me. He comes in peace! Please, if you'd only listen to me—"

But even as she tried to pull Ambrose off Constantine, her cousin suddenly shoved him back with a flashing burst of strength. The next instant, Constantine's sword hissed out, and the two men faced each other, both of them white-lipped with fury. Every man present drew his sword and eyed his enemy.

An eerie silence filled the air. Lianna's heart thudded as the twin scents of danger and death wafted about her.

One last time she tried to reach the man who held her heart, who owned it forever, if only he knew.

"Ambrose, stop being . . . such a fool. I never wanted . . . this. I knew about the army, yes, but that was *before*. Before I came to Blackenstar, before I fell in love with you—I wish you could only know how much I love you . . ."

He spun toward her, a stunned expression in his eyes. But at that same instant Constantine lunged, his sword swinging in a deadly arc straight at Ambrose.

"No!" Seeing the danger, Lianna hurled herself forward, knowing only that she had to protect Ambrose from the deadly blow. Constantine cursed and tried to turn aside the thrust, but the blade slashed through her cloak, and she gasped as the point pierced her flesh.

Lianna went down in a heap, darkness swimming before her dazed eyes. Pain burned at her shoulder, and warm, sticky blood flowed down her arm, soaking her gown and cloak.

"By all the saints! Lianna! Lianna, no!" Ambrose swept her up from the stony earth and cradled her like a doll in his arms. As long as he lived he would never forget the sight of her taking the blow that had been intended for him. Her face was still and white, whiter even than the snow that fell so lightly, like wisps of lace, melting upon her cheeks and eyelashes.

Constantine stood frozen. The sword fell from his numb hand. "Cousin!" His blue eyes blazed with a stark fear. "May the devil strike me blind, I never meant to hurt you."

"Of course . . . you didn't. My father . . . would be most . . . displeased," she managed to mutter with a bleary smile, but her glazed eyes were trying to focus upon Ambrose, upon his handsome face, ashen now in the starlight, his gray eyes studying her with undisguised fear and shock.

"Don't worry, my . . . lord . . . my . . . love. It is . . . nothing . . . it would take more than a simple wound to make me leave you," she whispered, and, reaching up, gently touched his beloved face.

Ambrose couldn't speak. Tears scratched at his eyes. Still cradling her, he tore off her cloak and tossed it on the ground, then carefully lowered her upon it. He ripped her gown at the shoulder to reveal the wound, and his shoulders sagged with relief as he saw that it wasn't deep, certainly not fatal. As Constantine came forward to clutch Lianna's hand, Ambrose ripped a wide strip from his own cloak and began to bind up the wound, as gently as he could, despite her slight moans and grimaces.

"We came here . . . Constantine and I . . . to stop the battle . . ."

"Quiet. Don't try to talk now. Save your strength."

Lianna felt herself sinking into dizziness and a thin, dark fog. The wound, the shock of it—added to her weariness from the grueling ride and her tormented heart—was exacting a toll. She felt herself weakening, slipping away. She fought to focus upon Ambrose's face.

"Listen to me . . ."

"No. Be silent. It doesn't matter, Lianna."

"Constantine, tell him . . ." she begged, even as she closed her eyes, letting the heavy blackness take her.

Dimly, through her faint, she heard Constantine begin to

tell Ambrose that they had indeed come in peace, that Lianna had ridden to the army's encampment and begged Constantine to call off the attack.

"She convinced me that she wants to remain with you. To remain the duchess of Blackenstar. I had gathered an army to rescue her, but she would barely take time to eat a single bite of bread—that though she was weary of riding all through the afternoon and evening. She wanted only to bring me to you . . . to explain to you . . ."

His words rose, fell, faded. In their place came the fairy song. Her grandmother's voice. The faint tinkle of the lost spell.

> *Catch yourself a falling star*
> *And love will blossom where you are*
> *Watch 'til dawn's new sun peeks through.*

"William, prepare a litter." Ambrose's voice broke through, sending the pieces of the spell spinning into murk once more, just as she was about to grasp them all. "We'll take her back to my tent."

"*No.*" Half sitting up, Lianna forced her eyes to open and clutched at his arm. "We must stay here. *Here.* 'Til dawn."

"Lianna, let him take you into the tent. You'll be warm, there are blankets—" Constantine began, but she shook her head weakly. Her gaze was locked upon Ambrose.

"Did you catch . . . the falling star?" she whispered.

He looked puzzled a moment, then suddenly nodded. "The star-brooch. You threw it to get my attention." He dug it out of the pocket of his cloak and stared at it. *Catch a falling star.* He shook his head and wrapped her cloak back around her, fastening the brooch in place once more. He lifted her so that she was nestled against him, his strong arms enfolding her. "It is safe. And so are you. Or you will be, once we get you out of this cold."

"No. We must stay . . .'til dawn. The spell . . . I feel it, Ambrose. My grandmother's spell. It is coming back to me . . . all of it. But we cannot leave here now, we must watch for . . . *there it is!*''

Ambrose followed her joyful gaze and saw, in a dazzling sweep of white, the shooting star that blazed through the blackness above and danced in a flash across the midnight sky.

''Comes the night of a falling star,'' she murmured, placing her hand upon his chest, ''send a heart's wish from afar. Then a kiss of love that's true . . . will banish evil's curse from you.''

The words tumbled out softly, pure and sweet and true as new snow. Ambrose drew her closer. He didn't fully understand, he only knew that this sable-haired princess had tried to save his life, that she was gazing at him with love glowing from her beautiful eyes. And he knew he couldn't go on for a single day without her.

''A kiss of love that's true,'' he repeated, and thinking of how close he'd come to losing her, he tightened his arms and leaned his head down toward hers.

The kiss was deep, sweet, and gentle as the dawn. All the coldness vanished. Pure warmth flowed between them, heat and light and tenderness that brought the sheen of tears to her eyes.

''A kiss of love that's true . . . will banish evil's curse from you,'' Lianna repeated the spell against the warm slant of his mouth.

They stayed there throughout the long, chill hours of the night. The soldiers brought blankets, and Constantine built a fire, and then all of Blackenstar's knights retreated. Constantine and his party went with them, leaving Ambrose and Lianna there upon the plain, with the moon and the stars as their companions, snuggled together while the hours tiptoed toward the dawn.

Early morning came at last, naked and sweet and golden against a shimmering lilac sky, and they watched it together, snug in each other's arms.

As Lianna gazed at the peaceful glow of color in the sky, as the chill of night faded and the new day began, the words came to her, softly, easily, every single one of them.

Breathlessly she murmured them, her eyes fixed upon the sun.

> *Comes the night of a falling star*
> *Send a heart's wish from afar.*
> *Then a kiss of love that's true*
> *Will banish evil's curse from you.*
> *Catch yourself a falling star*
> *And love will blossom where you are.*
> *Watch 'til dawn's new sun peeks through*
> *And all your dreams will fair come true.*

She closed her eyes and saw her grandmother's face, smiling, smiling.

The spell was complete.

"My heart's wish," she said, reaching up to stroke Ambrose's jaw. "I spoke it last night—that you should only know how much I love you. I didn't want to . . . but I gave you my heart, Ambrose the Barbarian. It is yours."

"And I give you mine, my beautiful, brave, and very stubborn princess. My heart, my life, my love. Forever."

A great rushing, flapping noise split the silence of the dawn, and, glancing up, they saw the sky grow black with crows. They swooped and darted, cawing and squawking, then wheeled away to the west, flying straight and fast and furious, leaving behind them an even deeper silence.

"The crows are gone from the keep." Lianna spoke with quiet certainty. "The curse is lifted."

"I hope that means we can leave this place now." He grunted and stroked a finger along the curve of her cheek. "Your shoulder must be throbbing. You must be cold, sore, hungry. Ready or not, Princess, I'm taking you home."

"Home." Lianna laughed as he lifted her in his arms. The twinge in her shoulder was nothing. Compared to the joy in her heart, it was nothing at all.

She thought of the keep that had so alarmed her at first, the place where she now wanted most to be. Alone in her sweet-scented chamber, with a blazing fire and the deep featherbed—and Ambrose. The two of them—safe, together.

She knew that a chance for peace now would grow across the land.

"Yes, my darling barbarian." Smiling, she wrapped her good arm around his neck as he began to carry her toward the camp and the horses and the men stirring from their sleep. "Let us go—*home.*"

EPILOGUE

"WHAT I DON'T understand is why this place is called Crow's Keep." Meeg glanced up from the five-month-old baby boy dozing in her arms and peered from Lianna's glowing face to Ambrose's beaming one. "I've seen larks, and doves, and gulls aplenty, but not a single crow in the fortnight we've been here."

"They're gone, banished—like all the other dark and ugly things in my life." It was Ambrose who replied. As he spoke, he leaned down and stroked a finger across the baby's cheek. His smile deepened as he stared at the dark fuzz of hair upon the boy's head and studied his peacefully closed eyes. "Thanks to this little fellow's mother."

King Penmarren's lips twitched in satisfaction. Constantine lifted his fair brows and smiled. But it was Lianna's laughter that rang like soft golden bells through the sundrenched castle garden.

"It was nothing, my lord," she retorted. And turning to Meeg, she said in a loud whisper, "He must want something from me. Whenever it is so, he resorts to flattery. In

179

the year and a half we have been wed, I've learned all his strategies.''

"All his strategies, eh?'' King Penmarren leaned back in the deep-cushioned chair that had been brought out to the garden for him, a twin of the one in which Meeg sat cradling the future duke of Blackenstar. The fragrance of a thousand flowers filled the air. "So great and renowned a warrior must have many strategies, my dear. How clever of you to have learned them all.''

"Not all.'' Ambrose suddenly tugged Lianna from the stone bench upon which she sat and pulled her into his arms. "Would you like me to demonstrate some you have not yet learned?'' he asked in a low, silky voice directly in her ear.

"Why, yes. But later, my lord.'' Her violet eyes sparkled. "This is hardly the time or place. We have guests.''

"Family,'' he corrected her. "Not guests. They won't mind excusing us. We have much to discuss—the entertainment for the banquet tomorrow. Jugglers or musicians. These things call for decisions.'' He wrapped an arm around Lianna's waist and glanced at each person in the garden. All chuckled and assured him that they were perfectly content to see him and Lianna excused.

"What more could we want now?'' Meeg shifted the baby in her arms as Marthe entered the garden with a golden tray of refreshments, which she set down upon a carved stone table. " 'Tis a beautiful day, like the May days of my girlhood. We have wine and cake and grapes. And I have this beautiful little one in my arms—happy and healthy.'' Her sigh of contentment was mirrored by the grateful tears that shone in her eyes. "All is well. Never did I think it would turn out this way!''

Lianna slipped free of Ambrose and went to her and kissed her cheek, as she had that long-ago night when she'd been taken from Penmarren as a most reluctant bride.

"Never did I think so either,'' she murmured.

"Will that be all, my lady?'' Marthe curtsied.

"Yes, Marthe. Thank you.'' Ever since the day that Beorn had killed poor Sir Gryford and tried to murder Ambrose, Marthe had found herself once more able to speak. The shock of seeing Lianna in danger had somehow shaken her out of her silent state, and though she remained for the most part quiet as a moth, she did speak now and then, especially to Lianna, to whom she had become wholly devoted.

As Marthe wove her way back toward the castle, Lianna bent her head and gave her son a kiss. "Now I believe it is my turn," Ambrose chuckled, and she rose to go eagerly into his arms.

"So that is what you wanted." Rising up on tiptoe, she brushed a kiss across his jaw.

"There. Will that serve, my lord?" she asked softly.

"For now." He took her arm and began leading her toward one of the peach-tree-lined paths that wound beneath the cliffs, away from the others, who were enjoying the May sunshine and the sweet profusion of flowers. "Constantine, will you be jousting in the tournament tomorrow?" he asked, as they passed the prince of Wyborn.

"That I will. Lady Else has been so kind as to give me her handkerchief as a token."

"Well done." Ambrose grinned. "And I suspect Sir William will have a token from the fair Lady Kira," he added as Sir William and Kira appeared on the path above, strolling together beneath the trees.

Lianna's ladies-in-waiting, Else, Kira, and Gwenlyn had all come to Blackenstar shortly before she learned she was with child and had been attending her ever since. But she would soon need to choose some new ladies-in-waiting. Gwenlyn had already been pledged to marry one of Ambrose's knights, and it appeared that Else and Kira would soon both be wed as well.

Something in the air at Crow's Keep—ever since the curse was broken—seemed to make love flourish.

At least, Lianna thought, it had been so for her and her Barbarian Duke.

As Ambrose led her to a secluded clearing that dipped off the path, out of the sight and earshot of those in the garden, she reflected on her life as the duchess of Blackenstar.

Not only had love flourished here at the castle, but peace had settled like a silken coverlet across the land. Those aligned with Beorn had been found and dealt with. The borders were secure, and Ambrose's enemies had turned their thoughts elsewhere, cowed by the strength of his new alliances.

And since little Rowan had been born, an air of laughter and contentment had seemed to shimmer right off the ancient stone walls of the castle—a joy almost tangible, for all to see.

The night of the falling star had brought the granting of all her wishes—hers and Ambrose's both.

"Now," Ambrose said, and touched the star-brooch that glittered at the shoulder of her topaz silk gown, "what do you say to jugglers first and musicians second?"

"I think musicians first and jugglers second," Lianna teased, then drew in her breath as his arms slipped around her waist, drawing her so close she could feel the strong, steady beating of his heart.

As always, her own heart began to thud in anticipation.

"As you wish, Princess," he murmured and cupped her face in his hand.

"If this is your strategy, my lord, to accede to all my desires in order to win my favor, and to flatter me and to . . ."

He brought his mouth down on hers and kissed her thoroughly.

"And to kiss me until I can't think straight . . ." she gasped.

Ambrose ruthlessly kissed her again. "That is my strategy exactly," he said.

"Then let me advise you." Lianna pulled his head down to hers and kissed him ardently, her mouth soft and pliant and eager upon his. Joy and love rose like soaring doves in her heart and shone from her eyes. "Proceed according to your battle plan, my lord. It is working splendidly."

THE CURSE OF
CASTLE CLOUGH

★

Ruth Ryan Langan

For Nora, Marianne, and Jill—true friends
And for Tom—best friend and love of my life

Prologue

Castle Clough, the Scottish Highlands

"GRIFF." SLIGHTLY OUT of breath, Lord Robert Cameron paused in the doorway of his father's library. Not his father's, he mentally corrected himself. It was his library now. As it had done for hundreds of years, everything at Castle Clough had once again passed from father to son. The land, the buildings, and everything in them. "I was busy with the herd when I got the message that you'd driven up from Edinburgh."

"Still playing the part of a gentleman farmer, I see." Griffin Mackenzie looked up from the ledgers he'd spread open across the desk and shot a challenging look at his former brother-in-law.

"I'm proud of the herds I've developed, Griff. They're the finest in Scotland. Maybe in the world. Now," Rob said tiredly, "I was in the middle of an important test. What is it you wanted to see me about?"

185

"It's about these." Griffin Mackenzie waved a hand over the ledgers. In his mid-sixties, he was thirty years Rob's senior. He was still a handsome man, with smooth, even features and dark hair graying at the temples. Over the years he had parlayed his knowledge of finance into one of Scotland's largest fortunes. He wore his success as easily as the perfectly tailored Saville Row suit and Italian leather shoes.

"What about them?" Lord Cameron crossed to the desk and glowered at the man who had dared to invade his private sanctum while he'd been busy in the fields.

"You'll find them interesting reading, Rob." Griff walked around the desk, then settled himself into a chair and stretched out his legs.

"All right, Griff." Rob crossed his arms over his chest. "You look far too smug to be here with good news. Why don't you tell me what I'll find."

"You'll find that your father's . . . vices were extremely costly."

Rob tensed. He knew all about his father's drinking, gambling, womanizing. "How costly?"

"More than fifteen million pounds."

Stunned, Rob sank down onto the desk chair and stared blindly at the ledgers. "And how would you know all this?"

"Because he came to me for the money."

"Which you were only too happy to lend him."

"I was, indeed." Griff's eyes glittered. He leaned forward, lowering his voice for emphasis. "You'll find that the documents your father signed are all legal and binding. If you can't repay the loans by month's end, the entire estate becomes my property."

Rob clenched a fist atop the ledger. "You know I can't raise that kind of money in only a few weeks' time."

Griff sat back and picked a piece of lint off his cuff. "A pity. But it should be some consolation that Castle Clough and all the surrounding land will still be in the family, in a manner of speaking."

"You aren't family, Griff. And you never were."

"I was married to your sister."

"And we all know why you married her." Rob's eyes narrowed. "I never realized until this moment just how much you resented me."

"I don't resent you, Rob." Griff closed his hands around the lions' heads carved into the arms of the chair, worn smooth by use over the centuries. The piece would be a fine addition to his office in Edinburgh. "I pity you. You had the misfortune of being born to a weakling father, who could never resist the lure of slow horses and fast women. He didn't deserve Castle Clough. You probably do, but now you'll never have it. It will all be mine."

"You said I have until the end of the month."

"I did. But don't get your hopes up." Griff smiled, though his eyes remained cold. "There isn't a bank in Scotland that will lend you a dime. Those I don't own outright, I control through stock or personal friendship. They'll do as I tell them."

"Then I'll sell everything." Rob glanced around at the elaborate coat of arms hanging over the fireplace. At the paintings, several of which were priceless and had been in the family for generations. "If I have to, I'll sell them for a fraction of what they're worth."

"I don't believe you." Griff leapt to his feet and stood facing him. "You love these things too much to sell them. It would kill you to part with them."

"I do love them. Not for their dollar value, as you do, but because they've been in my family for centuries. But I'd rather give them away than see them in your hands."

"Go ahead, then. Do what you please. But know this. When I take possession of Castle Clough, I'll retaliate by making the sale of your beloved cattle my first priority. Better yet, I'll have them all slaughtered."

He had the satisfaction of seeing Rob's face drain of all color. "And your pathetic staff will be out on the street. At their age, I doubt there'll be much demand for their services."

"You really are a bastard, Griff."

"A very rich one. And about to become much richer."
He sauntered to the door, then turned for one last thrust of
the knife. "I'll see you in a couple of weeks, Rob, old boy.
Have the keys to the estate ready to hand over."

1

"THERE IT IS, miss." The driver of the aged Rolls pointed to a break in the trees.

Estelle Sinclair leaned forward from her position in the backseat. At first all she could see was the curtain of rain that had been falling for the past hour or more. Suddenly lightning sliced the sky, revealing ancient turrets. The castle itself was hidden from view behind tall hedgerows and scattered woods. Then, as the car rounded a curve, she caught her breath at the sight of Castle Clough. She could see why it was often called the castle in the clouds. It was situated high on a hill, overlooking green, rolling meadows dotted with sheep. Despite the rain, the lovely pastoral setting made Estelle sigh with pleasure. At last she would see for herself the place she had been researching nonstop in her New York offices for the past four days.

Her heart raced at the rugged beauty of the Scottish Highlands. On the long drive from Glasgow she had seen the gradual changes, from long, lonely glens and open farmlands to craggy mountain peaks and wild, rushing streams. She had nearly wept at the sight of heather hills and cool, lovely lochs half hidden in dense woodlands and steep-sided glens.

The castle suited its rugged surroundings. With the mist-shrouded Highland forest behind it, it loomed like a fortress, dark and forbidding. The ancient stones had weathered to a dull gray. Though the towers were now empty, Estelle could imagine how they must have looked filled with Highland warriors holding their swords aloft, standing their ground against invading armies.

"Is this your first visit to the castle, miss?" The driver studied her in the rearview mirror as he swung the car through the open gates and up the wide, curving ribbon of drive.

"Yes." She met his eyes in the mirror and saw them narrow with speculation.

With a frown he brought the car to a stop and stepped out, then opened her door and offered his hand.

She accepted his help and stood admiring the ornate front entrance while he began removing her luggage from the trunk. He struggled under the weight of her first oversized suitcase and led the way up the wide stone steps.

Before he could lift the heavy brass knocker, the front door was thrown open and a tall stick of a man in a dark suit, crisp white shirt, and perfectly knotted tie stood glowering at them.

"What's this now, Angus?" he demanded.

The driver nodded toward Estelle. "The lass says she's here at the lord's request, Desmond."

Estelle stepped forward, eager to explain. "I'm Estelle Sinclair, with Smythe-VanPell Auction House in New York."

The older man looked down his nose. "We were told to expect you yesterday."

"Oh, dear. My original flight was delayed, and then I missed my connection. I see you haven't received the communication from New York about the change in plans."

Her driver reached into his pocket and produced an envelope. "I'll bet that's what this is, Desmond. I was told to deliver it with all haste."

"All haste, is it?" With a look of censure in the driver's direction, the man in the doorway tore open the envelope and read, then nodded.

When he spoke, his tone became brisk and business-like. "Come in, Professor Sinclair. Welcome to Castle Clough. My name is Desmond Snow." He turned to the driver. "Angus, you may leave the bags here. I'll see that they're taken to the professor's rooms."

Angus looked relieved as he backed away from the door and hurriedly retrieved the other bags.

As he set them down, he leaned close to whisper, "Be warned, miss. There are those, myself included, who would never dare set foot inside this place. There's a curse on it."

He looked up to see Desmond staring holes through him. He hurried back to the car. Within minutes he was driving away, the wheels of the car spewing gravel in his haste to depart.

Estelle looked after him thoughtfully. She'd read of the ancient curse of Castle Clough. Something about all the women dying young. But it was nothing more than an old wives' tale. It was difficult to believe that in this enlightened age people would still fret over such a thing.

Desmond stood aside, beckoning her in. "I'll show you to your room and see that you're given some tea and a bite to eat. I'm sure you'll want some time to rest after your long journey."

"Thank you. But I'd really like to see Lord Cameron. I'm eager to get started on my work here."

"I'm afraid that isn't possible right now, Professor Sinclair." His tone was brusque. "Lord Cameron is in a most important meeting. But I'll inform his lordship that you've arrived."

He led the way up a wide, curving staircase. Estelle couldn't help darting glances of admiration as she followed. The highly polished balustrade was hand-carved mahogany, each step of the staircase a slab of gold-veined marble. A chandelier was suspended on silver chains from four stories above. After a cursory glance, she estimated it to be the finest crystal, several hundred years old. The soaring walls were softened with ancient tapestries whose symbols of lions and stags and warriors may have faded through the centuries but were still excellent examples of superb craftsmanship.

Along the hallway leading to her room were portraits of lavishly dressed women and darkly handsome men. She had the odd feeling that they watched as she passed by.

Desmond opened a set of double doors, then stood back, allowing Estelle to precede him. Inside was a sitting room, with a mix of seventeenth- and eighteenth-century furnishings in remarkable condition. The room smelled of beeswax and ammonia, attesting to the fact that it had been thoroughly cleaned in preparation for her arrival.

"It's a bit drafty, with all this rain. If we had known . . ." He stopped and cleared his throat. It wasn't his place to criticize a guest's late arrival. "I'll have one of the lads sent up to start a fire." Desmond opened another door revealing a bedroom fit for a queen, with a huge four-poster bed decked with peach-and-white-silk bed hangings and an ivory comfortor adorned with what Estelle recognized as the Cameron crest.

He stood aside as she slowly circled the room, touching a hand to the silk hangings, pausing to study the signature on the painting that hung over a Louis XIV desk.

"I hope you'll be comfortable here, Professor Sinclair."

Despite his words, Estelle had the distinct impression that this man wasn't as much concerned with her comfort as with her untimely arrival. "Thank you, Desmond. I'm sure I will be."

She waited until he left. As soon as the door closed behind him, she kicked off her shoes and began slowly circling the room again, pausing to touch, to examine, to admire.

What a treasure trove. For someone like Estelle, who had spent years studying Scottish antiquities, this was the opportunity of a lifetime. She spread her arms wide and danced around and around before dropping onto a sixteenth-century chaise to catch her breath. Despite the less-than-cordial welcome, nothing could dampen her excitement at being here. And, she reminded herself, perhaps Desmond Snow was merely annoyed at being caught unawares. If he was in charge of the household staff, he probably took his duties very seriously.

Still . . . she considered her surroundings further. How could anyone remain annoyed at anything for any length of time in a place as regal as this?

At a soft tap on the door she looked up. Before she could cross to the sitting room, the door was opened and a brawny young man entered, carrying an armload of wood. Though such a burden would stagger most men, this lad carried the logs as though they weighed no more than a feather.

He looked at her, then quickly away. But in that moment she caught sight of his eyes. They had a strange, vacant stare.

He crossed the room to the fireplace, where he knelt on the hearth and deposited his burden.

Behind him trailed a boy of about twelve or thirteen. "Good afternoon, miss." The boy's cheeks turned a becoming shade of pink when he caught sight of Estelle in the doorway. "Desmond sent us up to start a fire and see to your comfort."

"Thank you." Estelle watched as the older lad carefully arranged the logs, then held a match to the kindling. His movements were slow and deliberate. Like someone who was sleepwalking. "My name is Estelle Sinclair. What's yours?"

"I'm Arley Barclay. And this is my brother, Fergus."

"It's very nice to meet both of you. Do you live here at Castle Clough?"

The younger boy laughed. "Oh, no, ma'am. We live in the village you can see from the window. Just down that winding road a bit. Dunfield, it's called. I help out here after school and on weekends. Fergus doesn't go to school, so he's here most every day." He studied the newcomer. "Will you be staying here long?"

Estelle shrugged. "I don't know yet. That depends on

Lord Cameron, and how satisfied he is with my work.''
She sighed. ''Though it will seem more like a holiday, living and working in such a beautiful place as this.''

The boy and his brother exchanged quick looks, before
glancing away. Estelle felt a shiver along her spine. Just a
quick tremor. But it left her with an uneasy feeling. As
though these two shared a secret. A not very pleasant one.

Satisfied with the fire, Fergus lumbered out of the room
and returned minutes later, handling Estelle's bags the same
way he'd handled the logs. As though they weighed nothing
at all.

''Bring them in here, Fergus,'' Arley called, leading the
way to the bedroom.

When the luggage had been deposited on a long wooden
bench, Fergus gave a nod of his head, then left the room.

Estelle stared after him. ''Can he speak?''

His brother nodded. ''Sometimes. A few words, though
not many. Mostly he just lives in his own world.'' He
seemed eager to change the subject. ''Desmond told me to
see to your things, Professor. Do I have your permission to
unpack your bags and hang your clothes in the wardrobe?''

''Of course. Thank you, Arley. But just the larger case.
The smaller one contains personal items. I'll unpack them
later. I'll just take this and go over some of my notes.''
Estelle picked up her briefcase and carried it to the sitting
room, settling herself on a sofa in front of the fire.

Just as she sat down, another knock heralded the arrival
of a stone-faced man carrying a silver tray.

''You'd be Professor Sinclair,'' the man said as he set
the tray on the table next to the sofa. He was a big man,
with broad shoulders and large, work-worn hands. His
white hair had been cut razor-sharp, adding to the harshness
of his stern, narrow face. There was a look of tension about
him in his stiffly held arms, in his brown eyes, which
peered unblinking, and in his mouth, which turned down
into a hard, tight frown.

''I'm Alfred Snow, Desmond's brother and the cook here
at Castle Clough for more than forty years.''

"It's nice to meet you, Alfred. I envy you living and working in such a beautiful place."

"Huh." That was the only acknowledgment the man made. But his frown, Estelle noted, deepened. "I hope this will hold you until dinner." Alfred lifted the linen covering to reveal a pot of tea, a tray of little sandwiches, and a lovely arrangement of sliced fruit.

"Oh, Alfred, that's more than enough. Thank you."

Estelle's smile elicited no matching response from the cook.

"I wonder if I might have a chance to meet Lord Cameron before dinner."

Alfred's lips thinned. "His lordship's still locked away in his meeting."

Just as he said that, a man poked his head in the doorway bellowing, "Alfred, where the hell is . . . ?"

He stared at Estelle, who jumped up and stared back at him. She had a quick impression of dark, flashing eyes, thick black hair, and a face that might have been handsome if not for the scowl that marred its features.

She knew from photographs she'd seen in her research that this was the new Lord Cameron. In his university days he'd been part of the wealthy and titled, following the sun and the parties around Europe. Now in his mid-thirties, he it was rumored to have rediscovered his roots and had returned to Scotland to raise prize cattle and carry on research in veterinary medicine.

His photographs hadn't done him justice. They didn't reveal the cleft in that strong jaw or the hint of danger that flashed in his eyes.

For several seconds he merely stared at her.

Alfred Snow said dryly, "Lord Cameron, this is Professor Sinclair."

The man frowned, running a hand through his hair in frustration. "Desmond should have told me the professor had arrived."

The cook gave a negligent shrug of his shoulders. "You were meeting with the bankers and told him not to disturb you for any reason."

"Yes. Well. I must return to the meeting. I just broke away for a moment." He recovered his wits and strode closer, extending his hand. "Welcome to Castle Clough, Professor Sinclair. Or should I call you Doctor Sinclair?"

He was tall, well over six feet. Estelle's own five-and-a-half-foot stature seemed small by comparison. When she placed her hand in his she felt a rush of heat and blamed it on their proximity to the fire. Or perhaps it was the anger she could sense in him. Anger mixed with frustration. "Those are such stuffy titles. I much prefer Estelle."

"Estelle." If he had any reaction of his own to her touch, he gave no indication. If anything, his frown became more pronounced. He dropped his hand to his side. Curled it into a fist. "My family and friends call me Rob. I prefer it to Lord Cameron."

"I'll remember." Estelle tried a smile, hoping it might put him at ease. "Now that you're here, perhaps we could talk about some of the things I'll be doing."

"I'm a bit . . . rushed at the moment." He bit off the words with a trace of annoyance. "Perhaps you could join me for dinner, and we can talk then."

Stung by his dismissal, she merely nodded. "Of course."

He seemed not to notice as he turned to his cook. "I'm looking for Fergus."

"This time of day he'd be hauling logs for the fire. I'll fetch him."

"Fine. Tell him to go up to my uncle at once. Until dinner, then, Profes—Estelle." Without a backward glance he strode out of the room.

Alfred Snow waited until he was out of earshot, then said dryly, "His lordship has a bit on his mind these days." He paused in the doorway between the sitting room and the bedroom, watching Arley hanging clothes in the wardrobe. Satisfied that the orders were being followed, he nodded to Estelle, then exited the suite, closing the door firmly behind him.

Estelle dropped down onto the sofa and stared into the flames of the fire. The notes from her briefcase lay forgotten on the coffee table. The tea and sandwiches no longer held any temptation. She'd arrived at Castle Clough as eager as a child at Christmas. This had seemed like the offer of a lifetime. A chance to see for herself all the lovely things that, until now, had never been viewed by anyone outside the Cameron family.

Now she was feeling more than a little uneasy. As though everyone around her knew a secret. A secret they had no intention of sharing with her.

What a strange reception.

Lord Cameron was either rude or distracted. She had, after all, dropped everything to come clear across the ocean at his invitation. Yet he couldn't even give her a moment of his time.

As for Desmond and Alfred Snow, they looked at her as though she were intruding on their turf.

Arley and Fergus seemed nice enough. But even they gave the impression of knowing something that she didn't.

She slipped off her shoes and curled up in a corner of the sofa, closing her eyes as weariness overtook her.

She hoped it was just the exhaustion of the overseas flight and the long drive from the airport. But she had the distinct feeling that something was very wrong here. Something dark and sinister was in the wind. And like Alice, she had fallen down a long, dark tunnel into a strange, alien world.

2

"WE'VE GONE OVER all the documents, Lord Cameron." Gordon MacKinnon was as round as he was tall, with soft, pudgy fingers, the nails carefully manicured. He sat hunched over the desk, tracing a finger around the rim of the bulging folder crammed with papers. "Each bank draught was signed by your father and properly witnessed."

"And the time limit? Is there any legal way to extend it?" Lord Cameron stared into MacKinnon's sad, hound-dog eyes.

"Perhaps . . ." The man shrugged and glanced around at the other men seated in the library, seeking their agreement. "Perhaps if you were to go to Griffin Mackenzie and ask for an extension . . ."

"He has already made it clear that it's out of the question. What about a loan? The estate is showing a profit. Certainly this house, and especially the land, can be used as collateral."

Bank vice president Maxwell answered in a gravel voice that grated like nails on a blackboard. "Your father already used the land and castle as collateral, your lordship, when he went to Griffin Mackenzie for money to finance his . . . various endeavors.''

Lord Cameron rounded on him, but before he could open his mouth to protest, Gordon MacKinnon interrupted. ''Maxwell doesn't mean to malign your father's reputation, your lordship.'' His voice was calm, soothing. ''He's just stating the facts, the same as the rest of us.''

''I know, Gordon. I know.'' Lord Cameron ran a hand through his hair as he studied the bank officials, all dressed in identical dark suits and crisp white shirts. His own scuffed boots and slightly frayed cuffs attested to the fact that he'd been working in the fields until their arrival. He had to keep working. It was the only way to hold on to his sanity.

''The fact is,'' Gordon MacKinnon said softly, ''your father, for whatever reason, chose to plunge his estates deeply into debt. We're not here to cast blame. We're here at your request, to help you find a way to hang on to your inheritance.''

The others nodded their agreement.

Lord Cameron lowered his voice. ''Thank you, Gordon. I appreciate that. But if the bank will extend the notes, I may have a way. I've sent for an expert on antiquities from Smythe-VanPell Auction House in New York. I'm told they're the best in the business. When Professor Sinclair has finished cataloguing the assets, I'll agree to a sale.''

The bankers' eyes widened in disbelief.

MacKinnon spoke for all of them. ''You refused to allow public tours of the castle, and you rejected out of hand the idea of turning it into an exclusive hotel. And now you're saying you'd strip Castle Clough of all its priceless antiques?''

''What choice do I have? I'd rather sell every piece of furniture, every rug and wall hanging, before I'd turn my home into something no better than a tourist trap or a cheap motel.''

''Hardly cheap.'' MacKinnon glanced at the others.

"People pay very good money to sleep in a castle. Especially one that's known to be haunted."

Annoyed, Lord Cameron walked to his desk and stared morosely at the thick file detailing the debt left by his father.

Gordon MacKinnon watched for several minutes before clearing his throat. "I know this is painful, your lordship. But Griffin Mackenzie is a very wealthy and powerful man."

"And you have no intention of going against his wishes."

MacKinnon pursed his lips. "Perhaps Griffin Mackenzie is just what Castle Clough needs. He can give the land and buildings the infusion of cash they need to properly represent our country in the next millennium. And at least it will stay in the family, so to speak. After all, he was once your brother-in-law. What is even more important, it will keep your family name free ,of scandal. The press need never hear of it. Your father's reputation need never be tarnished by rumors of debt and doubt."

He could see he'd struck a nerve. Lord Cameron winced and sank down into his chair.

Gordon MacKinnon pressed the issue. "I hope you'll give this matter your utmost consideration, your lordship. Griffin Mackenzie is the one man in Scotland who has enough influence to see that there's never a hint of scandal about this."

He paused dramatically before glancing at the others. "Gentlemen, I believe Lord Cameron has enough on his mind for one day."

The men got to their feet and shuffled toward the door.

A scowling Desmond Snow stood just outside the closed doors of the library, waiting to escort them to their waiting car and driver.

As Gordon MacKinnon took his leave, he turned and said softly, "When you've had time to think this over, I think you'll realize that Griffin Mackenzie is your best—your only—solution, your lordship."

●   ●   ●

"Ah, Professor Sinclair." Desmond Snow stood at the foot of the stairs, glancing at his watch as Estelle descended. "You're right on time. His lordship admires punctuality."

"So do I." She managed a smile. The nap had refreshed her. That and a long, scented bath. She had put aside her earlier fears, dismissing them as nerves. She'd dressed in a simple navy blazer over a navy wool dress and had pinned her hair into a no-nonsense knot at her nape. Perched on her nose were round glasses. On her feet were sensible pumps.

"If you'll follow me, I'll take you to the dining hall." Desmond led the way, with Estelle trailing behind.

He opened double doors and stepped inside. "Professor Sinclair is here, your lordship."

Estelle paused in the doorway. The room was enormous. Dark wood paneling, with great stone fireplaces on either end. In the middle of the room was a table massive enough to seat at least twenty or thirty people. It appeared incongruous with only three table settings at one end.

Lord Cameron had been staring into the flames. He turned to greet her, and she was struck by the look in his eyes. Sadness, she thought. Or worse, the very depths of sorrow. Then he blinked, and the look was gone.

He held out a hand in greeting. "Come and warm yourself by the fire. Will you have some wine?"

"Yes, thank you." She could feel such strength in his fingers as they closed around hers. It would seem that Lord Cameron was powerful not just in terms of wealth and social standing, but in physical condition as well. It was surprising, considering his life of ease. Perhaps, she thought, in recent years he had discovered the value of hard physical work. Or maybe he simply worked out with a trainer. Whatever his regimen, it seemed to suit him.

She took the seat he indicated, sinking comfortably into the oversize masculine wing chair. She glanced at an ancient sword, its jeweled hilt winking in the firelight. This man looked strong enough, and dangerous enough, to make use of it.

He handed her a glass of white wine. "How are your accommodations?"

"Just fine." She sipped. "Actually, they're better than fine. The suite is lovely. And finding myself surrounded by so many beautiful antiques is sheer bliss."

When he merely looked at her, she flushed and added, "As you know, my specialty at Smythe-VanPell is Scottish antiquities. Now that they're all around me, I can't help cataloguing them in my mind."

"I see." He nodded and settled himself into the chair across from her. "I suppose even when you're not working, you actually are, in a way."

"Exactly." She smiled, reminding herself to relax. There was something about this man that made it difficult. Perhaps it was those dark, piercing eyes, staring at her as though she were under a microscope. Or the tight set of his mouth, making her think he was wishing he could be anywhere but here.

He was distracted, she realized. Forced to be here while his mind was on other things. Or perhaps other, more interesting people.

He sipped his wine. "About this . . . cataloguing. Is it something you can do quickly? Or does it require a great deal of testing?"

"It takes a great deal of time and study and testing to determine the value and authenticity of most antiques. But I can often tell at a glance if certain items are worth the time involved. That sword, for instance. Though I'd have to examine it more closely, I'd estimate it to be from the fifteenth century."

He arched a brow, the only indication that she was correct. "Can you do the testing here? Or would you need to ship the items back to New York?"

"I'm qualified to do most of the work here, if you prefer. If I find anything questionable, I'll recommend that it be shipped to New York for further tests."

"I see." He looked up when Desmond entered.

Behind him was the lad Fergus, wheeling a chair. As he got closer, Estelle could see an old man huddled beneath a plaid blanket. A thatch of white hair topped a face that was deeply lined.

"Uncle Charles." At once Lord Cameron's tone softened, as did his eyes. "Thank you, Fergus." He dismissed the lad and wheeled the chair himself until it was positioned close to the fire. Then he knelt beside it and said, "We have a guest. This is Estelle Sinclair, from Smythe-VanPell Auction House in New York. Estelle, this is my uncle, Sir Charles Cameron."

"Sir Charles." Estelle offered her hand, and he accepted it, drawing her closer as he studied her.

"Did I read that you are a professor and that you earned your doctorate in Scottish antiquities?" Despite his age and infirmity, the old man's eyes were blackbird-sharp, as young and inquisitive as a child's.

Estelle smiled. "Guilty as charged."

He arched a shaggy white eyebrow. "In my day we never had any doctors or professors who looked like you, Dr. Sinclair." He glanced at his nephew. "Our expert isn't at all what we were expecting, is she, Rob?"

"Not at all." In fact, the picture he'd had in his mind was of someone old and doddering, and a bit eccentric. But there was no question of this woman's credentials. She had come highly recommended.

Rob stood to one side, watching the interaction between this stranger and his uncle. Charles had a way with people. He could cut through the walls they built around themselves and lay them bare, or draw them into the circle of his friendship in the blink of an eye. He'd always trusted the old man's instincts. "By the way, Uncle Charles, she prefers to be called Estelle."

"Estelle." The old man looked down at the hand resting in his. "Did you know that your name means 'star'?"

She nodded and gave him a smile before withdrawing her hand from his grasp. "Are you interested in names, Sir Charles?"

"I'm interested in anything and everything, my dear, no matter how trivial. It's always been my blessing and my curse."

He accepted a glass from his nephew and sipped, then nodded. "Scotch. Neat. Excellent, Rob. You never forget."

Lord Cameron winked at his uncle, then turned to their guest. "I'll need you to start first thing in the morning. Tell me what you'll need, and I'll see that young Fergus makes it available."

"The first thing I'll need is a workroom, big enough to set up some tables where I can examine the artifacts."

"A workroom . . ." He paused a moment, deep in thought. "Since time is of the essence, I'd hoped you could merely walk through each room and tag those items that are most valuable. As I explained to the director of Smythe-VanPell, I must complete the sale before the end of the month. In fact, in order to assure that I have the money in time, I'd prefer that the sale begin within the next few days."

She took a deep breath, choosing her words carefully. "I must caution you that you'll receive far less for these items if you sell them quickly, without a chance to have competitors bidding against one another. If you would allow our staff to take a year . . ."

"It's out of the question. Can you choose the most valuable items for quick sale?"

She nodded. "I can. I've brought along my computer and a digital camera, so I can take photos of the items you wish to sell, and send them to prospective buyers over the Internet. The buyers can respond in the same manner. But in order to authenticate each item, I'll still need a place where I can do a thorough examination. I suggest someplace where I won't be in the way. I will need a phone line for my computer's modem. And plenty of good natural light."

"How about the old playroom, Rob?"

"I don't think . . ."

Seeing that his nephew was about to refuse, the old man added, "It's big enough to set up several tables. A phone line was added years ago. It has those big windows. And it's certainly out of the way."

Lord Cameron started to shake his head, then gave a

grudging nod of approval before turning to his guest. "It's in the west wing, where it would get the benefit of afternoon light."

"Excellent." Estelle brightened. "Do you suppose I could see the room after dinner?"

"Of course. I'll take you there myself." He looked up as Desmond knocked and entered. "Is dinner ready, Desmond?"

"It is, your lordship."

"Tell Alfred he may begin serving." Rob wheeled his uncle's chair to the table, positioning it on one side, then holding the chair across from it for Estelle.

When they were seated, Alfred Snow entered, followed by Arley, who was pushing a serving cart laden with silver dishes.

They began with a clear broth to which spring vegetables had been added. Estelle felt her mood lighten considerably as she tasted it. Like the wine, the food was proving to be delicious.

Charles glanced at his nephew. "You're not eating, Rob?"

"Yes. Of course." Lord Cameron forced his attention to the food and made an effort to look enthusiastic.

Satisfied, the old man glanced at Estelle. "How is it that an American is an expert in Scottish antiquities, my dear?"

She smiled and lifted her wineglass. "It's all I ever heard from my aunt." The thought of her Aunt Rose brought a mist to her eyes. "After the death of my parents, she took me in and raised me as her own."

"It's what family does, my dear." Charles sipped his Scotch, watching her over the rim of his glass.

His nephew did the same.

She found the effect disconcerting.

"That's true. But it was quite a sacrifice on my aunt's part. She was single, with a challenging career. In retrospect I realize that she was passed up for promotions because of the demands of a child. Her private life suffered as well. She never married."

"All the more reason why she would have appreciated

having you in her life," Charles said softly. "I'm sure she was very proud of your accomplishments."

"I hope so. She spoke so lovingly about Scotland that when it came time for me to choose a course of study at the university, I never had any doubt what it would be."

Charles lifted a brow. "I'm surprised your aunt didn't accompany you on this trip."

"It would have been my fondest wish to bring her. She . . ." Estelle carefully controlled her tone. "She died last year after a long illness."

"I'm sorry, my dear." Charles reached across the table and squeezed her hand.

"I have a confession to make." She managed a shaky smile, grateful for his kindness. "When your nephew's letter came to the firm seeking our advice, I couldn't help thinking it had been guided by my aunt's hand."

"That's a lovely thought." The old man winked. "I've always believed in spirits myself." He turned to his nephew. "With good reason, wouldn't you say, Rob?"

Lord Cameron seemed relieved when the cook interrupted at that very moment, directing the serving of the main course. With a sigh the old man set about devouring a meal of succulent roast beef and potatoes, with biscuits warm from the oven.

"Alfred," he said between bites, "as always, you've prepared an outstanding meal."

"Thank you." Though he didn't smile, the cook did manage to nod his head before taking his leave.

A short time later he returned with crystal bowls of creamy caramel pudding and a platter of shortbread, as well as a pot of strong, hot tea. With an economy of movement he filled their cups, then nodded once more before exiting the room.

As if by magic, the moment their desserts were finished, Arley slipped silently into the room to retrieve their empty dishes. Estelle found herself wondering if the servants stood at attention just outside the door, counting the minutes between each course. The thought had the corners of her lips quivering with suppressed laughter.

When Desmond entered the dining hall, Charles motioned toward his empty glass. "I'll have another Scotch, Desmond."

The butler shook his head. "You know Dr. MacCallum left orders that you were to have no more than one a day, Sir Charles."

The old man scowled. "The bloody doctor probably has two or three drinks a night. But who's to tell him otherwise?" He waved a hand to his nephew. "I'd like to sit by the fire now. I'm beginning to feel a chill."

As his wheelchair was being pushed across the room, he said, "Didn't you say you'd like a drink, Rob?"

"Aye." Lord Cameron kept a perfectly straight face as he turned to their guest. "And you, Estelle?"

"No, thank you."

Lord Cameron nodded toward the butler. "I'll have a drink, Desmond. Scotch. Neat."

Desmond walked to a cabinet and opened the glass doors, pouring a generous drink into a tumbler, which he placed on a silver tray.

"Thank you, Desmond." Lord Cameron accepted the drink and waited until the butler left the room. Then he placed it on a table beside his uncle's wheelchair.

He turned to Estelle. "Perhaps you'd like to see the workroom."

"Yes, of course. I'd like that."

"Uncle Charles, would you like to accompany us?"

The old man waved him away. "It's far too chilly on that side of the castle. I'll just wait for you here by the fire."

Lord Cameron led the way across the room. While he was opening the door, Estelle turned in time to see his uncle lift the tumbler to his mouth and sigh with pleasure. When he caught sight of her watching him, he gave her an impish wink.

As Lord Cameron walked along a dimly lit corridor, he muttered, "I suppose you think I'm making light of the doctor's orders. But that little glass of whiskey is one of the few things my uncle actually looks forward to these days.''

"There's no need to explain. I understand completely. My aunt had a fondness for chocolate. Near the end, when the medicines had stolen her appetite, those little nighttime chocolate treats were often the only things she had to look forward to. It gave me such pleasure to be able to do something, no matter how simple, to ease her burden.''

He paused a moment, staring at her in that way that made her uncomfortable. "Yes. I suppose that's it. There's so little I can do for my uncle. And it gives him such pleasure to think he's getting away with something. Desmond is in on it, of course. But it would spoil my uncle's fun if he were to guess that. And so Desmond plays his part, and I play mine.''

As he turned and continued down the hallway, Estelle found herself wondering about this dour man. A man of such contradictions. Despite the fact that he'd offered a less than cordial welcome and had seemed thoroughly distracted throughout their meal, it was clear that he had a soft spot in his heart for his aged uncle. She was touched by the charade he and his butler were willing to play for the sake of one old man.

After many twists and turns along several different hallways, they paused outside a heavy oak door. Lord Cameron produced a set of keys from his pocket and unlocked it. The hinges creaked as he forced it open. Estelle waited while he switched on the lights, then stepped inside and looked around.

Like all the rooms in the castle, this one was oversized, with massive fireplaces on either end. The outer wall had three floor-to-ceiling windows that would allow a flow of natural light. In the darkness all that she could see beyond them was the tall spires of trees and the soft glow of moonlight.

The floors were covered with a layer of dust, but it appeared that they were made of wood. In one corner was a lovely Oriental rug that Estelle estimated to be at least two hundred years old. In front of the fireplace stood an ancient cradle, still draped in dusty fabric that looked fragile enough to shred if it were touched.

Across the room were toys that would have been modern several generations ago. A hand-carved rocking horse. A wooden wheelbarrow. A wagon, with smooth wooden wheels.

On one wall hung a child's sword, an exact replica of the one hanging in the great dining hall.

She began to circle the room, pausing to touch the dusty cradle, the wooden toys. "Did you play here as a boy?"

"Aye. Often. It was my refuge."

She found herself wondering what a boy of wealth and privilege could possibly need with a place of refuge. Perhaps he merely wanted to escape from a world of adults to one of childish pleasures.

She took some mental measurements, then nodded. "This room is more than adequate for my needs. If you can find a couple of tables . . ." She turned.

Lord Cameron was standing at the window, staring into the darkness. As though, she thought, searching for something just beyond the circle of light.

With an effort he pulled himself back. "I'll have Fergus see to them first thing in the morning. Now, if you don't mind, I think we should get back to my uncle."

"Yes, of course." She followed him out the door and back along the darkened hallways.

"Ah. There you are." Charles looked up with relief when they entered. "I was beginning to think you'd forgotten me."

"Not a chance." Lord Cameron smiled and hurried to his uncle's side. "Are you ready to turn in?"

"More than ready. I don't know whether to credit the whiskey or the warmth of the fire." He caught Estelle's hand. "Or maybe the lovely company. At any rate, I'm warm and content and eager for my bed. I should think you would be as well, my dear, after your long journey."

"Like you, Sir Charles, I need no coaxing tonight," she said with a laugh.

They looked up when Desmond entered. "Will there be

anything else before I retire, your lordship?''

Lord Cameron nodded. ''You can accompany my uncle up to bed.''

''What about you, Rob?'' Charles asked.

''I have some bookkeeping to do.''

''Give it a rest, Rob,'' the old man muttered.

His nephew's tone held a note of weariness. ''How I'd like to. But I can't keep avoiding it.'' He turned to Estelle. ''Good night. I hope you'll be comfortable here at Castle Clough.''

''I'm sure I will be.''

She followed Desmond, who pushed the wheelchair out the door. At the bottom of the stairs young Fergus lifted the old man out of his chair and began to carry him up the steps. Halfway up, Estelle turned to see Lord Cameron striding down the hallway.

He looked, she thought, like a man who was going to his own hanging.

3

Rob SAT AT the desk that had once belonged to his father, his grandfather, and his great-grandfather, and worked on the rows of numbers. The fire burned low in the grate. A tumbler of whiskey rested untouched on the desktop. A clock on the mantel chimed the hour. Two o'clock.

He looked up, running a hand through his hair in frustration. He was weary beyond belief. But he knew that if he were to go up to his room, sleep would elude him. He was too tense. There was too much at stake here.

How could his father have plunged the estate so deeply into debt? It didn't seem possible. And yet the figures didn't lie. There were the bank notes, all properly signed and witnessed, using Castle Clough and the surrounding land as collateral. Fifteen million pounds borrowed, and none of it repaid.

At the thought of what he could do with that much money he had to close his eyes against the pain. The improvements to the castle. The additions to the barns. As well as to the herd. More aid to the villagers who had lived for generations in the shadow of this place.

Instead, his father had squandered his family's birthright on his own weaknesses.

Rob picked up the tumbler and crossed to the fireplace, staring into the glowing embers. Time was running out. It seemed impossible to believe that something that had been in the Cameron family for more than four hundred years was about to be lost forever.

With a muttered oath he lifted the tumbler to his lips and drained it. He thought fleetingly about tossing it against the hearth, and having the satisfaction of seeing it smashed to bits. Then he reminded himself that it was Baccarat crystal. Like everything else in the castle, it would fetch a good price at auction. He could no longer afford to indulge himself. Even in a fit of temper.

He was about to set it on the desk when he heard a sound and turned toward the door. He saw a flutter of white as someone hurried past. Curious, he walked to the doorway and watched as the door to the butler's pantry closed.

With the tumbler still in his hand he made his way to the kitchen. "Alfred, while you're up, do you suppose you could . . . ?" His voice trailed off as he caught sight of Estelle. She had opened the refrigerator door and was pouring a glass of milk. She turned, and the light from the interior illuminated her eyes, wide with alarm.

"Your lordship . . . Rob. I'm sorry. I thought by now everyone was asleep."

"It's quite all right." Intrigued, he stepped closer. She didn't look anything like the woman he'd met earlier. That woman wore her hair in a plain bun and hid behind owlish glasses. Now her hair fell in wild disarray around her face and shoulders. And what glorious hair. It was a tangle of red-gold strands that would rival autumn leaves. Her face, without a trace of makeup, was absolutely stunning. All flawless, porcelain skin and the sort of high cheekbones a model would kill for.

He watched while she replaced the container of milk in the refrigerator. Then, needing something to do, he opened a cupboard and poured himself another drink. "Can't sleep?"

She shook her head, causing her hair to kiss her cheeks in a most provocative way. He had to curl his hand into a fist to keep from touching it.

"It's probably jet lag. I was exhausted a few hours ago. Now I'm wide awake."

"You'll be fine after a day or two." He took a sip of whiskey to soothe his parched throat. Up close, despite the modest terry robe, he could see the dark cleft between her breasts.

"I'm sure I will." She drank her milk, feeling distinctly uneasy at this nighttime encounter. She'd been as quiet as a mouse, hoping she could slip downstairs without disturbing the household.

She rinsed the glass, then turned and found him staring at her in a way that spread heat through her like slow, liquid fire.

"I'll say good night now."

"I was just going up." He tossed back the rest of his drink, then set the empty tumbler beside hers.

In silence they climbed the stairs. The only illumination came from torchères spaced evenly along the hallway.

At the door to her suite she reached for the knob, only to find his hand already there. At the touch of him she pulled away as though burned, then regretted her action when she looked up to see him watching her with a strange, knowing smile.

She swallowed and forced herself to meet his eyes. "Good night . . . Rob."

"Good night, Estelle. Pleasant dreams."

When the door closed, he continued on to his room, lost in thought. He ought to be grateful for this unexpected nighttime encounter. Up close, the good professor smelled like a field of wildflowers and had a touch that was as potent as a kick from an angry heifer. In a matter of minutes she'd managed to wipe all unpleasant thoughts from his mind.

He prayed the lovely image would last long enough to grant him at least a few hours of sleep.

Estelle awoke and lay very still, struggling to remember where she was. Then she smiled as sunlight peeked around the edges of the draperies and spilled across the bed.

Excitement rippled through her at the thought of what she was about to do. For the next few weeks she would be privileged to touch and feel and examine at length objects that had never been seen outside these castle walls. The Cameron family heirlooms had never before been catalogued. They were a collector's dream.

The unexpected encounter with the lord of the manor had threatened to rob her of precious sleep, but exhaustion had won. Now, too eager to remain in bed, she tossed aside the covers and made her way to the shower. A short time later, dressed in comfortable charcoal wool slacks and sweater, she descended the stairs, clutching her briefcase. Though the castle was still in darkness, she followed the sounds of activity until she found the huge butler's pantry, where Alfred and Desmond Snow were already hard at work.

They looked up in surprise. Though they appeared startled, they quickly composed themselves.

Alfred glowered, while Desmond, the more diplomatic of the two, managed to call out, without too much enthusiasm, "Good morning, miss." He indicated the dining hall. "Fergus has just started a fire. His lordship and Sir Charles won't be downstairs for a bit yet, but you're welcome to wait in there, and I'll bring you whatever you'd like."

"Thank you, Desmond. But all I'd like is some coffee. I'll take it with me to my new workroom."

"Yes, miss." He and his brother exchanged a look before he said, "Fergus has already set up the tables you requested. If you wish to go ahead, I'll be along shortly with your coffee."

"Thank you. I'd like that." Her wide smile betrayed her delight. "I can't wait to get started."

She followed the twists and turns of the hallways, hoping

she could remember the way. When she finally stepped inside the old playroom, she was surprised at the transformation. The floors had been swept clean, and the dust and cobwebs removed. A fire blazed at either end of the big room. In the middle were three long tables, spaced several feet apart.

She set her briefcase on the first table and removed pens, notebooks, and a handful of reference books. Then she opened her computer, plugging in the modem before turning it on.

She looked up when Desmond approached, carrying a silver tray covered with a linen cloth.

He set it in front of her and removed the cloth to reveal a carafe of coffee and a china cup, as well as cream and sugar and a plate of freshly baked scones and a little pot of jam.

"Would you like anything else, miss?"

"Oh, no, Desmond. This looks wonderful. Thank you."

"You're welcome." He took a step back, then glanced around. "What made you choose this room for your work?"

"Hmmm?" She poured coffee, then looked up. "I believe it was Sir Charles who suggested it."

"I see." He nodded, then continued looking around, as though in search of something. "If you should find it . . . not to your liking, I'd be happy to have Fergus set you up in some other room in the castle, miss."

"Thank you, Desmond. I'm sure this will be just fine. When Fergus has finished his morning chores, would you mind sending him here? Lord Cameron said that whenever you can spare the lad, he could help me by carting some of the heavier artifacts."

"Aye, miss. I'll send him right along. Which room will you be starting in?"

"Lord Cameron suggested I start with the rooms in the north tower, which haven't been used for years."

"Very good. Fergus can show you the way."

When he was gone, Estelle sipped her coffee and broke off a piece of scone, nibbling as she walked to the floor-to-ceiling windows. In the morning sunlight the view was breathtaking. The rain had washed the land clean, revealing undulating hills of deep green and, on the distant meadow, a carpet of heather. Beyond that was forest, wild and tangled, and falling from a high peak, a waterfall that tumbled into a loch far below.

What would it be like, she wondered, to awake to this each morning and know that everything, as far as the eye could see, was yours? What would it do to a man? Would he simply take it all for granted, as a king surveying his kingdom? Would it make him hungry for more? Or would he be content and wish nothing more than to remain here forever?

Though she heard not a sound, she sensed that she was no longer alone. Turning, she found Fergus standing in the doorway, watching her.

"Good morning, Fergus." She offered a friendly smile. "Have you finished with your morning chores?"

He nodded.

"Good. Lord Cameron suggested I start with the north tower. Would you mind showing me the way?"

He turned and started down a corridor. Estelle set down her cup and followed. She had no trouble keeping up with him. Despite his size and strength, he moved at a snail's pace.

Finally he paused and pulled open a door, then stood aside, allowing her to enter first. What she saw took her breath away.

It was a lady's boudoir, with a satin-covered bed and bed hangings and a matching chaise.

"Oh, this is just perfect." Estelle slowly circled the room, noting the crystal lamps, the mirrored tray on which rested a comb and brush of hammered gold. There were paintings hanging on the walls in soft pastels, statues in corners and on pedestals that appeared to be made of marble and jade, and pretty little boxes encrusted with semi-precious jewels.

She worked quickly, tagging those pieces she considered most important. "If you can bring these tagged items to my workroom, Fergus, I'd be most grateful. But I must caution you to be very careful. If they should be damaged, their value could be lost."

The lad nodded and lumbered forward, plucking two crystal lamps from a dressing table. Estelle continued on to the rest of the rooms in the north wing, delighted with the treasures she found in each. Then, while Fergus made dozens of trips back and forth from the various rooms, she settled down to begin the task of examining each piece and photographing it in anticipation of the sale.

As she picked up the first piece, the brush of hammered gold, she had to swallow the lump in her throat. It was true that the gold alone was worth a fortune. But what meant even more to her was the fact that it had been here, in this very place, for hundreds of years. How many women had held this in their hands and run it through their hair? Had a man commissioned this for his lover? His wife? Perhaps on their wedding day?

"Good. I see you've started."

At the sound of Lord Cameron's voice, she looked up sharply, the spell broken. "Yes. I . . . was just examining this brush."

"So I see." He'd seen much more. He'd been standing there for several minutes, watching her without her knowledge. It had given him a chance to really look at her. In the morning sunlight she appeared as clean and fresh as the flowers blooming in the meadow. Everything about her was so neat and tidy. Her hair was pulled back into a knot, without a single strand out of place. She had slipped on those round glasses, which only added to her prim and proper schoolmarm look. A look he found most appealing. She had rare beauty. A lovely oval face. High cheekbones. A perfectly sculpted mouth. The sight of it made his throat go dry, and he remembered their nighttime encounter with gratitude. It had caused him to see her in a way he couldn't forget.

She held up the brush. "I would advise you not to sell this to the first bidder. It's worth a fortune."

He walked closer and took it from her hand. At once he

felt the jolt and could see in his mind's eye the vision of his ancestor running it through a woman's hair. It had been part of their courtship ritual. The man had taken the pins out of the woman's hair, then had worked the brush through the long waves, all the while watching the reflection of her eyes in the mirror of the dressing table.

Rob blinked. The vision left him shaken. He managed to keep his voice unemotional. "It looks quite old."

"At least two hundred years. Maybe more. Do you know anything about it?"

He shook his head. "Afraid not. My sister, Patience, probably would have known. I'm told she made a detailed history of the place. It was the great passion of her life."

"How wonderful. Perhaps she'd be willing to help me."

"My sister died when I was just an infant."

"I'm sorry. Are there any other brothers or sisters?"

He shook his head. "Just the two of us. Patience was already married when I was born. Needless to say, I was quite a surprise to my parents, and to my sister. She died shortly after I was born. The child she was carrying died as well."

"How terrible for her husband."

His tone was dry. "He managed to survive. It was much harder on my parents. My mother never got over it. She died a few months later, leaving my father in a state of shock."

Estelle thought about the curse. No wonder that even today people believed such a thing. This story only added another layer to the myth.

"After my mother's death I'm not certain that the family could have held together without Uncle Charles, who is my father's younger brother. He pulled my father through a very rough time. As for me, it was always Uncle Charles that I turned to in times of trouble."

"Then I can see why you love him so."

"Aye." Up close, the round glasses seemed to magnify her eyes. Last night he'd thought they were blue. But he could see now that they were more green than blue. And her hair looked like fire in the sunlight. He itched to touch it. He had the most unreasonable urge to take the pins out of it and watch it tumble about her shoulders. And an even more unreasonable urge to kiss her. He stared at her mouth, mesmerized by the thought of those full, ripe lips crushed beneath his.

It was the brush, he thought. Just holding it had given him all sorts of fanciful ideas. He handed it back to her. "We'll be having breakfast when Uncle Charles comes down in an hour or so. I hope you'll join us."

"Thank you. I'm sure that by then I'll have worked up an appetite."

He nodded. "I'll send someone to fetch you."

As he walked away he passed Fergus, who carried a marble statue that would have staggered most men. He watched as the lad set it down on the table.

"My uncle has need of you now, Fergus."

The lad nodded before lumbering away.

For a moment longer Rob paused, watching as Estelle carefully examined the gold brush, then bent toward her computer to enter her remarks.

He had told her, in the space of a few seconds, more than he'd ever told anyone about his family. And though he'd revealed few secrets, he was surprised by even those simple admissions.

He turned away and found, to his amazement, that his hands were actually trembling.

He'd have to see to it that he got more rest in the nights to come. What else but a lack of sleep could explain his strange reaction to this woman? As for the vision of the brush, that was a bit easier. It was merely the strain of knowing that he would have to dispose of everything he'd ever loved in order that his father's reputation could remain untarnished.

Still, he would have to take pains to keep his distance in the days to come. He needed to focus all his attention on the problem at hand. The last thing he needed was a distraction. Especially one as tempting as Estelle Sinclair.

4

Estelle slowly lifted her head and studied Lord Cameron's back as he walked away. She let out her breath on a long, slow sigh of relief. Whenever he got too close, she had to struggle with the most unnerving sensations. She couldn't explain them. But she would have sworn that for one breathless moment he'd been about to kiss her.

Ridiculous. They had known each other less than twenty-four hours. He barely acknowledged her presence in his home. And yet she couldn't shake the feeling.

He had the most incredible eyes. Eyes that seemed to see clear through her. And he exuded strength. Not just physical strength, though that was apparent in the width of his shoulders, in the bulge of muscles that the sleeves of his sweater couldn't camouflage. This was an inner strength. She could sense in him an iron will and, despite his cultured manners, a keen edge of danger. He wouldn't be a man to cross.

"So. Have ye come to play, then?"

At the childish burr, Estelle glanced around. The boy was standing in a corner of the room, his face half hidden in shadow.

"I didn't hear you come in. How long have you been here?"

"Long enough to know ye're alone. I waited for the others to leave."

"Why? Are you shy around people?"

He laughed, a clear sound like the tinkling of a bell. "Ye might say that."

"What's your name?"

"Jamie."

She pushed back her chair and crossed to him, holding out her hand. "Hello, Jamie. My name is Estelle."

"I know." He placed his small hand in hers, and she felt a shimmer of heat.

She crouched down, studying him intently. "What an adorable costume." She ran a finger along the soft fabric of the wide-sleeved shirt, tucked into the waist of satin knee britches. On his feet were high stockings peeking out above well-worn boots. "Are you practicing for a play?"

"What's a play?"

"Make-believe. Acting."

"Ach. Nay. These are my clothes."

"I see. I'll bet you found them in a trunk. Are you some-one's grandson? Alfred's or Desmond's?"

"They've no family save the Camerons. That's why they're so sad. They fear they're about to lose the only home and family they've ever known."

"Why would they think that?"

"Because Lord Cameron is on the verge of losing every-thing he loves."

"What nonsense. Jamie, why would you say such a thing? Look around you. Why, he must be worth millions."

The boy stared up at her. "Ye dinna know? That's why ye're here, Estelle Sinclair. To prepare for sale the things that are most valuable, in order to keep Castle Clough from falling into the wrong hands."

She sat back on her heels, alarmed at what she was hear-

222 * Ruth Ryan Langan

ing. "I'm sure you're mistaken, Jamie. I think Lord Cameron merely wants to be rid of some of the things that are gathering dust."

"Why would ye think that?"

"He made it clear that he disdains his title. I assume he thinks even less of his family possessions."

"Then ye dunna know him at all. He rejects his title because of what it did to his father. And because he fears it will set him apart from others. He's a man of the soil. A man of this land. He's very good at hiding his true feelings. But his heart is breaking at what he's about to do."

"How would a boy like you know so much?"

He gave her a strange, knowing look. "I hear things."

"How?"

His lips split into an impish grin that tugged at her heart. "Most people canna see me. So they speak freely when I'm around."

"Really?" She was laughing now. This boy was delightful. "Do you make yourself invisible?"

"Aye."

"Professor Sinclair."

At the sound of Desmond's voice she looked up, then got to her feet.

"Lord Cameron wishes you to join him and his uncle for a morning meal."

"Thank you, Desmond. I'd like to bring . . ." She turned. Jamie was gone. She turned a complete circle, then circled again, glancing over her shoulder as she did. But he was nowhere to be seen.

"Yes, miss?" Desmond stood in the doorway, looking puzzled.

"Nothing. Thank you. Tell Lord Cameron I'll be there shortly."

"Yes, miss." The butler walked away.

When he was gone, Jamie gave his little laugh. Estelle turned to find him standing exactly where she'd last seen him.

"What sort of trick is this?" She wasn't so much frightened as she was annoyed. How had she overlooked him?

"I told ye. I can make myself disappear whenever I choose. For I only permit certain people to see me."

"Is that so? Then why me, Jamie? Why have you decided to let me see you?"

"I need . . . I need someone I can trust. And I think . . . Tell me. Can I trust ye, Estelle Sinclair?"

"That depends."

"On what?"

"On whether there will be any more tricks like that. Whatever you're doing, I want you to stop."

For a moment a look of contrition came over him. He folded his hands behind his back and hung his head. Then, just as quickly, the mood was gone, and he brightened. "Oh. Ye sound just like my mother. I knew I could trust ye." He surprised her by wrapping his arms around her neck and giving her a fierce hug.

"What was that for?"

"For scolding me. It's been ever so long since I've had anyone scold me. I've missed that. I have to go now. But I'll be back."

Estelle started toward the door. "I'll walk with you. I have to join Lord Cameron and his uncle for breakfast."

At the door she turned, expecting him to be trailing behind her. Instead, the room was empty. Though she peered into every corner, there was no denying that Jamie was gone and she was alone.

Puzzled, and more alarmed than she cared to admit, she made her way quickly to the dining hall, determined to tell no one of this. If Lord Cameron should find out, he might dismiss her on the spot, claiming she'd lost her mind.

"Ah, here she is, Rob." Sir Charles looked up from the table and smiled as Estelle hurried across the room. "We were just speculating on what was keeping you."

"I got a little busy." She accepted the chair Rob offered and waited to speak until he took his place at the head of the table. She continued to hold her silence while Alfred Snow served her plate.

Sir Charles cleared his throat. "Are you finding everything you need, my dear?"

"Yes, thank you. And I'm grateful that you could spare Fergus. He's very helpful."

Charles glanced at his nephew. "The lad has the strength of a bull and the heart of a warrior."

Estelle sipped her tea. "Why doesn't he speak?"

"He will when he has something to say."

She looked up. "You've heard him?"

"Once or twice." Charles dug into his eggs with a sigh of pleasure. Eating was one of the few things he could still enjoy. "Actually, Rob has heard him more often than anyone."

"He speaks to you?" Estelle turned to Lord Cameron.

He nodded. "When it's necessary."

Charles spread jam on a scone and popped it into his mouth. "How long do you think it will take to prepare everything for sale, my dear?"

"I'll try to complete a walk-through of the entire castle by the end of the week, tagging those items that I think will bring the highest offers." She turned to Rob. "As I explained, they won't bring nearly the money you'd get if you could circulate a catalogue that would stimulate excitement and then offer them at auction a year from now. Dealers from all over the world would be bidding against each other for such treasures."

She saw the pained expression on his face before he composed himself. In that moment, she knew that Jamie had been correct.

She noticed that he hadn't touched a bite of his meal. She realized she'd lost her own appetite as well. Suddenly she felt compelled to get back to work.

She looked up. "Would you be offended if I return to my workroom now?"

"Without eating?" Sir Charles looked up in surprise.

Rob shot a glance at his uncle, then shook his head. "Of course not. I have little appetite myself. I understand how compelling work can be."

Rob watched her until she had left the dining hall. Then

he turned to his uncle. "Griff is stopping by this afternoon."

The old man's mouth turned down in a frown. "So he can gloat?"

"Most likely. But I'm in no position to refuse, especially since he claims to know a way to save Father's reputation."

"Griffin Mackenzie never gave a thought to my brother's reputation while he was alive. Why would he care about his good name now?"

"Maybe because it will reflect badly on him as well. After all, Uncle Charles, he was once married to Patience."

"A mistake your sister lived to regret."

"You don't know that for a fact. You told me that she never said she was unhappy."

"She didn't have to. Every time I saw her I could read the misery in her eyes."

"Then why did she choose to start a family with him?"

"I've asked myself that. Maybe for the same reason your heritage will soon become Griff's prized possession."

"Are you saying he bullied Patience into conceiving a child?"

The old man shrugged. "Griffin Mackenzie has made a study of people's weaknesses. It's what has earned him millions. He knows what buttons to push. He knows, for instance, that you would never sell Castle Clough. So he had to get to your father before he died. I'd be willing to bet any amount of money that he dangled his fortune in front of your father's eyes, and in a moment of weakness, the wheels were set into motion that have now brought us to the brink of disaster."

Rob pushed away from the table. "For now, Griff is the only player in the game. I have no choice but to listen to his latest offer."

"Aye." The old man clasped his hands in his lap. "Just promise me one thing. Promise you won't sign anything."

Rob touched a hand to his uncle's shoulder. "You know me better than that."

As he strode away, the old man brooded. When Fergus came to take him to his room, he said, "Not yet, lad. I'd like to take a turn around the gardens. Maybe the sunlight will be just the thing to cheer me up a bit.''

Once outside, the old man huddled beneath his plaid blanket and dreamed of younger, happier times, when he'd raced across these lawns with all the grace and speed of a gazelle. He'd done so much in his youth. Lived. Loved. And lost. Then he thought of the bleak future looming on the horizon for his nephew, and lifted his face to the sun, struggling to dispel the chill that seemed to have penetrated his very bones.

He looked up to see Estelle in her workroom, head bent, eyes downcast, as she studied the object in her hands. There was something about the lass that tugged at him. It wasn't just the auburn hair and green eyes, though he'd always had a weakness for green-eyed redheads. There was a sweetness about her. A simple artlessness that was most appealing. Beyond her titles and degrees, he felt quite certain that she had a genuine love for this land and its artifacts.

Perhaps he would just drop by her workroom and spend a few pleasant moments before retiring to his room.

He turned to Fergus, who stood silently behind the wheelchair, staring off into space. ''I believe I'd like to go inside now, lad. And if you'd be good enough to take me to our young lady's workroom, I'd be grateful.''

Fergus pushed the old man's chair effortlessly across the lawn and into the castle.

''Sir Charles.'' Estelle looked up from her work and smiled in welcome. ''How nice to see you.''

''You don't mind that I'm interrupting your work?''

''I can't think of a nicer interruption.''

The old man signaled for Fergus to push him closer. When his chair was parked beside her table, Charles waved the boy away. ''Come back in an hour, lad. Oh, and you might ask Arley to bring us some tea.''

Fergus nodded before lumbering off.

''This is lovely.'' Charles picked up the jeweled box Estelle had been inspecting. ''I remember seeing this once when I was a lad. I believe it was in my mother's reading room. It held notepaper and a lovely crystal inkwell.''

Estelle shook her head in amazement. ''Even after all my years of study, I find it hard to believe that there are people who actually grew up surrounded by such beauty.''

''And we've taken it for granted all these years. We were quite spoiled, I fear. We wanted for nothing. Toys. Clothes. Amusements. My parents lavished my brother and me with love and attention as well. In our youth our father took us all across the Highlands, hunting and fishing. Even when we went off to university, we were always eager to return home.''

''I can see why. It's so lovely here.'' She accepted the jewel-encrusted box from his hands and set it aside. ''Did you ever marry, Sir Charles?''

He shook his head. ''There was a special young woman. We met at the University of Edinburgh, where I was teaching a class and she was working on her degree. We knew from the first that we were fated to be together.'' His eyes glowed with the memory. ''I can't remember a happier time.''

''What happened? Why didn't the two of you marry?''

''The time was wrong for both of us. She had obligations and was forced to leave the university. At the same time, my brother's wife died, and I realized he wasn't able to cope with the responsibility of raising little Rob alone. Maybe it's because my brother, Robert, was so spoiled as a child. Or maybe he was just born with a selfish streak. For whatever reason, he seemed unable to conquer his weaknesses. So I came back to Castle Clough to help in whatever way I could, thinking I could pursue my own happiness later.'' His voice lowered. ''But the years have a way of slipping by. When I tried to reestablish contact with the woman I loved and lost, my letters were returned. I suppose she grew weary of waiting for me and married someone else. I couldn't blame her. She had a right to happiness. But it taught me a painful lesson. We have but one chance in this world. We must seize it with both hands and live life to the fullest, or the opportunity for happiness could be gone forever.''

Estelle placed a hand over his. "I'm sorry, Sir Charles. Sorry that you lost her. And sorry that I asked such a personal question. I had no right to open up an old wound."

"Nonsense. It all happened a long time ago. I'm resigned to the fact that I can't go back and change a thing. So I'll not waste time on regrets."

"My aunt used to say that very thing." Estelle smiled. "You would have liked her. She had this childlike sense of wonder about things. She was curious, inquisitive, inventive. When I was very young, I used to wonder why I'd had to lose my parents. But as I grew older, I realized that I wouldn't trade a single minute of my time with my aunt. And I think . . ." She paused for a moment, wondering if she ought to be so bold. Then she plunged ahead. "I think it's the same for your nephew. Though he appears to have been a loving son, he truly loves you as well. He understands the sacrifice you made for him and loves you for it."

The old man cleared his throat. "Thank you, my dear. I can't think of a higher compliment."

They both looked up as Arley entered, carrying a silver tray. He set it on the table and removed a linen cloth to reveal a pot of tea and a plate of biscuits.

"Will I pour, Sir Charles?" the lad asked.

"Yes. Thank you, Arley." Charles accepted a cup of strong, hot tea and waited until Estelle lifted hers.

"How was school today, lad?"

"Fine, sir. But I was delayed by soccer practice, and Desmond isn't happy with me. I've left too many chores undone."

"Then I'll not keep you. You wouldn't want to make Desmond angry."

"No, sir." With a laugh the boy sprinted away.

"He's sweet." Estelle watched as he disappeared down the hall.

"Aye. His grandfather worked here at the castle when I was a lad. That makes him part of our family. And when he and Fergus lost their father, Rob insisted that we hire them so that they could help their mother a bit. He pays the lads far more than they could earn working in the village. Probably more than they're worth to Desmond. But it helps in two ways. It gives them spending money, and it eases Desmond's burden, now that he's getting up in years.'' He grinned. ''Not that I'd ever say that in his hearing, you understand. Desmond and his brother, Alfred, are very proud men. They'd not likely enjoy being reminded of their age. But they've spent their whole lives in service to our family. They deserve some help as they grow older.''

She thought of the things Jamie had told her. No wonder Desmond and Alfred looked so unhappy. They were in peril of losing the only security they'd ever had.

''What about Fergus?'' Estelle asked. ''Is there a story behind his infirmity as well?''

''Ah. The poor lad.'' Sir Charles sipped his tea for a moment. His eyes grew somber. ''Aye, a sad story. Fergus was hunting in the Highlands with his father just four short years ago, when he was twelve. They had no way of knowing that a company had come in to cull dead trees from the forest. Too late they heard a shout and realized a tree was falling toward them. They tried running to safety, but it was too late. The tree fell on both of them, grazing the lad's head, crushing his father. When the woodcutters arrived on the scene, they found Fergus lifting the tree in an effort to save his father. They came to his assistance and claimed it took four of them to do what the lad had done alone. But his superhuman effort was too late to save his father's life.'' He tapped a finger on the arm of his chair. His voice lowered to a whisper. ''The accident left the lad damaged as well. Some in the village think he's addled. But it isn't so. He's just a bit slower now. Head injuries do that, you see.''

''And your nephew hired him because no one else would.''

''Aye.'' He looked up when he heard the slow shuffle that signaled the arrival of the one they were discussing. ''Here you are, lad. Right on time. I believe I'd like to go up to my room now and have a rest.''

The young giant crossed the room and nodded to Estelle,

then took up his position behind the wheelchair.

Sir Charles patted her hand. "Thank you for giving an old man the gift of your valuable time, my dear. You've helped the hour pass very pleasantly."

"It was my pleasure, Sir Charles. I hope you'll drop by and visit often."

"I'd like that." He lifted his hand in a salute, as Fergus pushed his chair out of the room.

When she was alone, Estelle sat for a moment, staring out the window and thinking over all that she'd heard.

Lord Rob Cameron, it would seem, wasn't at all the dour, unemotional man she'd first thought him to be. He was kind and compassionate. And she was beginning to care about him, and his trouble, more than she wanted to admit. That fact disturbed her. After all, her job was to evaluate and prepare the artifacts for auction. She had always prided herself on her professionalism, which dictated that she had no right to become emotionally involved—with either the sale or the seller.

She pushed aside the troubling thoughts and returned to her work, more aware than ever that time was of the essence.

5

"Ach. what's this now?"

At the childish voice Estelle turned.

Jamie's head popped up from behind a marble pedestal. "I remember hiding behind this and watching while my little brother searched everywhere for me."

"You have a little brother?"

"I did. Once. He's gone now."

"Gone where?"

"Home." His voice grew sad and distant. "They've all gone home. All but me."

The look in his eyes nearly broke her heart. A shiver passed through her. This boy didn't appear to be ethereal. There was no puff of smoke. No passing through walls. He simply appeared and disappeared. And he seemed as much flesh and blood as she. But she knew without a doubt that he was from a spirit world. It all fit. The odd-looking clothes. The ancient manner of speech. The ability to come and go at will.

Sweet heaven, she hoped she wasn't losing her mind.

231

Still, she had to risk it. She had to verify what she sus-
pected. "Why can't you go home with them, Jamie?"

He paused a moment, looking perplexed. "There's something I have to do. Something I promised. And until I get
it right, I can't leave here. It's been such a long time. And
I really do want to be with them. I get so lonely sometimes.
It's been years since there were any children to play with."
Suddenly he brightened. "But now ye're here. And I've
found a new friend. Ye promised ye'd be my friend, Estelle."

"Yes, I did."

He pulled himself on top of the pedestal and posed, his
arms over his head. "Do I remind ye of that statue?"

Estelle couldn't help laughing. He was an adorable imp.
She nodded. "You do indeed. But the statue is prettier."

"I should hope so. I have na wish to be pretty like my
mother. I want to be strong and handsome like my father."
He hopped down and walked closer to the table, running
his hand over the objects that had been neatly tagged.
"These won't bring enough, ye know, to save Castle
Clough from foreclosure."

"How much will it take?"

"Fifteen million pounds."

"Fifteen million . . ." She pressed a hand to her mouth.

"Aye. Poor Rob. When the news gets out, his father's
name will be ruined, and all the generations of Camerons
to come will bear the shame."

"Is there any other way to save his estate besides selling
everything he loves?"

The boy shot her a quick grin. "I was hoping ye'd ask,
Estelle. Ye see, my powers are limited. But if ye were to
join forces wi' me, maybe together we could do what neither of us can do alone."

"Your powers . . ." Estelle decided to keep her thoughts
to herself. But the idea of one woman and a child—who
may or may not be a . . . ghost—solving this crisis was simply too much. She shook her head in denial. "I've wasted
enough time, Jamie. I must get back to work. But while I

do, why don't you tell me how you happen to be here while the rest of your family is . . . gone.''

"Aye. Ye wouldna have heard.'' He clasped his hands behind his back and began to stride around the room. "The castle was under siege. It was a terrible battle, made all the worse because it was with family, in a way.''

"In a way?'' She looked up.

"Aye. The warrior Donan was wed to my father's sister. But he had long coveted Castle Clough and the treasure it held.'' He glanced over. "Ye've heard of the Star of Scotland?''

Estelle's eyes widened. "Of course. It's the mythical star-shaped diamond said to have been worn by the first laird of Castle Clough in the thirteen hundreds. But there has never been any documentation to prove its existence. Scholars have declared it nothing more than a legend.''

"A legend, is it? If that's true, then I've seen this legend. And held it in my hands.''

Estelle lowered the magnifying glass she'd been using and turned to stare at him. "You're having fun with me now, aren't you, Jamie?''

"Nay.'' Agitated, he hopped up on the end of the table and began to walk along the edge, waving his hands like a tightrope performer. "My father presented it to my mother on the day they wed. It sat in a special place on her dressing table as a symbol of their love.''

"What happened to it? Was it stolen during the siege?''

"I think so. I canna remember. I've tried so many times to recall. But the memory is gone. I remember . . .'' He paused, staring out the window into the afternoon sunlight.

"What do you remember, Jamie?''

"I remember my mother telling me that Donan knew about the curse of Castle Clough.'' He looked up. "Surely ye've heard of it as well?''

She nodded. "All the Cameron women are doomed to die young.''

"Nay. That's not the curse.''

"It isn't?''

He shook his head. "The curse is this: Cameron men,

when they love, love so deeply that they can give their hearts but once in a lifetime. If a Cameron should try for more than one love, his fortune, and his very life, will fail.''

"That would explain what happened to Rob's father."

"Aye. He was brokenhearted over the death of both his daughter and his wife. He spent a lifetime trying to love again. But all he did was lose everything. And so it was, from the beginning of the clan. The enemies of the Camerons, knowing of the curse, use it to their advantage."

"How?"

"By threatening the life of the woman. They know a Cameron warrior would rather die than sacrifice the one he loves. My mother, realizing Donan intended to use her to snare my father, sent me to fetch the Star of Scotland and bring it to her in the great hall. She hoped to use it to bargain for my father's life. She told me I must not tarry, for Donan was a man of little patience."

"Did you do as she asked?"

"I tried. I remember racing along the long, dark hallways, the jewel in my hand. But then I heard a cry. It was my little brother. And as a warrior in training, I knew that I must save his life, even if it meant sacrificing my own. So I ran down to the playroom to save him. But it was too late. One of Donan's warriors had already come upon him and was laughing as he carried him away."

"Oh, Jamie! What did you do then?"

"I was torn between saving my brother and doing as my mother asked. I had my dirk at my waist and was skilled in its use. So I unsheathed it and followed the one who had my little brother. When I was close enough, I hurled it at him. But at the last moment he turned, and instead of inflicting a mortal wound, it merely pierced his shoulder, enraging him. In his anger he ran my little brother through with his sword, then came after me."

Estelle covered her mouth to keep from crying out.

"I knew then that I had squandered my chance to save not only my little brother but my father and mother as well. I started running toward the great hall, desperate to make up for the time I'd lost. I heard the pounding of feet behind me, and knew that Donan's warrior was still there. I felt the bitter sting of a sword and knew that I'd been mortally wounded. But as I fell I managed to trip him, and he fell forward, impaling himself on his own sword. He landed on top of me, and I feared I was goin' to die. But at last I managed to drag myself free. I crawled away and hid, for the castle was alive with warriors.''

Estelle glanced around. ''Where did you hide?''

He pointed to the far wall. ''There were some loose bricks there, where my brother and I used to play. I slipped inside. I must have been very weak. I don't remember much, except the sound of fighting that seemed to go on for hours, or perhaps days. Finally, when there was only silence, I slipped out of my hiding place and went in search of my family.''

He slumped down on the edge of the table and sat staring into space.

Estelle walked over and wrapped her arms around him. ''It must have been horrible, Jamie.''

''Aye.'' His voice was muffled against her shoulder. ''There was blood everywhere. Many of the rooms were smoldering, for our enemies had vowed to burn the castle to the ground.''

''And your family?''

''They were all . . . dead. My father. My mother. My little brother.''

''What about you, Jamie?''

She felt the shimmer of heat before he said softly, ''Aye. At least I thought I was dead. I could see my body there in the hiding place. But even after it was nothing more than dust, I was still here. And here I remain, sleeping in that same hiding place for all this time.''

''I can't see it.''

''About a hundred years ago the castle was remodeled. These walls were covered over with expensive panels of mahogany. So I simply pass through each night and return to my old place.''

''But you can't . . . go home?''

He shook his head. ''There's something I still must do.''

He pushed a little away and stared deeply into her eyes. "But I dunna know what it is. And I'm so weary. I just want to go home."

She picked him up and gently kissed his tearstained cheeks. "You will, Jamie."

"Do you think so?"

"I do. If there's any way I can help, I will. I promise." It occurred to her that, though he was hundreds of years old, his heart and soul were still those of a little boy. A very sad, very homesick little boy.

"What about the Star of Scotland, Jamie?"

He shook his head sadly. "I dunna know. It was my intention to hide it, to keep it safe. But I cannot remember. Perhaps I dropped it in my haste. Someone may have found it and carried it away. It was all so long ago."

They looked up at the sound of a deep voice from the doorway. "So. This is the professor of antiquities who is going to be Rob's savior."

Estelle felt the sudden chill and realized that Jamie had disappeared.

She crossed the room and extended her hand. "I'm Estelle Sinclair."

"I'm Griffin Mackenzie." He closed his other hand over hers, holding her when she tried to pull away. "Since I hold the mortgage on Castle Clough, I thought I'd take a look at your work and see just what you've uncovered."

She saw his greedy gaze sweep the paintings, the statuary, the gold and jewel-encrusted items.

"Such a pity that Rob will have to let go of some of his family treasures. I told him that if he really cares about such things, he should simply let them all remain within the castle walls. At least then they'll be here for future generations to enjoy."

"How generous of you." Estelle couldn't keep the ice from her tone. "Perhaps you'd be generous enough to extend the deadline. Then he could remain here where he belongs, surrounded by the things he loves."

At her boldness he gave her a long, slow, insolent look, then threw back his head and chuckled. "A word of warning, Professor. You're beginning to sound as though this has become a personal battle. There are those who might say you've overstepped your professional bounds."

"I don't live my life considering what others say, Mr. Mackenzie. Now if you'll excuse me, I have work to do."

"By all means, Professor. Please get back to it. After all, it's for my benefit as well as Rob's. Within a matter of a few weeks, all this will be mine."

Estelle watched as he sauntered out of the room. She looked down to find Jamie hiding behind her skirt. On his face was a look of pure terror.

"It's Donan. Come back to pillage."

"Nonsense. He said his name is Griffin Mackenzie."

"Aye. The name may have changed through the centuries, but his heart is still evil. I know this man. The same eyes. The same heart." He looked up at her. "Did ye know that he was once married to Lord Cameron's sister?"

"Patience?"

"Aye. When he married her, he thought he was marrying an only child who would one day inherit all this. The arrival of Rob, so many years after his sister, caught everyone by surprise. By that time Patience had already told her family of her expected baby. As I recall, when Mackenzie learned that her parents would be having a baby of their own, he wasna happy. He suggested that his mother-in-law was too old to give birth to a healthy child. He even went so far as to give his father-in-law a list of doctors, in case there were any second thoughts."

"Obviously they didn't take him up on the offer."

The lad nodded. "But consider this. Shortly after Rob was born, Patience suffered a terrible accident, and she was found dead. The babe she was carrying died as well."

"Are you suggesting that her death wasn't an accident?"

Jamie shrugged. "There was speculation that the marriage hadna been a love match. Now that there was an heir apparent to Castle Clough, Griffin Mackenzie had no need of a wife, or her child, for they could do him no good."

"You're frightening me, Jamie. Do you really believe he has waited all this time to steal the Cameron inheritance?"

"Ye tell me. Do ye think these things only happened hundreds of years ago? Or do ye believe that even today greed can drive a man to madness?"

Jamie's voice trembled. "For years, Donan was consumed with jealousy, until it drove him to kill all who stood in his way. For years, Griffin Mackenzie has coveted Castle Clough but has kept his distance. But a greedy man knows how to bide his time and how to use the weakness of others for his own benefit."

Estelle shivered. The boy made sense. But it wasn't her battle. She had been brought here for one thing.

To get her mind off her troubling thoughts, she forced herself to return to her work, picking up an ancient jewel-handled sword.

Jamie hopped up on the end of the table and began walking along the edge, staring at the sword as he did. "That belonged to my father, ye know. And one day it was to have been mine."

Hearing the pain in his voice, Estelle said, "I'm sorry, Jamie. I hate it that you and Rob must part with such special treasures. But he is . . ." She glanced up in alarm. "Be careful, Jamie. You're going to fall."

"Not a chance of it. It was always my little brother who couldna balance . . ."

Before he could finish the sentence he tumbled headfirst. Estelle scooped him up and hugged him fiercely. "Are you hurt? Are you bleeding?"

"Nay." He looked up and, seeing her concern, wrapped his arms around her neck. "Oh, it's been so long since anyone worried about me. You see? You're just like my mother."

She carried him back to her chair and sat down, cuddling him on her lap.

He snuggled against her for a moment, clinging to the warmth of her. "When you hold me like this, I see my mother's face. I even smell her." He reached up and touched her head. "But your hair is all wrong. Why do you wear it like this, Estelle? It should be all soft and loose." He pulled a strand out of the neat knot.

"Jamie, stop that."

Just as she reached a hand to his, a stern voice from the doorway had her stiffening in surprise. "So. The job has you talking to yourself already?"

She looked up.

Lord Cameron was walking toward her, looking at her in the strangest way.

"I was just . . ." She glanced down and saw Jamie grinning up at her. "Jamie and I were . . ."

At that moment she felt a cool breeze and realized that her arms were empty. Jamie had fled.

Rob crossed the room until he was standing directly in front of her. "Say that again."

She got to her feet. "It was nothing." She shook head, trying to pull herself together.

"You said 'Jamie.' Have you seen him?"

"Don't be sill . . ." She stopped. Started over. "You . . . know of him?"

He arched a brow. "Then you have seen him."

She swallowed and lifted her chin. "Yes, I've seen him. And I'm not crazy."

He smiled then, and she was amazed at the transformation. His eyes crinkled at the corners. His lips curved in the most enticing manner. He threw back his head and roared. "Believe me, Estelle. You're not crazy. I've seen him, too. Though I have to admit it's been years now. When I was a lad, Jamie was my playmate."

"Truly? You're not making that up?"

He nodded. "Jamie was my friend. My only friend when I was very young, and alone in this house with a father who hardly knew I existed. Jamie and I had some amazing experiences together." He shook his head, remembering. "I can't tell you how many times he got me into trouble."

"I can imagine. He's quite a little scamp. In fact, he was the one who tugged my hair loose just now."

She lifted a hand to push her hair back, but Rob closed a hand over hers, stilling her movement. "Don't. I like it better this way."

Estelle's eyes widened. At the mere touch of him, she

experienced a rush of heat that left her trembling.

"I'd like it even better if you'd let me do this." Rob reached up and removed the pins from her hair, watching through narrowed eyes as the rich red waves tumbled about her shoulders. It was as though he'd been cast under some sort of spell. And he thought fleetingly that Jamie might be the cause of it. Still, the scene when he'd held the brush flashed through his mind once more, conjuring an image he couldn't forget.

It seemed the most natural thing in the world to plunge his fingers into the tangles. He drew her head back and stared into her eyes. Saw them widen with surprise, then slowly heat as she realized his intentions. He lowered his gaze to her lips and tested himself for just a moment, holding back until he could almost taste them. Then he could wait no longer. Moving as slowly as though in a dream, he fitted his mouth to hers, and on a sigh he drank in the sweet, clean taste of her.

At that first contact Estelle felt the floor dip and tilt dangerously, and her hands reached out, clutching blindly at his waist. Though she tried not to react, she couldn't help the way her breath hitched, then released in a long, slow sigh. She could feel her pulse rate speed up and her blood begin to heat. Though she thought about resisting, she was afraid to move. Afraid that if she did, she would shatter like crystal. And so she stood, absorbing the most delicious sensations.

As he took the kiss deeper, all thought fled. All she could do was hold on while he took her on a roller-coaster ride of emotions.

He'd never met anyone quite so exciting to watch. He kept his eyes open, loving the way she responded to that simple kiss. Color flooded her cheeks. Her lashes fluttered, then lowered.

He changed the angle, keeping his mouth on hers, and found himself deeply aroused by the touch of her hands at his waist. The thought of them touching him everywhere aroused him even more. Though he was tempted to crush her to him and take what he wanted, he forced himself to go slowly, allowing the merest stroke of his hand along her spine. Her little shiver of delight only excited him more.

It took all his willpower to pull back. "I was tempted to blame this on Jamie. He was always getting me to do things I wanted to do, but was too cowardly to try." He smiled then, and there was an edge of danger in it. "But that would be a lie. This wasn't Jamie's doing. It was all mine." He tilted her chin, lifting her face to his, and brushed a light, butterfly kiss over her lips. "And you'd best be warned, Estelle. Given the chance, I'll do it again."

"Don't I have anything to say about that?"

He chuckled. "I didn't see you resist."

She felt the heat stain her cheeks. There was no denying the truth of what he'd said. Not only had she not resisted, but she had fully participated. And judging by the way her body was continuing to vibrate, she would gladly do it again.

"I wish I didn't have to leave to meet someone." Because his hands were shaking, he tucked them into his pockets and took another step back. It was dangerous standing too close to her. "Why don't you join my uncle and me in the library at six for drinks?"

"I . . . Yes. All right."

"Until then." He was, he realized, already looking forward to it.

He turned away and caught sight of Griffin Mackenzie standing in the doorway. When he realized what Griff had witnessed, his smile instantly disappeared.

Without a backward glance he stormed away.

6

"GOOD EVENING, MY dear." Sir Charles looked up from his position beside the fire. "You look lovely tonight." He glanced at his nephew. "Doesn't she, Rob?"

"Aye." Rob's eyes darkened as he studied her.

Estelle braced herself before meeting Rob's gaze. Ever since their kiss, she'd been fretting over how she would react in his presence.

"Wine?" Rob handed her a fluted glass, and as their fingers brushed, he felt a rush of heat that left him shaken. He tempted himself further by placing a hand beneath her elbow as he led her to a chair beside his uncle.

She felt heat stain her cheeks. She'd taken pains to look just right this evening. The dress was a vibrant shade of body-skimming green silk. At her throat was a single strand of pearls, a gift from her aunt. On a whim she'd brushed her hair long and flowing, but now she wished she had pinned it up. She suddenly felt silly and frivolous.

"My nephew was just telling me that you've met Jamie."

"I . . . Yes." What was happening to her? She was an intelligent, sensible woman who had slowly worked her way into a position of respect and authority in one of the finest auction houses in the world. She held art history degrees from two universities and was regarded as one of the most knowledgeable curators of Scottish artifacts. In less than two days, however, she had compromised her position by shamelessly flirting, and worse, was openly admitting to seeing and talking to a ghost in her workroom.

"I remember him as being such fun."

"Are you telling me that you've met him also, Sir Charles?"

"Of course. All the Camerons have met the lad, since his . . . demise in 1620."

"Have others outside the family seen him?"

Charles shrugged. "Only if he wants them to. Through the centuries there have been dozens of reported sightings. He's become an accepted member of the family."

"He told me the rest of his family has gone home. Why does he stay? Why doesn't he . . . join them?"

The old man shook his head. "I don't really know. It seems there's something he feels he must do before he can enjoy his eternal rest."

"He mentioned the Star of Scotland. Have you heard of it?"

"Of course. It was rumored to have been an important piece of Cameron history. But there are no paintings of it, no sketches, no written history of it. All we have is word of mouth handed down through the centuries. It appears to be more fiction than fact."

Estelle sipped her wine, considering what she was about to say. Then, after taking a deep breath, she turned to Rob. "Jamie told me that you've only agreed to auction off your belongings because you're about to lose Castle Clough. Is that true?"

His hand tightened on the glass, the only indication of his pain. "It is."

"I'm sorry. I can't even imagine what it must feel like to have to give up something this beautiful."

"It isn't only the beauty of Castle Clough that I'll lose. It's the land that has been in my family for generations. And the pleasure I take from my work."

"Not to mention," his uncle added, "all the people who live here and in Dunfield who depend on Rob to see them through the hard times. It's been a tradition for the Cameron family, one we take very seriously."

Now Estelle understood the sadness she could sense in Desmond and Alfred Snow, and Arley and Fergus Barclay. Then she thought about what Jamie had told her of the man who held the mortgage. "Jamie said that Griffin Mackenzie has long coveted your land."

"Aye." As always, when Rob's temper grew, his burr thickened.

Estelle knew that if she but closed her eyes, she could imagine Rob Cameron as a warrior of old, sword lifted, ready to do battle with his enemy.

She leaned forward. "There has to be a way to stop him from taking what is rightfully yours, Rob."

"Don't you think I've tried to find a way?" He stood and walked to the fireplace, resting a closed fist on the mantel. "I've been to every banker. I've had lawyers going over the documents, looking for a loophole. Griff was clever. Everything is legal and binding. And in just a few weeks, unless I find a pot of gold, everything I've ever loved will be his."

Estelle could hear the pain in his voice, could actually feel the sorrow he was feeling. It pierced her heart like a knife. She set down her drink and clasped her hands in her lap. "It isn't fair."

Rob stopped his pacing to look at her. On his lips was a heart-stopping smile. "No one ever promised that life would be fair."

Their gazes met and held.

"Jamie said that if we work together we may yet thwart our enemy."

"Ah. So now it's become your fight, too?"

Sir Charles sat in his wheelchair, sipping his drink and watching the interaction between his nephew and this young woman. Though he was certain they weren't aware of it as yet, he could sense a depth of feeling that went far beyond that of employer and employee.

Despite the seriousness of the situation, he felt a sudden lightness around his heart. It had long been his wish that Rob would meet someone worthy of him. Someone who would cherish his way of life and help preserve it. Who better than this woman, who had made a career of studying the very things Rob most loved in this world?

Maybe, he thought with a smile, there was more going on here than met the eye.

He cleared his throat, and the two young people looked his way. "It has often been my experience that out of even the most wretched of circumstances, much good can come." He gave them the benefit of his smile. "Who knows? Perhaps if we all work together, we may yet come up with a way to save Castle Clough."

"Miss?"

Estelle looked up from her work to find Arley standing in the doorway. "Yes, Arley. Come in."

"Sir Charles asked if you would deliver this to Lord Cameron." He held out an envelope.

She accepted it, noting that though it was sealed, it bore no markings. "Deliver it? Where is Lord Cameron?"

"Out in the field, miss. Working with the herd."

"Is it far?"

"No more than a kilometer."

"Is Fergus too busy to go?"

The lad shrugged. "I don't know, miss. I only know that Sir Charles asked that you deliver it."

She sighed. In the past few days she'd been given half a dozen such assignments by his uncle. Take this to Rob in the library. Take that to him in the dining room. Now she was being sent out to the field. At this rate, she'd never get her work done.

"All right, Arley. Tell Sir Charles that I'll see to it right away." She turned away and picked up a tweed jacket. Though the sun was shining, the air had a bite to it.

As she started off across the field, her spirits lifted. For days now she hadn't seen Jamie. In fact, she'd stopped looking for him. At first she'd missed his silly pranks. But now she was beginning to believe that he didn't exist at all. It was simply the sort of hysteria brought on by the power of suggestion. She'd read of the curse of Castle Clough, and because she'd misunderstood it, she'd simply conjured an image of a young ghost because . . . well, because all castles ought to have one.

There now. She felt better already. She was back to her old sane, sensible self.

As she came up over a curving meadow, she caught sight of Rob walking toward her. Slung over his shoulders was a newborn calf.

At the sight of him, tall and rugged, his dark hair mussed, his big hands holding the animal gently, her heart did somersaults.

"Estelle." He broke into a wide smile. "What brings you out here?"

"A message from your uncle."

He accepted the envelope and stuck it in his pocket.

"Who is this?" She reached up to stroke the velvet nose of the sleepy-eyed animal.

"This little guy's just a few hours old. The poor little thing will have to be hand-fed for a day while I treat an infection in his mother." He motioned behind him, and Estelle caught sight of a field hand leading a cow.

"Does he have a name?"

He shook his head and started toward the barn in the distance. "Not yet. Maybe you'd like to give him one."

Estelle kept pace beside him. "I've never named a calf. Tell me a little about him."

"His father is Brawny of Clough. One of the finest bulls in all of Scotland." Rob stepped out of the sunshine and into the darkness of the barn, strolling past several stalls before pausing before an open door. Inside, in a bed of straw, he gently settled the tiny animal and covered it with a blanket.

"And his mother?" Estelle knelt beside the calf and continued to soothe and stroke, while Rob filled a bottle with formula.

"A bonny heifer. This is her first birthing, and she came through it admirably."

He handed her the bottle, and she laughed with delight when the calf fastened onto it and began to drink. But she felt suddenly light-headed when she looked up to see Rob toss aside his shirt and plunge his hands into a bucket of water.

At the sight of his hard, muscled back, her throat went dry. When he turned, she could hardly tear her gaze away from the hair-roughened chest, the flat, trim stomach. The muscles of his arms bunched and tightened as he reached for a towel and dried himself before pulling on a clean shirt.

It seemed incongruous that all morning she had photographed priceless artifacts with a digital camera, sending the images over the Internet to prospective buyers, and now she was kneeling in a barn with a newborn calf, fighting the most primitive of all urges.

She looked down at the calf. "Oh, look, Rob. Look how bold he is."

"Is that his name, then?"

She arched a brow, considering. Pleased, she nodded. "He is bold. It suits him."

When the calf had emptied the bottle, Rob picked him up and gently draped him around his shoulders. "Come on, Bold. I'll take you to your mother."

With Estelle following, he carried the calf to another stall, where the mother stood waiting. As soon as he deposited the calf in the straw, its mother began nuzzling and coaxing, until the calf was standing beside her.

"Oh, Rob, aren't they beautiful?"

"Aye. But here in Scotland we say 'bonny.' "

"Bonny. Aye," she said, imitating his burr. "Mother and son are indeed a bonny pair."

He stood beside her, his foot resting on the crossed bar of the stall. For some reason he couldn't quite fathom, his heart swelled with pleasure. There was nothing she could have said that would have pleased him more.

She glanced at her watch. "I'd better get back. I'm neglecting my work."

"Wait." He pulled her close and brushed his lips over hers. It was the merest touch of mouth to mouth, but it had her blood running hot.

She savored the moment, loving the press of his hard, muscled body against hers, and the feel of his big hands moving along her spine. She realized that she would like nothing more than the pleasure of staying just so, with his breath warm against her cheek, and his firm, clever lips nuzzling hers.

"Until tonight, Estelle." He tucked her hair behind her ear, allowing his hand to linger a moment.

As she walked away, Rob tore open the envelope she'd given him. He read his uncle's familiar scrawl, then threw back his head and roared with laughter.

The old codger was playing matchmaker. He'd admitted as much in his note. He'd sent her out here for no other reason than to throw them together. And he'd added as an afterthought that he hoped his nephew would be sufficiently grateful for the favor.

He was, Rob realized. While everything around him was falling apart, while his whole world as he'd known it was shattering beyond repair, he was foolishly, and completely, losing his heart.

Estelle entered the dining hall and glanced around in surprise. Rob wasn't there. Sir Charles was sitting alone before the fire.

She felt a wave of bitter disappointment. She'd taken such pains with her dress. It was a soft white wool, with long, tapered sleeves and scooped neckline. She'd waged an argument with herself before deciding to pin up her hair in a neat knot. That way, she reasoned, she wouldn't look too fussy. Or too overtly sexy.

"Rob is late tonight, I see." She crossed the room and offered her hand to Sir Charles. Instead of squeezing it, he lifted it to his lips.

"He sent word that he'll be spending the night in the barn."

"Oh, no. Don't tell me there's something wrong with Bold."

"Bold?"

"Did he mention a calf, Sir Charles?"

"A calf?" The old man shrugged. "I believe he did. Something about keeping an eye on him . . ."

"Oh, Sir Charles. Would you mind terribly if I went to the barn to see for myself? I hate to abandon you, but this is the first calf I've ever named. He's very special to me. And if there's something wrong . . ."

"But of course you must go, my dear. I insist. Here." He lifted the soft plaid blanket that covered his lap and handed it to her. "Drape this around your shoulders to ward off the night air." Then he beckoned to Desmond. "Have you the basket of supper Alfred fixed for my nephew?"

"Aye." The old man lifted a basket from the table. With a slight bow he handed it to Estelle.

"Thank you, Desmond. Sir Charles, I won't be long."

"Now you musn't race back on my account. In fact, I'm feeling rather weary. I'll probably go up to my room any minute now and take my supper in bed. So take your time, my dear. Stay with my nephew a while so he won't be lonely out there in the night."

She started off, then thought better of it and returned to brush a kiss over his cheek. "Thank you, Sir Charles."

As she dashed out of the room, the old man touched a finger to the spot, then glanced at Desmond with a devilish smile. "You had Alfred add a second supper to that basket as I requested?"

"Aye, Sir Charles."

"Good. Good." The old man rubbed his hands together gleefully. "Now, if my nephew can resist all that, he's not the man I think he is."

The two old men shared a chuckle. Then, as he did every night, Desmond poured Scotch into a tumbler, set it beside Sir Charles, and went out, leaving him to his fire, his drink, and his memories.

7

"Rob."

At the sound of Estelle's voice, Rob turned to see her standing in the doorway of the barn, trying to locate him in the darkness.

"In here." He lifted a lantern from a hook and started toward her.

She raced forward, meeting him halfway. "Has something happened to Bold?"

"No. He's fine. Why?"

"Your uncle said . . ."

"My uncle." A flicker of a smile touched the corners of his lips. "I should have known. Bless his conniving old heart." He caught her arm and led her toward the stall. "I just wanted to stay here a while so I could keep an eye on mother and son." He held the lantern aloft so she could see for herself that the cow and calf were indeed fine.

"Oh, I'm so relieved." She set aside the basket and leaned on the rail, watching as the cow nuzzled her calf. "When Sir Charles said you'd be spending the night out here, I was certain something had gone terribly wrong.''

"Spending the night, am I?'' He hadn't planned on it, but suddenly it seemed like a fine idea. As long as he didn't have to spend it alone. "And you rushed out to keep me company.''

"Yes.'' She glanced over and realized he was studying her with a strange, intense look on his face. "What is it? What's wrong?''

"Wrong?'' He touched a hand to her cheek. "Nothing is wrong, Estelle. In fact, everything is so right. Especially where you're concerned. The way you look. So intriguing. One minute the prim professor. The next, a tempting little seductress.'' He drew her close and pressed his face to her hair, breathing her in. "The way you smell. Fresh and clean, like a field of wildflowers.'' He ran his hands down her back, sending little tremors along her spine. "The way you're willing to fight for me.'' He chuckled, and the sound sent a thrill racing through her. "I can almost see you marching headlong into battle, sword at the ready, determined to fight for what you believe in.''

She'd never known such amazing sensations. Icy tingles and shimmering heat. Fear and longing and a strange sense that everything in her life was about to change. And though it frightened her more than she cared to admit, there was a sense of anticipation, of wild exhilaration, as well. "I would fight for you, Rob, if only I knew how.''

"I know that. And I find it so . . . endearing.'' He caught a tangle of her hair and watched as the strands sifted through his fingers.

She felt the breath hitch in her throat and knew with absolute certainty that he was going to kiss her. Knew also that she wanted him to. Desperately. Still, she was torn between desire and a need to run back to the castle, where she knew she could be safe from her own weakness.

"You're so soft, Estelle. Everything about you is soft.'' He seemed fascinated by her pale skin, peeking out from beneath the cover of a blanket she wore like a shawl. With his eyes on hers, he ran a fingertip along her exposed skin, from her neck to her shoulder.

She shivered and started to draw the blanket tighter around her. But her fingers fumbled, and it fell to the straw at their feet.

"You look like an angel. My angel. Come to save me." He lowered his head, running wet, nibbling kisses along the sensitive hollow between her neck and shoulder until she moaned and pushed away a little.

Her eyes suddenly looked too big. She opened her mouth to speak, but no words came out.

"What's wrong, angel?" He smiled. But he seemed more dangerous than amused.

"I'm afraid."

"Of me?"

"No." She struggled to speak over the knot of fear that clogged her throat. "Of me. Of the things I'm feeling."

"Ah." There was a gleam in his eye as he lifted a hand to her cheek. "An honest woman. I'd expected as much." He stared down into her eyes before saying softly, "I have to kiss you, Estelle."

His arms came around her, drawing her close against his chest. His mouth hovered over hers for a moment, and she felt the jittery thrill of anticipation. Then his lips covered hers in a kiss that drained her even as it filled her.

As he took the kiss deeper, his tongue darted between her lips, dueling with hers, mating, while his hands moved seductively across her shoulders, down her arms. On a moan of pleasure he backed her up against the rough wood of an empty stall and continued raining kisses over her eyes, her nose, her cheek.

She was so hot she was melting. Each touch of his hands, each press of his lips, made her blood heat more.

At the whimpering, sighing sounds she made his blood pumped furiously. He could hardly see through the dark mist of desire that nearly blinded him. He couldn't remember ever wanting anything or anyone so desperately.

"Stay with me, Estelle." He spoke the words inside her mouth. "Stay the night."

"No. Wait. I musn't." She put a hand to his chest, struggling to think. But all she could think of was him. The way his eyes, hot with desire, met hers. The way those big, work-worn hands moved over her. All she could taste was him. A dark, mysterious taste that was like no other. And the need for him. Pulling at her. Tugging at her. Making her weak with the wanting.

"I can't wait. I don't want to." He dragged her close and kissed her again, until she was breathless. "You don't want to. Admit it."

At that she went deathly quiet.

He pressed his advantage. "If you tell me to stop, I will, though I swear it'll kill me. Tell me, Estelle. Tell me to stop. Tell me you don't want this, too."

She could feel the pounding of his heart against her palm. It was as wild, as erratic, as her own. He wanted her. Wanted her. The knowledge bloomed inside her heart until it felt as though it would explode. And the truth was, she wanted him. Desperately.

In the silence of the night he waited for her answer. Everything depended on her next words.

She let out a long, deep sigh. "I can't tell you I don't want this. It would be a lie."

He reminded himself to breathe. For the first time the tension left his voice, smoothed it out with a smile. "Thank heaven." He lowered his mouth to hers, avid, hungry. And he feasted.

She'd never had a man taste her like this, as though she were a banquet. He lingered over her lips, drawing out every drop of flavor, before moving on to nibble her jaw, and then lower, running hot, wet kisses down the long column of her throat.

"Oh, Rob." The words were more a sigh than a whisper.

His mouth found hers again, and he kissed her until they were both breathless.

With a moan of sheer pleasure she wrapped herself around him, returning his kisses with such fervor, she couldn't quite believe what she was doing. She'd never before thought of herself as greedy. But she wanted to touch, to taste, to savor every kiss, every jolt, every sweet sensation.

The purely male flavor of him poured through her, leaving her giddy with delight. In her prim, practical world there had been so little time to indulge herself. Instead of dinners and dates there had been field trips and seminars. Instead of flowers and candy there had been theses and exams. But now—now, she could indulge her woman's heart. With Rob, she could have what her heart desired. It was all here for the taking, in this man. This moment. And this, this taste, was only the beginning.

Her fingers fumbled with the buttons of his shirt. She could hardly wait to feel that hard, muscled flesh she'd seen earlier today. She slid the shirt off his shoulders and allowed her hands to splay across his chest, loving the ripple of muscle beneath her palms.

She felt the coolness of the night air as his fingers lowered the zipper of her dress. It slid off her shoulders to pool at her feet.

"Why, Estelle." His voice was warm with laughter as he realized that she was wearing nothing beneath it. "Who would have thought it of you?"

She found herself laughing with him, and marveling at the fact that they could laugh at a time like this. "I think I'll have to lay the blame at your feet, Rob. You make me feel like a woman."

"You are a woman. A beautiful . . ." He ran soft, nibbling kisses across her shoulder. ". . . desirable . . ." He brought his mouth lower, to her collarbone. ". . . absolutely fantastic woman." With a growl in his throat that sounded more animal than human, he closed his mouth around one erect nipple.

The jolt shuddered through her, and she struggled against a tidal wave of feelings that threatened to swamp her. All she could do was hang on as wave after wave assaulted her, leaving her trembling with weakness.

Each tug of his mouth, each clever flick of his tongue, had her climbing higher, then higher still, until she wondered how she could possibly survive any more.

She clung to him, weak and boneless, afraid that at any moment her legs would refuse to support her. Sensing her need, he lowered her to the blanket, then stretched out beside her.

Despite the coolness of the night air, her flesh was hot and damp, and quivering beneath the clever ministrations of his big, calloused hands.

He couldn't get enough of this soft, soft skin. Never in his life had he felt so thoroughly aroused. He had to struggle against the raging desire to take her quickly. Needs pulsed and throbbed, threatening to explode. But still he held back, wanting more. Wanting all.

"Rob, I . . ." She suddenly stiffened as, with just his tongue, he sent her soaring. It was the most incredible feeling in the world, and all she could do was fist her hands in the blanket beneath her, feeling the straw shift and move as she reached the first crest.

This was how he'd wanted her. Writhing beneath him, her eyes huge, her heart hammering. And his name on her lips. Only his.

"Rob, please. I need you to . . ."

"Shhh." With a hot, hungry kiss he stilled her words. "I know, love. I can't wait any longer either." He levered himself above her, fighting the urge to devour her.

As he entered her, she wrapped herself around him and began to move with him, climbing higher, faster, than either of them could have ever imagined.

Where had this strength come from? This intense energy? It nearly consumed them with its heat.

They moved together, hearts hammering, lungs straining, as they climbed higher and higher until they reached the moon. And shattered in an explosion of stars.

"You actually brought supper?" Rob lounged against the rough wooden boards of the empty stall while Estelle opened the basket and removed a chilled bottle of champagne, along with caviar and toast points, rare roast beef nestled in flaky rolls, and exquisite little fruit tarts.

"I see my uncle thought of everything." Rob couldn't help laughing.

"He said Alfred had prepared it for you. But there's enough here to feed half the town."

"The old scoundrel had it all planned."

Estelle's head came up sharply. "Are you saying he knew that I'd . . . that we'd . . . ?"

Rob kissed her before spreading caviar on a sliver of toast. "He couldn't know for certain. But I'm sure he was hoping."

Seeing the flush on her cheeks, he fed her, then filled two fluted glasses with champagne and handed one to her before sipping. He crossed one bare foot over the other and studied her by the light of the lantern.

She was wearing his shirt. Unbuttoned, it fell open, revealing pale, creamy breasts. Her hair tumbled about her face and shoulders in a riot of tangles.

She laughed, then a moment later found to her embarrassment that her eyes were swimming.

"What's this?" He wrapped an arm around her shoulders and drew her close, kissing away her tears. "Regrets?"

"Never." She shook her head, struggling for composure. "It's just that I've never experienced anything quite like this. Or experienced anyone quite like you."

"I could say the same about you." He traced his index finger around the outline of her lips. "You're the only bright spot in my life right now, Estelle."

She sighed. "I hate what's being done to you. It's so unfair. I feel so helpless."

"Helpless? You?" He nuzzled her cheek and lightly nipped at her earlobe. "There's such strength in you. I sensed it the first time I saw you."

"Did you?" She turned to face him, her eyes shiny-bright in the light of the lantern. "I figured, the first time we met, you never even noticed me."

He chuckled, remembering. "I'd been meeting with the bankers. They'd refused to offer me any shred of hope. Then I came upstairs, in search of Fergus, and found you, looking all neat and buttoned up. For hours after the bankers were gone, I was still seeing you in my mind. And hearing your voice. And smelling your subtle perfume."

"Amazing. I'd have never guessed. Jamie told me you're very good at hiding your feelings."

"What else did that little rascal tell you?"

"That he's lonely because there are no more children to play with. And that I remind him of his mother."

"You definitely do not remind me of my mother. Especially in that shirt. I've decided I like it better on you." He brushed his lips over hers, then spread more caviar, handing a piece of toast to her, then tasting his own.

She stared into her glass. "Something Jamie said keeps nagging at my mind."

"What's that?"

"When Castle Clough was under siege, he was told to fetch the Star of Scotland, in the hope that it could be exchanged for the lives of his parents. He was mortally wounded and doesn't recall much after that."

"So?"

"I know that the odds are very good that the Star was actually stolen during the siege. But, Rob, what if it wasn't? What if it's still hidden somewhere here in the castle?"

"Impossible. This old place has gone through extensive remodeling throughout the centuries. Someone would have come across it."

"But what if no one did? What would such a thing be worth today?"

"The Star of Scotland?" He shook his head, considering. "Absolutely priceless."

"If it were found here in Castle Clough, who would own it?"

He shrugged. "I suppose it could legally be claimed by the Cameron clan. But something that historic, that special, should rightly be put on public display, so that it could be viewed by all the people."

"If you were to own such a treasure, and you offered it to the government, wouldn't they, in turn, see that your father's debt was paid in full?"

He caught a strand of her hair and wrapped it around his finger. "That's a lovely fantasy, Estelle Sinclair, but a fantasy all the same." Then he drew her close for a long, slow kiss that heated his blood and started his heart racing again. "This, on the other hand, is real. And now that I've regained my strength, I'd like to go for seconds, if you don't mind."

Her own heart was behaving like a runaway train. Against his lips, she whispered, "That's a lovely, bonny thought, your lordship. I don't mind in the least."

And then there was no need for words, as they lost themselves in a world of soft sighs and long, lingering kisses. A world reserved for lovers.

8

"AH, HERE'S OUR lass now." Sir Charles looked up from his breakfast as Estelle rushed in.

Fresh from the shower, she wore creamy wool slacks and a cream-colored turtleneck. Her hair was still damp and curling around a face that was flushed with embarrassment.

She and Rob had sneaked into the castle like two errant children, their clothes in disarray, bits of straw stuck in their hair. The first person they'd run into had been Desmond. Though he spoke not a word, Estelle had seen the flicker of emotion in his eyes as he stiffened his spine, then continued on his way.

By now, she was certain the entire castle knew that she and Rob had spent the night together in the barn. And she could tell, by the gleam in Sir Charles's eye, that he was delighted with the part he'd played in all this.

"Well, my dear. You look as rested as Rob. Come. Join us."

"I . . . really can't stay." She brushed a kiss over the old man's cheek, then took the chair Rob held for her. As she

259

sat, he pressed a hand to her shoulder, allowing it to linger a moment before returning to the head of the table.

"Coffee, miss?" Desmond paused beside her.

"Yes. Thank you." She lifted her cup and sipped, aware that all three men were watching her.

"Now, tell us why you can't stay for breakfast." Sir Charles broke open a scone and smothered it with jelly.

"I've been checking my E-mail. The offers are starting to pour in on the items we've offered for sale. There's no time to waste. The deadline is almost upon us."

"Us." Sir Charles smiled. "I like the sound of that."

"I just meant . . ." She glanced up to see Rob sharing a grin with his uncle.

"Eggs, miss?" Alfred paused beside her and held out a steaming platter.

When she started to refuse, he spooned some onto her plate, then moved to stand beside Rob, and then Sir Charles. Without a word he returned to the kitchen, with Desmond following.

"Well." Sir Charles glanced at Rob, then at Estelle. "I'd say you've just been paid the highest of compliments, my dear. Alfred has rarely, if ever, taken the liberty of serving someone's plate. He must think you are special indeed."

She ducked her head, avoiding his eyes. "I can't imagine why."

"I'd say it's because he admires the way you're fighting to save this old place. It's something we all admire, my dear."

"I just wish I could do more." She ate a few bites, then pushed away from the table. "I'm sorry. I'd love to stay. But I have to get to the workroom and check my computer." She turned to Rob, and for a moment their eyes met and held. "I'll inform you of the first offers as soon as they're tallied."

He nodded, then surprised her by catching her hand and pressing it to his lips before releasing it. "I'll come by your workroom later."

When she was gone, he turned to his uncle. "I see the

grapevine has already begun buzzing about my nighttime activities.''

"I don't know what you mean." The old man seemed particularly intent upon sprinkling salt and pepper on his eggs.

"You old rascal. You're worse than Jamie."

Sir Charles looked up. His face broke into a wide smile. "Am I really?"

"Stop being so pleased with yourself."

"Have I reason to be?"

Rob threw back his head and roared with laughter. "I should be the one who's pleased. I can't remember when I've spent a more fascinating night. Or beheld a more beautiful sunrise."

"Then I'm happy for you." Sir Charles looked across the table at his nephew and smiled. "When you reach my age you realize what really matters most in this brief time on earth. Family. Honor. Love." He put a hand over Rob's and squeezed. "If a man should have all three, he is indeed blessed."

He beckoned to Fergus, who stood waiting in the doorway. "Come, lad. I think I'd like to take a turn around the gardens."

Rob waited until he was alone, then stood and walked to the windows, staring out at the stark, rugged Highlands. His uncle's words played through his mind. *Family. Honor. Love.* It was all that had ever mattered to him. His father had denied him the first, though his uncle had more than made up for it. As for honor, though he'd had his share of setbacks, he'd tried to lead an honorable life. And now, because of his father's weakness, even that might be sullied. As for the last, he'd feared it would forever elude him. Until Estelle. What a special gift she was.

With a sigh he turned away and headed toward her workroom, to face the figures that would determine his future.

"How are the numbers?" Rob paused in the doorway and watched as Estelle's fingers flew over the keyboard of her computer.

She looked up. "Not as high as I'd hoped. If only we had time for a bidding war."

He crossed the room and paused behind her. With his hands on her shoulders he pressed his lips to her temple. "I agree with what my uncle said. I like the sound of 'we.' I'm so glad you're on my side."

She closed one hand over his, then pointed to the computer screen. "Here are the latest offers."

She scrolled slowly, so that he could read the numbers. A quick tally told him they were far short of the amount needed.

"Add the paintings," he said tiredly. "And anything else that can interest a buyer."

"I've had a request for personal items from an American collector. He . . . mentioned a particular interest in your ancestors' sword and in the trunkful of clothes I found in the tower."

She saw the way his eyes darkened before he nodded. "All right. Have him make an offer."

"Oh, Rob." She stood and wrapped her arms around his neck. "I hate that this is happening to you."

"So do I. But it can't be avoided any longer." He kissed her, lingering over her lips, taking comfort in her warmth. "I'll be in the library, going over the papers. I expect that I'll be hearing from Griff before the day is over."

"My, my." At Griff's deep voice from the doorway their heads came up sharply. "Now isn't this a tender scene."

Rob stepped forward, placing himself in front of Estelle, as though to keep her out of harm's way. Once again she was reminded of an ancient warrior. "Why didn't you allow Desmond to announce you?"

Griff's tone sharpened with anger. "Don't play lord of the manor with me, Rob, old boy. I don't need to be announced like some mere visitor. Soon this will all be mine." He stared beyond Rob to the woman who stood just behind him. "Tell me, Professor. Have you managed to lure enough fools into bidding on these pathetic relics?"

She tucked her hand into Rob's, sharing her strength,

while drawing on his. "I don't report to you, Mr. Mackenzie. I work for Rob."

"Work for him? Is that what they call it these days?" He gave a short laugh. "Too bad you've chosen the losing side in this battle, Professor. I could have made your life extremely comfortable." His smile faded when he focused on Rob. "I'll wait for you in the library. I have an offer that might interest you."

"You have nothing that would interest me, Griff. If you want to talk, call my lawyer."

Mackenzie's eyes glittered with a dangerous light. "If you know what's good for you, you'll listen to what I have to say."

He spun on his heel and stormed away.

When they were alone, Estelle clutched Rob's hand. "Don't go. I don't trust him. I truly believe he could become violent. I can see it in his eyes."

He squeezed her hand, then brushed a kiss over the worried frown that marred her forehead. "Relax, love. Talk is cheap. It won't cost me anything to listen."

She watched as he exited the workroom. As she returned to the computer she couldn't shake the feeling of impending doom.

By late afternoon Estelle had tallied the final numbers, then printed them out. The thought of presenting them to Rob weighed heavily upon her heart. Even with the addition of the paintings and personal items, they were short of their goal. Which meant Rob would have to consider selling his herd.

She knew, from all she'd heard and observed, that the herd was much more than just his livelihood. It was his pride. His passion. It would be the cruelest loss of all.

"Bad news, Professor?" Griff stood in the doorway. On his face was a look of triumph.

Estelle took the papers out of the printer and clutched them to her, determined that he wouldn't see them.

"What's this? Secrets?" Griff was across the room in seconds. "So, Professor, what's the verdict?"

"You'll have to ask Lord Cameron."

"I'm asking you."

She started past him, but his hand shot out, stopping her in midstride. "Maybe you don't understand, Professor. I want that report."

She stared at his offending fingers, pressing painfully on her flesh. "You have no right to it."

"No right?" His voice was low with anger. "Don't you talk to me about rights. Do you know what it's like to have to claw and scratch your way out of the very bottom of a filthy hole, only to learn when you reach the top that there are others who will be allowed to push you aside? Not because they're smarter, or more clever, but because they were born to wealth. Born to it. And that gives them the right to fancy titles and special privileges the rest of us will never have. While I was still scrambling for my first dollar, Rob Cameron was sailing on fancy yachts and partying with royalty. Then, when he tired of that life, he came home to play the part of a country gentleman, reaping honors from his country for his precious herd of cattle. Well, he's about to get a taste of the cold, hard facts of reality. Now I'm the one with the money. And the power. And soon I'll have what should have been mine in the first place, if only he hadn't been born."

"So it's true that you resent him for simply being born."

"I hate him with every fiber of my being. And when I'm through with him, he will wish he had never been born." Griff tore the papers out of Estelle's hand and read the figures, then threw back his head and laughed. "Here." He shoved them at her, then turned away. "I've seen enough to know that by midnight tomorrow Castle Clough will be mine."

"Jamie." With Rob watching from the doorway, Estelle walked slowly around the workroom, calling softly, "Jamie, please come out."

After several minutes Rob shook his head. "I've told you, love. It's no use. No one has ever been able to entice

Jamie to show himself. He only comes out when he wishes.''

"Jamie.'' Estelle lowered her voice. "I know you're frightened of Griffin Mackenzie. I know he's the reason you disappear. But he isn't here now. There's no one here who will harm you. And we need you. Please show yourself.''

In the silence that followed, she closed her eyes, wishing with all her heart that she could coax the lad to come out. When the room remained empty, she turned away in defeat.

Rob held out his hand, and she started toward him.

"Did ye come to play, then?''

At the sound of Jamie's voice she spun around. A smile lit her eyes. "Oh, Jamie, I knew you'd come.''

"Ye woke me, Estelle Sinclair. I was havin' a lovely nap. Now are we goin' to play?''

She glanced at Rob, then nodded. "Yes, Jamie. I have a wonderful game planned.''

"A game, ye say?''

Estelle nodded. "That is, if you're willing to allow some others to see you.''

"Others?'' He backed up, looking alarmed.

"It's only Desmond and Alfred and Fergus.''

"They're not of the Cameron clan. I canna do it.''

"I'm not a Cameron either, Jamie. But you let me see you.''

"That's different. Ye remind me of my mother.''

"And what about the strangers who've seen you over the centuries? Not all of them were Camerons.''

"Aye. I did it to frighten them. Because I was tired of bein' alone.'' He paused, considering. "What's this game we're to play?''

"Come here, Jamie.''

She took a seat at the worktable, and the lad climbed up on her lap.

"From what you've told me, I have some doubts about what really happened that day of the siege. I believe you may have managed to hold on to the Star of Scotland after you were wounded.''

"What makes you think that?"

"Because you're still here. And you're a clever, feisty lad. What if, before you . . . gave in to the seriousness of your wound, you had the presence of mind to hide it?"

"I dunna know. I canna remember. Is that what ye want, Estelle? Do ye wish to search for the Star?"

She nodded.

"But why? I've had hundreds of years to try and I've never found it. What makes ye think we'll succeed tonight, when we've never done so before?"

"I don't know, Jamie." She tousled his hair and pressed a kiss to his temple. "Maybe because there's so much at stake. If we don't find the Star of Scotland tonight, Castle Clough will pass from your clan's hands into the hands of your enemy tomorrow. I thought that, with your help, I'd have Desmond and Alfred and Fergus work with us to rip apart some of the walls around the area where you sleep. Are you willing to try?"

He looked up into her eyes, then glanced at the man in the doorway. In a voice meant for her ears alone, he whispered, "Ye love him, don't ye, Estelle?"

She nodded. "With all my heart."

He pushed free of her embrace and slid to the floor, then took several steps across the room.

She sighed, wondering why she'd ever thought he would agree to her plan. But as she stood up, preparing to leave, he turned toward her.

"All right," he said softly. "Call in the others. But they'd better not laugh at me."

9

"THIS WAS WHERE I woke up after the siege." Jamie knocked on the wall, and the others could hear the hollow sound, revealing a hole behind it.

True to her word, Estelle had cautioned the others not to react with fear or humor when they first caught sight of Jamie. Desmond had maintained his usual stony expression, showing absolutely no emotion. Alfred's scowl had deepened as he'd studied the lad's strange clothes and heard his ancient manner of speech. But Fergus had surprised them all by his smiling acceptance of this stranger. It was as though he knew instinctively that Jamie was a friend. He knelt and offered his hand. And with a matching smile, Jamie accepted the handshake.

Sir Charles joined in by calling encouragement from the doorway, where his wheelchair had been parked out of the way. With crowbars and handsaws and assorted other tools, they began an assault on the walls, tearing the lovely mahogany away, to reveal ancient stone and brick.

At first they were infused with excitement as they peeled

away the wood. The keen edge of anticipation kept the adrenaline pumping as they pulled aside every loose stone and brick and piece of mortar, searching every crack and crevice that might serve as a hiding place for the jewel.

Shortly after midnight Rob noticed that his uncle had fallen asleep in his wheelchair.

"Fergus," he called softly.

The lad looked up.

"Take my uncle upstairs and see him safely to his bed."

The young giant set aside his tools and hurried to do the lord's bidding.

Half an hour later Rob touched a hand to Desmond's shoulder. "Desmond, you and your brother have done all you can. Go to bed now."

"An hour more, your lordship."

"No." Rob shook his head. "Fergus and I will search a while yet. But the hour is late. You need your rest."

Reluctantly the two old men turned away and went off to their beds.

Fergus, who had returned, surveyed the damage, then picked up a crowbar and attacked the last section of wall. Several hours later he slumped down in a corner of the room, his head nodding. Rob covered him with a blanket and left him sleeping, then walked over to Estelle and Jamie, who were digging in the rubble.

"It's no use," he muttered.

Estelle continued working.

He felt a sense of sadness tinged with respect when he looked at her. Her clothes, her hair, were covered with dust. Her nails were torn and ragged.

With an oath he hauled her to her feet. "It's over, Estelle. It was a lovely dream, but it isn't meant to be. Now it's time to admit defeat."

"I won't. I can't. You can't either, Rob. You can't let everything you love fall into Griffin Mackenzie's hands."

He touched a hand to her hair. "Not everything I love will be his."

For the space of a heartbeat she didn't understand. Then,

as the knowledge of what he'd said penetrated, she started to weep.

He pulled her into his arms and pressed his face to her hair. "I do love this place. And all the things in it. But they're not nearly as important as you've become to me, Estelle. Don't you see? Griff will have only things. But I'll have the memory of what we shared here." He lifted her chin and brushed a kiss over her lips. "And in the end Griff will have nothing. And I'll have everything."

As Jamie watched, he was overcome with bittersweet memories. Of a father and mother who had loved each other just this way. Who had bravely faced the inevitable with the same courage, the same stoic determination.

"Is that it, then?" he whispered.

"Aye." Rob looked at Estelle.

They both turned to Jamie and held out their arms, and the lad allowed himself to be drawn into their embrace. For just a moment, as he squeezed his eyes tightly shut, he was almost able to imagine he was being held by his own father and mother.

But then he opened his eyes and knew he was still here. Trapped between heaven and earth.

"Don't look so sad, Jamie." Estelle kissed his tears-tained cheeks. "If you wish, we'll keep on searching."

Rob shook his head. "You're exhausted. We all are. Go up and shower, and try to get some sleep."

"What about you?" She studied the weary look in his eyes, the dark stubble of beard, the slump of his shoulders. Though he had tried to keep her spirits up, his own were battered.

"I've told the bankers to be here at nine. The mayor of Dunfield, as well as the council and police chief, were included, since it will affect all of them. We'll formally sign the documents and turn over everything to Griff."

At the very mention of that, Estelle saw Jamie shimmer, then disappear. With a sigh of defeat she linked her fingers through Rob's and together they walked out of the room.

●   ●   ●

Estelle passed a hand over her eyes in a gesture of weariness as she climbed the stairs to her room. What a fool she'd been. She'd honestly believed that somewhere in that old playroom they would find the mythical Star of Scotland. She'd hoped that peeling away the wood and revealing the original walls might at least trigger some glimmer of memory in Jamie's subconscious.

What had happened during that terrible siege? Had Jamie panicked as he believed? Not that it was anything to be ashamed of. He was only a lad. And he'd loved his mother and father and little brother so deeply. It must have been a nightmarish ordeal for him. Still, the fact that he was still here seemed somehow connected to his actions on that fateful day.

She passed the portrait of his parents and paused. She could see why he was reminded of his mother whenever he looked at her. Like the woman in the portrait, she had the same auburn hair, the same green eyes.

She studied the lovely, flowing gown with long, tapered sleeves and a high circlet of lace at the throat. There had been dozens of such gowns in the trunks stored in the tower room.

Suddenly she had a flash of insight. Could it possibly work? She shook her head. It might prove to be just another dead end. But it was worth a try.

Her exhaustion dissolved as she raced along the hallway, taking the steps to the tower two at a time.

Estelle studied herself in the mirror, fussing with her hair until she was satisfied that it closely resembled the hair of the woman in the portrait. Then she stepped back to view the gown. The fabric was so fragile the seams were coming apart. But the neckline was the same, with a high, tight circlet of lace at the throat and long tapered sleeves edged with matching lace at the cuffs. The fact that the skirt was so long she was tripping over it didn't matter.

She caught the skirt in her hands and descended the stairs.

When she entered the playroom, she was surprised to see

that Fergus had already swept up the debris. It lay in several piles of wood and sawdust and broken bricks and mortar, to be carted away later.

A second pile of dust-covered toys lay nearby. The wooden rocking horse. The child's sword.

By now, she surmised, Fergus would be upstairs, helping Sir Charles to dress and prepare for the dreadful day ahead. And Rob. Rob would be facing his bleak future the same way he faced everything. With courage and dignity.

"Jamie." She walked to the middle of the room and slowly circled. "Jamie. Please come out. I need you."

Out of the corner of her eye she saw a movement and turned to see the little boy, his hand over his mouth, yawning loudly. He blinked, then, seeing her, opened his eyes wide.

"Mother. Ye've come for me."

"Aye." She swallowed, fighting a wave of guilt. It was a sign of her desperation that though what she was doing might save Rob, it would be seen as nothing but a cruel hoax by this tenderhearted lad.

"I knew ye'd come one day. Are we goin' home now?"

"Not yet, Jamie lad." She clutched her hands together tightly, so afraid her voice would break and give her away. "First you must prove yourself worthy."

"I will, Mother. I'll do anything. Just tell me what I must do."

"You must bring me the Star of Scotland, my son."

"But I dunna know where it is."

"Close your eyes, Jamie. Then search your mind. Think back. I know you'll remember."

Just as he did, a voice from the doorway startled her.

"What's this?" Griff stared around with a look of puzzlement. Then, as he saw the devastation to the room, the realization dawned. "You knew."

"Knew what?" Estelle stared at him blankly.

"I thought I was the only one who had the complete history of Castle Clough. Patience swore to me that she hadn't told a soul about her discovery."

"Discovery?"

"Don't act so innocent, Professor. Obviously you uncovered the same facts that my late wife did."

"Yes. Of course. The facts." Though she hadn't a clue,
she struggled to keep her features composed.

"Patience believed, from her research, that since the Star
of Scotland has never surfaced, it has to be still hidden
somewhere in this room. It was the last place the ghost had
been."

"Ghost? Are you saying there's a ghost in Castle
Clough?"

He seemed to notice her odd costume for the first time.
In quick strides he crossed the room and caught her by the
arm. "What game are you playing now, Professor?"

She tried to pull away. "I don't know what you mean."

"You know entirely too much. I was certain of it when
I first met you. And I knew, even then, that I should have
had you . . . eliminated, before you went any further."

"Let go of me, Mr. Mackenzie."

"Not this time, Professor. You've found the Star of Scotland, haven't you?" He plucked a small, thin object from
his pocket. When he touched a finger to a button, it opened
to reveal a razor-sharp blade. "If you value your life, you'll
give it to me. Now." He pressed the blade to her throat.

"Is this what you did to your wife?"

He laughed, a high-pitched sound that scraped her
nerves. "It wouldn't do to have the wife of the very successful Griffin Mackenzie found with her throat slit. I
merely broke her lovely neck, then pushed her down a flight
of stairs. It was neat and quick and final."

The ease with which he described such a gruesome event
made her shudder. "And how will you explain this?"

"Easy enough. A thief. One who saw the signs of digging for treasure and decided to help himself. The authorities will be convinced when they see these piles of rubble.
You surprised him, and he was forced to kill you before
fleeing." He pressed the blade until he drew a thin line of
blood. "Now give me the Star of Scotland, Professor. Or
do you think it's worth dying for?"

"Nay." Jamie appeared in a shimmer of heat. "Dinna harm my mother."

"What this?" Griff shook his head and tightened his grasp on Estelle. "What sort of trick are you playing?"

"It's no trick!" the boy cried. "Unhand my mother, and I'll give ye what ye seek."

Griff's eyes narrowed in anger. "I don't know who or what you are, but I'm not stupid enough to do what you ask. First you'll produce the Star of Scotland. Then I'll let go of the woman."

"All right, then." With tears nearly blinding him, Jamie raced across the room and picked up the child's sword from a pile of rubble.

"You think you'll fight me with that toy?" Griff threw back his head and laughed.

"Nay." Jamie grasped the sword by the blade and pointed to the jeweled hilt. There, in the center, was a star-shaped diamond the size of a walnut.

Griff's eyes widened as the truth dawned. Through all the centuries, everyone had looked for the treasure in some secret place. But all this time it had been in plain view, and never once had anyone recognized it for what it was.

"Oh, Jamie!" Estelle could hardly believe her eyes. "You finally remembered."

"Aye, Mother. All these years it had been wiped from my mind, but seeing you again gave me back my memory." He dug his chubby fingers into the hilt until the jewel slipped free and dropped into his palm. Then he walked toward Griff, with his hand outstretched. "Here's what you want. Now release my mother."

"Gladly." Griff shoved her roughly aside and reached for the jewel. As he did, Jamie reached up with his other hand, thrusting a dagger into Griff's stomach.

For a moment the man was too stunned to react. Then, enraged and in pain, he brought his hand out in a wide arc, intent upon slashing Estelle.

"Nay!" With a cry Jamie pushed her aside, taking the blow meant for her.

The force of it sent him staggering backward, the knife buried deep in his small chest.

"Oh, no! Jamie, no!" Estelle dropped to the floor, cradling the boy's head in her lap.

"Now I'll just take what's mine," Griff muttered as he started toward them.

"The only thing that's yours is a future in prison, Griff." The sound of Rob's voice stopped his old enemy in his tracks.

When he looked up, Griff saw Rob standing in the doorway, holding his ancestor's jeweled sword.

"Do you think you're man enough to use that?" Griff challenged.

Rob's voice was pure ice as he stepped closer, lifting the sword as he did. "There's only one way to find out."

Griff glanced beyond him to the doorway and realized that they weren't alone. Crowding in behind Sir Charles and Fergus were Desmond and Alfred, half a dozen bankers, and the mayor and police chief of the nearby village of Dunfield.

Knowing he was defeated, Griff lifted his hands in surrender.

At once the police chief strode forward and secured his hands with handcuffs.

"It was self-defense." Griff's voice rang with authority. "I'll never be convicted. It's obvious this woman is crazy. You can tell by her ridiculous costume. She attacked me when I walked in."

"Jamie is dying!" she cried, "and this is the man who inflicted the fatal wound." But she knew by the puzzled looks on the faces of the strangers in the doorway that they couldn't see the lad.

Griff shot her a look of triumph. "You see? She's absolutely mad."

"Rob." She turned to him in desperation. "Griffin Mackenzie confessed to killing your sister."

With a cry of rage Rob grabbed the front of Griff's shirt and aimed his sword at his heart.

"Please, your lordship," the chief said sternly. "Let the authorities handle this."

"Aye." With a long, slow hiss of anger Rob leaned close to whisper, "I wish you had given me the satisfaction of avenging my sister's death. But at least I know you'll pay, Griff. For the rest of your miserable life."

He tossed the sword aside and knelt beside Estelle, watching helplessly as she stroked the lad's cheek.

"Hold on, Jamie," she whispered through her tears. "You were so brave."

She looked up at Rob. "This is all my fault. I tricked him into believing I was his mother so that it would jog his memory about the jewel. But I never intended this. He took the blow meant for me."

Rob wrapped an arm around her shoulders. Against her temple he murmured, "Don't you see? It's what he wanted to do that first time, and couldn't. Now he's had his chance to get it right."

Her eyes widened as she realized the truth of it. And then, as they both watched, Jamie's eyes opened, and he smiled. "This is for you, Lord Cameron. And for all the Camerons through the centuries. Guard it well." He handed him the Star of Scotland. Then he looked over, and his smile grew radiant. "There you are, Mother. I've been waiting so long."

At first Estelle struggled with guilt, thinking she had once again deceived the poor lad. Then she realized that he wasn't looking at her. He was looking just beyond her. She turned to see a shimmer of light. And then, still smiling, Jamie began to glow, brighter and brighter, until the light was so brilliant that she and Rob had to shield their eyes.

"Are we going home now?" Jamie whispered.

There was a sound like the rushing of wind, and then the room went eerily silent.

While the others looked on without comprehension, Rob helped Estelle to her feet, then drew her into his arms, where she wept uncontrollably.

Epilogue

THE HOUSE WAS strangely silent. For a while the grounds of Castle Clough had been turned into a media circus as news photographers vied for glimpses of the notorious Griffin Mackenzie being led away. The authorities had conducted endless hours of interviews. A score of security officials from the government had already taken the Star of Scotland to a safe place, until the government could work out with Lord Cameron the details of its future. Though all agreed that the priceless treasure was the property of the Cameron clan, Rob had generously suggested that it was too important to be locked away in a vault. In time it would be put on view, presumably in a public building, for the whole world to admire.

Even now Rob and his lawyers were in the library meeting with representatives of both the government and the bank, and historians from several museums, reviewing the legalities involved.

Estelle folded the ivory wool dress and set it in her suitcase. She thought of the night she had worn it, then turned toward the window, deep in thought. Who would have ever believed that a few short weeks in Scotland would change her life so dramatically? She had lost her heart and for a while thought she was losing her mind. She would never see life in quite the same narrow way again.

Upon hearing the knock on the door she looked up.

Fergus entered, carrying an armload of logs. Without a word he bent and tended the fire, then stood, wiping his hands on his pants.

"Thank you, Fergus." She managed a smile. "I'll be finished packing soon. I'm expecting a car and driver within the hour. Could you come back shortly and carry my luggage downstairs?"

He nodded, then walked out of the room.

A few minutes later Estelle heard a knock at the door and hurried over. Sir Charles was seated in his wheelchair, with Fergus behind him.

"May I come in, my dear?"

"Of course, Sir Charles." She held the door while Fergus pushed him across the threshold.

Once inside, he waved the lad away.

"So." He glanced at her luggage. "It's as Fergus told me. You're leaving."

She nodded, no longer curious as to how the lad communicated. Perhaps he spoke. Maybe he used sign language. It wouldn't surprise her if he simply transferred his thoughts to others. Here in this fanciful place, anything was possible. "My work here is over, Sir Charles."

"Is it?" He pushed on the wheels of his chair, propelling himself around the room. "What about Rob?" He turned his head to study her carefully. "Do you love him?"

She swallowed. "Yes, but . . ."

"Do you think he loves you?"

"I think . . ." She chose her words carefully. "I think, now that his debt has been cleared, he will want some time to himself. Time to think about the future. As for me, it's time I got back to New York. To reality." A reality that didn't include life in a castle with a wealthy, handsome

Highland lord. That was for novels. It didn't happen in real life. Like everyone and everything else in this place, she had simply fallen under a spell.

"Ah, yes. New York. I'm sure one must be strong and . . . firmly grounded to survive there."

"Exactly. After a lifetime there, I know a little about survival."

He smiled then and halted his chair in front of her dresser. For long moments he stared at the framed picture of a young Estelle with a beautiful, auburn-haired woman. His smile faded, and he plucked the photo from her dresser.

She saw him trace his finger over the woman in the picture. "What are you doing, Sir Charles?"

"Remembering." He looked up. "I should have known. You look like her, you know."

"My aunt?"

"Aye. Rose. I wasn't certain, of course. You'd never told me her name. But the moment I saw you, I thought it was a possibility."

"I don't understand . . ."

"I told you I was in love once, and for that one brief summer, I was deliriously happy. But events happened that changed the course of both our lives forever. Her sister and brother-in-law died, and there was a child to raise. And my own family was in need of me."

Estelle's mouth dropped open, but no words came out. Finally she managed to whisper, "You and Aunt Rose?"

"Aye, lass. Did she never speak of it?"

Estelle shook her head. "She said only that she had loved once, and it was enough to sustain her for a lifetime. I always thought it too painful for her to talk about. But I never dreamed . . ."

"It was the same for me. It's the curse of Castle Clough, my dear. Cameron men love too deeply. They give their hearts but once. And that one woman is loved with a depth of passion that is all-consuming. So you see, when you wondered aloud if your aunt had a hand in getting you here, you now have the answer. You were meant to be here. With Rob." He pressed the photo to his heart. "And I was meant to learn the truth. My beloved Rose never married another. She went to her grave loving only me. Which means that if we couldn't be together in this life, we will surely be together in the next.'' He looked up at Estelle. ''Do you know what love, true love, really means?''

''I think I do.''

''If you do, you must know that Rob is under the same curse. If you go, you'll condemn him to a life of loneliness. Is that what you want?''

''I want . . . I want to do what's right. I want to give Rob a chance to enjoy this new freedom. I want . . .'' She was too overcome to speak. All she could do was shake her head. Suddenly chilled to the bone, she went to the fireplace and stood staring into the flames.

She didn't know how long she stood there. But when she turned, Sir Charles was gone. And Rob was standing behind her.

''Estelle.'' He saw the pain and confusion in her eyes and clenched a fist at his side. ''I wanted to come to you sooner.'' He ran a hand through his hair in frustration. ''So many demands on my time. So many interruptions. But all I really wanted was to be here with you. I can see that you've been deeply disturbed by all that has happened. For that I'm truly sorry.''

She turned back to stare at the flames. ''It really happened, didn't it, Rob? Even though the others swore they didn't see or hear any of it, we didn't just dream it, did we?''

''It truly happened. Jamie's gone, love. Our little scamp has finally gone home. And though I'm happy for him, I'll miss him.''

When she started to weep silently, he drew her close. Against her hair he whispered, ''Maybe we'll be blessed with a little scamp of our own. That is, if you'd be willing to uproot yourself and make your life with a country farmer in this lonely, out-of-the-way village in the middle of the Highlands.''

''How can you . . .'' She tried to laugh, but it came out in a sob. ''. . . be so sure? After all we've been through?''

"I've never been so sure of anything in my life. And though the time isn't right, and the setting isn't romantic, I'm humbly asking you to marry me."

"Oh, Rob." She offered her lips, and he kissed her with such tenderness, she felt her heart nearly break. "I don't need sweet words or romantic settings. What you've just described sounds like pure heaven. I can't think of anything I'd rather do than spend the rest of my life here in this magical, wonderful place with you."

"Estelle. My little star. I love you desperately." He pressed slow, deliberate kisses on each of her eyelids, her cheeks, the tip of her nose. "I couldn't bear to spend even one night without you. If you agree, I'll have the mayor of Dunfield do the honors tomorrow."

She wrapped her arms around his neck and gave a little laugh of pure delight. Then she caught his hand. "Come on, Rob. We'll go and tell your uncle. He'll be so happy."

"In a while, love." He lifted a hand to the buttons of her prim, high-necked blouse and slowly unfastened each one before pressing his lips to the hollow of her throat. "But first I just want to love you. The way all the Camerons have loved their women, from the beginning of time."

As she lost herself in his kisses, Estelle found herself blessing the one who had put such a tantalizing curse on Castle Clough. Because of it, she would one day die the happiest of women. But not young, she vowed. For that wasn't a part of the curse at all. The curse was love. Enough love to last a lifetime and beyond. Or at least until they had filled these lonely rooms with enough Camerons to carry on the tradition for generations to come.

STARRY, STARRY NIGHT

★

Marianne Willman

*For my sisters, Jane Clark, Elizabeth Clancy-Brown, and
Lowell Montgomery Clark*

*For my other sisters—Nora Roberts, Ruth Ryan Langan,
Jill Gregory, Karen Katz, and Laura Sparrow*

And for every dreamer who ever hoped and wished upon a star

1

Cornwall

LILY KENDALL WAS lost.

What had been a pleasant evening walk between the dramatic Cornish cliffs and the dark, foaming waves had become a dangerous venture. She'd strayed too far.

One moment the evening sky was a Van Gogh painting, all sapphire depths and bright, swirling stars. The next it was a blank gray canvas, as the fog came sweeping in from the bay. The sparkling indigo sea had vanished, and the craggy walls of lichen-covered rock had as well. It had seemed to happen in a literal blink of the eye.

And in the same time span, she had transformed herself from a sophisticated American traveler into a silly tourist caricature.

Somewhere behind her, the picturesque village with its narrow houses tiled in colorful slate and steep, cobbled streets was nestled cozily against a sharp upthrust of land.

Somewhere ahead—not too far, Lily prayed—lay the gentle slope up from the bay and along the strand to the lovely old hotel where she was staying. Exactly where, was the question. And the way back was strewn with great boulders and slippery, ankle-twisting stones.

Taking the shortcut along the base of the cliffs had been a miscalculation. A bad one. In fact, she thought distractedly, this whole trip was turning out to be a huge mistake.

She wished she were back home in her apartment in Washington, D.C., curled up in her fuzzy robe, watching an old movie on video. She would even trade her present adventure in for her familiar workaday world of fluorescent lights and gray filing cabinets, beige computers and worn metal desks.

But lately she had been feeling just as lost there, as if she were being smothered by layers of rules and protocol. The offer of promotion into the ranks of upper management had thrown her into a panic.

"My advice to you, Miss Kendall," her supervisor had told her, "is to take all your accumulated vacation days. Rethink your priorities. If you turn down this promotion, then they are certainly not here at the Department of Transportation."

This wild Cornish coast was as far removed from Washington's corridors of power as anything could be. The heavy mist clung to Lily, slid over her skin like a cool caress as she worked her way across the slippery strand. The breeze teased wisps out of her long blond braid as she struggled to get her bearings—a task that was increasingly impossible in the distorting layers of thickening fog.

Her supervisor's words had shaken her. She'd envisioned herself years from now, her identity gone, fossilized in the artificial world of work and career. How had she gotten so far from the dreams she'd woven for herself in college?

The decision of where to go to do this rethinking of priorities hadn't been difficult. Caribbean beaches seemed to be made for honeymooning couples, and the idea of joining a tour group lacked appeal. Her mother's ancestors had come from Cornwall. With its fantastic nineteenth-century bridge spanning the Tamar, its legends of Ygraine, King Arthur, and Merlin, that westernmost tip of Great Britain had always called to her—and how could she resist exploring a place with quaint names like Lostwithiel, Rump's Point, Land's End, and Mousehole?

She now stood on a shingle beach in a foreign country, lost, with an impenetrable mist rising like ancient wraiths around her.

Lily forced herself to listen. She could hear the sound of the waves rolling in to her right, could sense the massive bulk of the granite headland to her left, from the echoes bouncing back. A strange yearning filled her, a deep and terrible loneliness, as if she were the last person on the face of the earth. Wrapping her arms around herself for warmth, she headed in the direction that she thought led to the granite base of the cliffs.

The fog thickened and took on the texture and density of a damp wool sock. She was cold, cocooned in a narrow, alien world that was devoid of shape and color. The sound of her footsteps on the shingle beach was muffled, swallowed up by the thickening atmosphere. The sound of the wind was like a chorus of whispers, filled with a desperate, infinite longing. A shiver danced up her back.

Lily knew she had no business taking unknown routes in an unfamiliar landscape. She was a city girl, born and bred to concrete, asphalt, and taxis, to museums and theaters and high-rise apartments, and Chinese takeout on the corner. But hadn't that been part of the reason she'd come here to Cornwall, because it was far removed from her workaday life and totally different?

"Picturesque, and very restful," the travel agent had told her. "Calm."

A slimy tendril of seaweed snaked around Lily's bare ankle, and she yelped in alarm. "Calm, my ass!"

She kicked the attacking weed away. No need to panic. She was an intelligent and resourceful adult—and, she tried to tell herself, she was having an adventure. "I'll laugh at myself in the morning!"

The sound of her own voice was so comforting that Lily

almost convinced herself. Then another cold wave crashed against the shore, stronger than the last. It came hissing through the shingle as if it were alive, tugging at her ankles, urging her to follow it home to the sea.

Her canvas summer shoes filled with water, and before she could take them off to shake it out, another wave came swirling in. The sand sucked at her feet, and the cold water stung her bare legs. The lower half of her expensive embroidered linen dress was soaked and dripping. This wasn't the pleasant bay she'd seen in the brochures. Not by a long shot.

Squelching along in her sodden shoes, Lily moved up the beach toward the relative safety of the bluffs. Anything to get away from the increasing roar of the waves, the reach of the hungry sea.

All she had to do now was find the base of the cliffs and follow the headland around to the other side—without breaking a leg, getting caught by the tide, or succumbing to hypothermia.

Her right foot skittered on something slimy, and she recoiled. God only knew what disgusting things the waves might have cast up! Another wave slammed up the steep shore, and she lost her footing. The swirling, foaming water undercut the rocks beneath her feet.

One moment she was fighting to keep her balance, the next she was caught in a cold, salty wall of water, being sucked out toward the blackness of the bay.

Gut-wrenching fear gripped Rees Tregarrick as he braved the strong wind. No one from the village was fool enough to stray past Yearning Head by night. But there was a woman down at the base of the cliffs, picking her way through rocks as if she were out on a Sunday shell-gathering expedition.

He knew, beyond a doubt, that it was the woman who haunted his dreams. Whether ghost or reality, he had to know. If she was real, her danger was acute.

Atop the headland, the sky was unusually clear and filled with the largest, most scintillating stars he'd ever seen—

even at sea. The stars had drawn him out of the house toward the cliff's very edge. He hadn't gone there in the three years of his recuperation. Of his self-imposed sentence and exile. The house was his world. The sea—once his mistress, his lover—formed the bars of his invisible prison, locking him away on land.

But tonight he'd been drawn to the headland. No, had almost been forced here. While his mind was filled with tortured thoughts of loneliness and death . . . of Catherine . . . *she* had come lightly down the shingle beach, lost and out of her element, like a sea-maiden cast up from the waves onto the shore.

It was still a long way to the stairs carved into the granite of the headland. His stomach clenched. Would he get there in time, or would she be washed out with the undertow before his very eyes? He didn't think he could bear to see her white body thrown against the rocks. The urge to flee back to the safety of the house was almost as potent as the urge to save her.

Rees Tregarrick stumbled and cursed his way through the dark, wondering if he would be in time to rescue her from the cold, dark sea.

Lily's skirt snagged on the edge of a rock, and she wedged herself against it with all her might. When the wave retreated, she struggled to her feet again, barely managing to keep her shoes from being washed away.

Shivering in her light dress, chest heaving with exertion and fear, she scrambled away from the bay. Her situation was desperate, and she prayed to find her way safely back to the resort. Instead of a prayer, a jingle she'd learned in her grade-school days floated into Lily's mind:

> *Little star, do not hide*
> *Please come out and be my guide.*
> *Through rain and snow and darkest night,*
> *Guide me with your shining light.*

Lily lifted her eyes . . . and *there it was!*
It was incredible, the largest star she'd ever seen. And

the only one visible through the shifting layers of fog overhead. Instinct urged her to follow it, and she obeyed. With
every step the light led her farther away from the restless
murmur of the sea.

Thank God!

The nearer she got to the cliffs, the thinner the fog grew,
until it shredded on the rocks like old lace. She had never
realized that the air could have so many different shapes
and textures.

She was still disoriented, but the star led Lily on, away
from the increasing roar of the waves. Now and again the
star vanished behind the prowlike outthrust of the headland.
Each time, her heart turned over. She was terribly afraid
that she would lose sight of it for good.

A few more feet, and suddenly she stopped dead. This
couldn't be right. It seemed the star was leading her back
toward the water now. That felt wrong at best, and dangerous at worst. She hesitated. Foolish to trust her life to a
light that could be far out at sea for all she knew. Changing
her direction, she turned back toward the cliffs. She hadn't
gone ten feet when she heard a voice carried on the wind:

"Not that way! Tack around to your former position."

Lily was startled. The voice was deep, male, and urgent.
"What? Where are you?"

*"Damn it, keep moving toward the headland! The tide
is about to rush in. Hurry, or you'll be swept away!"*

The tide? *Jesus!* Her teeth chattered in fright and cold.
"Where are you? I can't see you."

*"Waste no time talking! Keep bearing to port, lass. No,
damn your eyes! That's starboard. Turn to your left! Ah,
that's right! Hurry now."*

The urgency in the man's voice spurred Lily to action.
She had to trust him. She could hear the waves roaring as
they smashed against the rocky shelf just past the headland.
Not much time! Dashing over the loose shingle, she turned
her ankle and swore as a line of fire seared up her leg.

"Come on, lass. You can do it!"

Half hopping, half sliding, and swearing fully, Lily followed the voice. The fog was thinning now, and she could

see the dark waves coming, row on row, against the foot of the cliffs ahead. She knew without looking back that the way behind her was already under water. Too late!

"Oh, God!"

"You're there! You've made it! Only another step . . ."

Lily stumbled over a snag of driftwood and pitched forward. Her hand touched something cold and scaly, and recoiled instinctively. Then she realized it was only a rusty metal handrail. There were stairs leading up, barely visible in the mist, and burning like a beacon above them was that single scintillating star.

Catching the rail, she hauled herself up the steps as quickly as her numbed feet would go. They were rough, carved from the cliff itself, but felt wonderfully solid after the shifting surface of the beach. The sea thundered up behind her, and she felt the wave break against the bottom step in a cold spray. Fear gave her the strength to bolt up the next steps. She was almost at the top when she heard the roar of an incoming wave, louder and higher than the last.

Despair and disbelief rattled her: *Jesus! I'm not going to make it!*

A hand reached out to grasp her arm roughly. "Easy, there, lass. I've got you!"

Now a second hand grasped her other wrist, pulling her off her feet and up against the slick granite surface of the rock. Her rescuer let one hand go free. Lily dangled helplessly, a sob lodged like a bone in her throat. The misty world reeled in a haze of vertigo. She smelled wet wool and male sweat. Then a strong arm wrapped tightly about her waist, and she was half hauled, half carried up and over to the top of the cliff.

She sat against a rock, gasping for breath, her fingers digging into the wet grasses. A hand brushed her cheek. "It's all right, lass. I wasn't sure for a moment if you'd make it free of the waves. But you managed . . . barely."

She was tired and weak with reaction. "Why didn't you help me sooner, instead of just shouting at me?"

"I would have, if I could."

For just a moment the fog swirled and shifted. She had a fleeting glimpse of a man in his prime bending over her: thick, dark hair, hawklike features, a firm, sensual mouth. He was dressed in a heavy fisherman's sweater of ivory wool and leaned on a crutch.

"Oh, God! I didn't know . . . I'm sorry!"

His voice was curt. "No more sorry than I. Come with me. Don't dawdle."

Lily was too cold and wet and frightened to argue.

She didn't even ask where they were headed. At the moment she would have cheerfully gone off with Norman Bates, Freddy Krueger, and the entire cast of a Hollywood horror film.

"Wait!" He stripped off his heavy sweater, then pulled it over hers. It came past down her knees. As Lily snuggled into the warm wool, the cold bite of the wind eased.

"Come along. We'll get you to shelter."

Her rescuer was strong, despite his limp, and his hand on her arm urged her forward with each flagging step. Shock and cold had taken a toll on her energy, and she stumbled on her injured ankle, but he covered the ground without a misstep.

"How can you see where we're going in this fog?"

"Fog?" He gave her a curious look, then shook his head. "I know every inch of this godforsaken place," he said, propelling her onward.

They passed through an iron gate set in a lichened granite wall. Once they were through it, the fog dissipated like magic. It was only then that Lily saw the lighted windows of a Victorian facade. Like the village houses, it was made of local granite and slate; but the lines were softened by porches and bays, gables and spires, and gracefully curved towers.

Light spilled from the far turret's beautiful and unusual window. Myriad triangles of golden glass radiated from a central diamond-shaped pane. It glowed in the misty haze, looking for all the world, Lily thought, like something from a Christmas card.

STARRY, STARRY, NIGHT ★ 291

"The star!" she exclaimed. "I saw it from below. I thought it was real!"

He didn't answer.

Lightning shattered the blackness in the distance, illuminating the roiling clouds with orange light. It was a startling sight, as if the night had cracked open, revealing hints of a molten sky. He stopped in midstride and tipped his head back defiantly. Another flash of lightning was reflected in his eyes. Lily thought he swore beneath his breath, but the wind snatched away the words.

His grip tightened on her elbow, and he guided her purposefully toward the house. Lily's ankle felt better, but she still had to hurry to keep pace.

She had her bearings now. The cliff road picked up at the end of the narrow drive. Just down the steep hill and around the bend, the village of St. Dunstan clung to the granite shore. But—shouldn't the red lights on the steel communications antenna above the harbor be visible from here?

With every step removed from danger, her survival instincts came more to the fore. There was no reason she couldn't continue on to her hotel. Even if the threatening rain did materialize, she would be no wetter than she was now, and the brisk walk would warm her.

She hadn't lived most of her life in Washington, D.C., without picking up a certain degree of cynicism: Compounding one mistake with another wasn't very wise. Her companion had rescued her, yes, but he was still a complete stranger.

They were almost to the porch when she pulled away. "Words are inadequate, but—thank you. I'm five minutes from my hotel. If you'd be kind enough to let me keep your sweater until morning, I'll be on my way," she said firmly.

"Don't be more daft than you've already proved!" he said sharply. "You'd not get far in this weather."

On the heels of his words a hard rain came rattling out of the night, and the wind tore through the trees. A scattering of twigs and dried leaves blew across the cobbles.

He brought her up to the door and turned the handle. It swung wide to reveal a paneled hall with a grand, winding staircase at one side and a thin woman in a dark dress standing anxiously at its foot.

When she saw them she went paper-white, and put a hand over her heart. "Captain Tregarrick!"

Lily was aware of how she must look, with water dripping from her hair and her dress plastered against her body. She started to shiver violently.

"The little fool was caught below the cliffs and almost washed away," he said harshly.

Without another word, the man the other woman had called Captain Tregarrick ushered Lily through the reception hall toward the stairs, past paintings in heavy frames and beneath the light of twin lamps.

The woman gathered her scattered wits. "What a start you gave me! I thought . . . Well, never mind what I thought. Thank the good Lord, you reached the poor girl in time!"

She hurried to Lily's side. "Come in, come in, poor dear. We'll have you set to rights before you know it."

"Where do you want her, Mrs. Penhale?"

"In the kitchen, of course. It's warmest there, and I've a kettle already on the boil."

There was something about the woman, with her welcoming blue eyes and concerned expression, that eased Lily's fears. No harm would come to her here.

As they passed the japanned sideboard by the staircase, she had her first good look at her rescuer in the warm light of the oil lamps. Mist beaded his thick, dark hair and clung to his lashes. His straight brows were drawn into a scowl above an aquiline nose, and he had the stubborn jaw and firm mouth of a pirate-hero from an old MGM swashbuckler.

He tossed his crutch onto a satin settee and snatched up a blackthorn cane from the large majolica vase used as an umbrella holder. Every movement was swift and economical.

Lily studied him. *Lean and stern as the granite cliffs of*

the headland, she thought. His hard-muscled body, beneath the rain-smoothed striped cotton shirt, seemed carved of the same material.

He was, Lily thought, quite simply the best-looking man she'd ever seen.

And, apparently, the angriest. That much was evident in the harsh lines that bracketed his eyes and mouth. He hadn't once looked squarely at her. Outside, those eyes had seemed darker than the night around them. But they weren't black at all. His irises were dark gray and blue flecked with white, like a wind-chased sea. She could sense, more than see, the bitter emotion that flickered in their fathomless depths.

"See to her needs," he told the woman brusquely. "Keep her out of my sight."

With those kind words of welcome, he handed Lily over into Mrs. Penhale's care.

2

Without so much as a good-bye, Captain Tregarrick vanished through the open door into what appeared to be a cozy study, and shut it behind him. The room seemed vastly emptier without his dominating presence.

Then Lily was whisked away toward the back of the house and through a green baize door. "Is he always so outgoing and friendly?" she asked, barely reining in her sarcasm.

"You'll not mind his ways," the woman said as they entered the warm kitchen. "The captain is not used to having strangers about. Nor has he ever been one to pass the time of day. Comes of being off to sea, no doubt. Grew up on the bay, he did, sailing his little boat from the time he was a lad."

The housekeeper plucked a colorful quilt from the back of a painted rocker and clucked over Lily like a hen with one chick. "Poor lamb, let's get you warm. Sit here, by the fire."

The kitchen was all whitewashed stone, scrubbed pine, and shining pots and pans. A fat lamp with a white opal-glass shade hung over the table. The heat of an ancient cooker—enameled a stunningly bright yellow—made the big room cheerful and as warm as toast.

The housekeeper dipped out a hearty serving of soup and took a thick slice from a crusty loaf of bread. "Eat up, while I serve the tea."

She smiled as she poured a generous splash of liquid from an amber bottle into the stout china mug. "You're new to St. Dunstan, Miss . . . ?" The woman managed to make the question seem like a friendly comment.

"Yes. I'm Lily Kendall. I'm staying at the Castle Inn."

"And I am Mrs. Penhale. I keep house for Captain Tregarrick."

"It's a big house to keep!" Lily said, stirring sugar into the tea. In its day, the mansion would have been filled with housemaids and parlormaids and scullery girls. "It must be difficult to manage such a large place these days."

"Oh, aye. It's been hard since the missus was lost, and I feared for him," Mrs. Penhale said, leaving Lily more than a little confused. "You finish that up, and I'll just have a word with the captain."

"Of course."

Lily wondered if Captain Tregarrick had suffered his injury in service to his country or if there was a more mundane reason. Now that the adrenaline rush of danger had waned, the warmth of the room and the tot of brandy in the tea lulled her senses. She had such a cozy, contented feeling that she didn't want to stir. Certainly not to go back out in the fog and rain. By the time the housekeeper returned, she was nodding.

"It's all settled," Mrs. Penhale announced. "Mr. Tregarrick has sent word down to the inn. You'll spend the night here, snug and safe, and Jem will drive you down on the morrow."

Lily didn't resist. "Thank you, Mrs. Penhale. And please thank Mr. Tregarrick."

The strangeness of the situation took on a surreal atmosphere. *I am having an adventure!* Lily told herself, and was glad that years of rigid routine hadn't rotted away her ability to sit back and enjoy the unexpected. More than ever, she was glad she'd taken a leave and come to Cornwall. Everything about it was so vastly different from anything she knew at home.

And now the fog, the threatening tide, and the handsome, brooding master of the manor only added to her wonderful sense of unreality.

Or perhaps, she thought belatedly, *it's the brandy.*

In any case, she wasn't about to turn down an offer to spend a night in this marvelous house. And, truth to tell, she was hoping for another encounter with the handsome and taciturn Mr. Tregarrick. *Just to thank him,* she told herself. *That's all.*

The housekeeper took a small lamp and led her up the staircase and down a hall. Lily caught a glimpse of herself in the mirror behind the desk, her blond hair turned mouse-brown with dampness, her fair skin several shades paler with exhaustion. At the sight, she cringed. "Drowned rat" would be too kind a description.

"I've put you in the Green Chamber," Mrs. Penhale said. "It's at the end of the hall. There's a fire laid, and to my fancy, it's the prettiest bedchamber of the lot."

Lily looked around. "Where is the big window that looks like a star?"

Mrs. Penhale stopped short and turned to her. "It's at the far end of the corridor and up the winding stairs. But please . . . don't think of going up there, lass. Mr. Tregarrick doesn't allow it."

"Why?" Lily smiled. "Is it haunted?"

"Only by him," the housekeeper said sadly. "Ah, lass, only by him."

She started off again, and Lily had to hurry to keep up with her.

Rees Tregarrick paced the floor of the study. He had been almost happy in his isolation. One by one he'd learned to wind his strong emotions down, furling them like unneeded sails. He'd vowed he would stay at Star House until Catherine sent him a sign that she forgave him. In three years no sign had come.

Until tonight.

It had come with the storm and wind and near violence, in the person of a small, blond-tressed woman, with a heart-shaped face and a softly rounded body. The question was, What was he meant to do? He stared out the window at the slashing rain.

After Mrs. Penhale went off, Lily lay beneath the down comforter in the Green Chamber, in the flannel nightgown the housekeeper had provided. Warmth seeped into her bones as she watched the small flames of the banked fire contentedly. She couldn't think of a cozier place to be on a night of such wind and rain. The windows rattled in the gale, but the room was exquisite, far nicer than the one she'd taken at the Castle Inn. Light flickered on the white-painted woodwork and the walls hung with pale silk in green and rose to match the bed hangings.

The soft linen pillowcase was edged with crocheted lace and carried faint scents of sun-washed air, of sea lavender and lemon verbena. Lily imagined Mrs. Penhale gathering herbs and flowers from an old-fashioned garden and making little sachets to tuck among the household linens. *As if she'd have time, with this big house to look after!*

There was something to be said for the slower pace of the days gone by, Lily thought. In this old house the past seemed very real, just as it did in the village. She wished she could see the rest of the house, but doubted that the taciturn Mr. Tregarrick would invite her back for a guided tour.

An odd man, her rescuer. There was no doubt in Lily's mind that he'd saved her life. And then, after bringing her home, he'd casually dumped her on Mrs. Penhale, as if she were a bedraggled stray kitten he'd found shivering in the rain. A strange man.

An interesting man.

She wondered what had happened to him. Not whatever it was that had made the crutch and cane necessary, but whatever it was that had made his eyes so dark and angry. Even now she could vividly recall the restless energy he radiated. Walking beside him had been like standing beneath a high-tension wire. Every cell in her body had been aware of every cell in his.

She had to admit that she hoped she would see him in the morning, and at the thought she felt her heart speed up just a little. No doubt about it, Captain Tregarrick was the kind of man to get a woman's juices flowing.

A log popped in the fireplace, sending a shower of sparks up the chimney. As she waited for Mrs. Penhale's promised return, Lily watched the flames. The peaceful atmosphere of the room fell over her like an enchantment. No ringing phones and faxes, no clacking printers. No muffled sounds of television from some neighboring apartment. Only the wind, the fire, and the settling of the house.

It was like stepping back in time. Surely, she thought, the place had looked much the same: candles in ormolu sconces bracketing the mirror above the fireplace, a tufted velvet slipper chair, even a needlepoint footstool with small gilt feet. It was, Lily decided contentedly, exactly like something out of *Jane Eyre*.

All it lacked was a madwoman, howling in the attic.

She slid softly into dreams—and was rudely awakened by the fearsome sound of a woman's screams.

3

Lily bolted upright. The sun was up—had been for some time—and the door to the corridor was open. A girl in a red sweater and jeans stood just inside the threshold. Her eyes showed white around the irises, and she was shouting down the house as if she was demented.

The sound of running feet came from beyond the door. Lily heaved a sigh of relief. Help was on the way.

"What's all this, Portia? Found a mouse in the mattress or the moth in the carpet?" a male voice said.

A young man with reddish hair appeared beyond the young woman's shoulder. "What in bloody hell . . . !"

The girl had stopped screaming. She took a deep breath. "Sorry, James. I thought for a moment that she was a ghost."

"Catherine T.? She does have a bit of the look of her, doesn't she? Well, go down and ring up Constable Polkenny. Tell him we've got an intruder on our hands."

He pushed past the girl in the red sweater and faced Lily,

arms akimbo. "What the bloody hell do you think you're doing?" he said.

Lily glared at him. "I *was* sleeping!"

"I can see that." He moved closer.

Lily edged to the far side of the bed. "Good. Now, would you please go away?"

"Aye, I will. And bring the constable back with me. Then we'll see how that sits with you."

She frowned and pushed back her hair. "Is everyone under this roof, except for Mrs. Penhale, stark raving mad?"

A thought hit her belatedly. Mr. Tregarrick had seemed more than a little odd last evening. Perhaps she'd just committed a terrible gaffe.

Lily edged to the far side of the bed, in case she had to make a bolt for it. "Ah, this . . . er, isn't a sort of place for . . . I mean a . . . *a rest home?*"

James gaped at her. "No," he said. "It's a bloody museum."

It was Lily's turn to stare. "Oh!"

Small wonder that everything looked so authentic. She tucked a strand of hair behind her ear. "How peculiar. I didn't know! When Mr. Tregarrick brought me here last night, it never occurred to me that this wasn't a private home. And evidently no one told you that I was here."

James was regarding her oddly. He backed away toward the door. The girl he'd called Portia was still standing there, frowning at Lily. The young man scratched his chin thoughtfully. "Mr. Tregarrick."

"He rescued me on the headland last night. Saved my life, really. I was almost washed out to sea by the tide."

James turned his head to Portia, but his eyes never left Lily's face. "You had better ring up Dr. Landry as well."

"Look," Lily said, "I'm fine. I don't need a doctor. I need my clothes. The housekeeper took them to dry—Mrs. Penhale said she'd hang them in the kitchen by the stove." She saw the blank looks on their faces. "Mrs. Penhale, the housekeeper."

Portia hadn't moved an inch. She put her hands on her

hips. "There is no Mrs. Penhale here, although there was once, a long time ago. I have her receipt books. And as for your Captain Tregarrick, there's been no one by that name under this roof in almost a hundred years."

Lily was dressed and sitting on the edge of the bed when the doctor arrived. Portia had brought her scalding-hot black coffee and shared the last stale donuts in a bakery box with her while they waited.

James had found Lily's clothes in the kitchen, just as she'd said, neatly pegged out on a line stretched across the room. Her shoes had gone missing, and Portia had obligingly fetched a pair of rubber thong sandals from a service closet.

"I got them at a jumble sale and wear them when I hose down the terrace," she said. "Or when I'm pottering about my grandmother's garden, at Old Cross Farm. You can drop them back here anytime. Just leave them on the side porch if I've locked the place up."

Lily sipped her coffee. "You take care of the museum, then?"

Portia smiled, looking younger than the twenty-two years she'd claimed. "I'm the curator. I've a degree from university, but in reality I do a bit of everything: keep the catalogues up-to-date, dust the knickknacks and hoover the carpets, schedule group tours, and generally see that everything is kept shipshape and in good preservation."

"That's a weighty responsibility."

The girl dimpled. "It's a family tradition, you might say. Ah, there's the doctor now. He's got an ancient Morris-Mini and you can hear him come sputtering halfway up the hill from St. Dunstan."

A short time later he came up the stairs and into the Green Chamber. Dr. Landry was a kindly-looking man, with a thick thatch of silver hair and a military moustache. Lily let him give her a brief examination. The situation had her baffled.

"Ticker working, lungs clear, oriented to person, place,

and time," he announced. "Although I gather that time was rather out of whack for you earlier."

"It seemed so real," she told him a little shakily. "I would have *sworn* that it was!"

"Let me see. Ah, you've quite a knot here," he said, probing the side of Lily's head. "My guess is that it took quite a blow to put it there."

"It must have happened when I lost my footing in the waves. I did a foolish thing," she told him. "I went walking along the strand and got lost in the fog."

He tugged at his silver moustache. "At Yearning Head?"

"Is that what it's called? How peculiar."

"The maps call the headland Dunstan's Head. No one here calls it that, though. It's been Yearning Head as long as any can remember. Some say it's because the waves sound like lovers' mingled sighs; others who've tarried there claim that they were filled with a great longing, like a terrible loneliness, when the wind blows in and the tide is just right. The old-age pensioners say that if you yearn for something hard enough there, it will come to be."

Lily remembered the strange feelings that had swept through her. "It is a beautiful spot, but very eerie."

"Yes. A dangerous one, too. You were fortunate. It was high tide last night. Others have been less so, and were washed out to sea."

Lily shivered. "And I would have been another, if not for Captain Tregarrick ... uh, rather, for the man who saved me, whatever his name. He saw me from the cliff and guided me to the stairs carved into it, just in the nick of time. I would never have found them on my own."

From the corner of her eye, she saw the doctor give her the same long, assessing look that James had. "Tell me about the man you called Captain Tregarrick. Could you describe him to me?"

Lily closed her eyes and conjured up his image. "He's tall. Strong. Dark-haired, with a patrician nose and a stubborn-looking jaw. Oh, and his eyes! I thought they were black at first, but in the lamplight I could see they were as many shifting shades of blue and gray as the waters of the bay.''

"A poetic description.'' Landry cocked his head. "Many artists come to St. Dunstan to paint the views. Are you perhaps among them?''

Lily shook her head. "When I was in college I wanted to paint . . .'' She broke off.

"Ah, now that's interesting. Not to *be* a painter, but 'to paint.' Your choice of words tells me that painting is something with a great deal of meaning for you—yet you say you became a design engineer. Tell me, do you paint now?''

"No.''

"Will you tell me why?''

"I tried. I haven't the talent for it.'' She frowned. "It never came out the way I intended it.''

"You're a perfectionist, then.''

"That isn't the reason I forsook my canvases.'' She laughed. "It was my stunning lack of talent. I wanted to be a dashing artist, blending shapes and colors with abandon and genius. Unfortunately I can only copy what I see, like a camera. But not nearly as well!''

A gleam came into Dr. Landry's eye. "Tell me, was your hotel room furnished with local brochures?''

"There were some in the desk.'' She shrugged. "I glanced at a few and put them back. I wasn't interested in doing the usual 'touristy' things.''

"I believe the mystery is solved, young lady. Come along to the drawing room with me, and you'll understand what I mean.''

He escorted Lily down to the ground floor and through a set of high pocket doors. She wondered how she had missed the strategically placed velvet ropes that kept people from getting too close to the matching Oriental cabinets in the main hall, or the sign welcoming visitors to Star House. Gently she touched the bump at the back of her head. It *was* quite a knot. It seemed less real than her invented memories of the previous night.

The doctor escorted her to a sunny parlor with white

wainscoting and pale blue walls. It had elegant proportions, with long windows on two sides and a fireplace at the far end. Dr. Landry indicated the portrait over the mantel.

"Is there any resemblance to your mysterious rescuer?"

Lily's jaw dropped. She frowned up at the painting. The frame was formal and unfamiliar, but the pose and the subject were not. The dark-haired man in the painting wore a thick ivory fisherman's sweater, like the one she had worn last night. His head and upper torso were depicted against a background of blue sky and a bluer sea. She recognized St. Dunstan Bay, obviously in another century, its surface dotted with assorted sailing ships.

Whatever the portrait's age, the man who had sat for it was almost an exact double of the man who had rescued Lily on the cliff.

"They could be twins," she said slowly. "Except for his eyes. They're the same dark blue and gray, with those little flecks of white, but the expression in them is totally different."

"What do you mean?"

"The man in this portrait is young and happy and carefree. The one I met was older. Stern and bitter." Lily stopped and reconsidered. "No, I think I used the wrong words. Perhaps 'burdened' is a better choice. As if the weight of the world had come crashing down on him."

"That painting," Dr. Landry told her, "is of Rees Tregarrick. He captained his own clipper ship and made a fortune in the China trade. He's the most well-known citizen of St. Dunstan, having contributed generously to the village. His picture is found on the cover of local tourist guides, as well as several area businesses."

"I hadn't noticed."

"Perhaps not consciously. But without realizing it, you had seen his face before. The artist in you took note. Later, when you injured yourself and stumbled upon the museum, his image was already impressed on your brain. Exhaustion and that bump to your head did the rest."

Lily's eyes were still on the portrait. It drew her against her will. She seemed unable to look away. "Is that a polite way of pretending you *don't* think I'm insane?''

Landry laughed. "People who are truly mad don't seem to be aware of it. They usually think they're perfectly normal. If need be, I'll attest that you're as sharp as I am, Miss Kendall."

Lily smiled back. "I'll take a census of local opinion, then, before committing myself."

He roared at that. "I'm afraid you'll find it sharply divided. I'm considered one of the local eccentrics," he told her. "I'm on my way to Penzance. May I give you a lift back to your hotel?"

"Yes, thank you." With a long glance at the painting, Lily allowed the doctor to escort her to the door.

The painted lapis-blue eyes seemed to follow her with their gaze. She felt self-conscious, as if he were actually there, watching her leave the room. What a powerful man Rees Tregarrick must have been, Lily thought, that even a painting of him could stir up something in her soul!

Portia and James were out on the porch, examining a loose railing, and waved cheerily as Lily and the doctor drove off down the steep and winding hill.

Dr. Landry pointed out a few places of local interest as his ancient car puttered down the cobbled streets. There were artists painting, their easels atop the granite wall. The view was breathtaking, overlooking the dull green and navy and cinnamon-colored slate roofs of the village, and the sparkling turquoise variations of the harbor beyond.

This, Lily told herself, *is the calm, picturesque place I wanted.* There was plenty to explore, while managing to stay away from isolated stretches of beach. And yet she knew she would go out to Yearning Head again. It called to something wild and lonely in her blood.

The car stopped for a fat tabby chasing a yapping terrier, then turned at a corner. The window of a small antiques shop displayed tin soldiers and Staffordshire pugs, and pair of striking blue-and-white vases.

"Those vases might have come over with Captain Tregarrick," Dr. Landry said. "He imported a great quantity of fine porcelainware."

But it wasn't the vases that had caught Lily's attention. "I thought there was a tea shop on this corner. I must be turned around."

Her companion glanced at her. "Are you sure you've never been to St. Dunstan before? There was a family-run tea shop there for generations. It went out of business when I was a lad, after old Miss Truro passed on."

"I suppose I might have heard it mentioned," Lily said doubtfully. But in her mind's eye she could envision lace curtains at the window, and a cozy tearoom done up in mauve-and-green chintz. Even a verdigris grasshopper on the ledge above the slate fireplace.

In less than five minutes she was standing in front of her hotel overlooking the harbor. Lily leaned down to the open window of the car and expressed her thanks to the doctor. "I know now that I imagined the entire episode," she added, "but I have to tell you that it still seems very real in my mind."

Dr. Landry smiled. "The human brain is capable of creating the glories of the Sistine Chapel, or sending men to walk upon the moon, Miss Kendall. It's small wonder, then, that it can make a dream seem like reality—often down to the finest details, no matter how seemingly bizarre."

"That's very true," she answered, shaking her head. "Right down to the crutch he leaned on!" She gave a little wave and started toward the door.

"Wait!" Dr. Landry called after her. "How did you know about Captain Tregarrick's injury?"

He was certain that there was nothing in the tourist literature about the tragic misfortune that had injured the captain and killed poor young Catherine Tregarrick.

It was too late. Lily had already vanished inside the Castle Inn. The doctor was still wondering about it when he passed the antiques shop on the corner, where the Grasshopper on the Hearth Tearoom had stood in his youth.

4

LILY WENT UP to her demi-suite with its papered walls, chintz curtains, and Victorian walnut furnishings. At least here nothing had changed. After a hot shower and shampoo, she put on a floaty dress of white cotton eyelet, threaded with blue ribbon.

The summer shorts and her jeans were still neatly folded in the drawer, untouched since her arrival. Somehow they didn't seem appropriate to the village of St. Dunstan. She felt cooler and more comfortable in the long, retro dresses that swirled around her slim ankles.

Only when she'd bound her long hair up into an old-fashioned coronet did she dare to lift the lid of the antique desk and remove the handful of pamphlets that discreetly touted the local wonders. Her fingers were unsteady as she spread them out on the desktop.

There were brochures of St. Dunstan village and other points of interest throughout the Cornish countryside: deserted tin mines, medieval monk's towers, rings of prehistoric standing stones, and the man-made moonscapes of white china clay.

There was nothing at all about Star House or Captain Rees Tregarrick.

Lily noticed the edge of a glossy leaflet peeking out from beneath the brown paisley lining paper. The front showed the slate-and-granite Victorian manor she'd seen through the fog, with gables and turrets and great starburst window. "Visit the Star House Museum." it read, "and take a Journey to the Untouched Past."

"Well, I certainly did that!" Lily turned it over.

Her heart gave a lurch that was not entirely unpleasant. There he was again, Captain Rees Tregarrick, in all his masculine splendor. The reproduction of a full-length sepia photograph was almost an exact likeness of the man she remembered . . . or had dreamed up—the wide brow, the strong jaw and aquiline nose, the firm, sensual mouth.

Again, only the eyes were different. There was no anger in them. And, Lily noticed, no crutch or blackthorn cane braced against his side.

She started to slip it back into the desk, then paused. Instead she tucked it into her purse.

Dr. Landry had recommended a nap: "Mother Nature's cure-all." But the sun was out, the sky a brilliant blue, and Lily felt absolutely wonderful. She hadn't come to Cornwall to nap, and her stomach was protesting its lack of lunch. Slicking pink gloss over her lips, she went down to the spacious dining room, with its rock-walled fireplace and tall windows overlooking the sea. It was still early, and only a handful of others were there.

"Good afternoon, Miss Kendall. Your usual place?" the hostess asked.

Lily hesitated. For the past four days she'd requested a seat in the sunny bay with the morning paper, and a view of the picturesque village. *Dear God, I've become such a creature of habit!*

She'd been running on the Washington gerbil wheel too long. She was in danger of making routine her god, change her enemy. No, worse, God help her! She was in imminent danger of becoming a career bureaucrat. And that wasn't the real Lily Kendall. Not really.

Was it?

She smiled at the hostess. "I think I'll change my routine today. I'd like a table with a view of the sea." *Of the headland.*

She didn't say it aloud, but she was given a table with a partial view of the harbor and beyond, the dark granite cliffs of Yearning Head. The sea was all slick, blue Bristol glass, rimmed with crystalline spray.

Star House was hidden by the headland's sharp uplift of terrain, and a frieze of stunted trees, bent sharply by the prevailing winds. Lily was almost glad of it. Despite Dr. Landry's explanation, she felt uneasy.

Portia had told her that the star-shaped window was no longer lit at night, to guide the ships home to port. "Cost, you know." But Lily could not deny the bone-deep belief that she'd seen the star guiding her to safety and heard Rees Tregarrick's rich, resonant voice leading her toward the granite sea-stairs.

Felt the warm, very human touch of his strong hand on her arm.

There she'd admitted it.

"Oh, I beg your pardon." She realized the hostess was holding out the handwritten menu. Lily took it and set it aside.

"Tell me," she asked, "have you ever been up to the Star House Museum?"

"My goodness, yes. I'm not from St. Dunstan, you know. I'm at university, and they take me on here for the summers. I visit the museum at least twice each season. You really should tour Star House. It's a fascinating place. Millions of pounds' worth of wonderful things."

Lily was surprised. "I thought it was just a restored manor. What kind of museum is it?"

"Oh, all sorts of treasures! Lovely Chinese porcelain and Indian furniture that Captain Tregarrick brought back from his voyages. Venetian glass, trinket boxes covered with semiprecious stones and mother-of-pearl, and snuff bottles carved out of amethyst and opal. My favorite is the Jade Room. It used to be the library.''

Lily remembered a glimpse of pale yellow jade when Captain Tregarrick had vanished into his study. But it was all fading, running together, exactly ike fragments of the dream that Dr. Landry had called it.

An elderly couple entered the dining room, and the hostess edged away from Lily with a polite murmur. ''If you go,'' she said over her shoulder, ''look out for the engravings done by Mrs. Tregarrick. She was a noted botanist— quite famous in her day.''

Lily hunched forward, as if a fist had punched her in the stomach. That's exactly how it felt. *Of course there was a wife in it somewhere.* Hadn't she come reeling off her last failed romance with the same discovery?

It took Lily a minute to recover. She'd felt as if all the breath had gone out of her. *Which is utterly ridiculous,* she told herself. *Why be upset over something that happened to a man who who lived almost a hundred years ago?*

She finished her meal and went out into the sunlight, strolling past shopfronts brimming with geraniums, up past the slate-and-granite houses, where the ubiquitous hydrangeas of Cornwall bloomed blue, and pink, and lavender in prodigal beauty. Ignoring a crowd waiting to get into the St. Dunstan Tin Museum, with its working model of the old mine that had gone out into the bay, far below the seabed, she turned south as if pulled by a magnet.

She climbed the cobblestones until she was high above the village, with the sea spreading out like a swath of crimped blue satin. Sequins of light glittered through the spume of brilliants the waves dashed up. Lily had never seen it look more beautiful. She stopped at the granite wall above the village, to watch the seabirds skim over the waves. Higher still, the dark bulk of Yearning Head towered over the cresting waves, drawing her back.

Rees Tregarrick stood at the star window and looked out at the headland. She was still there. Although the tree hid her from clear view, he could see the ends of her long blond hair, and the thin white of her skirt billowing in the breeze.

She had never appeared to him by daylight before. It had always been in starlight or moonlight that he'd seen her moving across the headland, or walking the strand below the cliffs, with her fair hair streaming out like satin ribbons.

He'd never managed to get close to her. Usually by the time he reached the front door she was gone. Then, lately, he'd been able to cross half the distance to the cliff's edge before she vanished.

Until last night.

He turned away from the window. *Until last night.* Those were the critical words. Until then, he'd turned his back on the sea and walled himself away in the house. His emotions had been as dead as poor Catherine. And then *she* had come, stirring up terrible memories, this mysterious woman who haunted his nights. His dreams. Terrible longings that had kept him awake till dawn. She hadn't had a stitch on beneath her summer frock, he was sure of it. *God in heaven, I am a man. And a lonely one, at that.*

Perhaps the sea had sent her to torment him, to lure him back to it. Why else had she vanished without a trace in the night? Cursing beneath his breath, Rees Tregarrick turned away from the window.

Lily had unplaited her hair and let the wind blow through it. The rubber thong sandals that Portia had loaned her were still in the canvas bag by her side, along with a notepad, a new copy of *People,* and the paperback of a favorite by Mary Stewart that she'd picked up on her way.

Lily had made no attempt to return the sandals, nor had she bothered to even skim the magazine's table of contents. She took out a pencil and sketched one of the flowers growing in the protection of a stunted tree. The rough bark made a pleasing contrast with the soft-textured pink petals of the blossom. Quite lifelike, she decided.

Soon, though, even the drawing palled. The breeze sighed, filled with invisible yearnings longing to be made real. Lily closed up the notebook and looked out over the sea.

The light was changing. The view had been like an Impressionist painting, myriad dots of color blending into one another. Now it was bold and crisp, each in-rushing wave distinct from the others. With the sun turning the air all crystal and gold, she was content to sit beneath one of the wind-gnarled trees. And wait.

She'd been waiting for some time when she felt his presence. Suddenly the light shifted, became clearer. The scent of some unfamiliar, exotic flower filled the air.

Lily didn't look up. She was afraid to.

She'd known that he would come. Known it deep in her bones.

Out of the corner of her eye she could see his boot, with grains of sand and a blade of fresh green grass clinging to it.

"Go away," she said. "You're not real."

"Oh, I'm real enough," Tregarrick responded. "Too damned real for my own good. It's you who are the ghost."

She looked up at that. "A ghost?"

He stared out past her, to the restless sea. The same aspects, changeable and fathomless, were reflected in his eyes. "Aye. You come and go like the moon through clouds, vanish like the mist."

"I've only been here once before. Last night, when you rescued me."

"Ah, no. I've watched you a hundred times before. I know the way your hair turns color in the light, and the whiteness of your skin beneath that dress."

He turned his head then and faced her fully. Her heart thudded painfully. Above the knitted fisherman's sweater his face, so handsome and intense, robbed Lily of breath.

"It's been more than a year since I had the first sight of you," he told her. "At the time I thought you were . . . someone else." A muscle ticked at his jaw. "Tell me, for God's sake! Why are *you* haunting me? If it were Catherine now, I could understand . . ."

He uttered a muffled oath and moved a little away. Lily watched him. The wind ruffled his thick, dark hair, the same as it did hers. His shadow fell across the tree's knotty roots, just as did hers. Surely there was a mistake some-where. He was as real as she. Lily rose to her feet.

"You *are* Captain Rees Tregarrick? The man who built Star House?" she asked. She was surprised her voice remained so steady.

"Aye, lass." He looked back at her, frowning. "Why do I think I know you? We've never met in this life."

"No."

And yet she had the same feeling as he. The crosswinds blew against the headland, and the soulful sound of the sea echoed up to them, like the murmuring of lovers. The air seemed to thicken, steeped with the echoes of old and powerful emotions.

Shivers ran up the back of her bare arms. Tentatively Lily reached out and touched his sleeve. Woolly, soft, and very real. As were the steely muscles of his arm beneath it.

"It's summer," she said, feeling the warm breeze against her face. "Aren't you warm in such a heavy sweater?"

He shook his head. Leaves skittered past his boot. "It's autumn," he told her. "You should be shivering with cold in your light frock. You'll catch a death of a chill."

Lily smiled. "Not if I'm a ghost . . ."

For a moment the air rippled between them. It was like looking down into the sunny tide pools of the bay as a light breeze ruffled the water over the rocks and moss and tiny scattered shells. She expected him to thin and disappear like fog in sunlight. The shimmer steadied, hardened.

He was still there.

Rees Tregarrick caught her hand in his, as if he were afraid she would run away. Or vanish like sea spray, among the sunbeams.

"Who are you?" he said. "*What* are you?"

Lily's breath snagged in her throat. "A woman," she whispered. "Just a woman."

5

Rees Tregarrick looked down at Lily with an enigmatic expression. "A woman."

The wind whipped her hair around them like a cloak. Without warning, he pulled her into his arms. She trembled in his embrace, as his hand splayed against her back. Her breasts pressed against him as he smoothed the light fabric of her dress down the gentle curve of her spine, along the lush curve of her waist and hip. His breath came quicker.

"You feel like a woman." His bent his head until his cheek grazed the top of her head. Lily heard him inhale. "You smell like a woman."

Then she was pulled tight against his chest, and his mouth came down on hers, warm and firm and incredibly sensual.

She was intensely aware of everything about Rees Tregarrick, from the scent of cedar on his clothes to the strength of his fingers against her back, the roughness of his jaw against her cheek. She clung to him while the world spun and rocked around her. Surely she was dreaming.

His mere nearness had triggered something between them. Now the heat of his hard body against hers was like an elemental force of nature, molding them together. Melding past and present, hinting of future pleasures, delicious and dark, and well beyond her own experience.

That first, hard kiss gave way to another, softer and yet more demanding. A shiver ran through her. As his embrace tightened, he took the kiss deeper, wilder. And she responded totally to the moment.

To him.

He broke the kiss and looked down at her. His eyes looked dazed and heavy with need. "Ah, God Almighty, but you taste like a woman!"

"I told you that."

"Yes." He wound his fingers into her hair, lacing them through it. "But I know I'm dreaming." He tilted her chin up until her eyes locked with his. The tip of his thumb grazed her full lower lip, and his eyes were dark as the sea.

"I'm real."

Rees shook his head. "You're a mirage. Or, if you truly are the woman who has been haunting my sleep, prove it. Make my dream come true. For the love of God, put an end to the curse, and to my hellish loneliness!"

How could she refuse his plea, especially when it was exactly what she craved herself? Lily stepped up on her tiptoes, and touched his mouth with her own. His lips were firm, then softened. He wrapped her close in his arms and kissed her again.

Lily had never been kissed so thoroughly, so passionately. It was a lost art, she thought weakly, a kiss for its own sake. Uncalculated and not a mere hasty prelude to something more. It was like an exotic drug in her blood. She wanted him with an ardor she had never known. Wanted him fully and completely.

Wanted him *now*.

His hand brushed her breast. She felt her body go liquid at its core as she leaned into him, and felt the potency of

316 ★ Marianne Willman

his response. Her fingers twined in his hair, pulling his mouth closer, drinking deep.

The textures of his mouth, the touch of his tongue were so real, yet she knew it was utterly impossible. *This can't be happening. It's a dream. I've fallen asleep beneath the tree,* she told herself, *and I'm dreaming.*

But his mouth was hot on hers, no less real than her own. His tongue followed the curve of her lower lip, and she sighed as it slid between her teeth. Her entire body shuddered with pleasure as something untamed and dark inside her responded. His leg nudged hers apart, and he pulled her closer, tighter, until she moved restlessly against him.

If this is a dream, Lily thought, *don't let me awaken.*

Her heart pounded against his chest, and she could feel the rough texture of his sweater against her straining breasts. His hand cupped one, weighing it gently against his palm. The tip contracted, hardened as he caressed it with his long fingers, and circled it with his thumb. She gave a tiny cry of eagerness, offering herself to his questing hand.

His skin was hot against hers, as he pushed down the strap of her summer dress and tugged it low. All the while his mouth worked against her, nibbling at her lips gently, then pressing them hard against her teeth until she reeled and ached with need. He was like the sea, relentlessly eroding her ability to think. She could only feel.

It was enough.

He worked the other strap down her shoulder, and they both shivered when it broke free in his hand. His lips moved from the corner of her mouth and down her arching throat. Over the delicate hollow at its base, and along her bare shoulder. Tasting. Teasing. Taunting.

Then he bent her back along his arm, and his lips touched her breast. So light, so light, it was like the brush of a butterfly's wing. The sensation was exquisite. Her body tingled with anticipation. Then he took the tip into his mouth and tugged, hard. There was nothing in the world but the cool kiss of the wind along her naked flesh, the heat of his hungry mouth upon her breast.

Lily lost control. Without warning she was thrown up and over the edge of reason. All conscious thought was washed away, overcome by waves of cresting desire.

He held her close until it passed, murmuring words in an unknown language against her flesh. When it was over, she lay limp in his arms. Lily felt shattered. And he hadn't really touched her. Not yet. Not the way she ached for him to do.

He lowered her to the sun-warmed ground, out of the breath of the wind. He didn't speak, but pressed a soft kiss against her throat. His hand kneaded her breasts gently, while he kissed his way back up to her lips. He kissed her deeply, plundering her mouth with his tongue until she was eager and wanton with desire.

Only then did he look down at her. His stern, masculine beauty struck her like an arrow to the heart—a sharp, sweet piercing surely as fatal to her peace of mind as any shaft of feathered wood. His eyes were ablaze with need that found an answering echo inside her.

Lily's lips were swollen from his kisses, and her breasts ached to feel his mouth once more. She touched his face, cradling the side of it with her hand. So real, so solid. She traced his lips with her fingertip, and he closed his eyes until she was done.

"Are you a witch?" he whispered, frowning down at her. "A creature sent by the sea to lure me back into her clutches?"

She could have wept with need and tenderness. "Only a woman," she said, trailing a hand along his jaw. "And who are you?"

He laughed without mirth. "Only a man. One you have driven half mad with desire."

"Then take me." She stretched her arms above her head, offering her breasts to his seeking mouth. "Make love to me. Even if this is nothing but a dream."

"If this is the dream, then I am the dreamer," he said, his voice rough with passion. "I have waited months to know the end of it.'' He caught her hands and kissed her fingers. "And I intend to make it end my way! Don't vanish on me now, woman, or I swear to God I'll go mad!''

Another ripple shuddered through the air, as dazzling as sunlight. Lily was afraid that it was he who would vanish, that she'd awake and find herself back at her hotel—or worse, back in her lonely apartment.

But, no, she was still dreaming. With her head turned seaward as he kissed her throat, she watched a freighter fade and wink out on the horizon. The newer houses high above St. Dunstan were gone, as if they never were and the bright blue bay was covered with sailing ships, their acres of white canvas billowing in the wind like cumulus clouds. It had to be a dream . . .

Yet he was so real, so ardent. He kissed her breasts, and the touch of his mouth was more genuine than the earth beneath her, or the twisted, sunlit branches above. Heat built up inside her, spreading through her limbs like warm honey.

"Hurry," she whispered. "Oh, hurry!"

He pulled his sweater off, and the sun gleamed on hard muscles sculpted by the rigors of the sea. Lily laughed in delight and ran her fingertips through the crisp hairs on his chest, watching his face flood with desire.

Stripping off the rest of his clothes, he slid her skirt slowly up her legs, caressing her skin as he worked it higher. "No stockings," he said, as if to himself. "No corset and no garters. Nothing but beautiful woman beneath this flimsy frock."

He shook his head wonderingly at her skimpy lace bikini panties, then tried to tug them down. Lily lifted her hips, and the fragile lace tore in his hands. She was free, naked and warm beneath him. He covered her with his length and lay still, breathing hard, like a long-distance runner. Waves of pleasure rolled over her, and he caught her in his arms as she trembled beneath him.

His chest rose and fell, and its mat of hairs tantalized her nipples, bringing them erect. He tightened his embrace and groaned. "Sweet vision, if you vanish now, I'll never find you again. And I will be doomed, lost forever in my lonely hell.''

Instead of answering, she brought his head down to her breast and arched against him. As he took the velvety tip into his mouth, teased it with his firm lips, she shifted her legs apart. He was hard and ready, and she couldn't wait any longer. The fear that she was dreaming, that he would disappear stabbed at her. *At least give me this*, she thought. This one moment of perfect joy.

She moved against him with a small, sharp thrust of her hips. A tremor shook his big frame, and he groaned again. "So impatient, love?''

"Yes.'' And so afraid to wake up and find herself alone. That the lover of her dreams was only, after all, a dream-lover. She moved against him, watching desire chase the shadows of pain from his face. "Love me, Rees. Now.''

He touched her, felt her hips shift up to meet his questing fingers. She was slick and ready, and he could no longer hold back. He took her boldly, lustily, as he sensed she wanted. Lily's breath hitched in her throat. Their joining was as ruthlessly fierce and beautiful as the land around them. Elemental as the sun and wind, powerful as the pounding of the sea.

When the moment came, intense almost beyond bearing, they rode it together, like hawks rising on the wind. Sensations poured through Lily, bright and dark, as he carried her up with him toward the sky. With every thrust her body arched to meet his, taking and demanding more. Then they were free-falling through space, and only his embrace kept her safe until they drifted gently back to earth.

Later she lay cradled in his arms with her hair splayed out over his naked chest, like a shawl of spun gold. She curled into the warmth of his body, afraid to move or speak. Afraid he would melt away beneath her like the mist rising through the trees. It would storm soon. She could feel the excitement of it in the air.

And what then?

As Lily lifted her face and looked down at him, he shimmered like a mirage before her eyes; but he was real and solid in her arms. She could feel the steady thrum of his heart against her ribs. All the tension was gone from his face. He looked younger, and so handsome and radiant she felt her heart might break.

He opened his eyes and smiled at her. "The sea gives and the sea takes away," he said slowly. "I asked for a sign of forgiveness . . . and you came to me, out of the fog and mist. I thought it was a trick of fate. I was afraid to trust that you were real." His hand closed on her bare breast. "But you are."

Leaning down, he kissed it, laved it with his tongue while she took in a deep, shuddering breath. No one had ever made love to her like this. She hadn't known . . . hadn't dreamed it could be so beautiful and so savage, so primal, yet so exquisitely tender. She kissed his shoulder, nipped the bronzed skin with its heady taste of salt and sweat and man.

His mouth moved lower, grazing the cleft between her breasts, moving down along her ribs. He planted kisses down the length of her, over the soft curve of her hip and the gentle swell of her belly, tasting her as he went. His lips brought trails of fire down her thigh, all the way to the delicate arch of her foot. And then he started to work his way up.

He bent his dark head and touched her with his mouth. She shivered beneath him, barely able to stand the deliciously intense sensations evoked by his darting tongue. A force was building in her, so hot and powerful she couldn't contain it. Passion exploded through her, pouring like liquid flame along her limbs. She bucked and shuddered against him, and then her blood was a bright torrent of sparks, racing hotly through her veins, melting any last remnants of her reserve.

He held her tightly until it was over, his hands cupping her possessively. When it was done she was deliciously weak and dizzy and spent. Her whole body seemed swollen with womanly response, ripe to bursting.

"Did you like that, love?" he murmured against her temple, as he pressed his mouth against her hair. "I knew you would. You've a fire in you that matches mine. It can't be quenched.'' His mouth slid down the curve of her jaw. ''It must be fed!''

Before she could speak, he twisted around and pinned her with his weight and kissed her. Sweet languor flowed through her, filled her with delight. The flame of need ignited once again. Lord, how she wanted him. Wanted to ease whatever sorrows had haunted him and banish them forever. His hand moved between her legs, and she shivered in delight and anticipation. Every atom of her body longed for him.

''Slowly this time,'' he told her. ''So that I can learn every inch of you, what you like and don't like. So that I can match the heat of your passions with my own.''

''Impossible.'' She laughed against his shoulder. She was on fire with need for him, burning with a wild, sexual hunger. ''But try.''

He took his time, exploring her body as he had promised. Memorizing every intimate curve and texture, making love to her with his eyes and his hands. Bringing her to the crest once more through sensual anticipation and his own passionate will. His fingers plunged deep, and she arched up off the ground, in pleasure so intense she was mindless with it. Again and again he brought her there and over, until she clung to his wrist to make him stop.

''Take me again,'' she said huskily. ''As hard and wild as you please.''

And he did, riding her through the bright fields of passion until they were both gasping for air, locked in each other's arms. Lily closed her eyes, inhaling the wonderful masculine scent of him, satiated and replete. She started to drift to sleep, lulled by the sounds of his breathing and the singing of the birds that had settled back in the trees.

Then a metallic *thunk* carried from somewhere in the distance. Lily's eyes flew open. Rees was still there. She could see his face alight with emotion as he gazed down at her, feel his weight pressing her down into the grass, the thrum of his heart beating in time to hers. But when she tried to tighten her embrace, her arms closed, on empty air.

She could still feel the pressure of his magnificent body, its radiant warmth, and the hard, protective circle of his arms about her shoulders; but the air shimmered, and she could see the wavery sky, the tremor of the high cirrus clouds through him, as if he were made of pebbled glass. In a moment he was gone, as if he'd never been.

"No!" The cry was ripped from her throat. Lily didn't want the dream to end. She couldn't bear it.

But as she sat up, the evidence was still there. The mark of his teeth on her skin. The taste of his mouth on hers. The sweet stickiness between her thighs. Even a few woolly threads of his sweater clinging to the bracken. But that was all.

"Miss Kendall?"

Lily heard her name called, and scrambled to cover herself. *Dr. Landry!* She pushed her skirt down and pulled up the straps of her bodice. Her breasts felt swollen and ached with tenderness from Rees's kisses. She glanced around for her lace panties, but they were gone, heaven knew where.

As she tried to loop her long hair back, Dr. Landry came around the line of stunted trees. "Ah, so it is you. Portia thought she'd spotted you out here earlier."

Lily wondered if he could see the wild beating of the pulse at her throat. "I came to bring her sandals back, and was seduced by the view." *Close enough,* she told herself.

"Yes, it's quite splendid, isn't it?" He leaned against the trunk. "Voices carry a long way. I thought I heard you talking to someone. Another tourist, perhaps."

Lily wrapped her arms around her shoulders to hide the red marks of Rees Tregarrick's hands on her upper arms. "I was singing," she said. That wasn't entirely untrue.

He leaned down and retrieved her fallen notebook. It fell open to her drawing, and Dr. Landry paused to examine it. "That's very well done! Have you ever given thought to becoming an illustrator?"

Lily shook her head. "It never crossed my mind. At any rate, it's too late for me to change careers."

"It's never too late," he told her, handing over the notebook. "You have a true talent, Miss Kendall. Don't dismiss it so lightly. I'm on my way to family gathering in St. Just. May I offer you a lift back to the village?"

"No, thank you. After I return Portia's shoes, I thought perhaps I'd take the tour."

"You'll find it worth your while. Captain Tregarrick brought back some wonderful treasures from his trips abroad."

When she was gone, Dr. Landry turned away from the sparkling bay and stared out over the placid farmland behind Yearning Head, the fields green and gold between their low rock walls. Some of those same fields were ancient, had been tamed and tilled since the Bronze Age. What a contrast they made with the bay, where the sea and land met violently, locked in eternal conflict.

Some people were like that restless seascape, mutable, shifting from moment to moment. Others were like the fields, neat and cultivated and all of a piece. Like Lily Kendall. At least on the surface. But what was she really like? People wore so many masks these days, it was difficult to tell.

Dr. Landry sighed. He was concerned about Miss Kendall, yet he couldn't say why. She'd gotten over that knock on her head without any untoward effects as far as he could tell. She seemed perfectly normal and levelheaded. But beneath the most placid of landscapes, volcanoes sometimes came bursting up through the earth.

He laughed at his wild fancy. "Too many National Geographic specials on the BBC," he told himself. Lily Kendall would be just fine. Meanwhile, a wonderful dinner awaited him at a restaurant in St. Just.

As he turned to make his way back to where he'd parked his battered mini, the wind blew across the headland, full of silent, urgent longings so keen that even a staid man of science could feel them. He stopped in his tracks.

The sun shone bright around him, and the air seemed

rich with the unmistakable scent of exotic blooms and recent lovemaking. Landry shook his head. "I'm imagining
things," he said.

Jingling his keys, he took a few steps toward the car.
Something crackled beneath his shoe. He looked down to
see what it was: a wisp of torn lace, and a handful of drying
leaves, looking as if they had been just been blown fresh
from some autumn garden.

6

"THIS IS CATHERINE, the first Mrs. Tregarrick," Portia said in her brisk, tour-guide mode. She'd set aside cataloguing the contents of various boxes from the attic to show Lily around. "The portrait was painted shortly before her death."

Lily was shocked. "She was very young!"

"Eighteen years and two months."

She didn't want to ask, but had to. "How did she die? Childbirth?"

Portia looked uncomfortable. "I suppose you'll have heard the gossip. Some people say she threw herself down the sea stairs carved into the cliff. Others say she was pushed."

"By whom?"

"Her husband, of course. Captain Rees Tregarrick."

Lily gasped. "And do they say why?"

Portia went on to another portrait, which showed Rees Tregarrick in formal attire. "Look at him. He was an adventurer. They say he wanted to live in the Sandwich Islands—Hawaii, one of your states now—but she refused to go.''

Portia smiled up at his likeness and dimpled. ''What a fool. If he wasn't my own great-great-something grandfather, I'd have gone off with him in a trice.''

Lily blinked. ''You're a descendant?''

''Not of Catherine Tregarrick. Of his second marriage.''

Again Lily felt that blow to her stomach. *Two wives in your life*, she said silently. *Did you love them both?*

She looked up at his painting, and those lapis eyes seemed to bore into hers. There were the lips that had crushed her own, that had suckled her breasts and driven her half mad with desire. And those were the skilled hands that had stroked her flesh, alternately soothing and inflaming her. She would swear it on her life.

I'm going insane, she thought with a sudden sense of panic. But her glance caught her trapped reflection in the mirror above the side table. Even with the strap of her dress in place, she could see the reddened place where his teeth had nipped. There was a small bruise on her inner arm where his thumb had pressed, and her body still tingled with satisfaction from his lovemaking.

Somehow, under Yearning Head's strange spell, Rees Tregarrick had crossed over from his time to hers and made love to her beneath the trees. She was as certain of it as she was of her own identity.

Curiosity warred with jealousy that she knew was totally ridiculous. ''Where is the portrait of the second Mrs. Tregarrick?''

''None are known to exist,'' Portia said wistfully. ''Neither paintings nor photographs. I should have liked to have known how she looked. If we might share some family resemblance, you know.''

Lily turned away. ''The people in the village say this house is haunted. Is it Catherine Tregarrick who walks about, rattling her chains?''

Portia looked offended. ''There are two ghosts, although I've seen neither one. The first is a 'woman in white' who is seen up on the headland. The other is Captain Tregarrick himself. James saw him once, standing at the star window, looking out to sea. He said he looked terribly sad—and rather angry.''

"Yes," Lily murmured. "That is how I first saw him."

"I beg your pardon?"

"Um . . ." Lily recovered quickly. "When I saw his photograph in the study, I mean. Could I see the star window? It intrigues me."

"It's really off-limits to visitors just now," Portia said, "but since there is only you today . . ."

She led Lily through a pair of wine velvet portieres and into another parlor. "This was the ladies' parlor." They went into a charming, sunlit room and finally up a flight of stairs. The window was in a turret at the very top.

Lily was amazed. The star window was much larger than she'd thought. Taller and wider than the stained glass windows in St. Dunstan's Church. It was a work of true genius. It gave the impression of being in three dimensions because of the masterful arrangement. The outer rectangle was formed of various shades of dark blue glass, the star inside composed of dozens of triangles of brilliant stained glass in bright yellow, shining gold, and rich, mellow amber. It was breathtaking, a magnificent work of art.

"Why here, away from the main living area?" Lily asked. "Surely they would have enjoyed it more in a place they would pass by frequently."

"There used to be a triple lantern hanging in front of the star, to light it in the night. It was a beacon," Portia explained, "a sign that could be seen far out at sea, welcoming Rees Tregarrick home. Guiding him to the harbor side of St. Petroc's Cathedral—that's what we call those sharp, toothy rocks that rise up out of nowhere past Yearning Head."

Lily remembered seeing the formation from the headland, protruding from the waters like a great granite claw.

The colors of the window fell across Portia's face. "On the day Catherine Tregarrick died, her husband's ship had been expected to make harbor for several days. The man at the helm always looked for the star window. Steering between Yearning Head and Tregarrick's Star, the pilot would know he was in safe waters, you see.''

She turned to Lily. "For some reason the lamps were unlit that night. The pilot said the beacon at Star House went out suddenly, and he lost his bearings. *Tregarrick's Star* was almost lost in the mist and rain. It came too close to St. Petroc's Cathedral and was almost dashed to pieces on the sharp rocks. It nearly capsized when they brought her about. Two men were lost overboard, dashed against the rocks.''

''How horrible!''

''Yes, and senseless,'' Portia added.

''But why wasn't the window lit up?''

''No one knows. Perhaps the wind blew the flames out. Or a jealous rival might have paid someone to sabotage it. The competition for the China trade was fierce. The servants reported that Captain Tregarrick reached home the next morning in a terrible fury. He blamed Catherine for not making sure the Star Window was well lit. There was a frightful row. Catherine ran out of the house, with Captain Tregarrick hot on her heels. Later the servants heard a woman's scream, and they ran out of the house. A fog had rolled in from the Atlantic. There was no sign Catherine or Rees Tregarrick. They'd ventured too near the cliffs, and weren't found for some time.''

Lily listened, appalled. So that was how he sustained his injury! ''What happened then?'' She was almost afraid to know.

''Rees Tregarrick was on the sea-stairs with his leg badly broken and his face raked raw along one side . . . as if by a woman's fingernails. Catherine was on the strand. By the time they reached her, she was beyond human help.''

''How very sad.'' Lily remembered the broken way Rees had uttered Catherine's name. ''How did they fall?''

Portia looked away. ''Captain Tregarrick claimed that his wife was suicidal. That she intended to jump from the headland, and that he tried to save her, but she fell to her death. He fell in the struggle to aid her. With Catherine dead, of course, there was no one to say any different.''

Something in the young woman's voice arrested Lily. "I see. And so a taint was attached to his name." She couldn't believe that he had murdered his wife. "I don't understand why he was blamed."

"It was an unhappy marriage," Portia said. "He wanted her to go to sea with him, as was frequently the custom. Unlike the second Mrs. T., Catherine hated the sea, hated Cornwall. She refused."

"Then why did she marry him in the first place?"

Portia laughed. "You've seen his portrait. Quite a man, I would say! Catherine was pretty and spoiled, and she set her cap for him. According to her diary, she was determined to make a splash in London society, and completely sure of her powers to persuade him to her will. Of course, his business brought them here."

"Quite a shock after London," Lily said.

"Oh, yes."

"He isn't a murderer," Lily said vehemently. "I am sure of it."

Portia slanted a look at her. "You've become his defender. Perhaps I should tell you the rest: Some say that Catherine was still clinging to life when they found her, bleeding and broken on the rocks. That she blamed her husband, and died with a curse on her lips."

Lily shrugged off the shiver she felt; but as they continued on the tour, she remembered Rees's words, how he had begged Catherine for a sign of her forgiveness. It went against her every instinct; but the knowledge weighed on her like a pall of lead.

They came upon James near the servants' stair, humping a large trunk down the worn treads. Light gleamed dully from the tarnished brass studs and double locks. He set it down on the carpet, dusting his hands of the stray webs that clung to old leather.

"This is the last of that lot beneath the north eaves. Shall I take it into your workroom?"

Portia looked it over. "Good quality. Look at that elaborate tin stamping. It doesn't appear to be an item one of the maids could have afforded. Perhaps it belonged to an upper servant.'' Her eyes lit. ''Or even a member of the family. Wouldn't it be wonderful if we found a photograph of the second Mrs. Tregarrick? There *must* be one somewhere.''

''There's only one way to find out,'' James said, leaning against the carved newel post. ''It awaits your pleasure, my lady.''

Portia's face shone with excitement. ''You never know what you might find—clothes, or letters and documents that might shed more light on the Tregarricks. One old valise was packed with remnants of a wonderful Oriental brocade, embroidered with gold thread. I've displayed some fans against a piece of it, in the case in the ladies' parlor.''

Lily caught her breath. For a moment James and Portia, the stairwell and the leather trunk, were overlaid with the image of shelves filled with rich silks and satins in every color known. She could smell incense and flowering plum outside the window.

She could see Rees Tregarrick nodding at the Chinese merchant, and turning to smile at her. So real she could reach out and touch his face.

The vision vanished, and Lily swallowed, hard.

Portia hadn't noticed anything unusual. She twisted the hitch that held the lid closed, and opened the trunk. Cedar and lavender filled the air, along with a scent of must. The inside held a woman's summer garments—tucked and frilled white organza and finely embroidered lawn—all neatly packed away in layers of silver paper. But on the very top, placed exactly in the center, were a pair of very modern-looking woman's canvas summer shoes.

Portia snatched them. ''How on earth . . . ?''

''How did they get into the trunk?'' Lily exclaimed, recognizing her missing shoes.

''Don't be daft, the both of you.'' James put his hands on his hips. ''There's nothing hocus-pocus about them. They had rubber-soled shoes like that for beachwear in Victorian times.''

''No, I don't think they had Keds back then,'' Lily said quietly, pointing to the inner markings. ''They're mine.

There's the place where I snagged the toe when I was almost caught by the tide. But I swear I have no idea how they came to be there.''

The air shimmered in front of Lily. For a disorienting moment she found herself in two places: She was standing at the foot of the staircase with Portia and James, staring at her shoes—and at the same time she was in a huge bedchamber, laughing as she slipped them atop the items in the trunk. There was a soft rushing sound in her ears, like the flow of fast water over smooth stones. She had to put her hand on the stair rail to keep her balance.

Portia shook her head. ''How do you explain the cobwebs over the lock?''

James made a sound of disgust. ''A busy spider. Nothing more.'' Portia glanced from the shoes to Lily, and gasped.

''What, have you been bitten, then?'' James took her hand in his and examined it anxiously. ''No. It wasn't that,'' Portia said shakily. ''When I looked at Miss Kendall just then . . .'' She paused and rubbed her eyes. ''For a moment I thought . . .'' She gave Lily an apologetic smile. ''I swear that it looked as if you had become transparent.''

''You need a vacation,'' James said, scowling. ''And no more episodes of *Twilight Zone* on the telly or reading those reincarnation books old Mrs. Polgelly sells to the tourist trade.''

He took the canvas sandals from her and handed them firmly to Lily. ''As to the shoes, you must have wandered into the attic that night, Miss Kendall, and left us a souvenir of your visit.''

''I suppose I could have,'' Lily said without conviction. ''I don't recall doing it, though.''

Portia bit her lip. She was still pale and agitated. ''If I didn't know better, I'd swear that trunk hadn't been opened in a hundred years.''

7

LILY RETURNED TO St. Dunstan after spending more time at the museum, staring at the paintings and photographs of Rees Tregarrick. As she wound her way down, her chance meeting with him on the headland seemed like a strangely vivid, erotic dream.

She wondered again if that was what it had been. Every time she did, she stopped to examine the small bruise his thumb had made on the inner side of her wrist, and the love-bite beneath the strap of her dress. He'd been real enough to leave them both.

Or perhaps I am imagining them as well, she thought with a tiny flutter of unease. She rejected it. Even in her wildest imagination, she could not have invented a man like Rees Tregarrick, or the marvelous things he had done to her as they made love.

The village was bathed in pale shades of muted gray and blue. *Like a Vermeer,* she thought, *but without the tranquillity.* She made her way down the steep, cobbled High

Street, past a few chattering tourists and the ubiquitous artists busily painting the view out over the quaint rooftops
to the sparkling turquoise bay. Beyond the Atlantic
stretched to the horizon like striped satin in tones of blue
and gray.

Since talking to Dr. Landry, she'd been thinking about
her love of art and painting. About how she'd turned her
back on it in despair when she realized she hadn't the talent
to take the visions from her mind and put them on canvas
to share with others. She'd gone into a field that was all
ruled lines and by-the-numbers regulations, a discipline
where everything was precise to the last degree. It was the
antithesis of everything she had once wanted. Small wonder
that she now felt so stifled.

And since Rees Tregarrick had touched her, bringing her
body alive with sensations she hadn't known existed, she
realized how barren her life had become. This trip to Cornwall had forever changed her.

A hard rain pelted down all afternoon and didn't let up
for two days. While the other tourists flocked to the local
cinema and the Tin Museum, or sat around the fire in the
quiet lounge over cards, she kept to her room. Except for
a brief courtesy call by Dr. Landry, she hadn't seen anyone
but the maid and the waiters from room service.

With her face against the cool panes, her body on fire
with need, she watched the gray silk rain and thought of
nothing but Rees Tregarrick.

He came to her in dreams, as she lay in the high tester
bed, bringing every inch of her alive and glowing. In
dreams her breasts tingled to his touch and ached for his
kisses. Time and again, her dream-lover brought her gasping to the edge between anguish and glory, and she would
awaken in the lavender dimness, sweaty and tangled in the
sheets, groaning with loss as the image of Rees Tregarrick's
strong, hard body and the lingering sensation of his strong
embrace faded from her mind.

The phone rang, startling her. It was the front desk.
"You haven't been down since early yesterday, Miss Ken-

dall,'' the head clerk said. "I took it upon myself to make sure that you're not ill . . . ?''

"Thank you, no.'' Lily tried to think of an excuse. "I've been catching up on my sleep and my reading, enjoying the quiet of the suite.''

"Very good. If you require anything you have only to ask.''

Lily replaced the phone and sat up. The clerk had sounded relieved. She wondered if the maid had said something about the way she sat at the window, staring over the cobbled waterfront to the gray, wind-ripped bay. Perhaps this was how Catherine Tregarrick had waited for him to come home from the sea, watching for him to make safe harbor.

She must have loved him when she married him, Lily thought. *Any woman in her right mind would have fallen in love with him.* Yet it must have been lonely for a young girl left behind, even by her own choice, while her husband sailed the oceans. *"She should have gone with you,"* Lily murmured to the falling rain. *"I would have."*

She wished she knew more about both of them. Rees Tregarrick was a powerful lover—could a man capable of such intense passion be capable of other, more violent emotions? A chill ran through Lily. She wrapped her arms around herself. She wanted to see Rees Tregarrick again. To ask him about Catherine. To have him take her into his arms and kiss away that very faint, lingering shadow of doubt.

Pacing the carpet before the windows that overlooked the harbor, Lily wept and cursed the rain.

The sun came out on the third afternoon, and St. Dunstan village bloomed once again with nasturtium and giant hydrangea, tourists in shorts with cameras slung about their necks, and artists dabbling in oils and pastels and watercolors along the quay. Her heart in her throat, Lily dressed eagerly, carefully, as if for a bridegroom. She'd done a lot of reading. A lot of thinking. She thought that she had finally figured out what she must do.

Leaving the hotel that had been both sanctuary and prison, Lily walked past the greengrocers and tea room to a little stationery store run by Mrs. Polgelly. It was a fascinating little hole in the wall, filled with postcards, artists' supplies, and souvenir books on one side, the latest magazines and paperback fiction, some old favorites, and a section of New Age books, crystals, tarot cards, and pamphlets on the other.

The rest was given over to everything from paperweights hewn from the local granite to miniature teapots and hand-embroidered tea towels. The proprietor bustled over and assessed Lily from head to toe.

"Visiting relations in St. Dunstan, are you?" she asked.

"No, just a tourist, I'm afraid."

"Ah, but you've Cornish blood, aye, and it's brought you back." The old woman fixed her with a bright blue gaze. "You've the look of the old Trelawnys about you. They have the farm up beyond Yearning Head. They've been at Old Cross Farm these three hundred years and more. Young Miss Portia who runs the Starr House Museum lives there." She wrapped Lily's purchases—a sketchbook and drawing pencils—nodding in satisfaction. "You've Trelawny blood. I'm never wrong, you know."

Bemused, Lily went out and started the long climb up the zig-zag street toward the headland. Could it be true that she and Portia Trelawny were some sort of distant cousins? That might explain her feelings of belonging in Cornwall, her sense of having come home. Or perhaps it was only Rees Tregarrick who made her feel that way. The nearer she got, the harder her heart beat with anticipation. Her excitement at the thought of seeing Rees Tregarrick again made her tremble inside. Whether he was man, or ghost, or illusion, she longed for him with such intensity it was a physical ache.

She sat beneath the same tree where he had come to her before and waited. Time passed, marked by the scudding clouds and the angle of the westering sun, but she felt no presence. She remained alone.

Lily tried to sketch the view, but her hands shook too

much, and her perspective was abominable. The vast expanse of the headland was empty. The wind soughed through the line of twisted trees, sounding like a woman's muffled sobs. There was nothing there but sea and sky, and the strange, intense longing that swirled through the very air along the headland. It seemed to emanate from the violent meeting of stern, unyielding granite and insistent, lapis sea.

Like doomed lovers. Lily thought, watching the waves. *Always meeting in passion, never able to hold on to the moment . . . or each other.*

Finally she gave up trying to sketch the wild Atlantic, rushing to engulf the great granite rock formation offshore that the locals called St. Petroc's Cathedral. Her waves were lumpy, not liquid, and her rendering of the delicate salt spume looked as thick as frosting on a cake. It was too much for her minor skills, she realized.

Setting her sights on something less grand, she concentrated on the wildflowers that dotted the grassy slope and clung to the lichened rocks. The colored pencils filled in the shadows and highlights as the flowers came to life on her page, but there was nothing else that stirred around her.

The sun lowered over the water, gilding the rocks and turning the wave-tossed sea to a cauldron of gold, and still Rees didn't come. Disheartened, Lily packed up her things and went back to the hotel.

Every morning for four more days, she went out to Yearning Head and spent the hours sketching the odd shapes of the wind-sculpted trees and the wildflowers that dotted the rugged headland. Every evening she returned to her hotel room with nothing but pages of carefully tinted sketches to show for her vigil, and a heart filled with aching disappointment.

By week's end she was anxious and out of sorts. Only three days of vacation left, and then she had to leave. How far away her life in the States seemed! How infinitely lonely. Once more she went along the strand and climbed the granite steps while the wind plucked at her skirts and pulled her hair loose from its clips.

She stood on the headland and lifted her face to the wind. "Where are you?" she cried softly. "Why won't you come to me, Rees Tregarrick?"

The sun warmed her face, a breeze kissed her mouth, but that was all. The doubts that had been growing in her heart loomed large. Perhaps Dr. Landry was right. Her loneliness and romantic imagination, compounded by a blow to the head, had conjured up what was nothing more than a vivid hallucination.

But, oh, the pressure of his hot mouth on hers, the feel of his warm hands upon her naked body, had been so wonderfully real.

Lily sat on the headland until well past dinnertime, and finally came to a decision. There was no use pining away over a man who'd lived a hundred years ago—and she couldn't face the boredom of returning to her job with the Department of Transportation. Not just yet.

She would wire her supervisor and request a leave of absence. Then she'd pack up and leave St. Dunstan, hoping her experiences would fade in time from sharp loss to a happily remembered dream. The world was full of other places to visit: Rome and Athens, Cairo and Capetown, Jakarta and Hong Kong. She would see them all. When her leave was up, she would know what to do about reshaping her life. One thing was sure, she wouldn't continue on the same worn path she'd been treading for years.

That decision made, Lily was still reluctant to leave Cornwall behind. She knew, with overwhelming sadness, that once she left she would never come back to St. Dunstan.

Two nights before she was to leave Cornwall, Rees came to Lily in her dreams once more, handsome and virile as before. She reached out to him, but he vanished into the gathering fog. The scene shifted in the strange way of dreams. Lily stood on the headland, wind whipping her hair against her face, while he watched her from the star window, his fists beating soundlessly against the stained-glass panes.

She wakened, drenched in sweat, heart fluttering with fear. And with hope. Lily lay awake till dawn, thinking. In the end, there was no real decision to be made. She knew what she must do.

On her last day in the village, Lily stayed in her room, packing. A quick call to the airline confirmed her flight home. She tucked in two of the sketchbooks she'd filled with her drawings, and placed the souvenirs she'd bought in her carry-on. Ignoring her half-finished letter to a friend on the desktop, she shot several pictures of her room with the new camera she'd bought in the little town. It was late in the day when she set out on a final pilgrimage to Yearning Head.

She walked briskly along the High Street and made her way to the strand. She reached the base of the cliffs as the sky turned from gold and pink to lavender. Twilight closed in, but she was not afraid. The water had gone out in the bay and shimmered in the distance like gray, watered silk. Lily couldn't help remembering her frantic scramble in the fog, racing the rising tide. The bright, burning star that had guided her footsteps.

The voice—*his* voice, calling her to safety. *Oh, Rees, my love!*

She smiled at the rich life of the tide pools, the colorful clumps of barnacles and limpets exposed on the rocks by the retreating waves.

"Good-bye," she said softly to the tide pool, and the silvery sea, and the great craggy bulk of Yearning Head.

As she rounded a jutting rock, her foot slipped on the loose shingle, and she went sprawling. Her sketchbook flew out of her hand. Lily ignored it. Before she could get to her feet, the air darkened and shimmered, and she knew. He was waiting for her at the head of the stairs.

She made the climb eagerly, grasping the rough railing to pull herself higher. When she reached the top of Yearning Head, there was nothing but a wide sweep of wind-bent grasses, the stunted trees to one side and the graceful lines of Star House against the rapidly darkening sky.

The wind grew chill, and she wrapped her arms around herself for warmth as night fell. Stars spangled the firmament, but the mansion's tower was a black bulk rising up like a threat, its great stained-glass window blank and unlit.

Lily lifted her arms to the sky. Love and a fierce longing flowed from her like an invisible force. The air crackled with tension.

"*Damn* you, Rees Tregarrick! Come to me. Come to me!"

The wind snatched her voice, carrying it inland, yet it seemed to echo from behind her, from the granite mass of Yearning Head. As those lonely echoes faded, a faint light bloomed in the tower, grew and blossomed before her eyes. Lily held her breath, afraid to move. Then the great star window lit the night, blazing in all its golden glory. "*Rees!*" she whispered.

And suddenly, miraculously, *he* was there.

He stood a little away. He looked older, and his cane was gone. His jaw was so hard, his eyes so angry that it frightened her a little. Was this how Catherine Tregarrick had seen him that fatal night? But, no, whatever it was that sparked in the depths of his eyes, she knew beyond doubt that he would never harm her.

"Rees!" She held out her arms to him, but his own stayed at his side.

"What do you want of me, woman?"

The harshness of his voice stung her. Lily went toward him despite it. All the longing in her soul welled up, compelling her to go to him.

He was no hallucination. He cast a shadow in the lowering sun, and she could smell his scent of cedar, see a few small whiskers he'd missed in shaving along his squared jaw. Her fingers itched to touch him, to reassure herself that he was really there. She restrained herself with difficulty.

"I've been waiting for you," she told him. "Calling for you."

He sighed. "I heard you tonight, in every sigh of the wind. Why are you tormenting me, woman? For the love of God, go away! Go back to wherever you came from and leave me in peace!"

8

LILY'S EYES WENT wide in surprise. "*I*, tormenting *you*? The shoe is on the other foot. You came to me, made love to me! And then you went away!"

He recoiled as if she'd slapped him. "A year and more has passed since then! I went out to the headland each day, for months afterward, searching for you. Waiting for you." He laughed bitterly. "I wanted to call out to you . . . and realized that I didn't even know your name."

Lily frowned. "Is it still autumn?"

"Spring," he replied. "Just after Easter week."

"It is still summer," she said slowly. "Only three days have passed since we met."

"Ridiculous!"

"What year is this?"

He looked confused. "What year? Why, it's the year of Our Lord 1881."

"Not in my world," Lily said quietly. She knelt and retrieved her handbag, pulled out the calendar in her wallet, and silently handed it to him.

"This is dated far into the next century!" he exclaimed.

Reaching in again, she took out several other items: a ballpoint pen, a credit card with a hologram on the front, a solar calculator, and showed him how they worked. He scanned her driver's license, her other I.D., and watched the hologram on the credit card change with the flick of his wrist.

His jaw tightened. "Are you saying that you are not a ghost, but a visitor come from the future? Like something out of Jules Verne?"

"Not exactly." Lily bit her lip. It was so difficult to explain. "I live in the future, yes. But it is you who have come to me, out of the past."

He touched her face. Her mouth. His long fingers outlined the contours of her lips until they trembled. "You are no illusion." His eyes darkened with desire. "And whatever—whoever—you are, Lily Kendall, you still make my blood run hot!" His hand dropped to his side. "Go away. Go back to wherever you come from and forget me. Perhaps that will end this curse."

"Why is it a curse?" she cried. "Are you afraid to love again? I'll stay with you, here in your time, if that is what you want. I don't know how, but I'll find a way!"

His face and voice were impassioned. "I can't ask that of you. It would destroy you, as it did Catherine. I took her away, out of her element, and she was driven mad because of it. I'm burdened with enough guilt for that."

Lily moved closer, so close that his breath stirred her hair. "I'm not Catherine. She was a mere girl. I am a woman. I'm stronger. And I want you, Rees Tregarrick! Not your position or your wealth. Only *you*."

She moved into his arms, pliant as a willow. With an anguished growl, he scooped her up. His kiss was as wild and defiant as the elements. She opened her mouth to him, sighing with relief. He wanted her, too. Lily's arms wound round his neck.

"I will never let you go," she whispered against his broad chest.

His limp was no impediment as he carried her down the grassy slope toward the house.

"No," Lily whispered against his cheek. "Portia and James are there."

"And who the devil are *they*?" Rees asked. "I tell you, there is no one at home today. It's St. Dunstan's fair, and all the servants have gone down to the village, even Mrs. Penhale."

When they reached the house, he kicked the door open and carried her inside. He mounted the stairs as if she were weightless in his arms. Lily barely had time to see that there were no velvet ropes before the cabinets, no advertising flyers on the table or blue-and-white vases by the parlor doors. The whole house was subtly different—but Rees Tregarrick was the same.

He pushed the door to the master suite open with his shoulder. "Not here," Lily murmured. "Not in her bed."

"Catherine never slept here," he whispered hotly. "I went to her. But you, Lily Kendall—I will make love to you here, as I've dreamed I have for so long."

And he did. His hands were rough as he stripped away her clothes, but gentle on her naked flesh. "I've aged three years, and you not a single day," he said. "Your breasts are as firm and high, your face as unlined as it was the day we met."

Lily noticed the faint sprinkling of silver at his temples. She ran her fingers through his hair, locked them into it and pulled his face down to hers. Her eyes were as fierce as her emotions.

"If this is all we ever have, we'll make the best of it! Love me, Rees Tregarrick, for I love you with every atom of my heart and soul."

This time they didn't bother with preliminaries. They were both more than ready. He slid inside her as if their bodies had been designed solely for one another. For a moment he just held her close to his heart.

"I'm so afraid you'll vanish again."

The moment the words were said, she felt a strange rushing sensation, as if she were being pulled backward through the air. She fought it and clung to him with all her might. Lily knew with terrible fear that if they were separated this time, they would never find one another again. Never in all eternity. And they would both be lost.

"Take me, Rees. Take me!"

As he lunged against her, the air shimmered. His voice was urgent, as if he shared her fear. "I love you, Lily Kendall. Love you with all my heart and soul."

She wrapped her legs around him, welcoming him, and he plunged deep. As their bodies joined, the air shimmered once more, fractured into shards of gold and rose and bright, electric blue.

She closed her eyes against the whirling colors, blocking out everything but Rees Tregarrick . . . the masculine smell of his body, the strength of his arms, the potency of his virile, male passion. Sliding his hands beneath her, he lifted Lily higher, thrusting harder, faster, with every beat of their hearts. They were flying like seabirds again, swooping over the brilliant sea, soaring up together over the bay and into the fiery sun.

He pushed her harder, and higher. "Don't leave me, Lily," he whispered against her ear. "Never leave me! Swear it!"

Lily felt the tension crackling in the air around them. She knew, without a doubt, that she had come to a crossroad in time. Once the decision was made, there would be no going back. Literally.

She arched up into him, taking him deep, and kissed his firm mouth. "Rees Tregarrick, I swear that if it is in my power, I will never leave you."

He filled her completely, claiming her as his own with every powerful stroke. The air shimmered once more, and although the sun shone outside the windows, a mighty crack of thunder rent the air. The lovers didn't care. Lost in each other, they rode the currents of desire higher and higher, until their wings were singed with the heat of their passion, and they fell spiraling back to earth, together.

He worshiped her with his body, grazing her skin with his lips, from the soft curve of her throat to the firm upthrust of her breasts and down to her thighs. He savored the taste of her, the scent of her, and brought her arching up into glory again and again.

Afterward, Lily lay in his arms, her head against his shoulder. "Tell me about Catherine. But only if it is not too painful."

"No." He sighed. "That wound is an old scar now. What is there to tell? She was young and beautiful, and I loved her despite her flaws, with all the ardor of a young man in his first infatuation. She was also selfish and shallow, but I was too head-over-heels to realize it. Catherine married me with no intention of settling at Star House. I didn't know that. I built it for her."

"Oh, Rees!" Lily heard only ghosts of the old pain in his voice, but the bewilderment was still there. She pressed a kiss against his shoulder.

"Were you never happy together?"

"It was all a sham. I think she was one of those women who loved herself so well, she had no love left for anyone else. But I was besotted. When she refused to go to sea with me, I brought her back all the treasures of the earth that I could find, hoping, I suppose, to buy her love. She didn't want them. And she didn't want me."

"She was a fool."

"Only young and ambitious. She wanted to be a dashing young London hostess, to spend her life at parties and balls, dancing away the hours. I was to be her tool, my wealth her entrée into the world she coveted."

He rolled onto his back and stared up at the ceiling. Lily ran her hands across the sculpted muscles of his chest, offering comfort. "You needn't tell me any more."

A long sigh answered her in the gathering darkness. "Some say I killed her, Lily."

"Yes, I know. I have never believed it."

He rolled over and took her face between his hands. "You should know this, then. I could have killed her when I learned what she had done! It was Catherine who snuffed out the lamps that lit the star window and sent the *Tregarrick's Star* onto the rocks."

"Dear God, why?"

"To rid herself of me!" The words were wrung from him. "So that she might return to London a wealthy widow and lose herself in a round of balls and mindless pleasures. For that I lost two men! Two good men, with wives and children in St. Dunstan. When she told me what she had done, I wanted to kill her, Lily! I wanted to throttle her with my bare hands!"

"But you didn't. You didn't!" She pulled him down and kissed him fiercely.

He laughed, with only a trace of bitterness now. "No. She ran out onto the headland, and I ran after her, thinking she meant to fling herself into the sea. Fool that I was! Instead, Catherine tried to trip me. She was insane with rage and thwarted ambitions. She meant for me to die that night, but she lost her footing. I tried to save her, and we both went tumbling down the sea-stairs."

His voice grew low and bleak. "She cursed me as she lay dying. 'May you never have a happy moment again, Rees Tregarrick, until you find a woman fool enough to give up everything else for love of you!' "

Lily kissed his chest, moved her lips teasingly over the crisp hair, and touched his nipple. "You've found her," she said, sliding atop him. "I will go where you go, live where you live. And," she said, as his body responded, "I will love you body and soul."

She straddled Rees and slipped down onto him, sheathing him inside her until he groaned and reached out to her. "Oh, Lily, I was such an imbecile. I never knew what love was until I met you. These past three years have been a lover's hell, waiting for you to appear again. Wondering if you ever would—or if I had conjured you up out of my loneliness."

"We'll make it paradise," she promised.

Placing his hands on her waist, he pulled her down, hard, and thrust his hips up to meet hers. She met him, jolt for jolt, her back arched and her head thrown back, reveling in the pleasure that she gave and took. The last fading light of the setting sun gilded the outlines of his splendid body, tipped her breasts with gold. As she cried out in sudden passion, he sat up, rolled her over, and took her with a fierce possessiveness that left them both spent.

Rees looked down into her eyes. "Lily, my love, my heart, will you come away with me? Will you leave this place behind and sail away with me?"

She smiled up into his beloved face. "Rees Tregarrick, I will sail with you to the ends of the earth."

9

DR. LANDRY CLIMBED out of his ancient automobile, feeling that he was on a fool's errand. For a moment he almost wanted to turn around and leave. It had been an exhausting morning, and he didn't want any more disappointments. But the note from Lily Kendall crinkled in his inner jacket pocket.

She hadn't signed it, but he recognized her writing from the postcards, and the woman who had left the note with his receptionist matched her description perfectly. Only a few sentences were penned on the neatly folded sheet:

> *Don't worry about me. I'm well and happy and more alive than I've ever been! Look behind the lining of the trunk that Portia opened at the Star House Museum while I was there—she'll know which one—and you'll understand.*

She'd vanished three nights ago, after having been seen walking briskly toward Yearning Head, her tote bag of sketching materials over one arm. Her ruined camera and rain-soaked handbag had been found among the rocks just above the tide line, along with the battered thermos from her picnic lunch.

As he would tell the coroner's jury, Miss Lily Kendall had evidenced no suicidal tendencies, as was shown by the letter she'd left half finished on her hotel desk, and the expensive new camera she'd purchased only the day before. She had confirmed her return ticket with the airlines.

The verdict would be only a formality: Miss Lily Kendall had been caught in the sudden squall that had blown up with unusual suddenness and been swept out to sea by the high tide. Like those previously lost on the beach at Yearning Head, no trace of her was likely to ever be found. A terrible tragedy.

And yet . . . The words of her note echoed through his head: *Don't worry. . . . I'm . . . more alive than I have ever been!* Somehow he felt it must be true.

Dr. Landry straightened his shoulders. He was wise enough to know that he didn't have the answers to half the questions that life posed. He was a man of science, never happy unless he'd investigated every avenue of inquiry.

Even if it turned out that he could never make the truth public, he had to find out for his own peace of mind.

He crossed the gravel car park and went through the side door into the museum, where he was one of the trustees. Portia looked up, surprised to see him. "Miss Kendall told me that you opened a trunk when she was here last. I have a particular interest in seeing it, if I may?"

"Of course." Sighing, Portia picked up her ring of keys. "I keep hoping we'll learn she went off to visit some other place and forgot to leave word."

The doctor avoided her eyes. "I don't think she's the kind of woman not to leave word."

"No, I suppose not." Handing him the key to the chest, she went back to her task of sorting out catalogue cards and entering them in her notebook computer.

The doctor passed through the door and into the museum's storeroom. The old trunk with the embossed tin

panels was against the far wall with other items to be catalogued and photographed. Light from the partially shaded
window behind it made it seem to glow. *I'm getting fanciful
in my old age,* he told himself.

Look inside the lining, Lily's Kendall's note said. Turning the trunk carefully toward the window, he unlocked it.
He found the small book nested inside the white organza
folds: *Unique Flora and Fauna of the Sandwich Islands,*
written and illustrated by Mrs. Lily Kendall Tregarrick. It
shook him profoundly.

Opening the pages, he admired the beautiful renderings
of birds and flowers in the engravings—each one so perfectly precise and lifelike that it might have been taken with
a camera. "So, you found your talent, after all," he murmured.

Landry ran his sensitive fingertips along the top lining.
Instead of a fine, smooth finish, the chest had a thin, rough
edge on one side of the floral panel. His heart gave a leap
of excitement.

He hunkered down and pulled out his pocketknife. Sliding the thin tip behind the liner, he worked it loose. There
were only six tiny nails holding the panel in place. He
popped the last one out and jumped as an envelope fell out
from behind it and landed facedown inside the chest.

When he turned it over, his hands shook just a little, as
he recognized his own name printed neatly in faded ink
across the front of it. The envelope was heavy. There
seemed to be a lot of papers in it, or perhaps old photographs.

Ah, yes. He pulled out a yellowed marriage certificate,
two birth records, a slim diary, and an ornate cardboard
frame, such as Victorian photographers had used. There
were several very like it in his collection of family mem-
orabilia.

It opened like a book. Inside were the ornate silver-
stamped name of a photographer in Honolulu, and two
sepia-toned photographs. One showed a dashing man and
a radiant woman, holding a bridal bouquet. The second was

a family grouping: the same couple, this time with two children.

To Dr. Landry, the baby looked like any other baby of three or four months, but the pretty toddler, with her wide eyes, deep dimples, and glossy ringlets, bore a startling resemblance to Portia Trelawny.

He smiled as he looked over at the wedding portrait again. The man's arm was around his bride with proud protectiveness. A happy bridegroom—Captain Tregarrick, certainly, but not the stern, unhappy man in the museum's portrait. Despite the hint of gray at his temples in the photograph, Tregarrick looked joyful, and carefree, and, Dr. Landry thought, almost amazed to find himself so.

And Lily Kendall—for despite the old-fashioned gown and hairdo and jewelry, he had no doubt at all that the woman with Tregarrick was truly she—how beautiful, how joyous her face was, with love and contentment shining from it like the sun!

Landry shook his head and smiled back. She had been right after all—and she had found her Rees Tregarrick, despite the span of generations that had separated them. His hands shook, just a little, but his world was shaken even more. Somehow Lily Kendall had managed to go back in time.

Ordinary logic had no rational explanation. He certainly had none himself. Perhaps quantum physics had the answer, and time and the universe were composed of a magical fabric, where every moment touched and blended into every other. Perhaps Yearning Head was one of those places where it was possible to step from one world into another.

Or perhaps, he told himself, he was mad as the proverbial hatter.

But no, here was Lily Kendall, in the portrait she had purposely hidden away a hundred years ago, for him to find today. Lily Kendall looking, as she had promised, happy and well and more alive than ever before.

Dr. Landry wiped his eyes. "Sentimental old fool," he muttered, and blew his nose in his linen handkerchief.

A small piece of yellow paper was tucked behind the

family grouping. The doctor pulled it out and read the words written in Lily's unmistakable handwriting:

Dear Dr. Landry,
I thought perhaps Portia would like to know how much she takes after her great-grandmother—even to the dimples!

There was no name, only the simple initial "L."

The tropical sun was clear and golden as the small sailboat cleaved the shining waves. The man at the tiller lifted his arm. "Look there, darling! A pod of whales!"

"Where, Rees?" As the prow knifed through the warm, tropical waters, Lily shaded her eyes from the bright sun and gazed out over the dancing waves.

"Oh! I see them now."

The sleek backs of the ocean giants glistened as the waves foamed and washed over them, darker shapes against the myriad blues and grays of the sea. One burst upward in a flash of strength and joy, then splashed back into the sea in a rainbow spray. A moment later she saw the misted-feather plume of its spouting.

"Can we get closer, Rees?"

He smiled at her from his place at the tiller, his eyes darker blue than the Pacific waters, his teeth white against his tanned skin. "As close as is safe. I'll not take any chances with you, my love."

Or the baby to come, Lily thought, smiling to herself. She hadn't told him yet. She wanted to be sure—but in her heart she already was. It would be a daughter, the first of the two children that she would bear him. Their son would be named Rees, like his father. But this one would be a girl, blond and dimpled, with laughing blue eyes. Her name would be Portia, of course. That was the name Lily had read in the records at the Star House Museum.

The small sailboat cut through the sparkling sapphire waters. Lily turned her face up to the warm December sun. Rising up in the distance, were the emerald-green humps of the Sandwich Islands, where they now made their permanent home.

In the eighteen months since their marriage, they had sailed to exotic ports of call, but now they had come back to Lahaina. If she strained her eyes, she could almost make out the white pillars of their home in the lush green hills above the town.

With the glorious flowers and balmy air, it was strange to think that it would be Christmas in little more than a week; but here everything was different—just as she was, since falling in love with Rees Tregarrick. Every day her love for him grew deeper, more boundless than the oceans they had roamed.

She glanced up at him, tall and tanned, against the azure sky. How handsome he looked in his white shirt, with the neck open at his strong throat and the sleeves rolled up against his sinewy arms. Lily's heart swelled with love for her husband. With gratitude to him, for the joy and love he gave her—and to fate, for enabling her to turn his life around as well.

It felt odd to know the outcome of their love story. That she and Rees would grow old together, surrounded by their children and grandchildren—and that someday, some of their descendants would return to Cornwall and St. Dunstan, and settle down in the little village whose cobbled streets and seaswept vistas she knew so well. To know that one of their granddaughters would marry Pen Trelawny, of Old Cross Farm, and their line would produce the eager young Portia Trelawny who ran the Star House Museum. A cousin would wed a Scots-Irish American named Malcolm Kendall and move to Arlington. But all that was still to come.

It would be many years, many generations until the circle of time, of fate, would be complete.

At the moment Lily was far more interested in the present than the past or future. They watched the whales at play for a while, and then Rees set their sail for a small and private island that they had made their own secret trysting place. He cut through the opening in the reef and dropped anchor in the sheltered lagoon.

The sands were white as sugar, the foliage as bright as the emeralds in Lily's wedding ring. Beyond them a crystal waterfall poured over a verdant green ledge like a veil of spangled tulle. Flowers garlanded the open-air bower Rees had built for her with his own hands, and tiny jeweled birds flitted past purple plumeria and deep crimson hibiscus, and the startling scarlet red of the high poinsettia hedges.

Lily knew she would never become jaded to the beauty of her adopted homeland. Or to her feelings for Rees. The how and why of their meeting was something they never discussed any longer. It was beyond their fragile human understanding.

Perhaps there were times—and places—Lily thought, when the barriers between past and present touched and mingled, like tendrils of fog melting into one another. Perhaps she and Reese had met on Yearning Head at such a magical moment.

Or perhaps the old St. Dunstan legend was true that, if someone longed for something with all their heart and wished for it in the crosswinds at Yearning Head, the wish would be granted. Theirs certainly had. Lily and Rees took it for what it was—a gift.

He made love to her in the bower, with dappled sunlight kissing their bodies and the music of the waves against the reef. He cupped her breasts in his hands and showered her face with heated kisses. His eyes shone bluer than the sun-tossed sea and as clear of the shadows that had haunted them.

He touched her cheek. "No regrets, Lily?"

"Not a one."

Rees kissed her hand. "Every morning and every night, I thank God for sending you to me. I don't understand how it came about." His fingers stroked her skin. "I don't care. It's enough to know you are here with me now."

"And to think you tried to send me away." She laughed softly.

"I was a fool," he said, pressing his mouth against her

breast, teasing the tender tip until she groaned and shifted beneath him.

"I wouldn't have gone," she told him as he slid his hand between her legs. She gasped in a deep breath. A single stroke of his thumb had her quivering with need. "Nothing you could have said or done, Rees Tregarrick, would have rid you of me. We are fated to be together."

The western sky turned to gold. The perfumed breeze caressed their bodies, as Lily and her beloved sipped wine and watched the tropical sun make its sudden plunge below the horizon. Stars sprang out against the velvet night. Huge, swirling globes of light, against a dome of sky like a hollowed-out sapphire. The sea glittered darkly around them, while night birds called and the surf murmured a soft lullaby. *Not a Van Gogh canvas.* Lily told herself, *but a painting by Gauguin. Paradise before the Fall.*

Setting down her crystal wineglass, she wound her arms around Rees's strong neck and arched herself against him. "Make love to me, darling."

His embrace tightened. "All night long, if you desire."

And he did, with all the skill and ardor he possessed. Afterward Lily smiled as she lay cradled in Rees's arms, sheltered and warmed by the heat of his body. He returned her smile and followed it with a passionate kiss.

"I love you, Lily Tregarrick."

"I love you more."

"Impossible!" he whispered, kissing her temple, her cheek, her soft and rosy lips.

The loneliness and sorrows of the past had been banished forever. Heart to heart, soul to soul, they celebrated their deepening love and joy in one another, all through the starry, starry night.